Dare dropped his voice to a suggestive whisper.

"Be patient but a little while. My friends will soon depart." He pulled Oriana close and kissed her parted lips. Her sudden intake of breath expressed surprise. He was conscious of her generous curves, his own superior size—and a simmering arousal.

Swiftly, she pulled away, her face expressing stunned dismay. "You're very bold, sir." She stepped back and bumped into a bookcase, but his hands seized her slender waist, and his mouth again locked on hers. Her body was rigid, unresponsive—then she trod sharply upon his foot. Startled, he released her.

In a cool, collected voice she inquired, "Are you drunk?"

"No. Did my friends advise you to play games with me? I'm a straightforward man; I prefer a bedmate with experience. You needn't feign virginal innocence to whet my appetite."

"I'm not a virgin," she stated with remarkable candor, "or a trollop. I am Oriana Julian. *Mrs.* Oriana Julian."

MARGARET EVANS PORTER

IMPROPER ADVANCES

AVON BOOKS
An Imprint of HarperCollinsPublishers

This is a work of fiction. Names, characters, places, and incidents are products of the author's imagination or are used fictitiously and are not to be construed as real. Any resemblance to actual events, locales, organizations, or persons, living or dead, is entirely coincidental.

AVON BOOKS
An Imprint of HarperCollins*Publishers*
10 East 53rd Street
New York, New York 10022-5299

Copyright © 2000 by Margaret Evans Porter
Map courtesy of Denise Robinson/Granite Image
ISBN: 0-380-80773-4
www.avonromance.com

First Avon Books paperback printing: December 2000

Avon Trademark Reg. U.S. Pat. Off. and in Other Countries, Marca Registrada, Hecho en U.S.A.
HarperCollins® is a trademark of HarperCollins Publishers Inc.

Printed in the U.S.A.

10 9 8 7 6 5 4 3 2 1

Acknowledgments

I must express my gratitude to the following people, whose contributions to this author and this novel were numerous.

Margot and Robert Pierson, for more reasons than I can list, including the technological assistance provided at the very earliest stages of this project in England and encouragement from afar as I neared the end.

Lisa and Dave Nixon, who have shared the Isle of Man in so many ways, and especially for a memorable and inspiring ramble through Glen Auldyn in the rain.

Alan Franklin of the Manx Museum, for a wealth of information on minerals and mining.

The Theatre Museum in London's Covent Garden and the National Horseracing Museum, Newmarket, Suffolk.

To Charles Beauclerk, the Right Honorable the Earl of Burford, for genealogical guidance as I pursued my interest in the St. Albans dukedom.

The talented Denise Robinson, for yet again creating the perfect map.

My most abundant thanks go to my husband, for all the joys we've shared, the endless support that smooths out my rougher days, and the companionship that brightens every moment of my life.

SCOTLAND

Edinburgh

Glen
Auldyn

Isle of Man

Liverpool

Chester

Matlock

Newmarket

London

ENGLAND

Prologue

London
May 1, 1799

"You're leaving town?"

Oriana could hardly believe it herself. "I decided that would be best—for everyone." She didn't know whether the earl disapproved of her decision or welcomed it, because his neutral tone and habitually austere expression revealed no emotion. Turning to her other guest, she said serenely, "Harri, please fill his lordship's glass."

When the pretty, black-haired young woman brought him the bottle of claret, Lord Rushton's keen, dark eyes studied her prominent bosom, thrust upward by her stays and spilling over her low neckline. While he was thus distracted, Oriana unfolded the letter in her hand.

"This, my lord, will allay your concerns." Skipping over the fond salutation—*My dearest, loveliest Ana*—she read out all that followed. *"My behavior last night was reprehensible. An excess of brandy is no excuse for my many indiscretions. I crave your pardon, and shall grovel before Liza when begging her forgiveness. When next you see me, I sincerely hope I'll be her husband. Yours faithfully, Matthew."*

1

She gave the earl a brilliant smile. "So you see, I pose no danger to your daughter's betrothal."

"I'm not convinced of that."

"Nor I," added Harriot Mellon. "Just because a man takes a wife, it doesn't mean he gives up his mistress."

"I'm *not* Matthew's mistress," Oriana defended herself. Their relationship was difficult to define; none of the usual terms seemed to apply.

"Few will believe that, after his outrageous behavior in your box at Covent Garden," Rushton pointed out.

"I tried to send him away."

"She did," Harriot confirmed. "But he was drunk and quarrelsome, and would not go."

"Is it true," the earl asked Oriana, "that he followed you out of the theater and climbed into your hackney?"

"I'm afraid so. I couldn't toss him out without making a bad situation much worse," she said reasonably.

Once inside the vehicle, the distraught and lovelorn Matthew had cursed and moaned. He was the unhappiest man in London. His debts were mounting. He'd grievously offended Lady Liza—who had never really loved him. His engagement was as good as over. At the conclusion of his woeful litany, he had burst into boisterous laughter and demanded that Oriana marry him.

Said the earl severely, "Until Powell and my daughter are standing in front of the vicar, hand in hand, I shall be very uneasy. His carelessness has done irreparable harm to your reputation. Your involvement with him has concerned me for many months, and I've repeatedly warned you not to encourage him."

Twisting one trailing auburn curl round her finger, Oriana responded, "Matthew needs no encouragement. Don't be such a bear, Rushton. I can remedy this problem by removing myself from town."

"Where exactly will you go?"

"To Chester."

Her reply startled him. "So far as that?"

"The Ladies' Benevolent Institution is sponsoring a charitable benefit concert—the money raised will support poor women who have recently become mothers. Mrs. Billington is unable to perform, and Mrs. Crouch won't. Ana St. Albans has been called upon to sing." She made a low curtsy.

"It is a worthy cause," he conceded.

"Afterward, I shall proceed to Liverpool to perform at the Theatre Royal—for my own enrichment. Harri's friend Mr. Aickin offers a salary large enough to defray the costs of my entire journey." With her brightest smile, Oriana concluded, "I expect the females of Cheshire and Lancashire to copy my attire as slavishly as any here in town."

She glanced down at the silk flowers and flowing ribbons—the St. Albans corsage—decorating her bodice. The hem of her gown was trimmed with a deep ruffle, a pale pink ribbon threaded through it—the St. Albans flounce. The shoes peeking out from under it were a shade known all over London as St. Albans blue. Her ability to create new fashions was unparalleled.

To the earl she said, "My friendly effort to repair your daughter's engagement is the reason I shall be absent from Epsom and Ascot. My one consolation is that I'll finally be able to see the horses run for the Grosvenor Gold Cup at Chester. I mean to return before July Meeting at Newmarket."

"Racing mad," he muttered. "I blame your Stuart blood."

Three sets of eyes turned to a portrait of King Charles II hanging on the wall near that of his much-loved mistress, Nell Gwynn of Drury Lane. Confronted by her famous great-great-grandfather's image, Oriana recalled that he had often disregarded the common good and followed his own selfish desires.

She was sacrificing her own pleasure, banishing herself at the very height of the social and theatrical and racing season. The prospect of leaving her confidante Harriot, her amusing friend Matthew, her comfortable Soho Square house, and all her many cherished possessions was a bitter one. But if she remained, she'd become enmeshed in a scandal like the one three years ago. Its damage had been lasting.

Moving to the sofa, she picked up her Neapolitan *mandoline*. Plucking the strings, she declared, "All my songs will be melancholy ones, and the audiences will be reduced to tears."

The earl's expression was milder when he said, "I stable my own carriage horses at the chief posting houses along the Chester Road. You may help yourself to them—I insist."

Although Oriana could afford to pay her own way, she saw no reason not to accept his generous offer. "Thank you. My maid and I can look forward to a most comfortable journey. Suke goes with me—her family live near Chester, and she's eager to see them again."

After Rushton wrote down the posting houses where she and her servant should stop, and supplied the name of the best inn in Chester, he took her hand. "To obtain the best service while visiting my shire, mention my name." His dry lips brushed her knuckles, and after a curt bow for Harriot, he departed.

"He's so cold and forbidding," Harriot commented as his lordship's town coach rolled past the drawing-room window.

"Before I knew him better, I shared that view. But he stood by me and supported me during my darkest days—

as you did—and I can never forget it. I do understand his dismay at all this trouble Matthew has caused."

Harriot sighed. "Mr. Powell is so lively and full of fun—he's the perfect match for *you*. And you're so fond of him."

"Fond enough to help him salvage his marriage to an heiress whose father intends to pay off his debts. He's desperately in love with Lady Liza; he merely threw himself at me to make her jealous. Six years a widow, and I've received only one *honorable* proposal—made in jest." With a soft laugh, she admitted, "I was tempted to accept, just to see how Matthew would wriggle out of it."

"You'll marry again," Harriot cheerfully predicted.

"Who will have the bastard daughter of Nosegay Sal, Covent Garden ballad singer, and the Duke of St. Albans? My great-great-grandparents were an actress and a King of England. My pedigree isn't likely to attract a respectable gentleman, and my profession only enhances my ineligibility. I'm 'that St. Albans creature,' whose every gown and hat becomes the rage among females who don't deign to notice or speak to me."

"Their husbands and their sons do."

"For all the worst reasons."

"I don't much care what sort of man I wed," Harriot confided, "so long as he's fond of me. And very rich."

After a brief silence, Oriana mused, "Perhaps I should copy the heroine of that absurd play we saw at Covent Garden, the night all this trouble with Matthew started. If I escape to a quiet, remote village and live there under a different name, I might impress some dashing fellow with my gentility and air of mystery."

"Silly, it's your beauty he'll notice first," said her friend. "When the Drury Lane season ends, I'll join you in Liverpool. All the merchants and manufacturers from miles around attend the theater. We'll each find a wealthy gentleman who will woo us and wed us and satisfy our every whim, no matter how expensive!"

Oriana's merry, high-spirited friend made her laugh away her cares and stave off despair. Unlike Harriot, it wasn't money she wanted. She craved companionship, understanding, affection—and the romantic passion described in the arias she sang. After so many years of waiting for the hero of her secret dreams, she was convinced she'd never meet him in her beloved London.

PART I

The wisdom, Madam, of your private life,
Wherewith this while you live a widowed wife,
And the right ways you take unto the right,
To conquer rumour, and triumph on spite;
Not only shunning by your act, to do
Aught that is ill, but the suspicion too....

—Ben Jonson

Chapter 1

Ramsey, Isle of Man
May 1799

This birthday, Sir Darius Corlett reflected from the head of the long table, was the last he would spend in his town house.

Within weeks, he'd move into the countryside villa he'd designed and built for himself. His spirits soared higher as he imagined some future dinner party in its elegant, oval dining room. He and his guests would converse and play cards in the spacious drawing room, surrounded by paintings of the Manx landscape—scenes of mountains and seaports and coastal cliffs.

As if guessing his thoughts, his architect cocked a grin and lifted his glass and they shared a silent toast. David Hamilton, a canny and talented Scotsman, had transformed Dare's rudimentary sketches into an impressive structure of locally quarried stone, with plenty of tall windows to take advantage of the views from Skyhill.

Wingate, the butler, opened a mahogany cellaret containing several decanters—cognac, brandy, rum, port. Familiar with each guest's preference, he served them with brisk efficiency. Then the birthday toasts began. Dare accepted congratulations on attaining his thirtieth year and endured many a jest about his advancing age. He received two bottles of whiskey, one from the Scotsman and one from the Irishman, and each of his fellow islanders presented him with a rock.

"For your collection," said his cousin, Tom Gilchrist.

Dare held the specimens close to the candelabrum. "Granite, veined with quartz. Graywacke, a common form of Manx slate."

"We couldn't think what else to offer the man who has everything," Tom explained.

"Buck and I considered providing you with another present," George Quayle stated, "which was certain to excite you—and satisfy you. But young Tommy disapproved of our plan." He sipped his rum, then asked, "What name have you chosen for that fine new dwelling of yours, Dare? Mr. Hamilton's plans and drawings are labeled *Villa for Sir Darius Corlett.* Surely you can improve upon that."

Tom leaned forward. "You say you'll not be happy till you're living up there on your hill. Perhaps you should call your place Happiness."

Dare frowned. "Sounds like something a woman would choose."

Accustomed to his habit of plain-speaking, Tom laughed.

Buck Whaley said, "When I christened my mansion, I chose a name with military connotations: Fort Anne."

The suggestion had merit. "My property was the site of a great battle, hundreds of years ago. Unfortunately, the Manxmen surrendered to the victorious Godred, who proclaimed himself king of the island. I wouldn't care to commemorate their defeat by an invading force."

"It's the new fashion to give island houses English

names," George Quayle pointed out. "The Elms, perhaps. Or if you prefer Manx, Ny Lhiouanyn."

Dare smiled. "That would be a cruel trick on my *Sostnagh* friends from across the water, whose tongues would never get round the Gailck. I've no prejudice against an English name. After all, the money that built the villa was carved out of my Derbyshire lead mines."

"Now that you've got the home of your dreams," said Hamilton, his voice thickened by a Scots burr, " 'tis time you found yourself a wee wife to share it."

"Dare? A *wife?*" Tom chortled. "He won't have one. His betrothal gave him a distaste for matrimony."

The architect, a devoted husband and proud father, wanted to know why.

"The young lady fancied my money more than she did me." Dare made a joke of it, yet his voice retained a hard edge. "If ever I marry, my bride's wealth must match mine. Better still, exceed it."

In a tone of reproof, his cousin said, "If you were wed, you wouldn't need to visit the house of pleasure in Douglas town."

"And if you ever went there yourself," he retorted, "you'd find out that most of the clientele *are* married gentlemen."

"Now that his building project is completed," said Whaley, "Dare has more time for his favorite diversion. What a pity there's no brothel here in Ramsey."

Quayle gave a rude guffaw.

Wingate entered on silent feet and approached Dare's chair.

"A visitor requests your immediate attention, sir. Should she return another time, or do you prefer to receive her now?"

A female, at that hour? "Who is she?"

"She seemed to regard the question as an impertinence. I can tell you only that she's English, and elegantly dressed."

"Old or young?"

"The latter, sir." The butler's meager lips stretched into a semblance of a smile. "Her features are most appealing."

"He'll see her," Buck Whaley stated.

Curiosity got the better of Dare. "I believe I will."

Wingate nodded, as if he'd expected that response. "She waits in your study."

Promising to return momentarily, Dare carried his brandy glass out of the dining room.

She stood before his desk, this unnamed visitor who had breached his well-guarded privacy, and frowned down at the jumble of handwritten papers. The elegance his butler had discerned was striking. Coils of auburn hair were intricately arranged atop her dainty head. Her profile was as pale and as cleanly cut as a cameo; her neck was long and white. She wore a long, flowing cloak of deep blue velvet, its hood hanging down her back. Her gown, doubtless very costly, was cut from a dark, shiny fabric and ornamented with a frivolous flounce at the bottom.

Picking up the shiny rock atop the stack of pages, she examined it closely.

"It resembles gold," he said, "but it's pyrite. Common sulpharet of iron."

Her face turned toward him.

He marveled at Wingate's talent for understatement, for she possessed an extraordinary degree of beauty.

After a burst of raucous merriment from across the hall, the lady said contritely, "I stole you away from your party."

Her voice, like sweet music, charmed him as much as

her glorious heart-shaped face. He had moved close enough to see that the hazel eyes returning his cautious scrutiny were a combination of malachite green and pyrite bronze, flecked with clay brown. Her mouth was delightfully shaped, full and rosy.

Alarmed by his susceptibility, he fought a losing battle against his desire to smile. "You're forgiven." He wanted to stand there gazing at her for the rest of the night, but felt it necessary to say, "I suspect you've come to my house by mistake."

"My instructions were explicit, and this residence fits the description I was given. Aren't you Sir Darius Corlett?"

He didn't need to ask who had given those instructions. Buck Whaley and George Quayle, ignoring Cousin Tom's protests, had clearly provided that exciting and satisfying birthday present. Where had they found this delectable doxy? Her refinement was unique for a member of her profession.

He dropped his voice to a low, suggestive murmur. "Be patient but a little while. My friends will soon depart." Taking her gloved hand, he pulled her close enough to kiss the parted lips. Her sudden intake of breath expressed surprise. Holding her, he was conscious of her generous curves, his own superior size—and a simmering arousal.

Swiftly, she pulled away. Her face expressed stunned dismay, and another emotion he couldn't identify. "You're very bold, sir. Do you know me?"

"I was beginning to," he responded.

"But you've never seen me before tonight?" she persisted.

"Never. I would certainly remember you." Not only her face and form, but the floral scent of her. He reached for her again.

She stepped back and bumped into a bookcase, knocking several fossils off the shelf. He didn't care. His hands seized her slender waist, and his mouth locked on hers. Her body was rigid, unresponsive—then she trod sharply upon his foot. Startled, he released her.

In a cool, collected voice she inquired, "Are you drunk?"

"Not entirely. Did they advise you to play games with me? I'm a straightforward man; I prefer a bedmate with experience. You needn't feign virginal innocence to whet my appetite."

"I'm not a virgin," she stated with remarkable candor, "or a trollop. I'm Oriana Julian—Mrs. Julian. I'll be spending several weeks on this island and require a lodging."

Laughing, he said, "And you accuse *me* of boldness! My dear, I'll gladly keep you here—if Mr. Julian doesn't object."

"*Captain* Julian died in the service of his country," she answered soberly. "Six years ago."

That disclosure hit Dare like a bucket of cold seawater. The enormity of his error silenced him.

Mrs. Julian stepped away, putting more distance between them. "If you'll stop chasing me around this shockingly untidy room, I will explain. Yesterday, I sailed from Liverpool. An hour ago, I arrived in this town. I asked the landlord at the King's Head whether he knew of any properties to let in Glen Auldyn, and he told me Sir Darius Corlett owns a villa there."

In his mind, a warning clanged as loudly as a storm bell. His wariness, temporarily overpowered by her physical attributes, reasserted itself.

A widow—with a weakness for the latest, most lavish fashions. One whose beauty was so seductive that even he, a hardened case, was affected by it. Here was a hazardous combination, positively lethal. She's trouble, he told himself, even as he focused on the parted cloak, revealing a well-formed bosom and a narrow waist. Better send her away—quickly.

"That villa will soon become my principal residence," he informed her. "Mr. Hinde referred to a small untenanted dwelling. Merely a cottage," he added, with a dismissive shrug.

"I don't mind. So long as it's situated in Glen Auldyn."

With some reluctance, he confirmed that it was. "If you seek an affordable lodging," he suggested, "you should inquire down in Douglas, the largest of our towns."

She shook her head, saying decisively, "I do *not* wish to live in a town. I chose this part of the island quite deliberately."

Moments ago he'd held her, he'd hungered for her. Now he wanted to be rid of her, as speedily as possible. He preferred a warm-blooded whore, eager to earn a few shillings, to a greedy huntress. Mrs. Julian's urgency, her expensive raiment, her dubious desire to live hidden away in a desolate valley alerted him to her true purpose in coming to the Isle of Man. In debt up to her pretty pink earlobes, he guessed. She must have left England in a rush, fleeing an army of creditors.

Cornelius Hinde, proprietor of the King's Head, had surely described Sir Darius Corlett as one of the island's wealthiest residents. This female, no doubt as clever and as calculating as she was desperate and beautiful, wouldn't be the first of that type to pursue him. Or the last, he thought fatalistically.

Plunging her gloved hand into her reticule, she withdrew a folded paper. Confidently she said, "This will help you understand."

Her handwriting, in contrast to her outward perfection, was atrocious. He struggled to decipher the scrawled phrases and gave up. "You'd better read it to me."

"Glion Auldin. This retired village makes a pretty appearance from the rocks around it . . . Sycamores thrive in it . . . This will be worthy the attention of a contemplative stranger; here he will perceive that happiness may reside clothed in a retired garb, and far distant from the refined luxuries of modern dissipation."

"You copied that passage from a tour book," he surmised. "Which author—Robinson or Feltham?"

"I have no idea. I found it at the circulating library in Liverpool. Before I finished reading it, I made up my mind to visit this island. Of all the lyrical paragraphs describing splendid scenery and beautiful vistas, that one tempted me the most."

"Are you so contemplative? You don't look it," he said daringly.

Her head came up, and she retorted, "Haven't you just learned the danger of judging solely by appearances?"

"In the scientific realm, observation is crucial to discovery. Your outward appearance cannot reveal the whole of your character," he acknowledged, "but it's highly informative. You employ a skillful and expensive dressmaker, and must have come from a large city where fine fabrics are easily obtained. Because you haven't an accent typical of Edinburgh, Liverpool, Manchester, or Bristol, I therefore conclude that you're a Londoner."

His discernment earned him a smile. "You know my city?"

"As well as I care to. I've not visited for many a year, and have no intention of doing so in future."

Her smile slipped, a sign that his frankness had wounded her. Making a quick recovery, she said airily, "Being thoroughly exhausted from the 'refined luxuries of modern dissipation,' I wish to spend a pleasant month in your quaint little cottage in the lovely, peaceful glen."

"You'd better see the quaint cottage before you make up your mind."

"I intend to, as soon as you permit. Are you at leisure tomorrow morning?"

Oriana returned to her chamber at the King's Head, gratified by her success but not entirely content. Sir Darius Corlett had reluctantly agreed to show his Glen Auldyn property.

He'd begun the interview by propositioning her—as though he'd known exactly who she was—and ended it disliking her because she'd asked to rent a cottage that needed a tenant.

As a public figure, and a notorious one, she was accustomed to improper advances. More troubling—and mystifying—was his behavior after she'd stated the purpose of her visit. Her simple explanation had wiped the smile from his arresting face and transformed his wry amusement to cool condescension. His failure to apologize for mauling her still rankled. Country manners, she thought derisively. His lack of finesse reminded her of the raw young squires who paid court to her—but none of them had kissed her so masterfully, or sparked a dangerous desire for more.

In future she would be careful not to arouse him.

Four weeks, she thought, entering her bedchamber. An entire month without employment or responsibilities. But no companion, either, for Suke Barry was enjoying a long leave of absence with her parents in Cheshire. Oriana missed her efficient, soft-spoken maidservant. She must also accustom herself to the absence of lively Harriot Mellon, solemn Lord Rushton, and amusing Matthew Powell. Even if the Isle of Man lived up to the enticing descriptions in the tourist guide, its beauties could not replace the pleasures of friendship.

She removed her bonnet and draped her velvet cloak across a chair, wondering what colors the London ladies, bereft of her example, would wear this season. At least she had the consolation of successfully introducing the St. Albans flounce to the female population of Chester.

The public, appreciative of London performers, had welcomed her arrival, and her charity concert on behalf of the impoverished mothers had been well attended. With soaring hopes she'd set out for nearby Liverpool, only to discover that Francis Aickin, the theater manager, had postponed her engagement. Preoccupied with hiring players for his summer season, he could not aggressively promote the appearance of the celebrated Ana St. Albans. Her concert, he said apologetically, could not take place until June. After agreeing to his preferred dates, she faced the dilemma of what to do with herself in the meantime. Her timely discovery of the guidebook had persuaded her to escape the bustle and coal smoke of Liverpool for Ramsey, this quiet backwater on the Isle of Man.

The chambermaid appeared with a pitcher of washing water. A poor substitute for Suke, she gawped at Oriana's nightgown, liberally trimmed with Belgian lace.

Oriana brushed out her hair and plaited it herself. Softly she hummed a haunting aria from the season's most popular opera. Next winter, she promised herself, she'd sing it in public, at the King's Theatre, to the delight of London's most fashionable citizenry and the chagrin of the Italian cabal, who regularly hissed English-born singers.

"Is Sir Darius Corlett a native of this island?" she asked the Manx girl.

"*Ta,* that he is, ma'am, but for a long time he lived

away. Two years ago he come back from Derbyshire to build his house. My brother, who works at the lead mine in the glen, says Mainshtyr Dare pays a good wage. His smelting works is right here in the town, and his ship is anchored in the bay. His man, Mr. Wingate, is very English. He comes into our taproom on his evenings off." The girl slid a warming pan between the bedsheets, and withdrew.

Crawling between her heated covers, Oriana reviewed her brief but telling encounter with the Manx baronet. Bold. Unchivalrous. Intelligent. Tactless.

Although he wasn't handsome by conventional standards, he was decidedly attractive—more so when he smiled. And he'd towered over her. She preferred dark men, the taller the better.

Sir Darius Corlett, whose demanding mouth and roaming hands had so greatly discomfitted her, was someone to avoid. She couldn't even put him in his place by boasting of her descent from the Stuart kings of England. That fact, like her profession, must remain a secret.

She didn't discount the dangerous possibility that some islander might have attended one of her London performances, or the more recent one in Chester. Dread of being recognized as Ana St. Albans had firmed her resolve to hide herself away in the secluded glen.

By adopting her married name she cloaked her identity. She'd rarely used it because it was connected to a bittersweet chapter in her life, a reminder of her shattering loss. Within months of their daring elopement, Henry Julian's regiment had been shipped off to India. There he remained, buried in foreign soil.

In imitation of the heroine in that ridiculous Covent Garden play, she would live in the country under an obscure name—albeit a genuine, legal one. After twenty-three busy years, she looked forward to leading a quiet, ordinary life. No admirers would demand her time and attention, her energies would not be depleted by vocal lessons and rehearsals and concerts. Best of all, she had escaped false rumors and the constant threat of renewed scandal.

Exhausted from her lengthy sea crossing, she slept the night through without waking.

In the morning, a thick mist hung gloomily over the port of Ramsey. Undaunted, she bathed in the steaming water delivered by the maid, who pressed the creases from a modish carriage habit of ivy green. In preparation for her new life, she simplified the arrangement of her hair. But she did reach for the cut-glass bottle of French floral water, as she did every morning, and touched her moistened fingers to her neck, her brow, her wrists.

She broke her fast with plain bread and bitter but sustaining tea, and drove away all thoughts of the immensely gifted Louis, her Belgian chef. On leaving the rickety table, she moved to the window to watch for Sir Darius. When she leaned out the casement for a better view of her surroundings, she saw plain buildings of white-washed stone and unpaved streets pitted with murky puddles. A large seagull marched across the slate roof; others clawed at the thatched tops of the dwellings.

Her escort arrived in a gig drawn by a bay pony—fourteen hands high, in her judgment—and halted in front of the inn.

Waving to catch his attention, she called, "Good morning, Sir Darius."

The baronet looked up, and touched his wide brim in perfunctory acknowledgment of her cheery greeting. A night's repose hadn't seemed to improve his mood, for he failed to return her smile.

Chapter 2

S he smelled like a garden of rare and exotic flowers.
   Dare, trapped in the fragrant cloud of her perfume, tried to identify it. Lilies, lilacs, roses? He couldn't guess what it was; he only knew it was damnably intoxicating.

"I had little faith that you would come, Sir Darius."

"I'm a man of my word," he declared.

Her head tipped back, exposing a slender column of a neck and the elegant curve of her jaw. As she eyed the low, heavy clouds scudding across the sky, she said, "It's not a promising day for a drive."

He let out a humorless chuckle. "If you're so easily deterred by damp, you won't like living on this island. Be thankful for a civilized mist—you might've had the more typical torrent of spring rain." He guided the pony around the largest puddles, to avoid splashing mud on his passenger's deep green skirt. "Have you ever lived in the country, Mrs. Julian?"

"Till now, I never wished to."

Dare imagined her being driven around Hyde Park in a fashionable phaeton, smiling and nodding to her acquaintances, or sweeping through London's lamplit streets in a closed carriage. "What made you change your mind?"

"A gentleman."

This disclosure deepened Dare's suspicions and, contradictorily, sharpened his interest. "He commanded you to leave London?"

"No, I went voluntarily. Extremely inconvenient, but very necessary."

He had to wonder if she made hasty departure in order to conceal the evidence of an indiscretion. But if that were so, she'd want to hide on the island for nine full months instead of just one.

"How far is Glen Auldyn from Ramsey?" she asked.

"Two miles. The whole island is thirty miles top to bottom, so there are no great distances." Fedjag, who regularly trod this stretch of the Sulby Road, slowed even before Dare tugged the left-hand rein. After negotiating the sharp bend, he said, "Here we enter the glen, which extends four miles southward. That field is called Magher y Trodden—the site of an ancient cemetery haunted by restless spirits."

"Trying to frighten me away, Sir Darius?"

He wished he could, but last night she'd demonstrated her tenacity. She turned her face away from him and gazed at the mountain on their right. Fog veiled the view but couldn't obliterate its beauty.

"You must favor hills and tors," she commented. "I'm told you have property in Derbyshire."

She *had* been asking questions about him, the little schemer. Affronted by this proof of her prying, he was determined to deflect further inquiries. "The locals identify Skyhill as the site of a fairy city. It's also a famous battleground—on that summit an army of Norsemen conquered the native Manx."

Her fascination killed his impulse to drive her away with a lecture on history—perhaps he should try geology. A soliloquy on the predominant characteristics of Manx slate would cause those pretty hazel eyes to glaze from boredom. By comparing and contrasting the Plutonian theory of the earth's origin—which he strongly supported—with the less worthy Neptunian example, he could force Mrs. Julian to leap out of the gig and run back to Ramsey.

The pervasive, garlicky odor of the ramsoms, pale flowers shooting up in shadowy places, would surely dissuade her from settling here. To his dismay, she complimented the precocious bluebells bobbing beneath the green canopy of tree branches, and admired the river, swollen by spring rains, as it splashed and foamed over the rocks.

To make certain she noticed that the glen was sparsely populated, he said, "There are very few crofters here."

"How do they support themselves?" she asked.

"You would regard their agricultural methods as primitive, but they manage to feed themselves and supply their livestock with adequate fodder. Lezayre parish is blessed with good farmland, and a quantity of grain leaves Ramsey port for England. Glen Auldyn used to be famous for snuff making, and some folk still grind tobacco with their hand mills."

His lead mine provided employment to two dozen men, but he didn't tell her that, or point out the pair of stone gateposts marking the entrance to his future home. He didn't want a fortune hunter to see his mining operations, or the unfinished splendor of his villa.

But he couldn't ignore the laborers erecting a stone bridge over the stream. Beyond them, another group shoveled gravel out of a wagon and spread it across his new drive.

"*Moghrey mie,* Mainshtyr!" the stoneworkers called.

"Good morning," he replied. He slowed the vehicle,

telling his passenger, "If I don't stop, they'll be offended."

Her gloved hands reached for his reins. "What's your pony's name?"

"Fedjag. Feather, in Manx."

"I can walk her up and down the lane till you return," she offered.

"No need, I'll only be a moment." As Dare moved away from the gig, he looked over his shoulder. Mrs. Julian, regal as a princess and twice as lovely, gripped the lines with unexpected expertise, forcing him to revise his vision of her progress through Hyde Park. He left her in the provocative feathered hat and the clinging habit of bold green, which complemented her milky skin and ruddy hair. But he permitted her to drive herself along the carriageway.

"Going to the mine?" asked Donny Corkhill. "When I saw Ned Crowe last night, his mouth was moving as fast as Auldyn stream. Said they'd hit a new vein of ore."

"I hadn't heard." If not for Mrs. Julian, he could investigate this promising development.

His mine's productivity couldn't match that of the Derbyshire operations he'd inherited from his grandfather, and it might be years before excavations yielded enough income to offset the expenses. But he could offer a job to those who needed one, either here in the glen or at his smelting house in Ramsey. The chief benefit to him was augmenting his collection of rocks and minerals with the specimens his men pried from the underground caverns.

Returning to the gig, Dare climbed up beside Mrs. Julian, and was assailed by that enticing aroma. Awareness of her swiftly seeped into him, until he felt thoroughly drenched by it. His shoulder brushed hers, and all those mad, carnal thoughts from last night resurfaced. He shoved them back down. His reluctance to have her for a tenant was at odds with his lingering desire to plunder her magnificent body.

Directly across from his new bridge stood twin stone pillars. Driving Fedjag between them, he announced, "Croit ny Glionney—Glencroft." He turned his head to catch her initial, unguarded reaction. She wouldn't care for the cottage. He was certain of it.

Her face revealed nothing during her silent study of the slate-roofed gray stone dwelling with twin chimneys at either end, and its adjacent barn. The boundary hedges were unruly and the surrounding meadow was over-grown.

"So many wildflowers," she commented with evident pleasure, before descending from the gig.

Dare observed her lissome grace as she approached the cottage, her dark green skirt brushing the upright heads of the bellflowers and yarrow. She moved like no woman he'd ever seen, and carried herself with supreme self-assurance. Kneeling, she plucked a handful of blossoms.

Wrenching his gaze from the queenly figure waiting for him on the doorstep, he looped the reins through the iron ring set into the stable wall.

When he joined Mrs. Julian, she declared, "I mean to fill this place with bouquets."

He fitted his key into the lock and turned it. Nothing happened.

"I hope you've brought the right one," she said, casting up wide, worried eyes. Little pearly teeth clamped down upon the plump lower lip.

Her pensive glance and wistful words dissolved his prejudice momentarily. "I did," he said, with a reassuring smile.

Their glances held. She drew a sharp breath, possibly of anticipation.

Dare returned his attention to the lock, and found, to

his dismay, that his fingers were shaky and his palms moist. It had been a long, long time since he'd stood so near a fetching—and fragrant—female.

He shoved against the door. When it failed to give way, he kicked hard enough to force it open. The grinding of the unused hinges was music to his ears. One glance inside, he told himself, and her enthusiasm for living in a quaint country cottage would vanish. Within seconds she would plead with him to recommend the best hotel down in Douglas.

Clutching her flowers, she preceded him into the narrow, dark hall, and found her way to the small parlor. The light streaming in from two small windows revealed white walls and a fireplace with an iron grate.

"Extremely rustic," said Dare, unnecessarily.

She ran her hand across a wooden chair back. "The furniture was made on the island?"

He nodded. The view of Skyhill had lured her to the window. After gazing out for a moment, she went into the adjacent room, which had barely enough space for its dining table and a few spindly chairs. He let her find her way to the rear of the house. A great stone-faced hearth dominated the kitchen. The dairy, dry and cool, contained rows of wooden shelving.

"I could have my very own milk cow," said Mrs. Julian. "And hens to lay eggs, and geese."

"Have you ever kept animals?" he asked.

"A dog, when I was a child. Rowley—my King Charles spaniel."

"Here, you'd need a cat. A good Manx mouser."

Undeterred by his implied warning that vermin infested these walls, she continued her explorations. He followed her up the narrow staircase, taking in every detail of her back view—the exposed nape of her delicate neck, the slender, tapering back, and gently swaying hips.

She peered inside the musty linen cupboard crammed into a corner of the smallest of the upper chambers and emerged wearing a frown, raising his hopes.

They proceeded to the principal sleeping chamber. Like the parlor, it offered her a view of Skyhill, and the bedstead was positioned directly opposite the window.

"Imagine waking up to that fine vista every morning!" Turning to Dare, she added, "I cannot comprehend why this dear little house is vacant."

"For most people, the rent is too high."

If her finances were dodgy, she wouldn't be able to afford it, either. Selecting a sum that she might well judge excessive, he said, "Twenty-five pounds per annum. Half a pound per week, on a short lease."

"I call that a bargain."

"You must take into account your servants' wages," he hastened to point out. "You'd need a woman to care for your poultry and cook all those eggs, to pluck and roast the geese. And milk the cow."

She thrust her flowers at him and her fingers delved into her reticule. "I'll pay you now. I've got five pounds."

This wasn't the outcome he'd envisioned. When she presented her banknote, he shook his head. "I meant five Manx pounds. Your English currency is worth more than ours."

"I've had no opportunity to change my money. The difference doesn't signify to me."

"Mrs. Julian, are you certain you're ready to commit to this project? I urge you to wait a few days—or longer—and acquaint yourself with the island. There are some very pretty towns along the coast, and many more glens."

"I'm satisfied with this cottage. What did you call it?"

"Croit ny Glionney. Glencroft."

With remarkable accuracy, she repeated the Manx words.

"I fear your life here will be very dull."

"That would make a pleasant change for me."

"And lonely," he persisted.

"I shall survive it." Taking back her nosegay, she declared, "For me, solitude is a novelty, not a hardship. And the episode at your house last night strengthened my resolve to avoid society."

Without overtly casting blame, she made him feel like a brute. She'd done it before—when informing him of her husband's demise. "Your arrival coincided with my birthday celebrations. When I found you in my study, I assumed my friends had arranged the surprise visit of a—a sporting female for my entertainment, who would—would—"

"Felicitate you? What naughty friends you have, Sir Darius." Prying up his coat lapel, she tucked the stems of her flowers through an empty buttonhole. "A belated present. I beg you to disregard the fact that these blossoms grew on your property and therefore belong to you already."

Her brazen gesture did nothing to allay his suspicions about her motives and solidified his determination to keep his distance from this delectable mantrap. Those limpid hazel eyes, that playful mouth, her lyrical voice and bright flashes of wit—surely they had been the undoing of many a less cautious fellow before him.

He wished he might see her without her modish green gown. His hands tingled as he imagined them cupping her bare breasts, sliding down her flat belly. The decadent curve and swell of her smiling lips brought back memories of hot kisses.

Oriana abruptly moved away from him.

This cottage would seem safer when it no longer contained the gentleman who gazed upon her with wolfish intensity. His dark eyes followed her movements, and if she weren't so certain of his dislike, she might believe he intended to resume the seduction he'd begun last night.

Soon, she told herself, she would occupy this chamber. She'd line her brush and comb and hairpins and scent bottle atop the wooden chest; her garments would fill its drawers. Tonight she intended to sleep in that very bed. Giddy with delight, her head so filled with plans that she felt it might pop, she returned to the window. After a lingering look at the cloud-covered mountain, she suggested that they return to Ramsey.

During their drive down the misty glen, she sought the baronet's opinion of the local haberdashers and victuallers who could supply her with necessities. His suggestion that she travel to Douglas to shop for goods and hire servants found no favor with her. Although she could not tell him why, she must avoid the island's most populous area.

"If the Isle of Man is anything like England," she said, "a city servant won't consider working in the countryside. I must find a woman from this parish."

"Mrs. Stowell, a pensioner of mine, managed my parents' household for many a year. She lives with her married niece in Barrack Street, and complained mightily of being coddled when last I saw her. I'll send her to the King's Head if you wish to meet her."

Oriana nodded. "Do you also know of a needy lad who might tend my livestock?"

"Young Donny Corkhill, who was helping the stoneworkers, lives in the glen. His family could use a few extra shillings."

He was motivated by concern for his candidates, she guessed, and cared less about her needs. Curious, that a man who had kissed with so much passion should possess such chilling reserve. Clearly he disliked being imposed upon. After today, she'd be careful not to do it again.

He delivered her to the inn. Oriana meant to climb down from the gig unaided, but he prevented her. Strong fingers manacled her wrist.

His eyes bored into her mercilessly. "Mrs. Julian, I can't help wondering about your flight from London. Earlier today you mentioned a gentleman. Did he do you harm? Are you afraid of him?"

A flush heated her cheeks, and her gaze locked on the wilted nosegay she'd impetuously bestowed. "He's one of the nicest people I know, but he did something very foolish. He asked me to marry him."

Her light tone belied her residual regret over Matthew's drunken, foolhardy proposal. More amusing than distressing, nevertheless it had revived bitter memories of Thomas Teversal, whose promise of marriage had made her believe in miracles—until his callous betrayal had destroyed her trust.

She would not share with this disapproving Manxman her shattered dream of matrimony, or her contradictory, incompatible longings. She hoped to reclaim her place on the opera-house stage, yet also wished to achieve a semblance of respectability. And although she desired a lasting love, she couldn't conceive of relinquishing her freedom.

Sir Darius Corlett did not need to know that she was Ana St. Albans, the Siren of Soho. And she could think of no good reason to explain why she intended to hide herself away in that dilapidated little cottage she'd rented for the ludicrously inflated sum of half a pound per week.

Chapter 3

$\sim\!\!\infty\!\!\sim$

The newly discovered vein of lead ore lured Dare to his Glen Auldyn mine day after day. Nearly five feet wide and ten feet high, it was a beautiful sight.

Holding a lantern up to the wall of glistening rock, he boasted to the manager, "This lode will be the making of us."

Tom Lace, one of the miners, grinned at him, teeth flashing white in his mud-slicked face. "Plenty o' lead here, Mainshtyr Dare."

Mr. Melton had come to the island from Dare's larger and vastly more productive Derbyshire mines. "We'll get some silver ore from it in addition to lead galena and blende," he predicted. "With the works at Foxdale abandoned, you've got less competition for labor."

"We must encourage our men to work diligently in these weeks before fishing season begins," said Dare. "When herring fever strikes, many will leave the mine for the sea." If necessary, he would raise wages to maintain production.

"I'd rather pass my days here, in the heart of the earth," Lace volunteered, "and my nights at home. I'm not one to make for the sea every sundown, hauling up *skeddan* and fighting gales. My wife won't have me on the water. Her father was a fisherman, a Douglas man, who went down

31

with the herring fleet back in '87." To Mr. Melton, he explained, "A great storm struck in the bay, and dozens of vessels were sunk or smashed on the rocks."

The persistent tap of a metal pick against stone ceased. " 'Tisn't so safe in here." The voice belonged to John Saile, working atop the wooden scaffold with young Ned Crowe. "We could all be blasted into bits from the gunpowder. If the pump failed and the water rushed in, we'd be drown-ded. Or a loose rock might strike any of us on the head."

Ned's hearty chuckle was a cheerful note in the gloomy darkness. "If you're so timid, John, you shouldn't be a *meaineyder.*" He edged along the plank, and the small flame of the candle set into his protective helmet flickered.

"Careful, Ned," Dare cautioned. "I promised your mother you'd come to no harm."

Dorrity Crowe had been comforted by Dare's deathbed assurance that he would stand friend to her fatherless son. Jolly and immoral, his Manx nurserymaid suffered many hardships in the course of her life, always returning to the Corlett family for support. One of Dorrity's many ill-judged liaisons had produced Ned, now twenty. He'd been blessed with his mother's merry disposition and warm grin, and his sprightly fiddle playing made him a universal favorite.

"Mainshtyr Dare," he called down, "I've got a *cliegeen* here for you."

Ned referred to all the bright bits of stone as jewels, though in fact they were mineral crystals that had formed within the deep cavities between the rocks. Like his fellow miners, he earned extra money by supplying the proprietor with pyrite, calcite, quartz, and spar. Dare welcomed every addition to a collection he'd begun in boyhood.

The stone Ned had found was passed along from man to man. Taking it from Tom Lace, Dare held it close to his lantern. Dolomite, he suspected, although he wouldn't be sure till he'd examined it in daylight.

He and Melton began their slow, laborious ascent from the lower level, working their way up the ladder. As they neared the opening, cool fresh air struck Dare's face. He liked coming out of the mine as much as going in. The towering chimney stack belched smoke no longer, for he smelted his ore down in Ramsey now, conveniently close to the docks. From there his ship *Dorrity* made her regular journeys, carrying his lead ore across the sea to Liverpool.

He inspected a recent repair to one of the launders, wooden troughs built on an incline to carry water and crushed ore from one location to another. A Manx pony, harnessed to a horse-wheel, powered the drainage pump.

While they strolled on to the offices, the Englishman said, "I met your new lodger yesterday."

"She came here?" Dare asked, his voice sharpened by displeasure.

"I met her walking along the glen, on my way back from the smelting house. Said she's taken Glencroft, on a short lease."

"Very short."

For three weeks more he must tolerate Mrs. Julian's tenancy, and pray that she wouldn't ask to extend it. Not once had he stopped by the cottage—he hadn't even ridden past it, lest he meet her. When he came to the mine, he followed a circuitous route. He crossed the stream at his new bridge and followed his graveled drive to a private track leading from his stables to this excavation site deep in the hills.

"Charming woman," Melton added.

Entirely too charming, thought Dare. *Mrs. Melton wouldn't approve of her husband's admiring tone.*

They stopped at the forge, where the sooty-faced smith crafted the necessary picks and shovels, and repaired any broken implements. A fresh supply of timber was stacked outside the carpenter's shop, waiting to be planed and sawed into planks for additional launders and scaffolds. Dare surveyed the revolving wooden waterwheel, the focal point of his small but bustling enterprise, and felt a rush of satisfaction.

Excited shouts interrupted Melton's commentary on the current price of lead ore. Workers from the washing floor raced past them, and Dare recognized their horrified, disbelieving expressions.

An accident in one of the levels.

He and the manager hurried back to the shaft operning.

"What happened?" he asked the Manxmen gathered round the ladder.

"Tom Lace called for help. Somebody fell from the platform."

"Who?"

No one could tell him.

Lace had been working near the scaffold—with Ned Crowe.

A cold, sick dread settled in Dare's gut. Regardless of who was involved, he would feel this same heavy regret. But with Dorrity gone, Ned had no blood relative to care for him. Or to bury him.

The waiting was unbearable. The mineworkers, understanding his concerns, at first tried to reassure him that all would be well. Dare pretended to believe them, his panic increasing with each second that ticked away on his gold watch.

A miner climbed nimbly up the ladder. "They're preparing to bring him up."

"Which man?"

"Neddy Crowe."

A helmet bobbed up. John Sail's eyes squinted from the daylight, then searched for Dare. "Mainshtyr, the boy fell. *Ta aggle orrym dy vel eh er ve er ny varroo.*"

"What's he saying?" Melton asked impatiently.

"He fears Ned has been killed," Dare translated numbly, as the miner backed his way down the ladder into the blackness.

An hour ago, Ned had laughed at John Saile's doleful complaint about the dangers of their work.

Let him live, Dare bargained with the heavens, *and I'll make sure he never goes into the mine again.*

"If they can't get him up the ladder," said the smith, "they can put him in the big kibble bucket. We'll pull him up the shaft like a load of rocks."

"No need for that," said the carpenter, peering into the gap. "Tom Lace is already bringing him—on his back. Fear not, Mainshtyr, I made this ladder sturdy as can be."

He could see Lace's head now, his hair wet and matted. The miner came up the ladder slowly, a rung at a time, with one muscled arm clamped around Ned's slender frame. Below them, a man supported the dangling, useless legs.

Half a dozen arms reached down, offering assistance as Lace heaved himself and his burden out of the hole. When they laid Ned flat on the grassy slope, his head lolled. Crimson scratches marred the pallid cheek, and the snub-nosed face was vacant, devoid of its habitual grin.

Dare reached beneath the wet shirt. Shallow breathing—a heartbeat. Cause for hope.

"*Ta,* he's with us still," panted Lace. "Missed his footing—fell. Arm's broke. Prob'ly his legs, too."

"He'll never wake up again," John Saile said dolefully. "He's on his way to meet his poor mother."

"Be silent, Saile," Melton snapped, "or you'll lose your day's wages. Get the master's pony and gig—be quick now!"

"The road is rough," Dare said, while the strongest men bore the unconcious youth to the vehicle. "Taking him all the way to Ramsey could do more harm than good. Glencroft is closer, and Mrs. Stowell is there."

"Shall I ride for Dr. Curphey?" the manager asked.

"I'll go myself. You stay here to restore order. Business as usual. I don't give a damn whether or not we bring up any lead today, but it will be better for our men to get back to work. And tell the carpenter to check that scaffold."

"Mainshtyr." Tom Lace stepped forward. "I'm staying with Neddy. He's my mate."

"We need you here, to point out exactly where Ned fell." He looked into the miner's sad and weary face, and said, "*Gura mie ayd,* Tom. Ned will thank you, too, when he's able. Later, if Mr. Melton gives you leave, you may come to Glencroft. But make sure you change into dry clothes first. You mustn't take a chill." He climbed into the gig and, with a command to Fedjag, put it in motion.

He held the reins in one hand and drove as slowly as he could. He used one arm to support the inert body and was careful not to jostle the injured arm. And even though the lad couldn't hear, he maintained a steady flow of speech.

"Your mother's life would've been easier if she'd followed her head rather than her heart. Once she ran off with the Duke of Devonshire's head footman—his livery won her affections. 'When he undressed,' she told me on her return, 'he wasn't near so fine.' She was proud of you, Ned, that I know. She felt no shame at your birth, nor her lack of a marriage ring."

His promise to Dorrity pressed painfully upon his conscience.

Glencroft, ignored and avoided for so many days, was a welcome haven now. Dare drove straight up to the door, crushing the wildflowers his tenant admired. A goose strutted out of the barnyard, honking incessantly.

"Mrs. Stowell! Donny!" he shouted over the noise.

The first to respond to his summons was the person he *didn't* want—Oriana Julian.

She emerged from the overgrown thicket clambering up the south wall of the cottage, clutching a pair of secateurs. "Sir Darius!" She noticed the slumped body in his gig, and her surprise was replaced by consternation. "What happened?"

"One of my miners is injured. Where's Mrs. Stowell?"

"In the kitchen. Oh, the poor man." She murmured something about the spare bedchamber and fresh linens, and scurried inside.

Relief washed over Dare when Mrs. Stowell appeared. He didn't care that her face was worn and creased by time, or that she had a hooked nose and wore spectacles. He wanted no hysterical, fainting female, for he was too heartsore to be civil.

She laid a wrinkled hand on Ned's forehead, praying in Manx, then said, "We must dry him off and make him warm. Carry him inside, Mainshtyr—Donny will help you get him up the stair."

With the stableboy's assistance, Dare delivered his charge to an upper room and laid him on the bed. Mrs. Stowell used her sewing scissors to cut away the soiled coat and damp shirt.

Mrs. Julian had stacked blocks of dried turf in the hearth. After she kindled them, she asked, "Is there a medical man in the neighborhood?"

"Dr. Curphey," said Mrs. Stowell, stripping away Ned's stockings. "At Ballakilligan, on the road to Sulby."

Dare didn't realize the Englishwoman's intention until

he heard her rushing down the stairs. He caught up with her as she retrieved her gloves and bonnet from a table near the door. "You don't know the road, or which house is Ballakilligan."

"Describe it to me," she responded calmly.

"I'm going. Stay here and make yourself useful—as best you can."

When he stepped outside, her goose darted after him menacingly, producing its infernal noise. He hoisted himself into the gig and gathered up the reins. Before departing, he glanced back at the cottage. The spectacle of the supremely elegant Oriana Julian flapping her filmy overskirt at the creature in an attempt to drive it away made him smile, despite his aching heart.

Dr. Curphey was at home, weeding rows of lettuces. "Has Ned spoken yet?" he inquired. "Opened his eyes at all?"

"Neither. He's breathing—feebly. He lies at Glencroft."

The doctor brushed the dirt from his palms. "I'll collect my instruments."

By the time they reached the cottage, Fedjag's mouth foamed, and her sides glistened from exertion.

Mrs. Julian came out to meet them. "Ned wakened—for an instant," she announced. "Hurry upstairs, Sir Darius. I'll tend your pony."

During the doctor's protracted examination, Dare went to the window and saw her vigorously rubbing Fedjag with a cloth. He couldn't fathom how this Londoner had acquired her knowledge of equine care. But what did he really know about her history? Only that she'd wed and lost a husband. And might have had another, if she'd wanted.

A pained murmur drew him back to the bedside.

Manipulating the upper portion of Ned's left arm, Dr.

Curphey said, "I must bind the fracture before he's fully sensible. Mrs. Stowell, strips of linen, if you please. I want you to mix some vinegar and water, so I can soak the bandages before applying them. I'll show you how to wrap the arm—just here, between shoulder and elbow."

"When will he return to consciousness?" Dare asked.

" 'Tis a case of watching and waiting, perhaps well into the night. If there's a swelling near the brain—" The doctor declared in a heartier tone, "But I don't despair yet, and neither should you, Sir Darius."

In order to watch and wait, he must remain at Glencroft.

When Mrs. Julian joined the sickroom vigil, he spied the water stains on one of her sleeves and similar splotches marking her skirt. Her cheeks were attractively flushed from activity. On hearing the doctor's report, her face sobered, and she nodded her understanding.

"I'm not certain when he can be moved," Dr. Curphey cautioned.

"He may stay here as long as necessary. Sir Darius, if you prefer that I vacate the cottage, I shall do so without delay."

Her graciousness shamed him.

"I would not inconvenience you to that extent." Avoiding her hazel eyes, he reached down to take Ned's limp hand.

The fingers trembled, then curled around his.

"Head hurts," Ned whispered.

"Well, well," the doctor said brightly, "this is promising." He placed his hand on his patient's forehead. "Neddy, my boy, lie still. You had a fall and injured your arm. It's broken—*t'eh brisht*."

Ned opened his eyes and studied the faces around his bed. "*Mummig?*"

"His wits are addled, and may be for some time," said the doctor in an undervoice.

"Your *mummig* is away," Mrs. Stowell replied. "Sir Darius is here, and I'll be staying with you. Bounced you on my bended knee, I did, when Dorrity was busy about her work. But you won't remember that."

"Gingerbread. Gave me gingerbread."

"That I did. And if you do exactly as the doctor says, and lie quiet while he tends your arm, I'll make as much gingerbread as you can eat."

"*Ta,*" he said. "And I'll play my fiddle for you and Mainshtyr Dare."

No one cared to point out that this wouldn't be possible for a very long time.

Ned Crowe's arrival enlivened Oriana's quiet retreat, and provided her with a variety of tasks. Like Sir Darius and Mrs. Stowell, she did all in her power to relieve the young miner's discomfort and followed Dr. Curphey's explicit instructions. She needed an occupation, for she was unused to leisurely days and idle evenings. In London, she dined with friends at her home or theirs, and when she didn't have a performance herself she attended some other theater. When she was at the races, her social round was still more hectic.

While the baronet spooned broth down Ned's throat, and Mrs. Stowell was busy in the kitchen, Oriana cut a sheet into strips for fresh bandages. Later the housekeeper carried a tray of food and a bottle of wine into Ned's bedchamber, for Sir Darius. As usual, Oriana dined alone, watching the darkness blot out Skyhill's bulge. She passed a quiet hour on the uncomfortable parlor settle, reading Ben Jonson's sonnets. She'd sent her only upholstered chair upstairs—the baronet needed it more than she.

On her way to her bedchamber, Oriana peeped into the sickroom. Sir Darius, coatless, was seated, propping his booted feet on a blanket chest. He stared at the motionless, sheet-draped figure stretched out upon the narrow bed.

When stepping away, she trod on a squeaky floorboard.

The dark head jerked around. "Come in."

She chose not to be offended by his commanding tone.

"I've no rum or brandy to offer you, but there's more wine here." Picking up his empty glass, she refilled it for him. "I'll send Donny to your house in the morning, to bring you a change of clothing and any other necessities."

"What's the book?"

"My favorite poet. Would you like to borrow him?"

"I doubt I could concentrate enough to read."

Leaning down, she tapped on his boot. "These should come off. If you tramp about on this wooden floor, you might wake Ned."

"You think of everything," he murmured.

"My mother was an invalid in her final years. Raise your foot." She curled one hand under the sole of his boot and with the other grasped the heel. Gently she tugged, sliding it down his calf. "Now the other one."

"You've done this before."

"For my father. For Henry, too."

"Your husband?"

Oriana nodded. On a few occasions, she'd performed the service for someone else.

Her untrustworthy mind carried her back to one particular night, when Thomas Teversal had insisted that she undress him from head to toe. First she had removed his boots, then his cravat, and next the shirt and breeches and stockings. He'd carried her over to the bed . . . Afterward, she'd asked if lovemaking would be as wonderful after they were wed. Most definitely, he had assured her, smothering her questions with his kisses.

The gentleman's quiet voice interrupted her aching reminiscence. "Is your father living?"

"He died when I was eleven," she replied. "At his house in the Rue Ducale."

"In Paris?"

"Brussels. His death came suddenly, unexpectedly. Mother was not so fortunate."

The sympathy that softened his brown-black eyes unsettled her. Confiding in him, she chided herself, was a mistake.

Not that she expected the Manxman to have heard about her father's demise. Outside the Beauclerk family, no one was aware that the duke's mistress and bastard daughter had accompanied his body to England. He'd been entombed in Westminster Abbey, near his similarly scandalous great-grandfather, King Charles II.

Gathering up her book, she said, "If there's anything else I can provide, you must let me know."

"Your company." He crossed to the bed on stocking feet. "Ned's sleeping soundly—our conversation can't disturb him." When he returned, he invited her to take the armchair, and he sat down on the chest.

Having endured many a lonely vigil at her mother's bedside, she recognized his need. "Ned is fortunate to have such a considerate employer."

"Dorrity, his mother, worked in my parents' household—when not engaged in the sort of amorous adventure that brought Ned into the world. Mother despaired of her morals, yet never failed to take her back into service. We were all fond of her." His broad shoulders lifted with a deep-drawn breath, and sank in a gusty sigh. "Ned wanted to work in the mine. He wasn't interested in house building, or tending the bellows in my smelting house, or any of the alternative positions I offered. I couldn't dissuade him. I'm supposed to take care of him—that's the promise I made to Dorrity. But I'm responsible for this—this *disaster*."

"You mustn't blame yourself."

"I do." After a pause, he continued, "Each miner's safety is important. They chose the work, and they need the money. I make no profit as yet, and don't care if I ever do. Grandfather Corlett endowed charities and hospitals and workhouses all over Derbyshire to assist the destitute. I established a lead mine on the Isle of Man. Because of me, Ned lies there, broken and in pain."

"It was an accident," Oriana insisted. Similarly burdened by guilt, she couldn't think how else to comfort him, except to say, "He will recover. The doctor told you so."

"Parenthood, I imagine, must require great fortitude. I wonder if I'll ever be ready for it."

"Are you planning to be married?" she asked in surprise.

He shook his head. "I don't know that I ever shall be."

How often had she spoken the same words to Harriot Mellon?

He was leaning forward, and his black-lashed eyes devoured her. "I've been waiting for my true love to find me—a lady of beauty and charm and wit."

Oriana's heart stilled as she stared back at his shadowed face. Was he going to kiss her again? Should she let him? Aware of the anticipatory thrum of her pulse, she couldn't decide. She always rebuffed a declaration from a man she hardly knew, yet she was responding amost as though she desired him.

"In addition," he drawled, "my bride must possess an impeccable lineage, a spotless reputation, and a fortune that exceeds mine. I'm sorry to blight your hopes, Mrs.

Julian, but until I meet this paragon, I shall remain a bachelor."

The implication of his silky speech was perfectly clear: She was not a candidate for the position of Lady Corlett. Conceited creature, he assumed that she wished to wed him!

Her pride scalded, she bobbed up from the chair. "Your matrimonial requirements," she snapped, "do not interest me in the least, Sir Darius." Head high, spine stiff, she moved to the door. Pausing, she spun around. "Here's a piece of advice. When you do meet that fine lady of your dreams, place *her* needs above your own, and you'll have a better chance of winning her heart. I bid you good night, sir."

She closed the door behind her with a bang, regretting it when she heard Ned Crowe's sharp cry of alarm, followed by the baronet's voice soothing him.

My refuge is safe no longer, she mourned.

When Sir Darius Corlett had hinted that he considered her beautiful, charming, and witty, her weakness had become all too apparent. She was barely acquainted with him, and she didn't want him for her husband. Yet his decree that she was unmarriageable, by his standards, wounded her.

Because, she thought unhappily, it was all too true. Not even as an *incognita,* her name and profession shrouded in secrecy, could she win the respect of a respectable gentleman. Disheartened, she retreated to a cold and empty bed.

Chapter 4

With feigned indifference, Oriana took her place at the dining table. The man she wished never to meet again was seated across from her, and she relied on years of stage training to overlay her enmity with an icy civility. His opinion of her was low enough already; she'd not lay herself open to a charge of bad manners. She should have felt at an advantage, for she'd slept on a proper mattress and was wearing a fresh gown. His rumpled garments were testament to the hardships he had suffered during the night. But his unshaven face heightened her awareness of his potent masculinity. Large, brash, broad-shouldered—this room seemed too small to contain him.

He reached for an oatcake on the platter Mrs. Stowell had placed in the center of the table, then pulled his hand away. "I was very tactless last night, Mrs. Julian. My judgment was clouded by the day's events, and the late hour."

His attempted apology for his rudeness failed to mollify her. The damage could not be undone by a few contrite phrases. He deemed her unworthy of a position she had not sought, and it disturbed her more than their first meeting, when he'd kissed her with a wild exuberance that she'd enjoyed far too much.

"I suggest, sir, that we forget the conversation ever took place. How is Ned this morning?"

"He's not much interested in the *poddash* Mrs. Stowell is trying to feed him, and says he aches all over. He doesn't remember his fall, or much else about yesterday."

"Dr. Curphey warned you that his memory might be impaired," she reminded him, pouring tea for herself.

"Tom Lace will have spread the news by now. It's possible he and some of the other miners will stop by. They're good men, but to your refined eyes and ears may appear rough in their speech and dress."

"If they speak Manx, I won't know what they're saying," she said reasonably. "I'm not so particular about the company I keep."

"I've noticed." He passed his hand along his jaw. "And despite extreme provocation, you haven't yet tossed me out of Glencroft."

His smile was devastating to her equilibrium. A powerful wave of emotion—complex and contradictory—crashed upon her.

"As you say," he continued, "my ill-considered remarks are better forgotten. I only hope they can be forgiven."

His conscience was uneasy; he sought absolution. *But he doesn't really deserve it,* thought Oriana bleakly. "Could you pass the cream jug, please?" Murmuring a perfunctory thanks, she returned her attention to her food. Her bread plate was less intriguing than the baronet's swarthy countenance but much safer to study.

For several silent minutes she wove an appealing fantasy, wherein her handsome table companion grew hopelessly and helplessly enamored of her. She imagined longing glances, whispered endearments, eager kisses, desperate persuasions—all of which she repulsed with dignified grace. And after declining a highly flattering proposal of matrimony, she boarded a ship for England, leaving the distraught and lovelorn Sir Darius standing on Ramsey docks.

While indulging in her vengeful fantasy, she spied a shabby stranger lurking at the window. He rapped on the pane and beckoned to her companion.

"Tom Lace—he wants me," he said unnecessarily, leaving the table.

She heard the men's voices, followed by the tramp of booted feet on her stairs.

Her planned retaliation was impossible. Hurt and angry she might be, but she couldn't follow Thomas Teversal's example, and torture the baronet with the sort of duplicity that had wrecked her own happiness. Besides, if she tried to entice Sir Darius into flirtation, she'd confirm his ridiculous assumption that she was chasing him.

Men, she fumed, invariably mucked up her serenity. If her father had tucked her away in a Brussels convent instead of supporting her mother's plan to put her on the stage, her life would be a great deal simpler. But, she conceded, her innate liveliness and taste for adventure wouldn't have served her well inside that cloister.

She wished she had access to a musical instrument. Learning a new piece, or an hour or more of demanding vocal exercises, would help her fling off her depression.

The clouds looming over Skyhill threatened rain—this was no day for a stroll. A chill might settle in her throat, or her lungs, and a lingering cold would affect her performance at her upcoming concert.

Leaving the table, she went to the parlor to pen letters to her relatives and friends back in England. From her sportsmen cousins Lord Burford and Lord Frederick Beauclerk, she requested racing news. To their father, the Duke of St. Albans, she scribbled her regret that her Liverpool engagement would prevent her from attending his birthday dinner. Harriot Mellon and Michael Kelly could supply the current gossip in theatrical and operatic circles; Lord Rushton might be amused by her humorous description of rural living. She dwelled on its delights and glossed over the inconveniences. Only to Harriot did she reveal her greatest aggravation thus far—the arrogant, brusque, conceited, masterful, and unfairly attractive invader of her privacy and destroyer of her peace.

He'd tried, he really had. But Oriana Julian cared nothing for his apology.

During a long and wakeful night of watching over the invalid, he had decided that a show of remorse was required. Unfortunately, it hadn't conveyed his sincere regret. Now he was even more determined to smooth the lady's ruffled feathers.

While Tom Lace chatted to Ned in a flow of Manx Gailck, Dare wondered what sort of friendly gesture or gift would earn his forgiveness.

She was fond of flowers. She *smelled* like flowers. But a floral offering was too loverlike.

She liked animals. He'd detected a wistful note when she'd mentioned her girlhood pet. Buck Whaley's household teemed with dogs—perhaps he could spare a King Charles spaniel. But that wouldn't do, either. For years to come she'd remember him every time she looked at it, caressed it, kissed it.

She enjoyed poetry. However, a book of poems, on any subject, would be too personal an offering. And ladies' fashion journals were unavailable in this part of the island. His scientific treatise describing the island's rocks and soils wouldn't interest her.

A lump of lead ore? He grinned, imagining her reaction if he gave her one.

Soon after Tom Lace departed, Dr. Curphey returned to

Glencroft and declared himself satisfied with his patient's condition.

"Did he sleep the night through?"

Dare nodded.

'You don't look as if you did. I'm sending you back to Ramsey—doctor's orders. Mrs. Stowell is here, and you couldn't leave the lad in better hands. As for Mrs. Julian—in Ned's place, I'd rejoice at having so lovely a nurse. Wouldn't you?"

Dare gathered that the question was rhetorical and didn't require an answer.

"Shameful, the way she keeps to herself. Mrs. Curphey agrees. Do you think she'd accept an invitation to dine with us at Ballakilligan?"

"I've no idea," Dare admitted.

"We must ensure that she returns to England praising our Manx hospitality."

His own failings in that regard chafed his conscience as he accompanied Dr. Curphey out of the cottage. The colorful wildflowers swayed in the breeze as they stood talking together. Then the doctor mounted his horse and trotted down the drive.

Dare studied the nodding blossoms, recalling Mrs. Julian's affinity for them. Before he could gather a handful for her, she opened the parlor window and summoned him over.

"Pardon my boldness, Sir Darius, but I require a favor."

"Anything," he promised rashly.

"When you return to Ramsey, could you post these for me?" She held out a collection of letters. When he took them from her, she thanked him, then cut off the conversation by closing the casement.

He called to Donny Corkhill to ready his horse and gig. He was ignoring the doctor's advice to return home and instead would drive all the way to Douglas town. Weather permitting, the mail packet to Whitehaven would sail that night, and Mrs. Julian's correspondence would go with it.

Curious about the identity of her English acquaintances, he halted outside the receiving office to study her letters. He had enormous difficulty deciphering the scrawled inscriptions; the locations were easier to guess than the recipients.

> To the Right Honorable Earl of Bumfold, the Jockey Club, Newmarket, Suffolk.
> Lord Frederick Beersleep, Vicar of Kimpton, Hertfordshire.
> To the Right Honorable Earl of Rustlip, Grosvenor Square, London.
> Miss Harriot Mellon, 17 Ruffle Street, London.
> Mica Nelly, Esquire, Lizard Street, London.
> To His Grace the Duke of Stallbarn, Muckfield Street, London.

An impressive list—discounting the obscure Miss Mellon and a gentleman who appeared to bear the name of a common mineral. He hadn't imagined that she was acquainted with a duke, a pair of earls, and a vicar who sprang from the highest ranks of the nobility. If any one of these personages was a blood relation of hers, then she was too aristocratic for a Manx baronet. Perhaps she was wealthy in her own right, a target of male fortune hunters.

Recalling his idiocy last night, he muttered a curse.

Even if he sought information from a borrowed *Peerage,* he doubted he'd find Bumfold and Beersleep and Rustlip and Stallbarn. Sorting through the collection of letters, he damned the person who had failed to teach proper penmanship to Oriana Julian. Here were clues to her background, and possible proof of her identity.

"Dare Corlett!"

Lifting his head, he found Buck Whaley grinning at him.

"What brings you into town? Lechery?"

"Chivalry," he replied, holding up the letters. "I'm delivering these to the post office for my Glencroft tenant. An English lady."

"When you've finished your errand, we'll go to the alehouse for a brandy and a smoke."

Sorely in need of a drink, the stronger the better, Dare accepted the invitation.

Ned Crowe winced when Oriana spread ointment on his bruised and scratched cheek, but he lay still as a statue while she removed and replaced the linen bandage wrapping his broken arm. What agony he endured she could only guess. After she completed the necessary procedure, he thanked her.

"Mainshtyr Dare will come here today, won't he?"

"I expect so. What does *Mainshtyr* mean?"

"Master." Ned sighed. "He won't let me return to the mine."

"Do you want to?"

"*Ta.* But he doesn't want me there," the young man replied with sad resignation.

"You suffered a severe injury, Ned, and need time to recover."

"I'm the one who slipped and fell, yet Mainshtyr accuses himself of being careless," Ned said, shaking his head. "He believes he broke his promise to *Mummig.*"

"What sort of work did you do, before you became a miner?"

"I'm a *fidleyr,* and make the music at weddings and wakes." The sparkle faded from his brown eyes, and he frowned at his useless limb.

"I'm a musician, too," she confided. "I play the pianoforte—the harpsichord as well. And the Neapolitan *mandoline,* a stringed instrument. I enjoy singing."

"Eh, I'm guessing you've got a sweet voice. I wish I might hear it."

She moved to the foot of his bed. Clasping her hands before her, she drew a deep breath. "Begone, Dull Care" seemed particularly appropriate—for each of them. As she trilled the familiar notes, Ned's fingers on the counterpane tapped out the tempo, tangible proof that he shared her craving for music.

So began one of the pleasantest hours she'd spent since arriving at Glencroft. She required very little urging to run through her repertoire of simple airs suited to *a capella* performance. Her voice filled the small room, and she had the satisfaction of an appreciative listener.

"What was that called?" he asked.

" 'Triumphant Love.' "

"People would pay money to hear such singing," he told her solemnly.

Oriana couldn't help laughing, for she earned over a thousand pounds in a good year. "Where I come from, it's considered unladylike to perform in public."

"I'll teach you some of our Manx songs," he offered. "Till my arm mends, I'm not able to play. But I can lead singing."

"When you're stronger," she replied. "You should sleep now. Later, I'll read to you from a comic play or a novel." She always traveled with the works of her literary acquaintances, Mrs. Inchbald and Mrs. Robinson.

"*Ta,* I'd like that."

She smoothed his sheets and fluffed his pillow, and left his chamber in a happier frame of mind.

For two days she'd been confined to the cottage, deprived of exercise, and was eager to resume her explorations. She intended to walk farther up the glen and view more of the natural beauties that had enticed her to make this her temporary home. And she needed to get away before Mainshtyr Dare, as Ned called him, arrived at Glencroft. The less she saw him, the better.

She had strolled only a short distance along the streamside lane when she met a Manxwoman leading a longhaired, sharp-horned brown goat. Smiling, she expressed her admiration of the exotic beast, and was startled when the barefoot crofter handed her the rope.

"I don't want it," Oriana protested. "Oh, dear."

"Croit ny Glionney?"

"Yes—*ta*. That's where I live. But—"

"I take her. You keep, Benainshtyr. Good *goayr*, this one." The woman held up four fingers. "Foor *skillin*."

A milking cow, a goose, and now a goat—the oddest she'd ever seen.

Walking onward, she laughed softly. Her noble cousins and Harri Mellon and the Earl of Rushton would be incredulous to hear that Ana St. Albans was collecting animals in place of admirers.

Chapter 5

Dare didn't crawl out of his bed until midday, and felt much better for the many hours of uninterrupted sleep. Wingate shaved him, helped him dress, and reported the latest developments in the persistent quarrel between his cook and the local butcher.

"Mrs. Crellin complains again that the kitchen floor tilts, sir."

"Assure her that all the floors in the villa are perfectly level."

"Indeed, sir. But she's sure to ask when you intend to leave this house."

"I'm damned if I know." Wingate held up a gray riding coat, and Dare slid his arms into the sleeves. Crossing to the mirror, he studied his appearance. His need to look his best today was rooted in his desire to secure Mrs. Julian's forgiveness. She dressed so exquisitely, perhaps the right combination of garments would help him win his way into her good graces.

He was sure she would be impressed by the horse he rode. Envoy was one of the most recognized—and coveted—animals in the island. An aristocrat among equines, the black had exceptional conformation and a showy gait.

His enemy the goose heralded his arrival at Glencroft,

waddling and honking, her wings flapping madly.

A shaggy Manx goat tied to the tethering ring began to bray.

"When did that beast take up residence here?" Dare asked Danny Corkhill.

"Mrs. Gill brought it a while ago, saying the mistress offered four shillings for't. Mrs. Stowell gave her the money."

Dare found the housekeeper in the kitchen kneading dough.

"Neddy's much better today," she informed him. "No wonder, for the mistress spent the morning singing to him."

"Singing?"

"A voice like an *ainle*, she has. I didn't think to hear such sounds till I get to heaven. Maybe it's because she eats so strange. Won't touch red meat, only fish and fowl. I'm thinking that's why her skin is so white and fine." She wiped her flour-caked hands on a linen cloth, saying, "I've made oatcakes, Mainshtyr—tell Neddy I'll bring them up with some buttermilk, soon as I set my loaves to rise."

Going to the spare bedchamber, Dare was delighted to find the young miner sitting upright, supported by his pillows.

"Here's an improvement," he commented, drawing the armchair nearer the bed.

"*Ta,* and a good thing it is. I'll be needing my strength, for Benainshtyr says I may teach her all my songs." With a sheepish grin, he asked, "Could you find a comb for me, before she comes again? I must be a fearful sight."

Dare perceived that he wasn't the only one whose peace of mind was disturbed by Oriana Julian.

With a low laugh, Ned said, "Eh, you needn't be worrying, Mainshtyr Dare, I've not lost my heart to her. She could never fancy a broken-up miner. She's an English lady, and the fairest I've ever seen. Her singing's so fine it makes me want to cry. But for all that, she treats me like I'm no different than her. Like you do."

Mrs. Stowell brought in a plate piled high with the promised oatcakes, and a mug of buttermilk for her patient.

"Where is Mrs. Julian?" Dare asked her.

"She went down the glen to buy Mrs. Gill's goat. But she's been a long time returning."

Lost in the hills, he thought ominously. "I'd better look for her." It was lucky he'd come on horseback instead of by gig; he could conduct a more thorough search of the neighborhood.

Dare returned to the stable yard and mounted Envoy once more. He soon reached the *claghan* used by generations of glen dwellers to ford the stream. Mrs. Julian must have crossed here. He imagined her moving from stone to stone, holding her skirts high to keep them clear of the splashing water.

A breeze stirred the green sycamore leaves. Farther on lay the broad path giving access to his mining operation. Guessing that she would keep to the main track, he pressed forward.

He was acquainted with the many hazards hidden among the splendors of this landscape. A flicker of alarm teased him as he recalled every disused mine shaft and abandoned cellar hole. There were countless paths, steep and treacherous, best suited to sheep—not delicate London ladies wearing frivolous shoes. If she slipped, she could twist her knee, or sprain one of those lovely slim ankles . . .

Pausing at each cottage, he questioned the crofters in their native tongue, but none had noticed the lady of Glencroft passing by. Deeply superstitious, these people expressed concern that she might have fallen victim to the *glashten* and *mooinjer veggey* and the *fer obbee* roaming the glen and uplands. Dare doubted Mrs. Julian's serenity would desert her if she did encounter a ghost or the little people, or even a wizard. She'd find a way to charm them into submission.

Envoy carried him deeper and deeper into hills golden with gorse, grazed by rough mountain sheep. A peregrine soared overhead, seeking young rabbits to feed upon. The zigzag track led him to remote crofts, and there he received encouraging news. A short time ago, Oriana Julian had crossed through the pasture and stopped to feed the pony a handful of grass. His sense of urgency faded.

"A while ago she came, that *ferrish,* as if from nowhere—like out of the old legends. I've sent *lhienno* to the house, so the fairy woman wouldn't steal them."

She'd probably prefer to have the pony, thought Dare. In Manx he asked her where the strange woman had gone.

"*Dys shen*—there." The crofter pointed him toward a meadow path.

Because it circled around to rejoin the lane he'd followed earlier, Dare expected to overtake his quarry. His faith was soon rewarded.

Envoy's thudding hoofbeats made the wanderer turn around. "Sir Darius." Her voice was expressionless, neither cool nor warm.

"Mrs. Julian." He bowed low.

"Why do you follow me?"

"I feared I might lose you."

"I daresay you'd be thankful if you could."

He swung himself out of the saddle. "One of the crofters thought you were a fairy woman, seeking to steal her children."

"I never noticed them. I was making friends with the pony."

He grinned. "As I suspected. Were you also being friendly when you offered Mrs. Gill four shillings for her goat?"

"I'd never seen that breed before, and tried to tell her so. She assumed I wanted to own it."

"You *do* own it."

"It's certainly decorative," she declared, taking an optimistic view. "And my milk cow will be glad of the company."

"I'm glad of this chance to speak with you," Dare told her. "I still haven't fully accounted for those unkind remarks I made the other evening."

"Quite unecessary; I understand perfectly. You assume that every female who crosses your path wants to be your wife." He detected more than a trace of mockery in the musical voice.

"It isn't conceit that makes me suspicious, but experience," he defended himself. "My wealth is a fact—and so is its influence upon others."

"You have my deepest sympathy. May I go now?"

"No," he barked. "I haven't even begun. After I realized you weren't a birthday toy my friends had provided for my amusement, I made another false judgment. I decided that you were a fortune hunter, probably in debt, intent upon luring me into marriage. I saw you not as a lovely woman—which you are—but as my worst nightmare."

"You mustn't flatter me, Sir Darius. Whatever else you feel compelled to say, I don't care to listen." She turned to go.

He placed himself in front of her. Grasping her arm, he declared in a heated voice, "You try my patience almost as much as that damned goose of yours." The surround-

ing greenery was reflected in her eyes, and in the wood-
land gloom her face bloomed white as a lily. A foreign,
inexpressible emotion held him in its toils, far more
tightly than he clutched her.

She regarded him fearlessly. "This is important to you."

"Immensely." At long last, he'd communicated something to her besides lust and disdain. "May I continue?"

She nodded.

He marched her over to a low boundary wall and made
her sit. He stepped away, taking time to collect his
thoughts.

"Grandfather Corlett married an English heiress, and
lived near Matlock, the watering place at the heart of
Derbyshire's mining and mountain district. My father,
enamored of his island heritage, chose a Manxwoman for
his wife. I was born in Ramsey and educated at Rugby
School in England. Between terms, I often stayed with
my grandfather. At the time, he was building a country
mansion on the grand scale, so I watched part of my
future inheritance spring up before my very eyes. Later I
attended Edinburgh University, where I studied geology
and mineralogy. But when my father died, Grandfather
insisted that I fully acquaint myself with my future
responsibilities. I learned the business of mining—from
the ground up, you might say. At social events in the
neighborhood of Damerham, I was besieged by young
ladies, all eager to claim the Corlett heir."

An image flashed in his mind—a pert and smiling face
with a pair of laughing eyes.

"One of them succeeded—Wilhelmina Bradfield,
daughter of a bankrupt china manufacturer. Her skin
resembled the finest porcelain. She had black corkscrew
curls, and dimples." Head bowed, Dare studied his
clenched hands. "Flirtation led to courtship. She was
receptive, and so was her family. But she didn't agree to

an engagement until my grandsire's long life completed its course. I inherited his mines, his mansion, and all his money."

She broke the silence, saying, "And you decided Miss Bradfield was after your fortune."

"Not then. My attention was divided among a prosperous mining operation, my geological pursuits, and a growing stack of architectural renderings for the fine house I intended to build for my bride. Willa never complained about my preoccupations. When I was overseeing my lead mines or cataloging rock specimens or visiting my mother, she was free to dally with her sweetheart. Long before she set her cap for me, she had pledged herself to the manager of Mr. Bradfield's china factory. When the business failed, she dutifully complied with her family's wish that she marry money. *My* money."

"Did she jilt you?"

"She couldn't risk it." Dare sat down on the stone wall, stretching his legs out before him. "She was carrying her lover's child. To save herself from disgrace, and to secure a fortune, she insisted upon a quick wedding. I preferred to wait. My mother wasn't strong enough to come over from Ramsey. The manager at Dale End Mine had given notice. Willa twice fainted in my presence, and I feared she was unwell. Marriage, her parents assured me, would be the saving of her. No time for banns—they begged me to get a license, immediately. I hastened to the Bishop of Derby," he said fiercely.

"You needn't tell me the rest," she said gently.

"I must." Staring into her troubled eyes, he said, "I've never revealed the whole truth to a living soul. On the eve of my marriage, the impoverished, unemployed factory man came to Damerham and made his confession. If not for him, I'd be shackled to a woman who couldn't love me, the lawful parent of a child not my own. Within a week of these events, Mother died—peacefully, in her sleep. She was spared the whole sordid story, for which I was thankful. At her funeral, I informed my Corlett and Gilchrist relations that my engagement had ended, by mutual consent. I've since acknowledged that Willa was a fortune hunter, but that's as much as anyone knows."

"Did her duplicity prejudice you against matrimony?"

"Against *mercenaries*," he corrected her. "Willa was by far the most determined, but she wasn't the only one. Ever after, when young ladies sought my company, I detected the calculation behind their glittering smiles and lowered lashes."

"Perhaps you misjudged them. As you did me," she said pointedly.

"I doubt it." He regarded her curiously. "Have you never placed too much faith in a suitor's avowals of love and devotion?"

"Yes," she acknowledged. "Even so, it didn't vanquish my hope of achieving perfect bliss."

"I suppose you equate marriage with blissfulness. Most women do."

"I give you my word, Sir Darius—"

"Dare."

"Sir Darius," she said firmly, "I do *not* covet your fortune or your possessions or your name."

He believed her. "I suspect I'm beneath your notice—my grandsire became a baronet late in life, and I'm only the second Corlett to hold the title. Your correspondents include a duke and two earls—your connections are far superior to mine." He added, "And I doubt your past contains an episode as unsavory as the one I've related."

A frown clouded her sublime countenance. "If it did, I wouldn't tell someone who already disapproves of me."

"I don't. I've no cause for it—I know too little about you."

"Perhaps it's better so," she said, faintly smiling.

Her reticence was a shield, swiftly raised to ward off prying questions. He ignored it. "You spent your youth in Brussels. You were wed and widowed. I should like to hear more of your history."

"My parents were eccentric, and my upbringing was unconventional. I thwarted my mother's ambitions for me at age sixteen, when I eloped with a young soldier. I loved him dearly, but our marriage was also an act of youthful rebellion. Henry's regiment went to India, and there he died, less than a year after we were wed. Sadder, but no wiser, I returned to my mother's house and the life I'd wanted to escape."

He sat quietly beside her, breathing in her flowery scent and watching the gentle, rhythmic rise and fall of her breasts. He'd humbled himself before a woman he'd wronged, and felt better for it. By telling her his terrible secret, he'd released much of the residual anguish he had locked away.

"My rudeness the other evening was inexcusable. I crave your pardon, and I hope that from this moment we can be friends."

She accepted his hand, but hers was quickly withdrawn.

When he suggested that she ride Envoy back to Glencroft, she said, "After this long rest, I don't mind walking."

"I can't let you stifle one of my rare chivalrous impulses."

Dare brought the horse over to her and lifted her onto his saddle. He shortened the left stirrup strap for her and was rewarded with a tantalizing glimpse of her foot when she placed it in the iron.

"Does he go fast?" she asked, threading the reins through her fingers.

"Very. But you can't try his paces till I've found a lady's saddle for you."

He released the bridle and away she rode. He followed behind, down the lane, across the stream, and through the gateposts of the property he had reluctantly rented to the fair rider.

With more politeness than enthusiasm, she invited him to come inside. "Ned wants cheering, and you're quite a hero to him."

But not to you, he thought regretfully.

"If you care to dine here," she added, "I'll tell Mrs. Stowell to lay another place at the table."

Dare cringed as the long-necked gray fowl hurled herself at them. "Might I suggest roast goose?"

Chapter 6

"**B**ooa."

"Cow," Oriana translated.

"*Kiark*," said Ned.

"Hen."

"*Goayr.*"

"She-goat." It was the easiest to remember.

From the front garden rose a loud honking. Grinning, her instructor said, "*Guy.*"

"Goose." Moving to the window, she discovered the cause of the latest disturbance—her landlord in his pony-drawn gig. "One day, Sir Dare will ride right over that creature."

He visited daily, pausing on his way to his hilltop house or his lead mine, stopping again on his way back to Ramsey. Usually he lingered, waiting until she offered him a cup of tea and Mrs. Stowell's gingerbread. He never turned down an invitation to dine.

Turning back to the bed, she asked Ned, "When will you teach me to speak full sentences?"

Mrs. Stowell applied her dusting cloth to the blanket chest. "*Yiow moyrn lhieggey*—pride will have a fall. A short and simple proverb, but none more true."

Oriana repeated the phrase. "Give me another, please."

"*Cha vow laue ny haaue veg.*"

64

"What does that mean?"

"The idle hand gets nothing. As I told the master many a time, when he was a lad. And this one: *Ta caueeght jannoo deiney ny share*. Religion makes men better." With a final swipe of her cloth, the housekeeper left the room.

Said Ned, "She's Methodist, very prayerful. Always worrying 'bout people's souls and salvation." After a thoughtful moment he said, "*Ta leoaie lheeah*. Lead is gray."

"I'm not likely to need that remark in the course of daily conversation."

She was still laughing when Dare entered the room. Warmth crept into her cheeks, for his intimate and admiring smile caressed her vanity.

"Is the lad setting up as a wit? What has he said to amuse you?"

"She's learning Gailck," Ned reported. "She can call her animals now and knows two of Mrs. Stowell's proverbs. And I've taught her three new ballads."

"I'm eager to hear them, Mrs. Julian."

Oriana's merriment was stifled by a *frisson* of alarm. Surely he'd recognize that her voice was highly trained—and that could lead to complications. They had been getting on so well lately, she hated to refuse, though.

"Perhaps another day," she said. "Ned is eager for news of his friends at the mine."

She darted out of the room, feeling that she'd escaped a lion eager to rip out her heart and feed upon it.

Absurd, she scolded herself. He wasn't the villain of an opera, nor was she a trembling ingenue. She must continue to behave like a sensible woman. Just as she'd forgotten—almost—the way her limbs had melted when he'd held her against his chest and kissed her, she must rid herself of this ridiculous desire to sing for him.

Did he like music?

Thomas Teversal had seldom attended her performances. He'd preferred to meet her afterward and whisk her from the opera house or concert hall to a rented room for an hour of pleasure. But that shaming final confrontation had occurred at the King's Theatre. Before a watchful crowd of elegantly dressed lords and ladies, Thomas had flirted blatantly with his betrothed—while Oriana, his former mistress, sang of love unrequited, ruinous passions, and cruel betrayal. Her pathos had summoned dozens of lace-edged handkerchiefs. She'd held back her own tears until she was alone and in bed.

"Lurking in the corridor—can you be eavesdropping? I'm appalled."

She spun around. "Whatever you and Ned were saying, I didn't hear."

"I was telling him his days as a bedridden invalid are numbered. Dr. Curphey says he can be moved soon."

"Where will he go?"

"I invited him to come to my house in Ramsey, but he refuses to leave the glen. Tom Lace and his wife wish to take him in, and he prefers to stay with them."

His reference to the doctor reminded her of a development she needed to discuss. "I had a note from Mrs. Curphey, inviting me to dine at Ballakilligan this evening."

"I know. I volunteered to collect you at the designated hour and return you to Glencroft."

"That's most kind of them—and of you. But I cannot go."

His black eyebrows arched. "You have a prior engagement?"

His question was a tease. He knew perfectly well that she was friendless, and her nights were free. "You should have explained my reluctance to mix with local society."

"How could I, when you haven't given me your reasons?"

Ignoring his complaint, she said, "I'll have to send a note saying I'm unwell."

"You'd soon have the doctor at your doorstep, and your fraud would be exposed."

She pressed fisted fingers to her mouth, considering her dilemma.

"I'm the only other guest," he told her. "Mrs. Curphey's dinners are widely praised, and I've already dropped a hint about your preference for fish and poultry."

"I haven't got anything suitable to wear," she protested, grasping at any possible excuse.

"That pretty jade green gown you wore the other night will do nicely."

He probably remembered it because the bodice was cut so low. "Do you mean to select my shoes as well?" she asked tartly.

"Gladly, if you need assistance. I'd like to see the entire collection, for I don't think you've worn the same pair twice. I'll wager you've even got dancing slippers. I mean to find out," he declared, and bounded into her chamber.

Determined to chase him out, Oriana followed. She was too late—he'd already opened the wardrobe, containing an array of garments ill suited to country life.

Fingering the crimson-silk gown she'd worn at her Chester concert, he commented, "I've not seen this. Or this." He held up a long sleeve of sapphire satin.

"You shouldn't be here," she objected. "What if Mrs. Stowell catches you pawing through my clothes?"

"This cottage is mine; I'm entitled to an inspection. I have to assure myself that my tenant is responsible and hasn't harmed my property in any way." He leaned down to peer into a dark corner of the compartment. "Ah." He picked up a pair of kidskin shoes with flat leather soles. "What have we here?"

"My personal possessions." She snatched her slippers from him and held them behind her back. "Go away, Sir Darius."

"Dare."

Oriana shook her head.

"We're alone—in your bedchamber. What better place for familiarity?"

"Ned could hear," she warned. "You'll make him suspicious."

"On this island, we're not so quick to the think the worst."

"No? As I recall, on first meeting me you assumed I was a trollop. Until quite recently, you regarded me as a fortune hunter."

He laughed, much too loudly. "Not any longer. The lavishness of these dresses proves that you've got plenty of money of your own, Oriana."

"I prefer that you call me Mrs. Julian," she said primly, although she couldn't repress a smile.

"Only in company. And when I escort you to the Douglas assembly rooms, I promise I shall behave with absolute propriety."

She'd never attended an assembly ball in her life. Stage performers were never invited to mix with gentry-folk and the nobility. She couldn't tell him that her only opportunities for social dancing had occurred at the public masquerades held at Ranelagh or in Vauxhall Gardens, where rakes and rogues and ladies of easy virtue supped together, listened to music, and dallied in dark groves and alleyways.

Marching over to the bed, he picked up the book she'd left there.

"Give it to me, she commanded.

He found the page she had marked, and began to read.

"Kiss again: no creature comes.
 Kiss and score up walthy sums
 On my lips, this hardly sundered
 While you breathe. First give a hundred,
 Then a thousand, then another
 Hundred, and then unto tother
 Add a thousand. . . ."

He looked up at her, eyes dancing. "You're a romantic."

She wanted to protest that characterization—or was it an accusation? Her affinity for Ben Jonson's verses was impossible to explain without mentioning her Stuart ancestors' court masques, or her plan to set her favorite sonnets to music. With her silence, she accepted the label he bestowed. It wasn't inappropriate.

Oriana was accustomed to seeing Dare in the coats and riding leathers and top boots typical of a well-to-do country gentleman. When he returned to Glencroft late in the day, he resembled the elegant stranger whose birthday dinner she'd interrupted. His cravat was intricately tied; he wore a patterned silken waistcoat with his dark coat and knee breeches. His eyes glittered devilishly when he complimented her green gown and insisted that she show him which slippers she'd chosen.

The doctor's family warmly welcomed them to Ballakilligan, and Mrs. Curphey sat them down in her parlor and served a cordial and sweet biscuits. Oriana, whose own dinner parties were attended by celebrated writers, witty actors, and gifted musicians, feared the conversation would prove tedious. It didn't, because it centered on the Cashins, a noble clan in the neighboring parish of Maughold.

"Lord Garvain's linen mill succeeds beyond expectation," Dare commented during dinner. "My friend Buck Whaley, one of the directors, boasts about the quantity of fabric being exported to England."

"Lady Garvain will be lying in next month," said Mrs. Curphey.

Dare nodded. "The Earl of Ballacraine must hope for a grandson, to carry on the title."

"That young couple are so devoted," the doctor declared, "his lordship will get a litter of grandsons *and* granddaughters in due course."

"Earls and barons live on this island?" Oriana asked, covering her alarm at this unwelcome news.

"We've one of each," Dare informed her. "And our very own duke as well. But the less said of Atholl the better."

"On the fifth of July, when Tynwald meets, you'll meet them all," the doctor declared. "As well as the full contingent of government officials."

"By that time, I shall be back in London."

In a fortnight she would give up her pets and pay off her servants, and leave the quaint cottage in the glen. Until then, she would avoid any gathering that might include aristocrats.

A maidservant bearing a soup tureen paused by her chair to ask shyly, "*Vel shiu er n'akin Ben-rein Hostyn?*"

Oriana looked to Dare for a translation.

"She wonders whether you've seen the Queen of England."

With a smile, she answered, "Yes—*ta,* several times. The King also. And they've seen *me.*"

Everyone at the table laughed.

Her host wished to know where her encounter with royalty had taken place.

"At the theater," she answered. "Their Majesties sit in their velvet-draped box, with the coat of arms carved upon it."

She'd been on the stage, singing for them.

After dinner Mrs. Curphey suggested that they leave the gentlemen to enjoy their brandy, and ushered her back to the parlor. A series of impersonal questions about the price of dress goods in London alleviated Oriana's fear of personal conversation. The good lady merely sought assurance of her favorable impression of the island—its residents, its scenic beauties, the cheapness of provisions.

"I've never lived any other place," Mrs. Curphey acknowledged, "so I've naught to compare it with. Sir Darius tells us you've lived in Brussels. Did you visit other cities on the Continent?"

"Paris and Vienna," Oriana answered, as Dare and the doctor entered the room. "And my mother and I spent several years in Italy."

She continued to dole out select morsels of her past for her Manx friends to feast upon, feeling guilty about the many facts she withheld.

Because Dare had posted those letters, and was hearing her vivid descriptions of foreign scenery, he had revised his opinion of her. In truth, he knew her no better now than when he'd believed her to be a marriage-hungry vixen. He pursued a friendship with respectable Mrs. Julian, well-connected soldier's widow. If she had visited his island as Ana St. Albans, he would either shun her or expect to sleep with her. She wanted no repetition of the indignities she routinely suffered in London.

During their moonlit drive through Glen Auldyn, Dare asked whether she'd enjoyed the evening.

"Very much." Spoiled by a lifetime in public view, she'd rather missed being the focus of attention. As long as the attentiveness was polite and undemanding.

"Confess, you're accustomed to more exalted company than a Manx country doctor, his wife, and the owner of a lead mine."

Secretly amused by his unsubtle attempt to elicit information, she replied calmly, "I occasionally dine in the home of a duke, yet I spent several months as a soldier's bride in a garrison town. Make of that what you will."

"Your time in Italy must have been interesting."

A soft laugh escaped her. "Too interesting, sometimes. Mother and I were constantly on the move. We wintered in Milan. We spent spring in Venice, summer in Florence, autumn in Rome, and Christmas in Naples. After the New Year, we returned to Milan and began again."

Lessons, recitals, performances—she had never worked harder. She'd sung for aristocrats, sometimes for royalty, in the most notable opera houses, and had provided entertainment for many a private fête. She'd sung in churches and convents. Although the Italian critics' assessments of her abilities had been encouraging, they saved their highest accolades for native divas. Her talent was remarkable—for an English girl, and one so young—but too many people believed that Italian opera was written for *Italian* voices. Yet she had her partisans, and because there was no debate about her budding beauty, she achieved a moderate success.

"Tell me about Mount Vesuvius. You must have seen it when you were in Naples."

"It's hard to miss," she told him. "There it is, looming in the distance, puffing smoke."

"Did you climb it?"

"Every tourist does. One evening we rode donkeys from Portici up to the very top of the volcano. We gazed into a deep cavern filled with waves of liquid fire—terrifying, like a vision of hell. A few weeks later, black smoke began pouring from the mountain. There was a powerful noise—loud blasts like thunderclaps, and red cinders bursting up toward the night sky. Afterward there was a great flow of lava down the sides of the mountain."

"I envy you that sight," he said. "I imagine the rocks of that region are very black."

She nodded. "I gathered up a handful, as souvenirs."

"You were happy there?"

"I wasn't unhappy. But four years was a long time to be away from London, and I was thankful to return to Soho Square."

The gig heaved up on one side and slammed down hard. Oriana fell against Dare, whose arm curled around her shoulders. Inwardly she melted, but her body went rigid.

Drawing away from her, he murmured, "Sorry. The wheel must've struck a stone."

Did he apologize for the bumpy ride, or for touching her?

She felt flushed all over, despite the bracing night air. The dangerous nature of the suggestive darkness, this deserted road, were suddenly obvious to her. He was a man, she was a woman. He wanted her, and his unexpressed desire wakened a similar need in her, but she must not give in to it. By letting him steal another kiss, whether tender or passionate or merely curious, she'd forfeit what peace of mind she had left. And tomorrow she would have to pack up her belongings and catch the next boat for Liverpool.

Her heart pounded wildly as she waited for him to pounce.

As soon as she saw Glencroft's gateposts, she said, "Set me down, please."

"In the lane?"

Reaching for the reins, she tugged them herself, and Fedjag obediently came to a halt. "Good night, Sir Darius."

"I do wish you'd call me Dare," he complained, as she climbed out of the gig. "Till tomorrow, Oriana," he called after her.

Beneath the green silk her skin prickled, and not because of the wind.

Two weeks of tomorrows, she thought, hurrying down the drive to the cottage. Fourteen days and nights of giving incomplete answers to his questions, of refusing to sing for him. And she must never put herself within reach of his hands—or his mouth—unless she wanted to lose the respect she'd desperately tried to cultivate.

Awfully tiresome, being ruled by prudence. Never before had she felt so restrained by propriety. When she liked a gentleman, she enjoyed flirting with him. Inevitably, the gossips turned any agreeable acquaintance into a tawdry affair. Those engravers who specialized in satirical prints would produce yet another grossly inaccurate bedroom scene and hang it in their shop windows.

On this island she was safe from those who caused her so much distress, yet she dared not take advantage of her freedom. For that reason, her convincing impersonation of a prim and proper widow was sometimes more of a curse than a blessing.

Chapter 7

Oriana presented her open palm and let the goat nibble the blades of grass she held. The animal's downy muzzle and blunt little teeth tickled her sensitive skin.

Her desire for companionship had driven her outdoors. The goose and the hens, busy with their own affairs, ignored her; the milk cow grazed at the distant edge of the meadow. But the goat welcomed her attentions, not caring that often she gazed distractedly toward the lane or that her affectionate murmurs subsided whenever she fell into reverie.

I won't fall in love with him.

She blamed her lack of music for this ridiculous, senseless despondency. While learning Ned's songs, she'd enjoyed a semblance of her London routine. Now the miner was recuperating in the Lace household. In her idleness, she was prone to unsuitable thoughts about her landlord. This strange mood was temporary; it would dissipate when she began rehearsing her concert. At Liverpool's Theatre Royal she'd be singing about the love and passion that eluded her off the stage. And by the time she returned to London, her interest in Sir Darius Corlett would have faded.

His broken romance had stirred her sympathy and roused a sense of comradeship. Willa Bradfield's deception and betrayal mirrored the actions of the callous Thomas Teversal, who had vanquished her scruples with promises and wrecked her peace.

On coming to this island, she'd cast off her name and shed past scandals. During her three weeks at Glencroft, she'd convinced Dare Corlett that she was a virtuous widow. For a few days more she must maintain her false—and very fragile—respectability.

She told herself it would be better if he stayed away. But every fleeting hour with him was precious, and she wanted to carry a hoard of pleasant memories back to England.

He didn't come in his gig, as she expected, but on his horse. Trotting beside Envoy was a dark pony, a sidesaddle strapped to its back.

"Meet Glistree," he called. "In English, Glitter."

"She lives up to her name." Oriana ran her hands over the animal's coat, then pried open her jaws to examine the rows of teeth. "Five years old?"

"Close to it. She works up at the mine, but for the next few days her stablemate will be in harness. I need to pasture her close by, and didn't think you'd mind the use of a docile hack—if your very crowded stable has room for one more beast."

"How did you acquire the saddle?"

"I borrowed it from one of my Gilchrist cousins, whose husband won't permit her to go riding while she's—until she safely delivers his firstborn. I'm taking you to the mine, and afterward we can visit Ned. Mrs. Lace doesn't coddle and spoil him as you and Mrs. Stowell did. She makes him stir her porridge and soups with his good arm, and he's responsible for a variety of simple tasks."

"I miss him," she confessed. "When you brought him here that day, I thought of my husband." She laid her cheek against Glistree's shiny neck. "If only I'd gone with Henry to India, I could have nursed him back to health."

"Did he die of a fever?" asked Dare.

"He was wounded in a skirmish with natives, and never regained consciousness. Or so I was told. I received a long letter from Henry's commanding officer, extolling his bravery and assuring me that his men respected and mourned him. Every soldier's widow has read those identical phrases, I'm sure. When Henry and I first met, at Newmarket races, he seemed infinitely older. Yet he was only twenty—the same age as Ned Crowe."

"What the devil were you doing at Newmarket?"

"Watching the horses run," she said matter-of-factly. "As I've done since I was a little girl, and used the *Racing Calendar* for my reading primer. My cousin Burford owns several racehorses, and—" She clamped her lips firmly together. Unwittingly, she had disclosed too much.

"Burford," he repeated. "Not Bumfold. This earl is your cousin?"

"*Distant* cousin." She cursed her carelessness, and was tempted to excuse herself from the excursion lest she compound her mistake.

Before she could, Dare's hands settled on her waist. She tried to tell him she could use the mounting block. Ignoring her tangled words, he vaulted her into the leather sidesaddle. His hands disappeared under her skirt, gripped her ankle—dear heaven, how he tortured her— and guided her foot to the stirrup. Her flesh tingled; her lashes fluttered. Busying herself with the reins, she threaded them through unsteady fingers.

They forded the stream together, their horses splashing through the rushing water, clipping the stones with their metaled hoves.

The lead mine was composed of stone buildings, an elaborate system of water troughs, and a series of entrances leading deep into the earth. Glistree's stablemate plodded a circular path around the horse-wheel. Dare explained that it powered a pump that drew accumulated water from the levels below, where the lead was mined. A chimney stack belching smoke and sparks marked the location of the forge.

"Can we go down inside the mine?" she asked.

"Definitely not."

"But I want to see veins of ore, and the scaffolds, and everything else Ned described."

"I'm sorry, I can't let you. Too dangerous for a female."

"I'd be careful."

"You couldn't make it safely down the ladder in that long skirt." His hand clenched on her forearm. "I've suffered enough guilt since Ned's accident."

"For no good reason," she told him earnestly.

"So says the lady who blames herself because her soldier husband had the misfortune to get killed in India."

"If not for me, Henry would still be alive," she confessed.

"What would you have done differently, Oriana?"

She couldn't tell him without opening a Pandora's box of secrets. Her parents' possessiveness. The demands of her profession.

"You loved each other, didn't you?"

"Very much." To help him understand, she admitted, "Our marriage infuriated my mother, who didn't want me following the drum. To part us, she purchased a prestigious captaincy for Henry, in a regiment bound for Madras. Her health was failing; she knew I couldn't desert her. The consequences of her stratagem were doubly tragic. After we received the letter notifying us of his death, remorse drove her into a decline from which she never recovered. For me, love has always brought loss."

"Better to have loved—and to have been so loved," he responded. "That's more than I can claim. But my luck might change."

Dare's hand settled on her shoulder, and her heart skipped at least two beats. Here it was again, that familiar breathlessness. Blindly she stepped away from him, pretending that she wanted to read the lettering on the brass placard on the door of the management office. Struggling for composure, she stared at the engraved words. CORLETT MINING COMPANY.

"Are we going inside?" she asked.

He opened the door for her. "Doubtless Mr. Melton is at home, having his dinner. He's your great admirer and will be sorry to have missed your visit. Step into my quarters—but I warn you, the untidiness rivals what you saw in my study the night you arrived in Ramsey."

Papers and books and magnification instruments littered every available surface in the proprietor's office.

Leading her to a long table, he explained, "Each of these specimens will be indentified and labeled, by mineral type and the location where it was found. This is my double-lens microscope." He pointed out its features before dragging her over to a row of bookcases. Their shelves held very few volumes—most of his books were stacked on the floor—and were used to display hundreds, perhaps thousands, of rocks. "When I move into the villa, I'll keep them in glass cases."

Sir Joseph Banks, Oriana's neighbor in Soho Square, had a similar collection, but not as large as the one Dare had amassed.

She moved to a slanted drafting table, and picked up an unfinished sketch of coastal scenery. "I didn't know you were an artist."

"My works are more notable for their accuracy than their feeling, and are merely a record of my observations.

In my view, the island's entire landscape, and many specific rock formations, confirm Dr. James Hutton's theory about the age of the earth. The Isle of Man contains a wealth of evidence to support my beliefs." Going to a cabinet, he tugged at the drawer pulls. "Somewhere in here I've got a printed copy of my treatise. You won't care much for the theoretical portions, but it includes descriptions of the island's scenery."

While he searched, she returned to the shelves and picked up some of the stones, replacing them exactly where she found them. She recognized pyrite, which resembled gold. The most beautiful of his samples were the clear, glassy rocks that sparkled like diamonds. "Are these valuable?" she asked, examining them.

"The crystals? They're quite common—quartz and calcite and spar. They grow inside the gaps between rocks. My men dig out more of them every day." He continued shuffling through his papers.

"They look like jewels," she said, holding one up to the light.

He brought her a pamphlet, bound and typeset. *Geology and Mineralogy of the Isle of Man, with a Defense of Hutton's Theory of the Earth, by Sir Darius Corlett.*

"You're an author as well?"

"I paid the printer's bill myself," he confessed. "But I like to think that someday, after I've revised and expanded it, my treatise will be published by the Royal Society of Edinburgh. Keep that copy—I have others at home. You'll be glad to have it, the next time you have trouble dropping off to sleep."

Taking it from him, she turned the pages. When she reached a section about mining, she read it.

The mines at Glen Auldyn are situated less than one mile from the valley floor. The height of the excavation is four to fifteen feet. The upper level, at a depth of one hundred yards, follows a vein nearly four feet wide consisting of quartz, common brown blende, lead galena, with lead the most abundant. Here is obtained common foliated lead galena with fresh lead gray coloring and strong metallic luster, somewhat rich in silver ore. The Duke of Atholl, as Lord Proprietor of the soil, claims from Corlett Mining Company, the lessee, one-eighth part of the gross profits from mining. The ores here obtained are smelted at Ramsey port and thereafter conveyed to Liverpool by ship.

She looked up to find Dare stuffing those bright, shining stones into a canvas pouch, by the handful.

"I want you to have these quartz crystals—they're remarkably fine."

Thomas Teversal had given her diamonds. They sat in her banker's vault, a lustrous, glittering array of crushed dreams . . . her hoard of frozen tears, which she'd banished to eternal darkness.

Their hands brushed when he presented his gift. Blushing like a schoolgirl, she asked, "Will you show me the washing area Ned described, where the ore is taken from the rocks?"

"Certainly." His dark eyes were bright with intimate intensity, and his tone was amused. Her discomfiture was evident, and he'd probably guessed the cause.

Seven days, she reminded herself, and she would sail for Liverpool with her sack of shiny stones, souvenirs of a charming holiday.

"Afterward," he continued, "we'll ride to Skyhill, and you can tell me what you think of my new villa."

"She refused, Buck. *Refused!*"

"Why?"

"Wouldn't be proper, she said. I couldn't sway her, not even when I swore that no one would ever know she'd gone there. I was annoyed—and said so. She went all silent and stiff, as though I'd insulted her."

"You said you wouldn't show the house to anyone," Buck Whaley reminded him, "until it's fully furnished."

"I thought she'd want to see it." He didn't admit how much he'd wanted to see her *in* it. Dare released his frustration by pounding his fist on the solid mantel of finely carved Carrera marble. "I'm determined to mend this rift between us before she leaves the island. I only wish I had some of your Irish eloquence. I'm too blunt and tactless. Everything I say comes out wrong."

Said Whaley, "I have no doubt you're persuasive enough to land a reluctant female in your bed. I assume that's where you want her."

"At this point, I just want a little encouragement. I'd like to know whether she finds me as irrresistible as I find her." Dare reached for his brandy glass and took a sustaining gulp of fiery liquid. "She's so skittish. If I touch her, she scurries out of reach. When our eyes meet, she's the one who looks away. But she's no innocent—she had a husband. And she came here to escape an unwanted offer of matrimony. It's possible, given her family's prominence, that she's a pawn in some dynastic chess game. Alternatively, if her relatives oppose this match, as they did her previous one, perhaps they sent her away for her protection."

"Sounds to me like you're the one in danger."

Facing his host, Dare said, "She fascinates me in so many ways."

Her bright beauty and her dark mystery enticed him, to be sure. But it was her independent spirit that held him in thrall. He had no desire to subdue it, but he definitely wanted to test its boundaries. He dreamed about making love to her, and in his desperation had even tried to sketch her—without any clothes.

Facing his host, he said, "She'll never be 'willin' fer a *skillin*,' like those lasses over in Douglas. Your knowledge of womankind exceeds mine, Buck. What should I do?"

"The only way to win her affection—and whatever else you desire—is to give her what she most wants."

"How do I find out what it is?"

"Ask her." Whaley crossed to the window and stared out at the broad sweep of Douglas Bay, its golden strand and deep blue waters. "When I first came to live on this island, I brought my mistress, the mother of my children. Because she wished it so much, we passed ourselves off as husband and wife. Though she used the name Mrs. Whaley, she went to her grave Miss Courtenay."

"Why didn't you wed her?"

"As a member of the Irish Parliament, I must cultivate useful political connections, and the best way to do it is through matrimony. Don't give me that look—how often have you said no bride for you, unless she's a great heiress?"

"I don't care about having more money. I'm trying to avoid fortune hunters."

"You're keeping this paragon of beauty and charm well hidden. You should bring her to one of the assemblies at Douglas and Castletown. Or are you afraid I shall steal her away from you?"

Dare didn't dignify this jest with a response.

From his friend's house, Dare proceeded to the Liverpool Coffeehouse to read the latest newspapers from England. Poring over a creased and much-handled copy of London's *Times,* he looked for items that might interest Oriana. A new play by Mr. Sheridan was causing a sensation, but most of the columns contained political reports.

His island was self-governing, so he cared nothing for the detailed account of Parliament's closing session. Back issues of the *Liverpool Advertiser* were more useful to him. He took out the memorandum book he always carried, turned past his field notes describing a coastal rock formation, and on a clean page scribbled down names and locations of furniture dealers and other tradesmen.

Then a boxed notice with a large typeface caught his eye.

> *Mr. Aickin, proprietor of the Theatre Royal, Liverpool, announces a series of gala evening concerts, commencing Tuesday, the eleventh day of June and concluding the following night. Madame St. Albans, the celebrated vocalist from London, will perform English, French, and Italian airs. This lady's talents have earned her the adulation of aristocratic audiences in the British capital, and she is a favorite with revelers at Vauxhall Gardens. Boxes, two shillings and sixpence. Gallery, one shilling. Seats may be obtained upon application to the box-keeper, Williamson Square.*

Precisely the sort of entertainment the music-loving Oriana would most enjoy. She was sailing for Liverpool about that time, and that's where he must go to purchase his new chairs and tables and beds and carpets, and everything else he needed to fill his new house.

Proceeding to the post office, he paused at the window where Miss de Grave displayed all the letters to see whether any had arrived for himself or his neighbors or his tenant since his last trip to town. He spied two bearing his name, both from Derbyshire. There was one with a London postmark directed to "Mrs. Julian, Glen Auldyn," penned in neat, feminine handwriting.

Dare went inside to pay the postage charges. The post-mistress's brother, who served as her clerk, received his money and took down the three letters.

Remembering that he needed to secure tickets for the concert, he borrowed a sheet of writing paper from Peter de Grave. Quickly he dashed off a request to a Liverpool acquaintance, requesting that he make the necessary arrangements on his behalf. He folded and sealed the letter, and surrendered it. "Can't miss the next sailing."

Stealth had never been his preferred strategy, but after considering his options he decided not to reveal to Oriana what he'd just done. As his gig carried him past familiar landmarks along the Ramsey road, he envisioned the day of her departure. He would gallantly escort her to his own dock, where they would board his vessel, the *Dorrity*. He imagined her astonishment and her delight when she learned that he had engaged a box at the Theatre Royal. There could be no doubt that a lady who reportedly had the voice of an angel would greatly enjoy hearing Madame St. Albans from London warble operatically in three languages.

Chapter 8

The gray goose responded to Dare's arrival at Glencroft in its usual fashion, shrieking insults as he climbed out of his gig. From Mrs. Stowell he received a more civil greeting. She sat in the afternoon sunshine, a large bowl of peas on her lap and a flock of scavenging hens at her feet. With lightning quickness, her aged fingers stripped the pods and tossed them to the ground.

"Mrs. Julian wants me to announce her callers," she informed him.

Dare muttered a curse.

She peered at him over her spectacles. *"Ta chengey ny host ny share na olk y gra."*

A silent tongue is better than speaking evil. Ignoring her rebuke, he took away her bowl. "Announce me, please."

While waiting the outcome of this new and, in his opinion, unnecessary protocol, he sampled the peas, popping them between his teeth.

When Mrs. Stowell returned, she regretfully informed him that her mistress was not receiving visitors.

This was a personal affront, for he well knew he was the only visitor his tenant might reasonably expect. With grim determination, he marched up to the door. He owned the cottage and would not be turned away at the whim of a capricious female.

Oriana was seated by the parlor window, reading. She lounged voluptuously on the upholstered armchair, feet propped on a low stool. Her russet skirt was bunched up to reveal a petticoat ruffle with a lacy hem and shapely white calves encased by pale stockings. She hadn't dressed her hair, which streamed over her shoulders and back in rippling waves of reddish brown.

When he came into the room, she looked up from her book, her eyebrows swooping down in an annoyed frown. In a glacial voice, she said, "I told Mrs. Stowell that I mustn't be disturbed."

"I won't create a disturbance. But if you're so determined to preserve your tranquillity, I wonder why you haven't yet wrung the neck of that pesky goose."

She was holding in a laugh; he could tell by the way her mouth flattened out, the skin at the corners of her eyes crinkled.

"I've brought something nice; it's in one of my coat pockets. Guess which, and I'll go away. If not, you pay forfeit."

"The left one."

Greatly relieved, he reached into the right one and held up her letter.

She reached for it eagerly. Breaking the seal, she carried the pages to the window.

Dare picked up her discarded book and examined its title page. *The Racing Calendar, Containing an Account of the Plates, Matches, and Sweepstakes run for in Great Britain and Ireland in the year 1798. Printed by H. Reynell, No. 21, Piccadilly and sold at the Publishers' Office, No. 7, Oxenden Street.* Included in the alphabetical listing of subscribers was the Right Honorable the Earl of Burford, alias Bumfold, Oriana's noble kinsman.

Refolding the letter, she released a small sigh.

"Bad tidings?"

"My friend was supposed to meet me in Liverpool, but she's been detained—indefinitely."

He welcomed the news. "I suggest you extend your stay at Glencroft until she's able to join you. Your friend's plans have altered. Why not yours?"

"Because I'm expected on a particular day."

Dare wasn't going to press the issue now. Choosing a more promising gambit, he said, "Time to declare your forfeit."

"I don't recall agreeing to your conditions," she objected.

"Too late to back out. You chose a pocket—that's tacit assent."

"Oh, very well. What must I do?"

"Go with me to the villa. Now."

"I don't understand why you are so determined to take me there."

"I'm not sure myself," he confessed.

Her hazel eyes regarded him thoughtfully. "No one will see us?"

"Not a soul. The place is deserted." He stared at her rosy lips, waiting for her response.

"I'll get my shawl."

"No need, the air is mild. But you'll definitely want these." He collected the shoes lying beside her chair.

Mrs. Stowell had gone into the *thie mooar* with her bowl. The chickens continued scratching among the discarded pea pods. Dare's long-necked gray nemesis had retired to her nest.

As he handed Oriana into his gig, she told him, "I want my fowls and the other animals to go to Donny's family. But I do think you should have the goose, as you're so fond of her."

"Only if she's plucked and trussed and ready for a proper roasting," he replied. He handed her his gloves. "Take these. You're driving."

The smooth-gaited Fedjag posed no challenge to her abilities, and with commendable skill she guided the vehicle between the gateposts and over the bridge. The metal-rimmed wheels rolled smoothly along his winding drive. As they swept around a bend, the classical façade of his villa came into view.

The basic design was his own, refined and embellished by David Hamilton. The structure, three stories high, had projecting bays at each end. Nearly all signs of construction had vanished, and grass sprouted in the level ground near the foundation.

Dare turned to Oriana, seeking her reaction. Was it larger than she'd expected? Smaller? He filled the silence by saying, "All the stone was quarried here on the property."

"Yours is the prettiest house on the whole island."

Although the compliment pleased him, he pointed out judiciously, "You haven't seen any of the mansions the wealthy natives and newcomers have built. After living at Damerham, I'm all too familiar with the inconveniences of a large establishment. This suits me better."

Dare began the tour at the stables and coach house. He released Fedjag from the harness, freeing her from the thick leather breast collar and belly bands, and guided her to a box strewn with green hay. Watching Oriana's fingers comb through the dark mane and glide across the gleaming neck, he wished that she could establish the same rapport with him.

Throughout his adult life, females had flocked to him, for all the wrong reasons. Now that he'd found one who pleased him, she shunned his company and spurned his touch. He couldn't even admire her self-possession, or her caution, because both prevented him from understanding her more fully. Having caught glimpses of a fascinating and complex personality, he was ever more desperate to break through her barrier of reserve.

In a sheltered area behind the stable was a stand of apple trees, the remains of a venerable but neglected orchard. "A rarity on the island," Dare said. He parted a cluster of leaves to show the small green fruit dangling from the gnarled branches. "That old cottage has been vacant ever since I can remember. I've considered knocking it down."

"Oh, you mustn't," Oriana told him. "Ruins are quite the rage in English parks, and yours is authentic. Have you named your house?"

"Not yet," he replied. "I'm Manxman enough to eschew a name that's overtly English, yet I want something appropriate to the setting. My cousin and my friends have offered numerous suggestions, but none of them seem quite right." He looked to the valley. "I've been considering Auldyn View."

Her gaze roamed across the ridge, barren save for the clumps of yellow gorse. "You could call it Skyhill House."

The skin at the back of his neck pricked. Wondering why he hadn't thought of that himself, he repeated, "Skyhill House." She had provided a perfect name, and he felt certain that he should choose no other.

He escorted her to the front entrance, adorned with columns; curving iron handrails bracketed the shallow steps. Nearly a month ago, they had stood together on the threshhold of Glencroft, Oriana watching intently while he fitted a key into a lock. Since that day, his opinion of her had undergone a profound change.

He swung the door open and led her inside.

Her auburn head tipped back as she admired the vaulted ceiling of the front hall. Dare, breathing in the mingled aromas of fresh paint and varnish, gave her sufficient time to study it before taking her to the drawing room.

He guessed she'd seen chambers far grander than this, but he hoped she shared his liking for its classical simplicity and elegance. A frieze of molded plasterwork, white with touches of sky-blue and gold paint, ornamented the walls; a pair of carved marble Corinthian columns supported the mantel. Light streamed in from the tall, south-facing windows.

Oriana crossed the wooden floor, her soles leaving prints in the white dust left behind by the plasterers.

"Here you see echoes of the Adam influence. You must be familiar with it."

"Oh, I am."

"This room will have colored draperies and upholstery—vibrant, but not too dark."

"Blue would be lovely."

"As for furniture, I want nothing heavy, or overly decorated."

"Hepplewhite," she said, nodding.

"Exactly what I had in mind."

"The primary decorations will be scenic paintings of the island. I've got quite a few but in my town house they're scattered all about; there's no single room large enough to hold them all. And last year I commissioned an artist to paint a pair of canvases to hang at each end of this room. Douglas Bay at sunset, and Ramsey Port in the morning—with my ship *Dorrity* at her mooring."

Next he showed her the breakfast chamber. The corner cabinet of fine-grained walnut, produced by the most skilled furniture maker on the island, would hold his mother's cherished porcelain figures and her favorite serving set.

The most notable feature of the rectangular sitting

room at the back of the house was the intricate parquet floor of varicolored woods.

"This is my study," he told Oriana, "twice as large as the one in my Ramsey house. My drawing table will go here, and my writing desk over there. And I want plenty of leather armchairs, for my friends."

"Like a gentlemen's club."

"Exactly."

"I once asked Rush—a gentleman I know—why he belongs to White's Club. Because it has the most comfortable chairs in London, he said."

Giving in to her womanly interest in the domestic regions, he took her down to the kitchen and pantry and scullery, the servants' hall and their sleeping quarters. After leaving the cool, empty gloom of the cellars and other storerooms, they climbed the main staircase to view four bedchambers of various sizes and his dressing room.

He saved his library, his masterpiece, for last.

The balcony level, enclosed by a wooden rail, had benchlike seats positioned at each window.

"Up here, I want glass-fronted cabinets and display tables for my collection of rocks and minerals. Down below, as you see, the bookcases are already in place."

Oriana began a gradual descent of the spiral stair, one hand trailing along the oaken banister rail. At the bottom lay a large bundle of canvas, the dustcover the painters had used to protect the floorboards. She sat down on the last step.

Dare joined her there. "Fatigued?"

"No," she said, elbows on her knees, one palm supporting her chin. "I wanted to gaze upon your magnificent room and imagine how it will look when it's filled with your books and collections." After a moment, she added, "You are the most fortunate person I know."

"Why do you say that?"

"You possess more money than you can count. You belong to a respected family. You're well educated, your mind is capable of understanding—and explaining—important scientific theories and concepts. You designed this wonderful house. By anybody's definition, yours is an enviable existence."

Her remarks probably held a few clues about those aspects of her life that she'd concealed from him. But at this moment, Dare didn't want to probe her mysteries—he needed to take advantage of her proximity.

"I haven't felt at all fortunate lately," he replied. "Just when we reached a friendly understanding, you changed. You've been avoiding me—don't deny it. Am I the only man to receive such cool treatment, or do you freeze all who seek to know you better?"

"Nearly all," she admitted.

"Not your Captain Julian. You eloped with him."

"I was sixteen, madly in love. Running away was the only way we could get 'round my mother's objections."

"Do your grand relatives oppose your latest suitor?"

"I never asked their opinion. In some respects Matthew resembles Henry, but I didn't care to wed him."

"You see something of your late husband in every man. Do I remind you of him?"

Oriana, alert to the jealousy underlining his bitter observation, turned her head. That, she immediately realized, was a mistake. His face had tensed, his eyes blazed. He was drawing quick, shallow breaths.

With Henry, she'd always felt safe. Dare Corlett posed some indefinable danger, and when he was near she must maintain her defenses. Especially when his hand was on her knee.

"Answer me, Oriana."

"You're not like anyone I've ever known." That was why she feared him so much.

"Good." His fingers traced an invisible line from her kneecap to her thigh. "You must concentrate on me, only me, when I touch you." His arm hooked her waist, pulling her closer. "And hold you." His mouth hovered over hers. "And most of all, when I kiss you."

The press of his lips pitched Oriana into violent turmoil. She wanted this contact with her whole being, there was no use pretending that she didn't. The fire of longing flooded her veins, and she was dizzy with a need that would not be denied and could not go unanswered.

His hands molded themselves against her face, even as her fingers sought the shape of his features—hard cheekbones, firm jaw. First their playful lips teased and taunted, and then their tongues. All the while they murmured blissfully—and with increasing desperation.

"From the moment I met you," he rasped, "I wanted this. I wanted *you.*" Palming her breast, he closed his eyes as if from the sheer agony of his hunger for her. His dark lashes cast small crescent shadows on his tanned skin.

She responded to his delicious assault with a wild kiss that expressed the complex emotions he had roused in her: pent-up desire, contrition for every fact she withheld from him, and the joy of discovering that she could inflame him as he did her. And she communicated her willingness to do more.

Dragging his lips from hers, he muttered, "Make me stop now, if stop I must. Or else I won't be able to."

His blunt but belated attempt at gallantry made her smile. If he wished to take her here and now, in this vacant, cavernous room smelling of oiled wood and fresh plaster, she wouldn't prevent him. What she dared not do in London was safe to do here. No prying eyes, no wagging tongues—none of the publicity that had proved fatal to her reputation.

Shakily she confessed, "I can't let this end. I want more." She craved all he could give her, having gone without for so very long.

As his mouth roamed her neck, she reminded herself that he couldn't break her heart because she hadn't given it to him. His curiosity and his need would be satisfied, as hers would be. And he might succeed in obliterating so many hurtful memories from her past. By sharing her body with this man, she could cut the ties that still bound her to the dead husband he knew about and the living lover whose existence she'd never revealed.

Seeking no additional justification for an act of impulse, she let her lips communicate her willingness, with kisses more eloquent than words.

Dare stripped away his coat. With an impressive economy of action, he slid one arm beneath her legs and wrapped the other around her waist, scooping her up and setting her down on the softer canvas bundled on the floor. The tight fabric of his breeches revealed his intentions, and her breathing became even more erratic.

He loosened the cord that laced her bodice and gained access to her breasts, spilling over the top of her corset. His lips traversed every inch of her exposed and heated flesh.

"You're exquisite. Too beautiful to be real."

She was a quivering mass of unrelieved lust. All her senses were alive, aroused by his caressing hands and mouth, the murmured endearments, the glow in his eyes, and the taste of him on her tongue. Inserting her fingers through the gap in his shirt, she felt crisp hair covering the solid muscles. She felt his powerful chest contract and expand. He slid his breeches down over his hips, revealing his erect and hardened shaft. Now his hands were moving up her legs, settling on her mound, making her writhe in anticipation. Boldly and seductively he stroked her inner flesh, already moist from wanting him.

With a groan of pleasure, he pressed himself into her cleft.

Oriana wrapped herself around him as he dived into her repeatedly. She'd assumed she could live without this, only to discover how wrong she'd been—and how bereft.

No exchange of promises bound them, no expectations, only their physical craving for each other. She didn't understand why this was happening, but this was not the time to make sense of it.

Content to let him set the pace, she patterned her motions on his. Kissing when he kissed. Surging forward to meet his thrusts. Lying still when he paused to savor the intimate contact.

Realizing how tightly she clutched his shoulders, she relaxed her fingers.

Dare startled her by abruptly seizing her wrists and pushing her arms back toward the canvas that cushioned them, pinning her beneath him with a tender savagery. His half-lidded, possessive eyes stared down at her, and he increased the tempo of his surging hips, intensifying her delight but also frightening her. This was, she sensed, a deliberate attempt to fuse not only their bodies, but also their destinies. And it was disastrously effective—that mysterious yet highly sensitive bud of her anatomy burst into sudden, fiery bloom. Her joy was so intense that it drew a wild cry from her throat, immediately echoed by his ecstatic moan.

He collapsed against her, panting, his cheek pressed against hers. His mouth found her earlobe and nibbled it.

"Delectable," he whispered. "I could feast upon you forever."

A glorious prospect, but impossible. Dare's lovemaking—terrifying and exhausting in its thoroughness and intensity—had been no overture.

It was a finale.

Chapter 9

Oriana's wanderings often brought her to the edge of Liverpool's docks. Pausing at the end of Red Cross Street, she gazed at a flotilla of ships, recently returned to port or preparing for the next voyage. Among them, she knew, were vessels that traveled to and from the Isle of Man. A fortnight past, she'd made her escape aboard the largest of them, *The Duke of Athol,* setting sail from Douglas. In a newspaper list of weekly arrivals, she'd spied the familiar names *Belle Anne* and *Peggy* and *Eliza,* which traded out of Ramsey. And the *Dorrity,* bringing lead ore from Sir Darius Corlett's smelting house.

She stopped a well-dressed merchant strolling in her direction. "Can you tell me where I might see the Manx trading ships?"

"I fear not, madam," he replied. "I'm an American, lately arrived from Boston, and haven't yet got my bearings."

The innkeeper at the Legs of Man could tell her what she wanted to know. Many weeks ago, Mr. Radcliffe had arranged her passage to Ramsey. Not only could he recite the names and owners and tonnage and cargo of every Manx vessel, he knew when they departed and where they anchored. But the likelihood that he was in regular contact with a certain mine owner interested in her whereabouts had kept her away from his establishment.

Within hours of the passionate interlude in Dare's library, she had fled Glen Auldyn. By inviting him to make love to her, she'd shattered his illusions about her respectability, and the only way to salvage her pride was to hasten to Liverpool.

She studied the fluttering pennants on each tall mast, searching for the Isle of Man's distinctive three-legged emblem, as her treacherous mind carried her back to the hillside villa.

After lying in Dare's arms as long as she dared, she'd laced up her bodice. He had pelted her with questions: Was she angry, offended, regretful? Reassured by her denials, he had bestowed many more intoxicating kisses. She had insisted on returning alone to Glencroft. And by the time she reached the cottage, her decision was made.

Forlornly waving Harriot Mellon's letter, she had informed her housekeeper of her intention to sail for Liverpool as soon as possible. With efficiency acquired from years of travel, she packed up her belongings. While Donny Corkhill loaded them onto his father's hay cart, she retreated to the parlor and sat down to compose a brief note for Dare, laden with apology but light on explanation. Never one to encourage false hopes, she stated that she would not return to the Isle of Man. To bid him farewell in writing rather than in person was preferable, for she'd convinced herself that a man so blunt would dislike an emotional parting scene.

She presented Mrs. Stowell with a golden guinea and the fashionable feather-trimmed bonnet that had elicited so many admiring sighs, entrusting her with a handful of coins for Ned Crowe.

No visitor could lawfully depart the island without the requisite pass signed by the Lieutenant Governor, which she purchased from the landlord of the King's Head in Ramsey, for nine shillings. Mr. Hinde sent her off in his carriage to Douglas, where she had the best chance of finding swift transport to England. Throughout her southward journey she fingered the piece of quartz she carried in her reticule. Of the two dozen sparkling stones Dare had given her, she'd kept only one as a memento of her visit to the mine.

In nine months' time, she thought ruefully, she might have another keepsake. But this week her breasts felt tender, and her temper grew shorter by the day. On several occasions she'd snapped at Mr. Aickin, manager of the Theatre Royal. With the onset of these symptoms, her fear of pregnancy subsided.

Turning her back upon the docks, she retraced her steps. By the time she reached Castle Street, the tower bells of St. George's pealed the opening notes of a hymn, followed by two long booms to mark the hour.

She was late for her rehearsal.

Frantically, she searched the broad and busy thoroughfare for a hackney coach. There was none to be had, and she was a long way from Williamson Square. If she walked too quickly, she'd have no breath to sing with.

While fighting her way through the crowd of clerks, servants, and wives belonging to the city's prosperous merchants, she carried on a familiar debate with herself over the wisdom of writing to Dare. She couldn't shake the feeling that she'd treated him unkindly. In her last days on the island, he'd proved himself her friend. At another time, under different circumstances, he might have become much more. His ship was in Liverpool— surely she could prevail upon a mariner to deliver a letter for her. Or should she wait till she was safely back in London?

Flushed and footsore, she arrived at the theater, and

humbly begged the assembled musicians to forgive her.
"The time slipped away from me," she told them apologetically. "I shall sing as well as I can, so you can all go
home early and have a long rest before tonight's performance." To her relief, none of the men appeared to be
vexed—they returned her smile and bobbed their heads.

The manager could fine her for tardiness, but wouldn't.
She was Ana St. Albans.

Tossing her cloak onto a chair, she took her position at
the front of the stage, careful to avoid the worst of the
warped and uneven floorboards. This theater, she
reflected, must be the shabbiest and most ill managed in
all England, and she found her best friend's enthusiasm
for performing here incomprehensible. The empty seats
of the pit, boxes, and gallery were tattered, faded, and
stained. The air was foul, and there was a pervasive
atmosphere of decay and gloom. But Harriot's career had
begun in provincial playhouses, in far worse conditions.
She, on the other hand, had toured the elegant European
opera houses, where crystal chandeliers illuminated gold-
painted panels and velvet hangings and satin upholstery.
The ladies' heads and gowns had glistened with jewels,
and sparkling buttons and badges had encrusted their
escorts' dress coats.

"Shall we start?" ask the harpsichordist, his hands
poised above the keyboard.

With sprightliness and verve, she sang, "*No nymph
that trips the verdant plains, with Sally can compare, she
wins the hearts of all the swains, and rivals ladies
fair . . .*"

One of the first tunes she'd learned, a tribute to her
mother's charms. Her father had never tired of it, and it
was a great favorite with her Vauxhall audiences.

She ran through her carefully selected repertoire of
English ballads and Italian arias and French *chansons*.

Francis Aickin didn't care what she sang, or in which languages, so long as she filled his auditorium for the two nights he had engaged her. The absence of Drury Lane performers, Harriot Mellon among them, had inconvenienced him. Mr. Sheridan's new play *Pizarro* was the greatest theatrical success in living memory, and he could spare none of his players until it ended its unprecedented run.

While singing the melancholy verses of "The Disappointed Lover," she thought about Dare Corlett.

"Most affecting," the harpsichordist commented when she finished. " 'Pon my life, Madame St. Albans, you'll have all the ladies sighing."

Oriana raced through a snippet from an opera, full of trills and vocal flourishes, the showy sort of song her audience would expect of a London performer. She was determined to give them their money's worth.

Nearly done. The musician brought forth the mournful notes he'd devised as a prelude to her final offering.

Her lips parted, and she sang the words that Ned Crowe had taught her.

> *"Te traa goll thie, as goll dy lhie*
> *Ta'n stoyll foym greinnagh mee roym*
> *Shen cowrey dooid dy ghleashagh*
> *Te tayrn dys traa ny liabbagh.*
>
> *My Ghuillyn vie, shegin dooin goll thie*
> *Ta'n dooie cheet er y chiollagh*
> *Te gignagh shin dy goll dy lhie*
> *Te bunnys tra dy ghraa, Oie vie."*

The stringed instruments came in softly, adding texture to the accompaniment as she continued with the English version.

"It's time to go home and go to rest
My stool is making me want to rise
This is a sign that we should move
Drawing us nearer to bedtime.

Come, my good lads, for we must away
Darkness draws in upon the hearth
Telling us all that we must go to rest
The time for saying good night."

Her accompanist beamed at her.

Wouldn't young Ned be amazed if he knew she would conclude her concert with his song? She had repeatedly sung it to the harpsichord player, who had recorded each note and composed an arrangement for the full orchestra. During their collaboration, he had admitted that she had defied the musicians' expectation that the visiting vocalist would be a termagant and difficult to work with. The local performers resented the annual invasion of London players—all but Miss Mellon, who was universally adored. Their friendship, Oriana guessed, was responsible for her warm reception here. Hardly a day passed without someone sharing with her an amusing anecdote or fond reminiscence about Harriot.

"Madame St. Albans." Francis Aickin stood in the wings, beckoning. "I beg a moment or two—meet me in the box-keeper's office."

She gathered up her cloak, wondering if he was going to fine her after all. Should she protest the punishment, or accept it?

He invited her to take the only chair that could be crammed into the tiny space he'd chosen for this interview. "I was a little acquainted with Sally Vernon years ago," he told her in his smooth, Irish-flavored voice, "when I performed at Covent Garden and Drury Lane.

And during my brief career as a hosier in York Street, I was fortunate enough to secure the patronage of your father, the Duke of St. Albans."

Familiar with his manipulations, she perceived that he wanted something from her.

"And now his lovely daughter graces the theatrical firmament. Our brief association has proved most pleasant—and promises to be profitable. This season finds my company sadly depleted. Mr. Sheridan's great success with his new play—a masterpiece, I'm sure—has deprived me of dear Miss Mellon and other leading players from Drury Lane. The people of Liverpool tell me, 'London actors, or none!' and I must oblige them."

"Your company includes Mrs. Chapman from Covent Garden," Oriana reminded him. "And Mr. Young. And the comedian, Mr. Knight."

"Nevertheless, I am in need of reinforcements. For that reason, I plead with you to remain in Liverpool."

"For how long?"

"Until August."

"I'm sorry, sir, but I cannot stay. At the end of the month I begin my annual summer engagement at Vauxhall. I have a prior commitment to Mr. Simpson and Mr. Barrett to sing once every fortnight."

"Could you not stay with us for another week? I'll make it worth your while."

She very nearly advised him to spend his money improving this ramshackle theater, but she held her tongue. "I'll consider it," she replied, knowing perfectly well that she must reject his invitation.

On her way back to her lodging, she composed a letter to Dare Corlett.

To Sir Darius Corlett, Ramsey, Isle of Man. Sir, I trust this letter finds you in good health and spirits . . .

Too formal.

Dear Sir Darius, I apologize for my hasty departure, and hope you can forgive me for . . .

Renting his cottage in the glen? Encouraging him to make love to her at Skyhill House? Running away from him?

My dearest Dare, You are constantly in my thoughts, day and night. My life seems dull and dreary without you. If only you were here to talk with me, and make me laugh, and hold me in your arms, kissing me until I'm witless, just as you did when we . . .

Realizing that she'd walked past Mrs. Woodell's house, Oriana turned back.

Reaching into her cloak for the door key, her fingers brushed the quartz Dare had given her. She let herself in and climbed the staircase. On the landing she paused to look at the stone, a new habit of hers, and held it so the light would strike the facets.

From above, a high-pitched voice called, "Here at last! I've been waiting forever!"

Startled, she dropped the quartz. "Harri! You're supposed to be in London!"

The actress bounded down the steps to embrace her, laughing all the while. "We arrived today, on the mail coach. Mother was thoroughly rattled, but she's sleeping now."

"I want all the news from town. But first I must find my treasure." Kneeling down to search, she found it by the wainscoting.

"Oh, how pretty! What is it?"

"Quartz crystal. It came from Sir Darius Corlett's lead mine."

Harriot noted the softening of her friend's voice, the yearning in the fine hazel eyes, and drew the only possible conclusion about her relationship with the mine owner.

She followed Oriana to her chamber, the nicest one in the house. The singer never had to economize, or share her bed. She could afford to travel by post chaise instead of the mail coach, without counting the cost.

Her interest in Oriana's latest romance went unsatisfied, and she was forced to answer questions about recent events at Drury Lane theater. "*Pizarro* is all the rage," she reported. "Kemble is better suited to his role than his sister Mrs. Siddons. She plays a camp follower, in a most majestic fashion. Sheridan is once again the most celebrated playwright in the realm. It's his greatest achievement in twenty years, and the theater is packed to the heavens every night. But I worried that I'd be stuck in town forever, with nothing much to do—another actress understudies Mrs. Jordan. When I reminded old Sherry that I was wanted at Theatre Royal in Liverpool, he let me come."

"Mr. Aickin will be glad. He'd rather have you than me. An actress is more useful to him than a singer."

It pleased Harriot to hear that she was appreciated here in Liverpool, after listening to her mother's bitter comparisons of herself and her more famous friend. She needed no reminders of Oriana's superior talents, or her beauty, or her aristocratic Beauclerk cousins. According to her mother, Oriana was sluttish and immoral, and therefore didn't deserve her successes. Harriot knew that she'd strayed from the path of virtue only because she'd believed in Mr. Teversal's promise to wed her. And she'd seen that a brilliant career and having a duke for a cousin couldn't mend a broken heart or restore a sullied reputation.

Studying the lovely, solemn face, Harriot tried to think of a rallying quip to make Oriana smile. "How lucky that

Mother and I arrived in time to witness your Liverpool debut."

"And I'm fortunate to have you here. I'm more nervous than I should be."

"You, nervous? Absurd!"

"It's my first time here. Expectations are very high."

That a singer so gifted and renowned could doubt her ability to please a Liverpool audience was incomprehensible to Harriot. She wondered if that mine owner was responsible for Oriana's dispiritedness.

"Aren't you going to tell me about your Manxman?" she asked.

Her question brought a sudden flush to Oriana's pale cheeks. "I already did—in my letter."

Actress that she was, Harriot could distinguish between feigned indifference and the real thing. "You said he was arrogant and disagreeable. Did he make an indecent proposal?"

The auburn head drooped. "He got what he wanted without ever asking."

Harriot couldn't think of a reply that wouldn't sound critical or judgmental—like her mother.

"I wanted so much to earn his esteem," Oriana continued. "And I did. I wasn't burdened by my fame, or my notoriety. I was a prim and proper widow, leading a quiet life in the country with her fowls and her cow and her goat. We became friends. He confided his darkest secret and shared his highest ambitions. He is a brilliant man, with a very sharp wit. But we spent too many hours alone together," she said wretchedly. "A sort of madness came over me. Afterward, I couldn't bear to see him again, so I took the next packet boat for Liverpool."

"Oriana, if you'd stayed, he might have proposed!"

"How could I accept him, after concealing my identity for four weeks? I had a concert to prepare here, and must return to London and rehearse at Vauxhall. All this work was supposed to help me forget. Only I haven't."

"Perhaps you don't really want to," said Harriot, feeling very wise, and terribly sad.

"Here we have a set of mahogany chairs in the highest style, for the dining room. To be covered in whatever material you desire."

Dare ran one hand across the carved back of one chair. *Damned uncomfortable against the spine,* he reckoned. "Not quite what I had in mind."

Directly behind him, Wingate gave a faint hum of concern. The butler carried a long list of necessities, and after nearly an hour in the furniture warehouse, very few items had been crossed off.

"Your new house, does it have a library?" the salesman inquired.

"Certainly." And Dare would never again enter it without remembering Oriana Julian.

"We offer an extensive selection of map tables and folding steps."

"I've seen enough. For today," he added, so the man wouldn't feel slighted.

A tedious and uninspiring business, stocking his villa with chairs, tables, carpets, and everything else it lacked. He should be enthusiastic about the task, but Oriana's disappearance had stolen the luster from his project. In his daily wanderings along Liverpool's crowded streets, he'd paid closer attention to the female passersby than the goods on show in the shop windows, seeking an oval face of surpassing beauty, framed with auburn curls, and a pair of clear hazel eyes set beneath exquisitely arched brows. But it appeared only in his fitful dreams, and nowhere else.

"Shall we stop at the carpet seller's, sir?" suggested Wingate, after they exited the warehouse.

"Tomorrow," Dare decided. "You're dismissed for the rest of the afternoon."

Four days ago he'd disembarked from the *Dorrity* with every intention of finding Oriana, confident that he could locate her in this familiar city. But his systematic and, in his opinion, brilliantly orchestrated search, had turned up not a speck of evidence that she was here now, or ever had been. Mrs. Julian was not included on the subscription list for the largest circulating library. Not a single maker of musical instruments had ever heard of her. She was not, he had determined, a benefactress of the local infirmary, the Seaman's Hospital, or the charity school—he'd visited all. He'd attended the most recent gathering in the Town Hall Assembly Rooms, to no avail; he hadn't encountered her there. None of the dressmakers or shopkeepers recognized her name.

Each time he pieced together the events of their last day together, desperate to make sense of them, he inevitably failed. The Mellon woman's letter had distressed Oriana. She had responded to his lovemaking with uninhibited passion. And after making him the happiest—and most hopeful—of mortals, she'd vanished from his glen.

Tonight he would continue the hunt at the Theatre Royal.

He might as well use those concert tickets his friend had procured at his request. A review of the first performance had appeared in this morning's newspaper. Disregarding the flowery compliments to the London vocalist and rebukes to the unruly spectators, he'd scanned the names of the most celebrated attendees. No mention of a Mrs. Julian, but his hopes had soared when he learned that a Miss Mellon and her mother had been spotted in the audience. If Oriana's friend was in Liverpool, she must be here also.

Until he saw her again and received the explanation he was due, he must endure this hateful uncertainty. His dismay at her abrupt departure had given way to a burning indignation, and he suspected that listening to an overweight soprano screech in gibberish at the top of her lungs—for hours on end—was only going to make it worse.

Chapter 10

◦─◦◦◦─◦

The dressing room lacked a door, affording no privacy whatever, and the stage manager had failed to rig a curtain. Oriana hadn't bothered demanding one, though, for she'd arrived at the theater fully dressed and had spent all her time on the stage. And with no acquaintances in the house tonight, Oriana wouldn't linger in this dismal little room.

Francis Aickin rushed in, crying exultantly, "Another triumph! Gad, I thought the clapping and shouting would never cease!"

Oriana arched her brows. "During my recital, or after?" She would remember this night's audience as the most unruly she'd ever faced, far worse than on Tuesday evening. In a contest with the Italian cabal at the opera house, she would choose the Liverpudlians as the more disruptive group.

"I hope your warm reception in this city has softened your resolve to leave it so soon," the manager went on. "Won't you agree to an additional performance, out of consideration for those poor souls who had not the privilege of securing tickets?"

His question was so blatantly self-interested that she burst out laughing. Her work was finished, and she was so glad to be free of Aickin that she found his persistence—and greed—more humorous than aggravating.

Turning toward the door, the Irishman said invitingly, "My dear sir, if you identify yourself, I'll gladly present you to Madame St. Albans."

Still smiling, she turned around to see who was there.

"No need for introductions," said Sir Darius Corlett, his voice harder than Manx granite. "She knows who I am."

A thunderous tide of alarm washed over her. He'd followed her to Liverpool—had actually attended her concert. Dear heaven, he'd looked as though he wanted to strangle her, and no wonder!

The manager's speculative gaze darted from Oriana to her visitor and back again. He grinned and winked at her, then said, "I'm sure you and your gentleman prefer privacy. We shall continue our business discussion at another time."

His insinuation sparked her temper. "No need to scurry away till the matter is settled," she said sharply. "As I've told you repeatedly, Mr. Aickin, I cannot sing again in Liverpool. I should be most grateful if you would pay out my fee immediately, so I can depart for London." It was lowering to plead for her salary in front of Dare, but her pride must not get in the way of her livelihood.

"Certainly, certainly. My treasurer is still reckoning tonight's receipts, and tomorrow you'll receive your share." With a shallow bow to Oriana and another to the baronet, Mr. Aickin made a speedy exit.

Nervously playing with the tassels dangling from the gold cord around her waist, she admitted to Dare, "For the past two days, I've been writing a letter for you."

"How very thoughtful." The stony voice contradicted his polite words. "My compliments on your remarkable performance. Not only here, but also while you lived at Glencroft."

"You've every right to be angry. But I had a very good reason for—for—"

"Duping me?"

"There was no deception, Dare. Not exactly."

She felt so odd standing before him in her green-satin stage dress, designed to resemble Turkish attire, her cheeks rouged and powdered, brilliants in her hair.

"Where were you seated? I didn't notice you down in the pit."

"My tickets entitled me to a box, but I neglected to send my servant to hold my place, and someone stole it. I was high up in the one-shilling gallery, squeezed between two boisterous fellows who made such ribald comments about your anatomy that I wanted to shove my fist into their leering faces."

A sharp rap on the doorframe interrupted their tense dialogue.

Tentatively the harpsichordist asked, "Madame St. Albans, may I beg a moment of your time?"

She moved across the room, giving Dare a wary glance as she swept past him.

"It's unlikely we'll meet again, and I wanted you to have this." The musician presented a rolled-up paper tied with a crimson ribbon. "I made a clean copy of our music for the Manx song."

Blinking back a sudden rush of tears, Oriana said, "Thank you, I am most grateful—and shall always treasure it."

"Playing for the *protegée* of my idol, the great Haydn, has been an honor. And a pleasure."

Touched by this accolade, she replied, "If you ever seek employment in London, come to my house in Soho

Square. I'm on good terms with the managers of all the theaters, and the opera house."

"I'm not sure my wife would care to live anywhere but Liverpool," he admitted, before taking his leave.

When she turned back to Dare, his face was even grimmer than it had been before the interruption.

"That fellow knows more about you than I do," he fumed. "He was speaking of Haydn the composer?"

"Yes. During his residence in London, he befriended me."

"And how many other men have done so?"

If Dare was jealous, she reasoned, his discovery of her identity had not obliterated his affection for her. On a faint laugh, she said, "Herr Haydn is an old gentleman, very grandfatherly. There was no impropriety in that or any other professional relationship."

"You never sang for me," he said bitterly. "Were you hoarding your talents for the paying customers, Madame St. Albans?"

Deep in her abdomen, she felt a painful twinge. Being a female had its hellish moments, and this was definitely one of them. Soon her emotional turmoil would be compounded by the grinding ache that came once a month.

"This face paint and satin gown are the real disguise—it's what my *paying customers* expect to see. Underneath, I'm the same person who sought refuge in your glen. I did not lie to you, I never told an untruth. Oriana Julian is my lawful name. I eloped with a soldier, who died in India. It was my choice to give out only those essential facts. Do not forget, you didn't extend the warmest of welcomes. And I'm unaware of any law, English or Manx, requiring me to share my full history with an unfriendly stranger. Which you were."

"My attitude changed, as you well know."

"I'm not in the habit of confiding in people," she replied.

"Or trusting them?"

"In London I am constantly scrutinized and criticized. During those weeks I lived in your glen, I found the solitude I had been seeking."

"At the moment, Oriana, I care very little for the differences between your public and your private persona."

He *did* care. If he were indifferent, he would have left the theater without confronting her.

"At our last meeting," he continued, "your famous reticence was notably absent. We achieved a particular closeness." He moved in, lancing her with his dark eyes. "Your hasty departure from Glencroft, was it prompted by that letter you received, or what we did together in my library?"

She braved his piercing stare. "Both. I was expected here in Liverpool. With Harriot stuck in London, we risked losing our rooms at Mrs. Waddell's house. And then after my—my recklessness complicated the situation, I didn't want you thinking I'd set a snare to trap you and your fortune. Knowing you wouldn't care to see me again, I left."

"You assumed I *wanted* to be rid of you? If so, why in hell's name would I make love to you?"

The answer was so obvious that she didn't bother to voice it. He was a man, one accustomed to having whomever or whatever he desired.

He vented his frustration in a gusty huff. "You understand me about as well as I understand you. Which is to say hardly at all. When you offered me that most precious of gifts, was it because you were bored by country living? Maybe you were seeking physical gratification, or perhaps settling a score. Or is that the way you typically bid a gentleman friend farewell?"

She flushed from her crown to her toes. "No!"

"Then why, Oriana? I deserve an honest answer."

Marching up to him, she declared, "Because at that moment, I was greedy for all the things I had either lost or had sacrificed. Warmth. Affection. Desire. With you, I felt so alive."

"Behold me at your service. After my two-week nightmare, I require a bit of enlivening myself. Let us instantly retire to my hotel. Or, if you prefer, to your lodging house."

She couldn't tell whether he spoke in jest, or in earnest. "I'm no whore," she informed him frostily. "A common assumption, but I assure you that singing is my sole source of income."

Sordid rumors about the Siren of Soho and her string of lovers must be circulating here in Liverpool—why else would her concerts fill the theater? She wanted to hasten away from this smoky, busy city before Dare heard about her sullied reputation. And if he was the type to boast that he'd had his way with Ana St. Albans, she preferred not to know.

Seizing her shoulders, he growled, "Nevertheless, you are wickedly, shamelessly cunning. I might find a way to forgive you for keeping your damned secret, but not for deserting me."

His kiss was angry, overflowing with recrimination. When her tender breasts brushed against the solid wall of his chest, she recoiled.

Dare released her with a dissatisfied sigh. Glancing at their surroundings, he complained, "Christ, this is the *ugliest* room I've ever seen. How can you bear it?" Taking her cloak from the back of a chair, he said, "I suggest we continue this conversation in a more comfortable and civilized location. I'm staying at the Royal Hotel in Whitehall, a short walk from here."

"I might be recognized. Meet me tomorrow—I'm at Mrs. Waddell's house in School Lane, Number Thirty-three."

"Oh, no, Madame St. Albans. I won't have you repeating your furtive escape from Glencroft. You might slip away from your lodging in the middle of the night."

"I won't," she promised. "I *can't*. Mr. Aickin hasn't paid me. When he does, I'll depart for London. Unless you knock me senseless and stow me aboard your ship, you can't prevent me from leaving Liverpool."

Flashing a grin, he said, "An excellent suggestion. I would greatly enjoy holding you hostage, and exerting some form of punishment. Taking away your clothes—confining you to my cabin—keeping you in my bed."

Her heart fluttered. If she weren't careful, this bold and aggravating gentleman would steal it from her.

"I should think you'd want to toss me overboard," she said. "You've already declared me guilty of duplicity and treachery."

"I'm feeling more merciful now. Your logic is deeply flawed, but your contrition moves me. A few more of your enchanting smiles, a glass of brandy, and perhaps I'll absolve you of any deliberate intent to wound me. But I withhold final judgment until I've heard the complete history of Ana St. Albans."

Thick, heavy clouds spread slowly across the darkening sky overhead, as Dare escorted Oriana towards his hotel. Mindful of her desire for privacy, he avoided busy Whitechapel and took her down a lesser thoroughfare running to the south of Williamson Square.

In the month of June, nightfall came late, and there was enough light left to study her as she walked silently beside him.

Her poise and grace and her blue-velvet cloak were all that remained of the lady who had lived at Glencroft; in every other respect, she was different. A thick, ropy braid, anchored with diamond-studded hairpins, circled her aristocratic head. Real gems, or paste? Her own purchase, or a lover's gift? The torture of speculation was driving him mad.

He'd left his island to search for her, a mad notion of marriage whirling about in his mind. When she'd stepped onto the stage, a vision of loveliness in shimmering green satin, his vague but persistent dream of winning her had dissolved.

Her voice, which he'd longed to hear, was incomparable. Its range and power astonished and moved him. His knowledge of music was sketchy, and he'd been too stunned and outraged to take pleasure from her performance, but he had heard in her singing the same passion and need that she had expressed with her lovemaking.

I was greedy for all the things I had either lost or had sacrificed. Warmth. Affection. Desire.

Her superior talent had made her famous, but the price of her fame was the loneliness.

Coming to Church Street, she halted, and said miserably, "I can't do it."

"Do what?"

"Go to that hotel. My mind was muddled. You'll get your explanation, but you'll have to wait."

"I want it tonight, Oriana. Here and now, if necessary." His assertiveness, and choice of words, made it seem that he was demanding something more. And in a sense, he was.

"St. Peter's lies just ahead. I go there to listen to the

organist practice, or whenever I want to avoid Mrs. Entwistle."

"Who?"

"Harriot Mellon's mother. She has a foul temper and she dislikes me, because my advice to her daughter invariably contradicts hers. And because I'm—for other reasons. She has convinced poor Harri that if she achieves enormous success on the stage, she'll catch a rich husband to pamper them both." Shaking her sparkly head, Oriana said, "It almost never turns out that way. And not just any rich suitor will do, for Mrs. Entwistle says that Harri's father was a lord—although she refuses to reveal which one."

She paused when they came to the church steps. "We can talk here."

"Your friend's parentage doesn't interest me," said Dare, seating himself. "Now—tell me about yours."

Chapter 11

Clutching her scroll of music, Oriana faced him like a reluctant witness forced to give evidence before a magistrate. "Like Harriot, I'm baseborn."

That possibility had never occurred to Dare.

"My father was George Beauclerk, third Duke of St. Albans. If you've studied your English history, or ever read Mr. Pepys's *Diary,* you know about pretty, witty Nell Gwynn, the actress who was mistress to King Charles II. She bred a pair of sons in quick succession, and insisted that their father provide surnames and titles. The eldest was designated Earl of Burford, and his father was later persuaded to bestow the dukedom that eventually descended to my father."

Her lineage was not merely noble, he marveled, it was royal—albeit on the wrong side of the blanket. Earl of Bumfold, Duke of Stallbarn—Burford and St. Albans.

"After a year of wedlock, my father separated from his duchess. Like his great-grandsire, the Merry Monarch, he failed to sire a legitimate heir. His many mistresses proved fertile, and supplied him with bastard children. He preferred to live in Brussels, and while there achieved a brief reconciliation with the duchess, during which he was flagrantly unfaithful—singers were his great weakness. After the failure of his marriage, he paid a visit to London, where his fancy lighted on Sally Vernon, a performer at Drury Lane. She became his mistress, and my mother."

"You have theatrical connections on your maternal and paternal side," he observed.

She nodded. "Mother was herself the bastard daughter of the tenor Joseph Vernon. As a child she roamed Covent Garden selling flowers and singing ballads— everyone called her Nosegay Sal. When she was older she provided other services, for an extra shilling. One of her lovers, a popular actor, put her on the stage. The duke was her most exalted conquest, and she made sure everyone knew by continuing to perform for the duration of her pregnancy." Smiling, she acknowledged, "While still in the womb, I was creating my first scandal. My father bestowed on me the name Oriana Vera, and rewarded Mother with the freehold of a Soho Square house, and an increase in her allowance. My earliest memory is sitting at her harpsichord, pounding at the keys and trying to sing."

Her appreciation for the music that filled her home, coupled with a uniquely mature voice, convinced the duke and his mistress that they had a prodigy on their hands. St. Albans, opera lover and lover of opera singers, agreed that his tiny daughter's talent should be cultivated, and promptly departed for Brussels.

"Grandfather Vernon was my first vocal instructor," she went on. "I wasn't very old when Mother loaned me to Mr. Sheridan to fill children's parts at Drury Lane. At age six I became instantly famous—I quelled a riot in the pit by bursting into song. Sheridan was quick to publicize the fact that I was Nosegay Sal's little girl, 'direct descended from Nelly Gwynn and King Charles.' My popularity was assured. Before I turned ten, I performed a Vauxhall Gardens concert with my grandfather. The

Prince of Wales attended, and the next day he sent me a puppy, a King Charles spaniel. Mother said I must call him Rowley, after my great-great-grandpapa. It was His Majesty's nickname."

St. Albans, believing that Oriana was worthy of Continental audiences, invited her—and her mother—to join him in Brussels. Her lighthearted anecdotes of the Rue Ducale household revealed a deep affection for her father, and an awareness of his many faults and vices. Burdened by massive debts at home and abroad, he was so hopelessly insolvent that Brussels shopkeepers refused to extend credit. Whenever the duke required a fresh supply of beer, or ham, he had it sent over from Glassenbury, his estate in Kent. During Oriana's public recital at the Théâtre de la Monnaie, he'd leaned precariously over the edge of his box—not to obtain a better view of his daughter, but to ogle a luscious female. Sally, restored to favor and alert to possible rivals, had made a scene. Their quarrel, highly entertaining to Belgian high society, had distressed Oriana.

"Undeterred by his lack of funds, he started building a grand castle on the outskirts of the city." Fondly she recalled their shared excitement when a shipment of fruit trees and shrubbery arrived from England, destined for his new pleasure garden.

"This was his last gift to me," she said, parting her cloak to exhibit a gold brooch pinned to her bodice. "I always wear it when I sing, for luck. His family crest—a lion standing guard, wearing a ducal crown and collared with three roses. The motto is engraved below—*Auspicium melioris aevi*. A pledge of better times. He was still waiting for them when he died."

His grace's will made no provision for Sally Vernon or her daughter. They had the London house, furnished at

his expense and stuffed with treasures from the Beauclerk collection: portraits of the king and the actress, old
master paintings, antique jewels—the diamond pins in
Oriana's hair had belonged to Nell Gwynn—rich carpets,
fine furniture.

"The next duke died within months of inheriting the
title and properties. He was succeeded by a cousin, Lord
Vere of Hanworth, an art collector. He came to Soho
Square and offered to buy back some of the Beauclerk
heirlooms. Mother refused, saying they were my legacy.
Cousin Aubrey took an interest in my career, and invited
me to Hanworth, near Windsor Castle, to meet his family.
He'd lived in Italy, and suggested that Mother take me
there for more extensive training."

"You were there a long time," he recalled.

"Four years. In London, I had won accolades. But in
Naples and Rome and Florence and Venice and Milan, I
couldn't overcome the prejudice against my national-
ity—my voice and style were too 'English' to suit Italian
audiences. I wasn't a failure, but I wasn't a success. Back
to London we went, fully expecting that I was experienced enough for the King's Theatre. Mr. Kelly, who
directs the operas, fed me many compliments but he was
blunt: he wanted Italian singers. The King Charles and
Nelly Gwynn mythology was no longer useful to me. I
was only sixteen, and had spent a decade in the public
view—I knew no other life."

"But you persevered," said Dare.

"Mother gave me no choice. There were other venues
in which I could perform. In summer I sang at Vauxhall
and during Lent I performed in oratorios. Herr Haydn
urged me to rest my voice, and concentrate on the
pianoforte. But Mother was determined that someday I
should be a *prima donna*."

He tried to imagine a younger Oriana—well traveled, disillusioned, living in the Soho Square house with her controlling and ambitious mother.

"That's when you decided to elope with Captain Henry Julian."

She nodded. "Burford, Cousin Aubrey's son, played matchmaker at Newmarket."

"You described your marriage as a rebellion. Against your mother?"

"And her plans for me. She was urging me to marry an Italian—preferably a singer or musician, but almost any Italian would do. As a *signora*, I could conceal my Englishness, and pass as foreign. It was her obsession. I decided to run off with my handsome young captain— salvation in a uniform—and let him fight my battles for me." After a pause, she said, "Henry's love for me cost him his life. Please, Dare, don't make me dredge up that tragedy."

"You might have shared these facts weeks ago," he told her. "Why didn't you?"

"Because I'd wearied of men treating me like a whore—as you did when you found me in your study and decided that I was your birthday present. I'll not be your Nell Gwynn," she said with determination, "or your Sally Vernon."

"I made no such suggestion."

"It wasn't necessary. When you were kissing me a while ago, I could tell what you were after. I've been fending off improper advances for many years now."

"Successfully?"

"Yes. Not that it's any concern of yours."

"It concerns me a great deal." Watching her closely, he commented, "Very well, the respectable Widow Julian and the celebrated Ana St. Albans are one and the same. I require clarification on exactly two points. Which one was rolling around on the library floor with Sir Dare Corlett of Skyhill House? And who left a gift of two dozen quartz crystals behind at Glencroft?"

Pulling her hand from his grasp, she inserted it in her cloak pocket. "If you'd counted, you would have found this one missing."

In the absence of bright light, the pale stone she held up was lusterless. But it restored his faltering hopes. He kissed her, plunging his tongue into the warm recess of her mouth, and his hand crept beneath the folds of her cloak, seeking her breast.

She pulled away from him. "Do you enjoy making females weep?"

"I never have done—you'd be the first." He watched her fumble with the reticule dangling from her dainty wrist. "What's this?" he asked when she handed over a silver coin.

"The price of your seat in the gallery. I want no profit from this great mess I've made."

"A wasted gesture," he said, and flung her shilling aside. "I'm taking you back to Glen Auldyn."

Oriana surged up from the bench. "When you see Ned Crowe, tell him how I've been using those songs he taught me."

"Tell him yourself. I won't sail for Ramsey without you."

"I don't belong there. Mrs. Julian's holiday in the glen has ended. London is home to Ana St. Albans." She rose onto her toes, her lips touching his in a hasty, off-center kiss. "I shall enjoy thinking about you, living in your beautiful villa on top of the hill, adding interesting minerals to your collection, warding off all those fortune hunters . . ."

Watching her walk away, he wished she *had* actually been chasing him to get his money. The motive of greed at least would have made sense to him. Her rejection did not.

Six weeks ago this Oriana, this enigma, had drifted into his life, roused his suspicions, won his affection, made love to him. And yet again, she was leaving before he could express the volatile emotion trapped inside him, roiling and burning like lava.

In some respects her lengthy recitation had enlightened him, but she was as much a mystery as she'd ever been. There was so much more he needed to know. Her love of singing was genuine, but did she derive true satisfaction from her profession? Her strained relationship with her mother, and the loss of her young husband, had scarred her. She was starved for affection, and yet every time he offered it she turned away from him.

She couldn't leave Liverpool yet, he reminded himself. She hadn't received her salary. As her retreating figure grew ever more distant, he wondered whether he could rely on the assistance of the oily manager, Aickin, to delay her departure. Failing that, he'd have to steal the theater's cash-box.

"You're the most ungrateful daughter in all Christendom, and I the most miserable parent!"

Harriot Mellon, the object of her mother's fury, clamped her jaws together. It never did any good to defend herself against such a harsh charge; that merely prolonged the tantrum. She stared at the skirt flounce she hemmed and, with shaking fingers, completed a few more stitches.

"Have you nothing to say for yourself?" Mrs. Entwistle shrieked.

Say nothing. Sit up straight. Don't cry.

"Your selfish disregard for my feelings pains me, Harriot. All your life I've worked hard—your stepfather, too—all on your behalf. We rescued you from the drudgery in Mr. Stanton's theater in Staffordshire, and took you to London and Mr. Sheridan. Through sheer stupidity, you almost lost your chance for a place at Drury Lane. I had to go back to him and debase myself, begging and pleading."

The incident had occurred four years ago, and Harriot was never allowed to forget it. "There was no vacancy in his company."

"When people in Hyde Park mocked your shabby dresses, I hoped it would send you back to plead with Sheridan. But no, you were too proud, never mind that your poor parents were beggaring themselves to keep you in the city. And when Drury Lane found room for you, I proved my devotion by accompanying you to the theater and back to our lodging—every day, on foot. And twice a day when you had rehearsals and performances both."

The constant exercise had proved beneficial, for Harriot's figure was—in her own estimation as well as her mother's—overly plump. "Yes, I know," she responded, thinking back to those early days in London, and the scoldings she'd endured while trudging to and from her place of work, where she'd labored for thirty shillings per week. She'd been relieved when they moved into a house in Little Russell Street, directly across from the theater.

Her progress in her profession was slow. She played secondary roles—merry, warm-hearted country girls—and understudied the popular Mrs. Jordan's leading parts. She could sing and dance. But because she was so unlike the elegant, sylphlike Oriana, or the majestic tragedian Mrs. Siddons, she shared her mother's fears that she would rise no farther in the theatrical hierarchy.

Continuing the tirade, her mother held up Miss Farren as an example of the good fortune that could come to a clever actress. The lovely Elizabeth's salary had soared to thirty guineas a week before she retired from the stage to wed the Earl of Derby. Harriot nodded at intervals. Lifting her eyes from her sewing, she feigned attentiveness, though in fact she was eyeing the water stain on the parlor ceiling and mentally straightening the framed aquatint on the wall.

But when the shrill, cutting voice uttered the name Ana St. Albans, Harriot could no longer shut it out.

"Mark this, my girl. If you don't escape the influence of that saucy slut, you're bound to come to grief. Unless you heed what I say, do as I tell you, you'll end your days in a workhouse, a fat and pitiful woman, without a penny or a friend to your name."

This was more than she could bear. "You're wrong about Oriana. And about me. I've *always* been grateful for your care and devotion, Mother. I *am* obedient. But however hard I try to please, you call me foolish and ignorant. You say I've put on too much weight and cultivate the wrong sort of people. But I remember when you encouraged my friendship with Oriana. You wished I could be exactly like her—beautiful, admired, successful. Only after you learned about her affair with Mr. Teversal did you warn me to keep away. She was heartbroken and distraught, and in need. I couldn't desert her."

She left the room hurriedly to evade the vicious tongue-lashing her defiant words would provoke. If she remained in this house one minute longer, her mother would hunt her down. Blinded by tears, she opened the front door and bolted outside. Her escape ended as she started down the steps, when she collided with a solid mass of flesh and bone.

The object blocking her way was a man—very tall, attractively dark. Blinking her eyes to clear them, she sent the tears rolling down her cheeks.

"I've finally done it."

"What?" she asked.

"Made a lady weep."

"Oh, no, sir, I started before I bumped you." She dried her eyes with the dangling end of the kerchief tied over her bosom. "So sorry."

"No apology necessary," he said pleasantly. "You must be Miss Mellon. I'm looking for Mrs. Julian—Madame St. Albans—Oriana—whatever she answers to this morning. My name is Corlett."

When he smiled, he was even more handsome, and she wished she had happier news for him. Flustered, she replied, "She's not here."

"Has she left for the theater?"

"No, sir. She's gone to London."

"I might have guessed."

The cold fury of his reply was just as unsettling as her mother's explosive rages. Then his expression changed, and his face looked as bleak and bereft as Oriana's had been that morning as she climbed into the post chaise to begin her long journey.

PART II

Let us not then rush blindly on unto it,
Like lustful beasts, that only know to do it:
For lust will languish, and that heat decay,
But thus, thus, keeping endless holiday,
Let us together closely lie, and kiss,
There is no labour, no shame in this;
This hath pleased, doth please,
and long will please; never
Can this decay, but is beginning ever.

—BEN JONSON

Chapter 12

Oriana, her face shaded by her hat's excessively broad brim, strolled with her cousin beside Hyde Park's ornamental river. Brilliant sunshine glanced off the Serpentine's calm waters, and she was trying very hard not to squint. Too many people were watching her.

"Your first Vauxhall night was successful?" Lord Burford asked.

"A good beginning to what I trust will be a profitable summer."

"But you'll be at Newmarket, I hope, to see your favorite run. Combustible finished third at Brocket Hall, her first race," he boasted. "My brother Fred offers himself as jockey for her next."

"A racing clergyman—what must his bishop think?" The energetic Lord Frederick Beauclerk's passion for sport made Oriana smile. "When last I saw him, he boasted of having a saddle built into his pulpit at St. Michael's so he could preach as though on horseback. The parishioners must be relieved that he doesn't give his sermons while swinging his cricket bat."

133

Burford was as typical an English nobleman as could be found in the park this afternoon. After serving his king and country in the army for more than a decade, including a stint in Canada, he'd stood for Parliament. When not occupied with countryside matters, he attended sporting events. In the earl's face, as in her own, Oriana could trace the unmistakable imprint of Nell Gwynn, their legendary ancestress—plump, soft lips and pointed chin, prominently arched brows, and hair that was tinted with copper. A passionate interest in Newmarket racing was another St. Albans legacy.

He'd found her in her music room, fingers dancing across the keys of her pianoforte as she sang from the depths of her lonely heart. After she had performed a pensive Manx song in a minor key—which swelled her nostalgia for the island—he had invited her to join him in a jaunt through the park. She had accepted, for what was the point of having a new promenade gown if she wasn't going to show it off?

To maintain her place in the forefront of fashion, she'd called in her seamstress. This extravagant enterprise, like her constant vocal practice, helped to fill a void that hadn't existed before her Isle of Man holiday. Suke Barry was a grateful recipient of her cast-off garments. All the ladies who so slavishly followed her modes would hurry to their own dressmakers when they saw that Ana St. Albans had bestowed last season's wardrobe upon her maidservant.

As Oriana and her cousin strolled along at the edge of the busy carriageway, sharp feminine eyes studied every detail of her attire, from the number of nodding plumes atop her large hat to the deep, lace-edged flounce of her indigo gown. The gentlemen also looked at her. The riders slowed their hacks as they went by, the drivers whipped up the teams pulling their curricles and phaetons in an effort to impress her. One bold pedestrian stopped, ostensibly to ask the earl's opinion of the costly and pampered horseflesh on parade. But she and Burford both knew that his real purpose was to flirt with her.

When they walked on, she searched for familiar faces among the fashionable throng. Any combination of dark head, broad shoulders, and exceptional height never failed to catch her attention, and inevitably caused her pulse to race.

Stop being so silly, she chided herself. There was no chance that she'd find Sir Darius Corlett in this gathering. He was far, far away, either in Liverpool still, or back on his island.

Ignoring the display of privileged humanity, she let her mind carry her off to a distant glen, undisturbed by carriage wheels or chattering voices. Its silence was broken only by birdsong—or the honk of a territorial goose. A gem of a house stood atop a green hill. Its owner was closeted in his study, composing another treatise on the origin and antiquity of Manx rock formations.

"Looking for someone?" Burford inquired.

"No, no," she answered briskly.

Dare Corlett had once followed her across the Irish Sea, from Ramsey to Liverpool. It was madness to suppose he might travel all the way to London, a place he professed to dislike, after so firm a dismissal. Besides, by now her infamy had surely been revealed to him. Henceforth he would regard her as a fallen woman—a duplicitous one—unworthy of trust or affection.

She often wondered whether he had wanted her for his mistress, as she'd assumed, or his wife. His precise intentions would remain a mystery. If, like Thomas, he needed a willing bedmate, he'd have to look elsewhere. And if he had marriage in mind?

Impossible, replied her more rational self. The disclosure of her illegitimacy and her profession, combined with her uninhibited behavior in his library, had destroyed any chance of his making an honorable proposal.

As though reading her thoughts, her cousin abruptly announced, "Fred believes you ought to find a husband."

Oriana laughed, and asked idly, "Has he got someone in mind?"

"We agree you should have a chap with heaps of money and a string of racehorses, who wouldn't mind your larking about London."

While he was describing the perfect match for her, she made up her own list of desirable husbandly attributes. Perceptive eyes, appreciative of her beauty but never dazzled by it. Strong arms to hold her close, a chest as solid as a Manx boulder. Masterful hands that could smooth her hair or dry her tears or worship her body. An ability to make her laugh, whatever her mood. Devotion, honesty. Physical strength combined with a formidable—and invigorating—intellect.

A passing horse kicked up a piece of quartz-flecked gravel, which dropped into Oriana's path. She paused to examine it. Deciding that it was pretty enough to keep, she stuffed it into her reticule.

"That's the third stone you've picked up. Starting a new fashion?" her cousin teased.

"Not intentionally."

"Look there," said Burford. "The Earl of Rushton bows to you. Wishes he were walking with you, I'll wager."

"I doubt it. He's too respectable a personage to seek my company in a public place."

He gave her arm a consoling pat. "You make too much of other people's opinions. I'm calling on my father and sister before I leave town. Care to accompany me to Mansfield Street?"

Whatever her observers thought as she exited the park, she had the secret satisfaction of knowing that her destination was a ducal residence. Her connection to his grace of St. Albans could not shield her from wagging tongues and rampant speculation, but it would always be a source of comfort—and a reminder of her pleasure-seeking parent.

Dare leaned wearily against the tall iron railing that enclosed a spacious garden at the center of Soho Square. He was surrounded on all sides by neat town houses, varying only in their doorway architecture or the number of sash windows set into the facade.

Across the way, a stout female in a shabby riding habit trotted over the raised pavement. Dare, determined to accost her and question her, stepped away from the rail— just as she darted into a corner house.

"I've got a new toy."

He turned. The small, high-pitched voice had risen from the garden shrubbery and belonged to a boy with plump cheeks and cherubic golden curls.

"Show me," he said encouragingly.

The child emerged from the thicket of leaves and branches. Tucked under his arm was a miniature horse with uniformed rider, set on wheels. He set it on the pathway and tugged on the attached string. As he pulled, the toy rolled forward. The mechanical horse lifted its forelegs, and the calvaryman raised his sword arm.

"It came from Hamley's shop," the boy explained.

"What a lucky fellow you are," said Dare.

"I know. I'm Merton Pringle."

"Do you live nearby?"

"Over there." The lad reached through the iron bars and pointed in the general direction of Frith Street. "Mamma is Lady Pringle and Papa is Sir Walter. My brothers board at the academy on the other side of the square. Walt is called Pringle Major and Antony is Pringle Minor."

Dare decided to cultivate his new acquaintance. "You have many neighbors in this square. Do you know their names and houses?"

Young Merton's bright head bobbed confidently up and down.

"I'm looking for a lady who lives here. Do you know Ana St. Albans?"

Said the child solemnly, "I'm not s'posed to talk about her."

"No? Whyever not?"

"Mamma says she's wicked and immoral and *depraved*. I don't know what that means, but it's something bad. Lizzie, our housemaid, told me Madame St. Albans has many lovers. Lovers are men who like to kiss ladies. Is kissing depraved?"

"Sometimes," Dare responded grimly. "Depends who's doing the kissing. And how it's done."

Many lovers. Immoral and depraved. This information contradicted his own impressions of Oriana, and refuted her statements to him. *I'm no whore,* she'd said when refusing to accompany him to his Liverpool hotel. *I've been fending off advances for many years now,* she'd claimed during their conversation in the dark churchyard.

Oriana's elusiveness infuriated him, and the demands of her profession were bothersome, yet they hadn't quenched his need to possess her. Her collection of gentlemen was an unexpected complication, though.

"Sometimes I see Papa kissing Lizzie behind the parlor

door, and in that shadowy place under our staircase. I think he must be a lover."

"I daresay," Dare responded absently. The intrigues within the Pringle household were of no interest to him. He was trying to decide how to wrest Oriana away from her assorted paramours.

"Mamma calls the ruffle on her skirt a St. Albans flounce. Lizzie had one, too, but Mamma wouldn't let her keep it."

"Show me the house where Madame St. Albans lives."

"That one over there," said the boy, pointing his stubby finger.

"With the drawn shutters? Or the one beside it, where the carriage is stopping?"

A masculine figure had emerged from the vehicle.

Merton whispered, "He's one of the lovers. A lord, Lizzie says. I think he might be Thomas, the man in the song."

"What song is that?" An elderly manservant had answered the door, and the visitor was going inside.

In a piping treble, the child enlightened him.

"Of all the beauties in London town
  The dark, the fair, the slender or round,
  There's a songbird who makes the most
     glorious sound
  Her name is Ana St. Albans.

  Vainly do gentlemen sigh for her charms
  They suffer heartburnings and many alarms
  But she's happiest locked in wild Thomas's arms
  The lovely Ana St. Albans."

When Dare had learned the ugly truth about Willa Bradfield, the evidence had been presented all at once.

With Oriana, there was a steady stream of damning information.

The lovely and charming widow who had shied away from his kisses had turned out to be a famous stage performer, and was the bastard daughter of a dissolute duke. She and one of her many lovers had inspired a naughty song. Her current protector was an aristocrat who owned a fine coach with a crest on the door panel, and he visited her in the middle of the day.

Just like Dorrity Crowe, he thought, flitting from man to man. Insatiable, ever seeking fresh amusement, unwilling to settle down. And worst of all, thoroughly deceitful.

"I must go," he told the boy abruptly, and marched across the street.

Grasping the brass door knocker, he banged out his anger and frustration.

The aged servant, startled by the violence of his summons, asked his business.

"Inform your mistress that an acquaintance wishes to pay his respects. And don't tell me she's not receiving, because one caller has already gained entry."

Taken aback, the butler—or steward—said meekly, "Step inside, sir." Gingerly accepting Dare's hat, he handed it over to a young footman wearing buff livery trimmed with blue. "What name shall I give?"

"Corlett."

Dare made a circuit of the small antechamber, absorbing every detail. The arrangement of the chairs around the hearth was informal, and the presence of a gate-leg table indicated its use as a breakfast parlor.

He peered into the adjoining room, much larger and filled with evidence of Oriana the singer. A pianoforte with a straight-backed chair, sheet music stacked upon a tabletop, a wooden music stand in the corner, and a guitarlike instrument lying on the sofa. This, he surmised, served her as both music room and library. The majority of the volumes in the bookcases were extremely old. On a lower shelf were some antique folios, very tall—musical scores, perhaps. A selection of theatrical pictures adorned the walls. Sally Vernon, clutching a nosegay, smiled saucily at him from one frame. He found Joseph Vernon, Oriana's grandfather, hanging between two brass sconces.

In this attractive, cozy dwelling, Oriana sang and played and dallied with her lovers. Despite his pain and fury, he was conscious of how clearly it was marked by her personality and her interests and her background. In her womanly way, she'd created a home whose warmth and style he coveted. His own house, grand though it was, had no history yet—nor any contents.

Hearing movement on the stair, he turned away.

"Madame St. Albans will see you," her servant announced, not quite able to conceal his amazement.

Up the staircase he went, his heart thudding in unison with his heavy footsteps. Would she be angry? Alarmed? Ashamed?

He entered a drawing room. She occupied a settee and spoke earnestly to her visitor, a slender gentleman with gray-flecked temples. Her appearance was remarkably angelic. Her high-waisted gown was a white cloud formed by many layers of diaphanous material, its scooped bodice exposing a wealth of creamy flesh. A pale ribbon held her loose auburn curls away from her face. Her casual attire, combined with her guarded expression, fired his rage.

"Sir Darius, this is an unexpected pleasure." Her voice

was soft, but with an undercurrent of dismay. "What brings you to London?"

Before Dare could answer, the nobleman said, "My dear, it's perfectly plain. *You* do."

Chapter 13

"I can speak for myself," Dare said.

His abrupt answer made Oriana smile, and her companion frown.

Throughout his long and tedious journey from Liverpool, Dare had carefully composed his declaration. Now that he was with her again, the words had flown from his mind. And it didn't even matter, because he hadn't found her alone.

"What do you want of me?" she asked serenely, leaving the settee.

Oh, she knew *exactly* what he wanted. And he hadn't even kissed her yet.

"Assistance. I'm here to obtain furnishings for my new house, and therefore wish to know the names of London's best workshops and warehouses. I'd hoped to find satisfactory goods in Liverpool, but failed to do so. That, however, was the least of my disappointments during my stay," he said harshly, recalling her stealthy escape.

He yearned to run his fingers over each sharply defined collarbone. His lips hungered for her. And here he stood talking of furniture, when all he really cared about was getting her into bed and showing her what she'd missed by abandoning him.

"Lord Rushton," she said to the gentleman, "I present Sir Darius Corlett, of Derbyshire and the Isle of Man."

The Earl of Rustlip—Dare had delivered a letter with that inscription to the post office in Douglas.

In his well-bred drawl the earl remarked, "I recall one Corlett of Damerham, who requested my donation to a philanthropic project some years ago. A connection of yours, Sir Darius?"

"My grandfather."

"I regret to say that we never met, but by all accounts he was highly respected. Am I correct in thinking he was an industrialist?"

"He owned lead mines. Near Matlock."

"And this furniture you require is for your Damerham property?"

"No, my lord. I've constructed a rural villa on the island and now must fill it." Was it a good sign or a bad one that Oriana had failed to mention his existence?

She said, "You would admire the setting, Rushton—a secluded valley, with mountain views."

"It sounds delightful. You will find the town very crowded just now, Sir Darius, but it will empty soon enough. I hope you had no difficulty finding a desirable lodging."

"Nerot's in King Street." It ranked among the most fashionable and expensive of London's hotels, and he hoped the quizzical Lord Rustlip was impressed.

"Not your first visit, I take it."

Dare had met this type before—worthy, wealthy, impeccably turned out. From his cropped, silver-dusted head to his leather soles, Lord Rushton was the model of an English nobleman, as excruciatingly correct in his behavior as in his dress.

Looking to Oriana, the earl said pleasantly, "I had better leave, that you may confer with Sir Darius. My daughter demands my escort to the Park—her Mr. Powell is in Wales, administering to a sick relative—and I must not fail her, else she'll be cross. Shall we see you there this afternoon?"

"Not today," she replied.

While her noble guest made his farewells, Dare wandered over to examine the pair of portraits hanging on either side of the window. Charles II, attired in formal robes and doublet, smiled enigmatically, his black eyes half-lidded and his long black hair hanging down his shoulders. His swarthy complexion and curling moustache gave him a piratical appearance. Nell Gwynn, painted *en déshabillé,* placed a floral garland around a lamb's neck; the white bedgown drooped from her shoulder, revealing one plump breast. Her pink, pouting lips reminded him of Oriana's, and her curls were a similar shade.

From across the room, she told him, "I was afraid you might come." Now that they were alone, her agitation was evident.

Facing her, he said wrathfully, "You have cause to fear me. Because this is one of those moments, Oriana, when I wish I could torture you as you've tortured me. Mercilessly."

"Quiet, my servants will hear you."

"I don't care if the whole of London hears me. What's the point of discretion? You're Ana St. Albans, your lovers visit the house in broad daylight, one after the other. I'm surprised there's not a queue outside your door."

"You needn't be jealous of Rushton," she snapped. "He's not my lover, and never has been."

"That's not what I've heard. Is his name Thomas?"

She shut her eyes as if pained by the question. "No, it's Richard—but I've never called him that, our friendship isn't that intimate. Who told you about Thomas?"

"Merton Pringle."

"I don't know him."

"Lady Pringle's youngest son." Taking her wrist, he drew her to the window. "He's down there, playing in the garden."

"That little boy?"

"He can't be more than eight or nine, but he knows all about you."

"I doubt it." She freed herself, saying, "He may have heard some silly rumors."

"He entertained me with a ballad. I can't remember all of it, but that was your name in the refrain."

"I know the one. Oh, this is worse than I imagined." She pressed her palms against her face, warding off his accusing stare. "I didn't want you to know. I could have told you myself, in Liverpool. But I fully expected that you'd find out."

"Are you admitting there's truth in that stupid song?"

"Yes."

Oriana wished she could have given him the denial he so clearly wanted, but she wouldn't lie to him.

"Was your liaison with Thomas another of your youthful rebellions?"

"No. It was a mistake," she said. "As I've told you, while mourning my dead husband, I nursed my dying mother. When I lost her, I was desperately lonely. I didn't believe I could ever fall in love again. In my third year of widowhood I met Thomas. From him, I wanted all that Henry had offered—love *and* marriage. Only after he asked me to be his wife did I accept his presents, and after much pleading on his part, I proved my affection for him in the way that he most desired."

Dare wouldn't look at her.

"My happiness lasted only a few weeks. Mrs. Mountain fell ill on one of her Vauxhall nights, and I was called in to replace her. Thomas turned up with a large party of fashionable people—he was attentive to a very pretty girl. And that's how I learned of his prior engagement to another duke's daughter—a legitimate one, with a courtesy title and a fortune. The next time he visited my house, I refused to receive him." After a pause, she asked, "Did you see Willa Bradfield after you learned the terrible truth about her?"

"I didn't want to."

"That's how I felt, too. Out of spite, he told his friends that I'd been his mistress—just when I'd finally been offered a position at the opera house. He attended my debut, with his betrothed and her parents. I've never felt so exposed as I did that night, or so outraged. The claque was out in force. They loathe any singer who's not an Italian, and they shouted the rudest comments imaginable. After that hideous incident, every rake in town claimed he'd made love to me. *Falsely.* I was furious."

His expression of outrage told her that he shared her feelings. And she was relieved to see his hard eyes soften with compassion. "Your longing for privacy," he said. "I understand it better now."

"My name turned up in a book listing the most renowned females from the brothels and the alleyways round Covent Garden. 'The Siren of Soho,' she quoted bitterly, " '*a duke's by-blow, is an armful of delight and much in demand. This sprightly, auburn-haired maiden has an inviting countenance and melting eyes. She is a skilled musician and singer, in bed proves herself a zestful companion.*' I paid the publisher a hundred pounds to edit me out of subsequent editions. And after finishing my season at the King's Theatre, I never returned."

"Didn't your aristocratic relatives step forward to quash the scandal?"

"They couldn't. Society, hungry for the most salacious stories, labeled me a fallen woman—and still does. Wagging tongues inevitably couple me with nearly every gentleman who can claim an acquaintance with me, and just as many who can't. I've grown resigned to it."

"I don't believe you."

He was right to contradict her. "Well, if I retaliated by announcing that all those prominent men who boast of sleeping with me are a pack of liars, I would harm only myself. As a performer, I'm too dependent on the goodwill of the public to make enemies. My only defense against slander was my virtue."

"I was your only lapse?" He sounded pleased.

"I've no right to make demands, after the way I've behaved. But I beg you, Dare, don't tell anyone. *Please.*"

"Christ, Oriana," he said impatiently, "have a little faith in me. Your secret is safe." He seized her forearms, and gave her a little shake. "I want your promise that you'll stop running away from me."

"I've nowhere else to go. Except Newmarket, to watch the—"

He silenced her with a kiss that melted her limbs.

Her arms curled around his waist, and she surrendered herself to a losing battle between emotion and reason. Dare Corlett knew the worst now, and judging from his hungry lips and roving hands, his passion for her had not diminished.

As her body quickened with desire that must forever go unfulfilled, she remembered the joy of yielding herself to him. She must put an end to this immediately, for her own sake and for his. But his kisses were too potent, or else she was too weak.

"Ma'am, the dressmaker wants to know whether you'll want—"

Horrified, Oriana tore herself from Dare's arms.

Her maid stood in the doorway.

"What were you saying, Suke?"

"I thought you were alone, ma'am." Rattled by finding her mistress wrapped in a stranger's embrace, the servant continued nervously, "Your seamstress sent a message asking whether she should finish the cream-colored silk gown for your dinner party, or the green one."

"The cream," Dare suggested to Oriana, in a carrying voice. "I've already seen you in green, several times."

Suke stared at him.

Poised between mirth and annoyance, Oriana informed her servant of her preference—which just happened to coincide with Dare's. "And I want you to take all my pearls to the jeweler for restringing."

"As you wish, ma'am," Suke replied before making a speedy retreat.

Dare swept Oriana's hair aside, exposing her neck.

"You are the most shameless—that tickles."

"When is your party?"

"Next week."

"You'll be devastating in that new evening gown, wearing your pearls," he murmured, his mouth moving against her skin. "Must you deprive me of the chance to see you in all your splendor? I'm a stranger in your city, fully dependent on your goodwill and hospitality. . . ." His lips touched her forehead, as lightly and gently as the flicker of a moth's wing.

He was thrusting himself into her life. She was unable to muster a defense as he distracted her with his kissing and caressing.

"How would I explain your presence to my cousins, my friends?"

"To repay my *many* kindnesses during your stay in Glen Auldyn, you invited me to dinner."

"That will make my numbers uneven." Mentally reviewing her guest list, she said, "If you come, I must get another female. Rushton won't want his daughter coming to my house. Even if he permitted it, I couldn't have Lady Liza without Matthew Powell—they're betrothed. He's the man who wanted to marry me."

"Rustlip's daughter is pledged to one of your admirers?" He raked his fingers through his black hair. "Oh, to hell with all of them—I'm too exhausted to make sense of your intrigues."

Counting on her fingers, she ran through the other names. "Cousin Aubrey and Lady Catherine Beauclerk. Michael Kelly and Mrs. Crouch will sing for us afterwards. I know—my friend Miss Banks appreciates fine music, and so do Sir Joseph and Lady Banks."

"Not the same Joseph Banks who voyaged with Captain Cook? The president of the Royal Society?"

She nodded. "He collects rare plants and scientific books, and catalogs them as you do your minerals."

"That's not all he does," Dare said. "How did you become acquainted with him?"

"He's my neighbor." Leading him over to the window, she pointed to the corner house. "His sister Sarah Sophia and I have much in common, mostly notably singing and horses. She's teaching me to drive four-in-hand."

"A large woman in riding clothes? I saw her." As Dare stared at Sir Joseph's residence, he yawned.

"When did you arrive in town?"

"Today, after three nights on the road. Sleepless nights, no thanks to you. Do you keep brandy?"

"With that queue of gentlemen at my door, I'd be foolish not to."

His hand cupped her cheek. "My apologies for that. I was angry."

This time his kiss was tender, contrite. Hers was forgiving.

How long, Oriana wondered fatalistically, before this dangerously intense friendship would be publicized by the *Oracle* or the *True Briton,* or one of the newssheets? She trusted Dare's promise of discretion. But despite her servants' similarly good intentions, she had scant faith in their ability to keep silent. In London, any new-minted gossip about Ana St. Albans was currency too valuable to waste.

Chapter 14

***

Oriana planned Dare's first shopping excursion as rigorously as a general prepared his military campaign, leaving nothing to chance.

"Why did you make this list?" he asked, as they cut across the square. "It's no use at all—I can't read a word you've written. Whoever formed your penmanship did a miserable job of it."

"My parents provided me with many a music master, but I never had a governess. I learned my letters from Mother, and Mrs. Lumley, our housekeeper, showed me how to use a pen." With noticeable self-consciousness, Oriana admitted, "You might say I educated myself. I was schooled at a convent in Brussels very briefly. My mother told me if I didn't succeed as a singer, I could become a postulant—because my father needed someone to pray for his soul."

"What did the sisters teach you?"

"Prayers and hymns. When I lived in Italy, I sang at a convent ceremony. Several wellborn young women were being received into the church—they were magnificently dressed and covered in diamonds. I always wonder what their lives were like after they bade farewell to the wicked world to live in the cloister."

"Do I detect a note of envy?"

The curling plume on her bonnet waved as she shook her head. "The peace of the place would appeal to me only if I could have my pianoforte and music books. I suspect I'd soon pine for the theaters and concerts, and race meetings. The worst of it would be wearing the same black dress every day."

Although she laughed when she said this, he could tell she meant it. "Is that ruffly bit hanging from your skirt the famous St. Albans flounce I've heard about?"

"It is."

"And what do you call that fetching little jacket?" He liked the way the shiny yellow fabric outlined her splendid curves, flaring out slightly above her hips.

"A St. Albans spencer."

"How fortunate I am to have the guidance of the best-dressed lady in London. As well as the most beautiful."

"With the worst handwriting," she said airily, brushing off the compliment. Coming to the corner of a broad and busy thoroughfare lined with shop fronts, she announced, "This is Oxford Street."

Dare consulted the paper in his hand. "The first cabinetmaker listed here appears to be called Abdomen Wreck."

"Abraham Wright."

Mr. Wright's establishment offered a variety of handsome household objects, carved from the finest woods and exquisitely finished. After studying the pattern-book, Dare roamed through the showroom. Everything he saw, he liked—especially the beds.

His craving for Oriana was at odds with her determination to keep their relationship platonic. Never doubting that she was aware of his ulterior purpose, he saw no reason crassly to state it and risk a certain refusal. He had no rival to defeat; the only obstacle in his way was Oriana herself. Somehow he must win out over her vigorous independence and her dread of scandal. She'd stated plainly, with a bluntness he could respect but not like, that she wouldn't be his mistress. His campaign of seduction must be subtle. For the time being he must be content with flirtatious banter and, in his bolder moments, a furtive kiss.

Ta'n dooinney creeney shaghney marranyn, Mrs. Stowell had often told him. The prudent man avoids mistakes.

Steering her toward a bedstead, he asked, "Do you prefer four posts and curtains, or a half tester? What about this tented version?"

"You must decide which style suits *you* best," she responded, clearly reluctant to discuss what, for him, was a topic of abiding interest.

Whether he selected a frame that was simple or grand, it would support the best goosedown mattress—large enough for two to tumble about on and covered with sheets of soft Manx linen.

Well, he could dream. Impossible not to, when every time he turned he found another bed, each one reminding him of the ecstasy he'd found with her in his library.

From his perspective there was no impediment to the relationship he aspired to. She was sensitive about her tattered reputation, for reasons that he could understand. He could do nothing to mend it, but neither could he cause further damage. With a steady income and a house of her own, she possessed an unusual—but pleasing— measure of independence. Oriana Vera St. Albans Julian could be the perfect mistress, if only she would stop pretending that a bed was made only for sleeping.

"Mahogany or rosewood?" he persisted. "Plain wood, or gilded? Too many choices, and you're not being very helpful."

"It's your house," she reminded him, before wandering off to inspect the clothespresses.

Yes, his house. And because of her, he didn't even know when he'd see it again. He'd left the seclusion of Glen Auldyn to pursue a deliciously seductive and damnably elusive female.

After inspecting a set of drawing-room chairs, Dare asked for the tradesman's engraved card. He and Oriana exited the shop, and once again he tried to decipher her scrawl. "Where do we go now—is it Deer Street?"

"Dean Street. Just round the next corner."

A few minutes later they walked past a small hotel. Intrigued by its proximity to Soho Square, and its tidiness, Dare made a mental note of it. A pair of urns with trailing ivy and scarlet flowers marked the entrance, the door gleamed with fresh paint, and the windows shone in the sun.

"We'll cross over here," said Oriana. "The address we want is on the other side. Number Fifty-two, Mr. Weatherall's."

"Is that what it is? Looks like Wormwiggle."

While exploring the sizable workshop, he found a pair of Pembroke tables that were perfect for his library. Encouraged, he described to one of the artisans the glass-topped display cases he required, and sketched an example of what he wanted.

"Three tall cabinets with shelves and glass doors," he said, and jotted down the dimensions. "Three lower ones with glass tops that lift up, and an inner compartment lined with green baize."

He placed the order, and collected another trade card.

"How will you transport your purchases to the island?" Oriana asked him when they proceeded to the next shop.

"By water. Wind and tides permitting, my *Dorrity* will

reach Deptford docks within ten days. She won't be needed for the Liverpool run. Now that the season for herring fishing has begun, Mr. Melton has fewer men working the mine."

In Broad Street, Oriana paused to admire a pianoforte displayed in the window.

"Owen and Cox—this shop doesn't appear on your list."

"I didn't think you had any use for what they make here."

"My drawing room is large enough for musical parties," he improvised. His drinking cronies—Cousin Tom Gilchrist, Buck Whaley, George Quayle—would be astonished if he ever invited them to attend a concert in his home.

"You'll do better elsewhere. Broadwood makes a grand-pianoforte—five and a half octaves, two pedals, English action. I purchased mine last year, and am delighted with it. I'd like to have a new harpsichord as well, for they're not so popular as they used to be and there's no saying how much longer they'll be made. But I can't afford one just now."

"I thought you earned vast sums for your performances."

"In comparison to others, I do. But my income waxes and wanes, and I cannot bear to run up debts. Since returning to town I've spent a great deal of money on new gowns."

"I'll buy that harpsichord for you. Cost is no object to me."

"I never accept gifts from gentlemen."

He didn't press the point, although he penciled the name "Broadwood" at the bottom of the list as a reminder.

Mr. Thomas Sheraton's showroom came next, and there they lingered. Dare studied a recent edition of the famous *Directory,* containing sketches and detailed narrative descriptions, until his head swam with images of chairs, settees, and sideboards. He examined the sample furnishings on display and wrote down the dimensions of a handsome dining table before he and Oriana visited the shops on Gerrard Street and Berwick Street.

"I can stock Skyhill House without ever leaving Soho," he commented as they emerged from yet another cabinet-maker's.

"You'll want to look round St. James's also," she replied. "Somebody at Nerot's can direct you to the upholsterers in Jermyn Street and New Bond Street."

"You won't go with me?"

With a sweeping gesture that took in the bow-fronted shops and brick residences, she said, "This is where I'm most comfortable. I rarely stray into the most fashionable part of town, unless I'm on my way to the Park for air and exercise. Or to exhibit a new walking gown."

"An excellent suggestion," he approved. "We've breathed in enough varnish and sawdust for one day."

"You'll have to go without me. My feet are too weary—yours would be too, if you'd been walking about in these." She raised her skirt a few inches to show him her narrow, sharply pointed slippers.

"With ankles like those, I wonder you didn't become an opera dancer."

She dropped her gown immediately. "Dare Corlett, you're a terrible influence! Whenever we're together, I find myself doing the most outrageous things."

"Yes, I remember one thing in particular." Leaning down, he added, "When shall I have my tour of *your* library?"

Up came her head, and she smiled no longer. "Here we must part. I've much to do at home, with a dinner party to plan. And my Vauxhall concert the next night—I must keep practicing for it. Not to mention packing for a week in Newmarket."

"If I promise not to behave outrageously, will you walk with me in the Park tomorrow?"

"It depends."

"On what?"

"The weather."

A succession of showery days forced him to seek indoor pursuits. He submitted to Wingate's insistence that he visit the most eminent tailors; though his wardrobe was appropriate for Ramsey and Liverpool, in London he was very much behind the mode. Making a foray to the financial district, in the City, he established his account at Down, Thornton, Free, and Cornwall of Bartholomew Lane. When he declared himself a client of its partner bank in Matlock, Arkwright and Toplis, he received prompt and respectful attention. In Ludgate Hill he found the jewelers Rundell and Bridge, and spent a pleasant half hour gazing upon the sort of pretty, sparkly, costly items that Oriana was certain to refuse.

How could he convince her that he was different from all the other men who had courted her favors? Undaunted by her reluctance to be his mistress, he intended to follow Buck Whaley's advice and offer whatever she wanted or needed. Not money, not gemstones.

He hadn't much practical experience of courtship. Willa Bradfield, attracted by his wealth, had been an easy conquest. The genteel young belles of Matlock and Douglas had always sought his company, and though he might partner them in a country dance, he had no intention of courting them. The attentions of those lively lasses in the island's brothel had been his for a few shillings. They liked him, they satisfied him, and he'd felt a shallow affection for his favorite, before she left to seek her fortune in Liverpool.

Accustomed to being pursued, he eagerly embraced this unfamiliar and interesting role of pursuer.

During his rainy-day outings, he supplied himself with a smart pair of patent shoe buckles, a new hat, and had himself measured for new clothing, thereby winning his servant's approval. Wingate was less pleased by his abrupt decision to change his lodgings, but Dare turned a deaf ear to all protests.

When the sunshine returned to London, Dare walked to Soho Square. On the way past the garden, he saw young Merton Pringle's golden head poking through the black-iron railing.

"Do you ever leave your cage?" he asked.

The child reached through the bars, tiny fingers curled into a claw, and growled. "Did you kiss Madame St. Albans yet?"

"A gentleman never tells," Dare replied.

"If you come into the garden, I'll let you play with my soldier."

"I wish I could, but I have an engagement."

Merton's cherubic face suddenly bore a striking resemblance to that of a gargolye, and he stuck out his tongue before ducking back into the shrubbery.

Dare proceeded to Oriana's door. "Good morning, Lumley," he greeted the elderly retainer. "A splendid day, isn't it?"

"For some," the man responded heavily. "Me missus has been pouring beef tea down me throat—says it's strengthening. You'll find Madame St. Albans in the music room."

He'd already guessed that; he heard her soaring soprano, accompanied by strings.

When he invaded her santuary, her music ceased.

"Is that a lute?" he asked, studying the instrument she cradled. At the top of its long neck were eight tuning pegs, four on each side; the bowl-shaped body was made of inlaid wood.

"This is a *mandoline*. I learned to play it when I lived in Naples. Mine came from the best workshop, it's made of rosewood and fir. As you see, it has double strings, and they're tuned in fifths, like a violin. The top ones are gut and the lower brass." She plucked to demonstrate the difference in sound.

"What do you use to pluck them?"

"A raven's quill. I trimmed it down myself. Some players prefer ostrich."

As she laid the instrument aside, he said, "Don't stop. Play for me."

Her left fingers dancing between the frets, she serenaded him in Italian, with such sweet wistfulness that he assumed it was a love song. When she finished, she tucked the bit of quill into a space near the bridge and placed the *mandoline* on the sofa cushion beside her.

"I know now why they call you the Siren of Soho— your magical songs have surely lured many an unwary gentleman to his doom. But you're out of place in the city. Those sirens who gave Ulysses and his mariners so much trouble lived on an island." And so could she, if only he could persuade her to exchange London for Glen Auldyn. "Will you perform that tune at Vauxhall?"

"No. I'll have the accompaniment of a full orchestra. Today I'm practicing for my concert in Bury St. Edmunds, which takes place after the racing at Newmarket."

He perched on the armrest of the sofa and hovered over

her. "You smell like a rose garden. Whom were you expecting?"

Her cheeks went pink. "Nobody. I always use floral water."

"There's a military review at St. James's Palace today. Afterward, we can go walking in Hyde Park. The next fine day, you said."

"You've got a habit of persuading me to do things I shouldn't."

"I haven't even *begun* to persuade you," he responded. "And I won't. I'll not have you come along just to be civil. I thought you might enjoy being outdoors on so warm and bright a day. If not—"

"I can't be seen with you, that's all."

Gazing at his feet, he said glumly, "New coat, new waistcoat, new breeches—and these very elegant shoe buckles. Wingate seems satisfied—I hoped you might be, also."

"Oh, Dare, that's not what I meant. I'm not concerned about your clothes, but about our reputations."

"I haven't got one," he pointed out. "Nobody in London knows who I am."

"Your anonymity will suffer if you take me to the Park," she warned him, leaving the sofa.

For some reason she felt the need to change the placement of her figurines and straighten one of the prints hanging on the wall. He watched her in silence while she moved about.

Her inner struggle was brief. Facing him, she said, "Until you see what indignities I endure, you'll never completely understand why that guidebook description of Glen Auldyn was so tempting. I'll go with you, to the review and the Park, and anywhere else you suggest. I hope you won't mind if my maid accompanies us."

"Certainly not."

Suke Barry, pretty and mannerly, had soulful blue eyes and soft brown hair. She appeared to be her employer's contemporary, and was almost as elegantly dressed. Head demurely bowed, she trotted behind Dare and Oriana, responding with a shy smile whenever he glanced over his shoulder to see if she was still there.

"How long has she worked for you?" he asked Oriana.

"Three years. Rushton recommended her—she grew up on his estate—and I agreed to take her on. She was apprenticed to a milliner in Chester, but when the business failed she found herself without a place. I'm fortunate to have her."

Had the earl's intervention in her household been as disinterested as she implied? Possibly he'd placed Suke Barry in Oriana's household as a spy. But Dare's tendency to leap to conclusions had already caused great strife, so he made no mention of his suspicion. Her easy friendship with the toplofty peer troubled him, but a show of jealousy and possessiveness would alienate her.

"The Lumleys have been part of my life forever," she went on, "and Sam, the footman, is their nephew. My chef is a Belgian who cooked for my father—a very devout man, he goes to mass every day. The scullery maid is a pert little thing, and drives my older retainers to distraction."

Outside the gates of St. James's Palace, he had his first encounter with royalty. The Duke of Gloucester, brother to King George, presided over the parade of soldiers. The gold buttons and fastenings of their scarlet coats glistened in the sunshine; the sprightly march carried well in the humid air. The crowd gathered at the edge of the streets cheered the procession, and Dare's mood was similarly buoyant, till he noticed Oriana's still face.

Her Henry, her beloved husband, had been a military

man. If he'd remembered that sooner, he might have spared her a heartache.

Taking her elbow, he said, "I've seen enough."

She glanced up at him. "But they've only just started. It's a large regiment."

"And a great deal more impressive than the Manx Fencibles," he admitted. "If you don't mind, I'd like to go to the bookshop I noticed the other day—on Piccadilly."

"Hatchards? Yes, I know it." She crooked her finger at Suke.

Gentlemen's clubs and fashionable shops lined St. James's Street, which extended from the redbrick palace to busy Piccadilly. At the bookseller's, Oriana purchased a monthly journal, the *Universal Magazine of Knowledge and Pleasure,* in addition to a selection of new music. He kept the clerk busy hunting for scientific literature, and left with Rashleigh's *Specimens of British Minerals.*

They arrived at Hyde Park in advance of the fashionable promenade, but already it was populated with smartly dressed pedestrians and stylish equipages. Many of the women were handsome, but none could eclipse his companion—the cold, disdainful glances she attracted were surely provoked by envy. He, too, received curious stares despite being an unknown—or rather, because of it. He hadn't been watched so closely since his forays into the Matlock Assembly Rooms, where the young ladies had studied his every move.

A group of gentlemen crowded round Oriana. In rapid succession, he was presented to Misters and Sirs and Lords, all of them looking at her in ways that made his blood simmer.

"You'll be at Newmarket?" asked one excitedly.

"When's your next Vauxhall appearance?" another wanted to know.

"Saturday evening," she responded.

"We missed the last one. Will you dine with us after your performance? Do say yes, just this once!"

"Pray do not ask again, Mr. Launceston. You know I must decline."

"Cruel Ana. Have a care, Corlett, she'll break your heart as she did mine."

Oriana listened patiently to their competitive banter, neither inviting nor discouraging their attentions. When Mr. Launceston sought her opinion of his horse, she was complimentary. On being assured that she'd been greatly missed during her absence from town, she declared that she was happy to be back among friends.

"But you've made new ones," observed Launceston caustically. He glared at Dare before cantering away on his bobtailed gray.

No sooner did the mob of young bucks disperse than Oriana gave a mournful little sigh. "Oh, no."

"What's amiss?"

"The Prince of Wales is here. The portly, fair-haired man in the blue coat."

An equerry approached Oriana and informed her that His Royal Highness wished to speak with her. With an apologetic glance at Dare, she followed the messenger along the pathway.

"I gather this commonly occurs when your mistress walks in the Park," Dare commented to Suke Barry.

Her head moved up and down. "Those gentlemen— Mr. Launceston and the others—they cannot leave her be. Nor me. Sometimes they seek me out and give me letters for her, and I've received money for delivering them. The first time it happened, I told her. She laughed like anything, and said I might keep whatever I was given. I use the notes to light my bedroom fire."

"You must pocket a tidy sum."

"I do, sir."

"Does Lord Rushton ever bribe you for information?"

"Bribe me? Nay, sir. In the spring he did ask me how often a particular gentleman called at the house, and I told him. But he didn't pay me."

"Which gentleman?"

"Mr. Powell, sir. The man who will wed his daughter."

Dare decided there was nothing terribly sinister about a man ascertaining the habits of his future son-in-law. "I gather there's no Lady Rushton."

"Not for many a year. Her ladyship died soon after Lady Liza was born, and his lordship didn't wed again."

When Oriana's audience with royalty concluded, Dare went to meet her.

She apologized for abandoning him. "I couldn't present you to the Prince without his requesting it."

"I was content to gaze at him from afar."

When they made their way to Hyde Park Corner, she turned her hazel eyes upon him and asked, "Now do you see why I was so reluctant to come? I'm so very weary of all these predatory gentlemen. Even though they often amuse me, they are an annoyance."

"Is your fame always so burdensome?"

"There's a difference between fame and notoriety," she replied. "The quality of my singing receives less attention from the public and the press than the affairs I'm supposed to have had and the gowns I wear. The bucks of the town flock 'round because they assume I'm an easy conquest. The Prince beckons from a belief that flirtation with me enhances his reputation for gallantry."

"And because he wanted a closer glimpse of your lovely face."

"At least he doesn't want me for his mistress. He prefers ladies who are older—and married."

A hackney coach returned them to Soho Square, and

on entering Oriana's house they discovered a chaotic scene.

Her elderly butler was seated on the staircase, clutching the rail, while his wife held a feather under his nose.

"What happened?" cried Oriana.

"Me legs turned all wobbly," the sufferer reported. "And there's a buzzing in me ears."

"I told him to lie abed," Lumley's spouse huffed. "Where's Sam with that brandy?"

The footman was coming down the hall, and Oriana went to take the glass from him. She presented it to Lumley, who took it in a shaking hand.

"Your wife is correct, you should be resting."

"Aye, well, so I would, ma'am, if there wasn't a dinner party tomorrow. The silver service wants polishing, and I need to choose your wines."

"Never mind any of that," she interrupted. "Louis knows his way around the cellar. Sam will clean the silver, and wait at table." Oriana rose and descended to the entrance hall, where Dare remained. "I have a domestic crisis, as you can plainly see."

"I'm confident that you'll rise above it. Unless there's anything I can do, I'll leave you."

She untied her bonnet ribbons. "We'll manage. Somehow."

Regretting his uselessness, Dare left the house.

"Lover, lover, lover!" Merton Pringle taunted.

He wished he could exchange the pesky brat for that damned noisy bird Oriana had kept at Glencroft. Given a choice, he much preferred the goose.

Chapter 15

On the day of her dinner party, Oriana rose earlier than usual and dressed with uncommon haste. The doctor, after identifying her butler's ailment as a fever, had recommended bed rest and regular doses of hot beef broth, and when she went belowstairs she found Mrs. Lumley was enforcing this regimen, despite her husband's protests that he felt better.

"I mean to get up and be doing me duty tonight," he assured Oriana.

"Listen to him," scoffed Mrs. Lumley. "As if she'd want you handing 'round her best dishes in your condition. Besides, what you've got might be catching."

Said Oriana, "You must do exactly as the doctor said, Lumley."

"Very well, ma'am. But take me missus out of here, I can't abide all her cosseting and carping."

"I've better things to do," retorted his affronted spouse, nose in the air. "Till I'm home from the greengrocer's, Annie will wait upon you." Turning to Oriana, she added, "After an hour of so of being tended by that wench, he'll be glad to have me cossetting him again, won't he?"

The maligned scullery maid glared at the housekeeper.

After Mrs. Lumley departed, basket on her arm, Oriana

conferred with her chef. The Belgian, whose opinion of himself was as large as his person, blithely informed her that the food, at least, would be impeccable, no matter how badly it was presented. This thoughtless comment made young Sam blanch. Oriana took him to her parlor, where they would be safe from interruption, and soothed his rattled nerves as best she could.

"You know what needs to be done—this party will be no different from any other."

"Yes, ma'am. I've put fresh tapers in all the drawing-room sconces, and moved the *torchère* nearer the harpsichord. When Suke finishes ironing the cloth, I'll lay the table."

"Excellent. If you stay busy, you won't have time to worry."

She fully intended to follow her own advice and not fret about the disarray in her household. Her guests, she hoped, would be generous enough to excuse any deficiencies in her arrangements. If Sam could refrain from spilling food or drink all over the diners, she'd count the evening a triumph.

The pounding of the door knocker sent Sam rushing from the room, before she could tell him she wasn't receiving. If the caller turned out to be Dare Corlett, she would have no qualm about sending him away at this most inconvenient time.

When Sam returned, a stranger accompanied him. The man, of medium height, had pewter gray hair and wore somber black clothing.

"My master, Sir Darius, sent me. I'm Jonathon Wingate."

A horrifying possibility occurred to her. If Dare was unable to come, her numbers would be ruined—she'd need to find a gentleman to replace him. "Are you delivering his excuses?" she asked, waiting for the sword to fall.

"No, madam. He instructed me to assist you and your servants in every conceivable way. Not only am I here to help with preparations for your dinner, I shall wait at table. In addition to valetting Sir Darius, I'm his butler."

The relief on young Sam's face was comical.

"I'm most grateful to Sir Darius," confessed Oriana. Salvation had arrived in the form of this pleasant and competent being. "Sam, never mind laying the table, you must carry a note of thanks to Nerot's."

"Sir Darius is no longer there, ma'am. He has moved to Morland's Hotel in Dean Street."

"Morland's?" She couldn't imagine why he would leave the most elegant establishment in St. James's, if not all of London, for a lesser hotel in Soho.

Her surprise must have been obvious to the butler, who declared, "He finds this neighborhood more to his taste. Mr. Morland set up his establishment just last year, and his lack of custom allowed him to grant my master's wish to have the entire second floor."

Oriana crossed to her writing desk. Without sitting down, she plunged the pen into the inkstand and scrawled upon a sheet of notepaper, *I doubt that I can ever fully repay you for what you've done, but I shall try.* She folded it and handed it to Sam. "Off with you to Morland's—quickly."

After the footman left the room, Dare's servant asked, "Will this be a large party?"

"No, only eight persons." She reeled off her guests' names. "We'll have two courses, with a cold collation as a supper, after the musical entertainment. I've got the menu here—somewhere." She searched her desk.

Wingate moved to the fireplace and removed a paper

on the mantel shelf. "Might this be it?" He studied the list of dishes, and nodded approval. "You employ a French cook?"

"A French-speaking Belgian. After a decade in London, he speaks perfect English—when he's in the mood. Louis is monarch of the kitchen, and a culinary genius. He'll tell you so himself."

"Ah, yes. Monsieur Louis sounds much like my master's cook. I'll take care not to disturb his equanimity. Have the wines been chosen?"

"Not yet. Here is the key to the cellar. The plate has been moved from the butler's closet and laid out on the long table in the servants' hall. If you don't find everything that's necessary, ask Mrs. Lumley. Oh, and you have my permission to snub Annie, should you be tempted—and you will be. She's the scullery maid, the plague of our lives. Sam, whom you just met, is very reliable. But too much responsibility discomfits him, so I'm glad you're here."

"Likewise, madam."

For the remainder of the day she practiced her *mandoline* and perfected a new piece on the pianoforte; then she perused the journal she'd bought at Hatchards. Suke Barry popped into the music room at intervals to report on Wingate's activities. Amazingly, he had endeared himself to the two persons most likely to be prejudiced against his intrusion, the cook and the housekeeper. Sam, his minion, was performing his duties with great efficiency and eagerness.

"Mr. Wingate even spoke with Mr. Lumley," the maidservant informed Oriana. "He wished to know his opinion about whether the Frontenac would be better for the beginning course, or the first-growth claret."

That diplomatic effort would serve him well, thought Oriana, lifting her teacup to her lips. Entirely at leisure, she was indulging her appetite with a plate of chocolate puffs fresh from Louis's oven.

She wondered how Dare was spending his afternoon. Visiting the shops, in all probability, selecting fine furniture to adorn his villa.

What she'd given him once, he desired again. But if she repeated the indiscretion she'd committed at Skyhill, she would suffer for it. When Dare completed his necessary purchases, he'd sail back to his island, depriving her of his bracing company, his candor, and those kisses that burned her brain and turned her limbs to water and made her heart leap. As he'd done in Liverpool, he might invite her to go with him.

Although she had enjoyed her weeks in Glen Auldyn, and the temporary respite from work, she didn't belong there. She was bound to Soho Square—this was home. All her life, she'd trained to become a *prima donna.* For the past several years she'd labored in London's concert halls and pleasure gardens, dreaming of the day when the manager of the King's Theatre would summon her back to the opera. What folly it would be to relinquish her long-held ambition because of a Manxman, for her past loves had always ended with loss.

But Dare Corlett was not a military officer. And she knew, with wistful certainty, that he would treat her more considerately than Thomas Teversal had done. His vibrant personality would buoy her whenever she was at low ebb, either in her private or her professional life.

No matter what the future held, she could never forget that he'd offered to purchase a new harpsichord for her. He'd done it on impulse, because he could afford to— without realizing the significance of his gesture. And yesterday, he'd asked her to sing for him. Of all the men in her life, only her father had nurtured her talents, and cherished them. Henry had cared more about soldiering than music; Thomas had poured diamonds into her hands but had rarely bothered to attend her performances.

Dare had been curious about her mandoline, and had wanted to carry her off to Broadwood's.

She wouldn't delude herself into hoping his intentions might be honorable. Whenever she found herself speculating about marriage to Dare Corlett, she reminded herself that he wanted no wife like her. He'd stated the qualities his bride must possess with wounding bluntness: impeccable lineage, a spotless reputation, and a fortune that exceeded his. If he scoured the globe, he couldn't have found a lady who contradicted that description as fully as she did. His ambitions weren't matrimonial and never would be. He wanted her for his mistress.

On the island, loneliness had made her vulnerable to his admiration, and she'd let a passionate impulse push her into committing an imprudent act. In London, she must be stronger, and wiser. She must conquer this desire he'd roused in her, a force as dangerous as it was unpredictable.

Dressing for dinner, she felt the same rush of excitement that she did preparing to go on the stage. On private occasions she dispensed with vibrantly colored, richly spangled garments, and could strive for a more subtle form of elegance. Her new gown of creamy silk crepe was perfection; the overskirt parted at the waist to expose a pale petticoat finished off with a St. Albans flounce of Brussels lace, to match the appliqué on her bodice.

Suke swept her hair up into a chignon, covering it with a pearl-encrusted fillet. Oriana placed a strand of pearls around her throat and inserted the large drops into her earlobes.

"He'll think you the loveliest lady in all London," Suke murmured, offering the scent bottle.

"Who?" asked Oriana, as though she didn't know.

"That gentleman you walked out with yesterday. The one who kissed you."

Oriana's reflection in the glass wore a secretive smile, for Dare had done far more than kiss her. Her maid's supposition that she dressed for him tonight should have troubled her, but didn't. Rising from her chair, she said, "I must speak with Wingate, to make sure all is in readiness."

"He thinks of everything, ma'am. Do you know, he persuaded Annie to put on a fresh cap and apron without ever raising his voice."

"A miracle worker, beyond doubt."

The Earl of Rushton, the first arrival, expressed regret that he must depart immediately after dinner, as the House of Lords was sitting late.

"Shouldn't you be at Westminster now?" Oriana asked him.

"I'll take my place later. Knowing what pride you take in your arrangements, I didn't wish to impair your seating plan."

"I'm sorry you must miss the duets Mr. Kelly and Mrs. Crouch will sing for us later."

Her Beauclerk cousins, the next guests to arrive, greeted her with affection.

"A charming gown," Lady Catherine approved. "Your seamstress is assured of a comfortable retirement, whenever she decides to give up her trade."

"I hope she hasn't any plan to do so," Oriana responded. "Without her, I'd never set another fashion." Smiling upon the Duke of St. Albans, she said, "Cousin Aubrey, I look forward to hearing about *your* latest purchases. Did you buy the marble vase, or the bronze?"

"Both—as you'll see when next you call in Mansfield Street." His pale blue eyes scoured the drawing-room walls. "You've moved those canvases you bought at my auction."

"You'll find the Rembrandt in my music room." Lowering her voice, she added, "Because the bacchante is rather a saucy girl for mixed company, I'm keeping her in my private chamber."

The duke laughed.

The pair of paintings had cost her nearly four hundred pounds, but she didn't regret last year's extravagance. The Poussin, *A Bacchante Crossing a River,* had been the costlier investment but a valuable addition to the collection she'd inherited from her father. Rembrandt's *Matron Giving Advice to Her Daughter* had been a sentimental choice; the great Dutch master had depicted the mother and daughter in a pose that inspired nostalgia for the times when she and her mother had been at peace.

Michael Kelly—tenor, composer, *bon vivant*—entered the drawing room with his duet partner, Anna Maria Crouch, who shared his home in Lisle Street. Their marriage was prevented by the existence of Mr. Crouch and their Catholic faith, which prohibited a divorce. Mick Kelly directed the singing at Drury Lane and the King's Theatre, and Mrs. Crouch was that rarity, an English *prima donna.*

In her sweet voice she told Oriana, "Mick brings you glad tidings—but I shall let him share them."

"Later," the Irishman promised, twinkling at Oriana. "Mustn't discuss business on an empty stomach."

Oriana wouldn't build her hopes too high, for without an Italian surname she wasn't likely to be offered a position at the opera house. Most likely he wanted her to preview one of his latest compositions at Vauxhall.

"Will you have some wine?" she offered, as Wingate approached with his tray.

"I'm no enemy to the juice of the grape. A new servant?" Kelly asked, after the butler retreated. "I wish you better luck with him than Mrs. Crouch and I had last year, when we increased our domestic staff. A stranger recommended a man to us, but we had to turn him off when we began to suspect he meant to rob us. Scurvy criminals, the pair of them—in league with a gang of housebreakers. One went to Newgate, the other had his neck stretched, poor soul. Take care, my dear Ana, and be sure you can trust the person who introduced him to your household."

Before Oriana could explain that Wingate's presence was temporary, her gathering increased by three persons: Sir Joseph Banks, his wife, and his sister. Because the eccentric Banks ladies preferred their riding habits to any other garments, Oriana was always amused when she encountered them in evening attire. Lady Banks wore her yellow-diamond marriage brooch, surrounded by white-diamond pendants, but Sarah Sophia Banks wore no jewelry.

"Madame St. Albans, such a pleasure," her ladyship gushed. "As I was telling Sir Joseph, this is lavish repayment for having you in for potluck during Eastertide!"

The baronet broke in to say, "A mystery beyond solving, why you'd want a crusty old scholar like myself at your entertainment."

"You are my neighbor here in Soho Square," she responded, "and the duke's neighbor at Windsor."

"But we rarely see him since Hanworth Park burned down. I must ask him about the progress of his rebuilding project." When she offered wine, he shook his silvered head, regretfully stating that he was a martyr to his gout.

"Tonight you'll meet a newcomer to London," she informed him. "A Manxman. He's knowledgeable about geology and mineralogy and has written a paper on the history of rocks on the Isle of Man."

Where *was* Dare? What had detained him?

Her guests mingled; the drawing room filled with their pleasant chatter. Wingate, after making a final circuit with his tray, withdrew to the dining room to oversee the final preparations.

Oriana's gaze continually wandered to the doorway. While listening to Lady Banks describe recent additions to her china collection, she eyed an ormolu timepiece that had formerly graced her father's Rue Ducale residence in Brussels. If she told Louis to hold back the meal even a quarter of an hour, he'd be outraged. Not even the masterfully tactful Wingate would be able to break the news of a delay without disturbing the tempestuous Belgian.

Please come soon, she begged Dare silently, as the minutes ticked on.

Her reputation as a superior hostess could not be brought down by the tardiness—or the absence—of a single guest. But she needed to prove to her clever, country-loving admirer that she was a creature of the town, actively social, her days and nights crammed with activities. She had no time to spare for dalliance. Once Dare realized that, he would leave London. Until he did, she'd live with the constant fear that his persistence and personal magnetism could overcome her reluctance, leading to another passionate entanglement like the one that had taken place at Skyhill.

She cast a vague smile at Sir Joseph, for she hadn't heard what he'd been saying. Because his thick gray brows were set so low, he seemed to glower. He was, she realized, studying the figure in the doorway.

And an impressive figure it was.

As Dare strode into the room, the old gentleman asked, "Is this the fellow you were telling me about? I've seen him before—at a Lord Lieutenant's dinner in Derbyshire, I believe it was. Who is he?"

"Sir Darius Corlett." Her fingers tightened around the stem of her wineglass.

"Corlett?" Banks repeated. "I'm sure I knew his grandfather, for the King granted our baronetcies in the very same year."

Mindful of her duty to a guest, she went to welcome Dare, adding in a confidential murmur, "Wretch, you might have told me you already knew Sir Joseph."

"That would be an exaggeration," Dare replied. "We met once, a long time ago."

"He recognized you."

"I didn't expect him to," said Dare.

"You're late," she accused him.

She couldn't even remember why it mattered. Her reaction to his appearance was shallow, but she didn't care. His evening clothes were beautiful—form-fitting black coat with long tails, clearly cut by a master tailor, burgundy-and-white-striped waistcoat, white-silk breeches.

"I'm unaccustomed to dressing for grand occasions without my valet's assistance," he explained. "I had to rely on two of the hotel servants, and I'm still not sure I'm properly put together. If Wingate comes over to adjust my cravat, I'll know I failed."

"You look"—she swallowed to cure the dryness in her throat—"exactly as you should."

What was the matter with her? For two months she'd known him, had encountered him in various situations, some ordinary and some not.

"Come and meet my relations," she invited.

She proceeded with the necessary introductions, presenting him to each of her guests in order of their precedence, beginning with the duke. If Rushton was surprised to see him, he hid it well.

Here was a man she could proudly introduce to her company. Her repeated claim that she was repaying

Dare's hospitality was a harmless, thoroughly plausible description of their connection, unlikely to incite speculation among the people who knew her best.

Or so she hoped.

Chapter 16

A t the proper time, Oriana shepherded her guests into the dining room. The table, covered by her best cloth, was laid with the best china and crystal and silver, gleaming in the light of chandelier and candelabra. She placed herself at one end of the table, and the duke took the chair opposite hers. Oriana had placed Rushton on her right, Miss Banks beside him, then Mick Kelly and Lady Banks. To her immediate left sat Dare. Also on his side were Mrs. Crouch, Sir Joseph, and Lady Catherine near her father.

Oriana could not compete with her famous neighbor's popular assemblies, at which men of knowledge, wealth, and distinction gathered to discuss topics of mutual interest. But she prided herself on bringing together so brilliant a collection of minds, talents, and titles—science, politics, society, scholarship, music, and industry were represented at her table.

Wingate paused at each place and filled the glass with the white wine he'd deemed suitable for their first course, consisting of *soupe* Lorraine, salad, French beans, young artichokes in a white sauce, bisque of pigeons, salmon in lobster sauce, and a savory veal pie. To her supreme satisfaction, her guests relished the exquisite fare Louis had prepared, and the many dishes that followed were similarly well received.

Rushton carved the haunch of venison, served up with truffle sauce. He speared a slice and offered it to Oriana.

Shaking her head, she told him, "None for me, thank you."

With an apologetic smile, he replied, "I was forgetting your preference for fish and poultry."

Dare, having expertly quartered a roast duckling, presented her with a portion of breast meat, which she accepted.

"Sir Darius, have you purchased the household items you required?"asked the earl.

To conceal her interest in the answer, Oriana delved into her peas *françoise*.

"I've bought a number of pieces," Dare stated, "at the Soho shops, and also in St. James's."

"Then you'll not reman in London for very much longer," Rushton hazarded.

"Probably not," said Dare coolly.

Oriana could not have said why his announcement disturbed her. A short time ago, she'd hoped to learn of his immediate departure. Stealing a glance at him, she saw him pass Mrs. Crouch the plate of cherry tarts topped with Belgian cream.

At the conclusion of the second course, all dishes were removed and the cloth lifted from the table. Fruit and cheese were laid out on the rich mahogany.

Oriana soon signaled to Wingate to bring in the brandy and port decanters. Rising, she conducted the other ladies to her drawing room. The after-dinner separation of the sexes was her least favorite of England's social customs and offended her Continental sensibilities, but she conformed to it.

She and her friends discussed books recently read and entertainments enjoyed at the Little Theatre in the Haymarket, while sipping from tiny glasses of sherry or cordial and nibbling lemon biscuits and macaroons. Mrs. Crouch, who had lately recovered from an indisposition, recommended her physician to Lady Banks, concerned about her husband's gout. The robust Miss Banks reported on her latest excursion to the Park in her new phaeton. A gifted and daring driver, she spent vast sums on her carriage horses, and invited Oriana to ride with her one day and try them out.

"I'd like that very much." Crossing the room, Oriana joined Lady Catherine, for whom she felt a cousinly fondness. In a low voice she made an inquiry about the progress of her ladyship's secret romance with the duke's chaplain.

"I haven't yet told Father that Mr. Burgess and I hope to marry," Lady Catherine confessed. "Since my mother died, I've been responsible for the household, and while he rebuilds Hanworth, with all the attendant frustrations, he depends on me to maintain domestic tranquillity."

Oriana's heart went out to her lovelorn kinswoman. "How much longer can you hide your true wishes?"

"Burford knows. He and my James are firm friends, and we have his support. At thirty-five, I'm too old for a long delay."

Oriana tried to imagine herself at that age. Twelve years from now, would she be alone, still waiting for a man who could offer marriage? Very probably.

And doubtless Dare Corlett would be living at Skyhill House, surrounded by a large and affectionate family. His progeny would climb the apple trees in the orchard, swinging from the gnarled branches. They would race their Manx ponies across the ridge. And the rich, beautiful, aristocratic Lady Corlett—

Abruptly she curtailed her reverie, already jealous of Dare's nonexistent future wife.

A hearty burst of masculine laughter sounded from the

dining room. A few minutes later, Lord Rushton stepped out.

"I stayed later than I intended," he told Oriana, "testimony to the pleasure I've had this evening. But duty tears me away."

Responsibility for amusing Oriana's company fell upon the singers. She sat with the Beauclerks, her chaotic thoughts temporarily lulled by the sublime combination of Kelly's rich tenor and Crouch's lilting soprano. At the end of their recital, her drawing room echoed with praise and applause.

Her cousins departed soon afterward. Mrs. Crouch suggested to her partner that they also take their leave. Had she not, thought Oriana, the convivial Michael Kelly would have remained indefinitely, gabbling on about his adventures abroad and his professional associations with eminent musicians—Mozart, Haydn, and Paisiello.

"Bless me, I quite forgot to tell you the happy news," he said, shaking his dark and woolly head. "There'll be a place for a first woman singer in the opera company this season. Mr. Taylor says I must go abroad to look for her. It doesn't suit me to travel just now, so I'm hoping that the Siren of Soho might accept the position—if it should be offered."

It was the great chance she'd hoped for, ever since the Teversal scandal had driven her from the opera-house stage. To encourage him without sounding desperate, she said noncommitally, "I carefully consider every offer that is made to me. Until I know all the details of the engagement, I can't say more than that."

"Very well, Madam Prudence. But be assured, you are my choice, and I shall be your most vigorous champion."

The crowd of ten had dwindled to five. Only her Soho guests—the trio of Bankses, and Dare—remained to indulge in the light collation of cold meats, cheese, and jellies. The gentlemen discussed Derbyshire affairs. Miss Banks, between forkfuls of cold sliced beef, complained about a recalcitrant and unsatisfactory butcher. Lady Banks appeared to be stupefied by an abundance of food and the lateness of the hour.

When the dialogue between the two baronets shifted to science, Oriana followed it even more avidly.

"You met Dr. Hutton?"

"Frequently. I attended university in Edinburgh and was privileged to attend his lectures on geology. My youthful enthusiasm must have amused him, but he welcomed me into his illustrious circle of like-minded acquaintances. I assisted them when they conducted their field studies, cataloging specimens and making sketches. My knowledge of mineralogy was sound, but Hutton helped me increase my powers of observation. Under his tutelage I became more adept at interpreting the relationships of rock types."

"I had not the honor of knowing him."

"He possessed sharp eyes, a brilliant mind, and an engaging manner. His enthusiasm for his discoveries was positively infectious. Everyone liked him—his popularity among his fellows is perhaps the greatest testimony to his greatness."

"Indeed it is. Men of science can be as petty and jealous and argumentative as the rest of humanity, if not more so." Sir Joseph regarded Dare shrewdly. "I'm surprised your colleagues neglected to propose you for membership in the Royal Society of Edinburgh."

"When we met I was merely a scholar, and family obligations prevented me from taking my degree. I'm still very much an amateur scientist."

Oriana would not let his modesty prevail. "As I mentioned earlier this evening, Sir Darius has composed a treatise describing his island's geology."

Said Sir Joseph, "As president of the original Royal Society, I can arrange for you to tour its premises." With a nod to Oriana, he added, "This lady's royal ancestor, King Charles II, founded our organization, and his bust occupies a prominent place in our meeting chamber."

Dare replied to the invitation with appropriate gratitude. He climbed to his feet and politely thanked Oriana for an enjoyable evening. Knowing him so well, she detected an undercurrent of discontent flowing beneath his civilities.

A few hours ago she'd wanted him to leave London— now she felt desolate because he had deserted her drawing room.

His departure broke up the party. Her neighbors, echoing his thanks, trooped down the staircase to the front door. From her parlor window she watched them cross the square.

Oriana sank wearily into an armchair. Slipping her feet out of her tight silk pumps, she flexed her cramped toes. She chose not to return to her empty drawing room, no longer ringing with music and cheer. The bittersweet aftermath of a party was inevitably a solitary experience, for not since her mother's death had there been anyone to share it.

Her spirits should be uplifted by Mick Kelly's implication that she was his chosen candidate for the vacant place at the opera. But all she could think about was Dare's stated intention of returning to the Isle of Man.

Hearing footsteps in the stairwell, she called, "Everyone has gone, Wingate. You may go up to clear the table."

"I'm not Wingate." Dare came into to the parlor.

Rising quickly, she said, "I thought you left for Morland's!"

"I went no farther than your wine cellar, and stayed

until the coast was clear. Wingate wanted to show me a cask of muscadet he's partial to."

"If he wishes to drink it all, he certainly may. After everything he's done this day and night, he deserves the reward."

Dare's hands moved to his neck, and he began unwinding his cravat. In her shoeless state, Oriana could hardly object.

Tossing the length of creased linen over a chair back, he said, "You look more beautiful tonight than I have ever seen you. I couldn't leave without telling you so."

Her heart expanded. "You chose this gown."

"There I was, conversing with one of the eminent scientific minds of the age, and all I could think about was holding you. And touching you."

When he came nearer, she said unsteadily, "My servants are about."

"I don't see any."

She felt his breath on her cheek, warming it. Lowering her head, she watched his tanned fingers slide across the shiny fabric and lace inserts of her bodice.

"I've waited all night for this—I won't be denied."

His lips claimed hers, insistent, caressing. Her eyelids drooped, her neck arched, and as long as the delicious contact lasted, she wallowed in bliss.

She wanted him so desperately that it hurt. But by admitting that simple truth here and now, she would concede defeat in a battle she had waged before, unsuccessfully. Unless she defended herself, her body would be forfeit. And then the entire bastion would crumble— independence, pride, self-respect.

"If you loaned your butler for the evening in the belief that I'd lie with you—"

"I didn't. But I won't insult your intelligence by pretending that seduction isn't my purpose now. It most certainly is—we both know that."

"You should go," she told him, her voice a raw whisper.

"And I shall." But still he held her. "My desire and your unwillingness are incompatible. I won't stop wanting you, Oriana. But I won't stay here and become a nuisance like those chaps who mobbed you in Hyde Park."

"Is that why you told Rushton you'd be leaving London?"

"I'm going because you want me to."

"I'm not sure what I want," she confessed. "In Liverpool everything seemed so much clearer. When you turned up here, I decided to give you a taste of my real life, thinking you'd find it unpalatable."

"As you do?"

"I'm used to it."

"So the walk in the park, and including me in your dinner party, were intended to repel me?" He shook his head in bewilderment. "You spent the first month of our acquaintance concealing your identity. Now you're using it to fend me off."

"I must," she cried unhappily. Still, she couldn't help asking, "Will I see you again before I leave for Newmarket?"

"Only if you're prepared for the consequences." He kissed her hard, his solid legs straddling hers.

An existence free of risk, devoid of excitement, had never appealed to Oriana. She felt happy when Dare was near and less happy when he was not. The attraction mystified her, because their backgrounds and habits were so unalike. His respectable obscurity found its opposite in her notoriety. He was a scientist and she an artist. His area of expertise was mining, hers was music. And none of those facts could quiet her turbulent mind and hungering body. She burned for him with a ferocity that terrified her.

"Do I have a reason to stay, Oriana?"

"Vauxhall," she mumured.

"What?"

"Meet me there, after my concert. You'll get your answer then."

When he left her, she opened the desk drawer in which she'd placed his geological treatise. Turning up the oil lamp, she sat down to read the introduction again.

> *The chief portion of the Isle of Man, perhaps three-quarters, consists of a barren soil overlaid upon graywacke slate and on clay slate. In the northern portion, light sand rests upon a bed of common clay. The mountainous areas are formed of clay slate strata—with veins of quartz—upon mica slate overlaying granite. The slate is chiefly gray in color, weathering to brown, light green, deep blue, or black. These appear to be sedimentary rocks formed in a deep ocean bed by compacted silts, mud and sands. The layered nature of this material is clearly visible at Maughold Head, and elsewhere, in the folds and fissures created by subterranean events. The granite is primarily composed of feldspar, mica, and quartz.*

By hiding away in Glen Auldyn, she'd deprived herself of the natural wonders he described—mountains, rivers, beaches, entire towns. Perversely, she wished she could see them, but doubted she ever would.

In just a few days, she would either send Dare back to the Isle of Man or accept him as her lover.

If only she could give him all that he desired from her—and she from him—without losing anything essential to her contentment. Could they perhaps find a compromise, reach an accommodation, that might bring them together?

To find it, they needed time. He was a very impatient gentleman, and she was a very cautious lady.

She stared thoughtfully across the square to the Banks residence. The lights were still on.

Bounding up from her chair, she hurried into the hall. Sam, an apron tied over his clothes, was coming down the stairs with items from the dining room.

"After you've carried those dishes to the scullery," she said, "I want you to deliver this pamphlet to Sir Joseph."

It wasn't until Sam had embarked on his impromptu errand that Oriana's qualms surfaced. Her effort to justify her act continued through the long night.

Dare had printed his arguments and distributed the copies to geologists in Edinburgh—how could he object to a review by the most prominent supporter of scientific discovery? He deserved recognition, not only by Sir Joseph, but all the members of the Royal Society, and every other person who learned enough to appreciate his diligent work. If they could hold him here in London to explain his theories about Manx rocks, so much the better for her.

Chapter 17

Promptly at eight o'clock, the conductor bobbed his wig-covered head at the other musicians. The opening bars of the concert drew Dare—and Vauxhall's music-loving visitors—closer to the gothic-styled orchestra stand. Swags of colored lamps hung from the structure, and a multi-branched chandelier threw a soft light upon the rows of powdered heads and glanced off the towering organ pipes at the back of the pavilion.

All walks of life were represented in this crowd: common prostitutes, shopgirls, prosperous merchants, members of the gentry and nobility. Like the rest of them, Dare had crossed the River Thames and paid two shillings to enter the gardens. But he felt infinitely superior, for he had been bidden there by the soloist they had come to see and hear.

His tour of the grounds earlier had taken him to the vast Rotunda, the site of masquerades and musical entertainment during inclement weather. Before tonight, he'd never imagined, much less seen, two thousand glass lamps blazing at once. They hung in festoons from the sheltering colonnades and the semicircular dining pavilions, and the effect was impressive. He'd promenaded along the stately elm-lined Grand Walk, and the Cross Walk, and the Italian Walk—spanned by three triumphal arches—and the Hermit's Walk.

At the farthest reaches of the park was an unlit Lover's Walk, and he hoped to stroll there later with Oriana.

This place, beloved by Londoners and greatly admired, struck him as an odd combination of the tawdry and the tasteful. He could have dispensed with the *trompe l'oeil* paintings, sham ruins, transparencies, and other stage-craft illusions. The beauties of nature required no such adornments; he preferred to contemplate them in soli-tude. He might have appreciated Vauxhall's magnificence more if there weren't so many people getting in his way.

A foursome nearby talked over the music, so loudly that he could hear every word of their conversation. The pair of young ladies—first-time visitors—marveled at the splendor of the orchestra pavilion. Their gentlemen, more interested in flirtation than in a concert, tried to entice them away from the throng and into the shadowy avenues of trees.

"Oh, do come along, Hetty," said one impatient swain.

"Not till I've seen the gown she's wearing."

"Makes no matter," said Hetty's confidante, "for nei-ther you nor I could afford one like it. We haven't rich lovers like *she's* got."

Both young women cast critical glances at their escorts.

"Remember, Miss Hetty, I purchased your entrance ticket and I've another shilling yet to pay for your din-ner."

"All for a paltry shaving of meat," the other gentleman complained, "and a roasted chicken no bigger than a sparrow!"

"If you think you can find a lover who's richer than me," Hetty's chap said bitterly, "give it a try. I'll be on the watch for a girl who'll appreciate a hardworking brewery clerk."

"Don't be cross, Ralph," Hetty pleaded. "We can wander through the Dark Walk after I've heard a few songs. I promised Aunt not to stray from the Grove, and I fear she'll quiz me about the concert."

"Willy and I will stay for the first part and tell you what you missed," her friend offered, "and we'll amuse ourselves while you listen to the second half."

Ana St. Albans came to the forefront of the pavilion balcony as Ralph and Hetty, hand in hand, threaded their way through the throng unnoticed. She acknowledged the calls and applause by inclining her glossy auburn head, decorated with pale, glittery flowers. The tiny brilliants sprinkled across her transparent overskirt twinkled in the light, and her jade green petticoat shimmered. The gold brooch engraved with the St. Albans crest gleamed upon her breast.

A pledge of better times, that was her family motto. Exactly what he hoped to win from her tonight.

When her audience's enthusiastic welcome faded, she smiled at the conductor to indicate her readiness, and his musicians provided a few introductory notes.

The words of her first song were incomprehensible to Dare, but her magical voice created notes of perfect clarity and piercing sweetness. Ignorance of the stylistic differences between Italian and English singing couldn't hamper his enjoyment. He knew what he liked, and he liked what he heard. The rest of Oriana's listeners were similarly enthralled, judging from their rapt, upturned faces and approving smiles.

She retired from view during an orchestral piece. On her return, she performed a selection of the Manx songs she'd learned from Ned Crowe, resulting in a request for an encore. When she withdrew from the stage a second time, a bell rang, signaling the nine o' clock intermission.

The crowd pushed and shoved its way along the path leading to the Grand Cascade. Dare, curious about this celebrated and highly regarded spectacle, let the sea of humanity bear him toward the viewing place.

A decorative curtain rose upon a miniature stage and revealed a painted landscape, artfully lit, which contained a small house, watermill, and a road. Cheers rose from the onlookers when a mechanical waterfall began to pour forth with sufficient force to revolve the little mill wheel. The substance used to simulate the stream spilled and foamed with astonishing reality. Tiny automatons—pedestrians, riders, animals, and a mail coach—traversed the bridge spanning the waterway.

Dare questioned a bystander about the mechanics involved.

The man shrugged. "Stage trickery," he muttered before shuffling away.

After a ten-minute interval, the concert resumed. Oriana sang a lengthy aria, and with a deep curtsy she bade her admirers farewell. A quartet of male glee singers took her place.

Dare had positioned himself near the door through which the performers entered and exited. As he expected, Oriana soon darted out, swathed in dark velvet.

She raised the hood of her cloak to cover her flowery head. "Let's move away, I don't care to be recognized," she explained, taking his arm.

"Quite a large crowd," Dare observed. "Is this usual?"

"For a Saturday night it is. Drury Lane's season ended earlier this week, so this is the first night Vauxhall doesn't compete with Mr. Sheridan's *Pizarro* for an audience."

The supper boxes and alcoves were already crammed with persons eager to sample Vauxhall's famous thinly sliced ham and cooked chicken. A regiment of waiters moved about, vigilantly performing their duties. A band of pipers and flutists was playing, and a party of roving musicians wound its way through the gardens, pausing to entertain the diners when requested.

"Did you see the Grand Cascade?" asked Oriana. "It fascinated me when I was a girl, and the magic wasn't spoiled when I was shown the clockworks that make the figures move. The moving-water effect is created by very thin strips of tin. Very ingenious."

"I preferred the music."

A bald-pated gentleman, overhearing him, came up to say, "Our attendance always rises, sir, when Madame St. Albans performs. Mr. Barrett and I wish we could afford to have her sing for us every week rather than fortnightly."

Oriana presented Mr. Simpson, Vauxhall's master of ceremonies. He welcomed Dare to the gardens, shaking his cane so excitedly that the silver tassel dangling from its knob bobbed up and down. "Do you dine here this evening?" he inquired. "I can secure one of our finest supper boxes for you both."

Guessing that this plan was at odds with Oriana's preference for privacy, Dare responded, "Would it be possible to take away a selection of food in a hamper, and a bottle of your excellent champagne?"

"Permit me to make all necessary arrangements for you, Sir Darius; it would be my pleasure. Anything else I can do to make your enjoyment of Vauxhall complete, I shall. Madame St. Albans will tell you that we pride ourselves upon the quality of our entertainments." Mr. Simpson tucked his *châpeau bras* under one arm and bowed so low that his shirt frills grazed the knees of his tight-fitting breeches. He marched away, waving his cane to signal an attendant.

"Your refreshments won't be ready for quite some time," said Oriana.

"*Our* refreshments."

"Vauxhall portions are scandalously meager; you'll not get enough food to share."

"Then you shall have all—you must be ravenous. I'll be too busy to eat." Tugging at his hat brim, he added, "I'm your oarsman tonight."

Eyeing him from head to foot, she commented, "I'll wager you didn't ferry yourself across the Thames—not in those clothes."

"No. The man who rowed me over was so industrious and entertaining that I tripled his fare. He said I might have the use of his craft for the rest of the night, and took a carriage home."

"Dare Corlett, you're a madman."

"A Manxman."

"One and the same, as far as I can tell. Why would you want to row a boat all the way across the Thames, when you can hire someone else to do it?"

"I'll get you safely to the other side, I promise—I've been around boats all my life, and salt water flows in my veins. But before we take to the river, you can show me the Lover's Walk."

"I'd be glad of some fresh, cool air," she told him. "The stage lamps are hot and bright, and they smoke so badly that my eyes water. Did you purchase more furniture yesterday?"

"No, I visited another Bond Street tailor, at Wingate's insistence." He cast a rueful glance down the open front of his double-breasted evening coat, adorned with rows of shining gold buttons. "I asked him whether he'd prefer working for a town gentleman, someone who would do him greater credit. He thought about it for a while, before replying that he intended to make *me* more creditable, but it might take rather longer than he expected. He was vastly disappointed when I postponed today's fitting with a hatmaker to visit the British Museum. The collection in the Mineral Room is immense—fossils and gems from around the globe, and the representative rocks of England, Scotland, and Ireland."

"Were there any from the Isle of Man?"

"No—a glaring omission. I must donate some choice samples of galena, quartz, and calcite. Rock specimens, too. Manx slate, Peel sandstone, Castletown limestone, basalt from the Stack of Scarlett."

"What about pyrite? And granite—isn't that the most common of all the rock types?"

"Madame St. Albans, did you perchance read my description of the island's geology?"

"Every word," she declared triumphantly. "I daresay you didn't think me clever enough to make sense of it."

"I didn't think you'd be *interested*," he admitted.

"It's worthy of being published by the Royal Society."

Laughing at her naive but flattering opinion, he said, "I'm not so certain of that, although I'd like to think my theories would interest the membership. Now that I've conversed with Sir Joseph Banks, perhaps I'll feel more comfortable inaugurating a correspondence with him. But for the time being, I've abandoned my geological research to complete a study of animal behavior."

"Really? What sort of animal?"

"An exotic female of the human species. I'm keenly interested in learning how the subject of my investigation will respond when separated from her pack and isolated in a dark, remote area," he said—for they had left behind the colonnades and gaudy illuminations, and were entering the shadowy alley where amorous couples roamed.

Chapter 18

The overhanging branches of densely planted trees formed a leafy canopy, thick enough to block out the sky and stars.

"We've entered the most disreputable part of the gardens," Oriana said, as they ventured down the long, narrow alley. "The Druid's Walk, it used to be called."

"A popular place of assignation, I gather."

"Here the lightskirts parade their wares before the gentlemen of the town, and many an innocent girl has met with ruin. I've not come to the Lover's Walk for several years." Her hood fell back as she gazed up at the treetops. "Did you hear? A nightingale!"

"Poor creature, she must have felt sadly inferior when you were signing."

"Oh, Dare," she sighed, "that's a lovely compliment."

"Allow me to improve upon it." He studied her shadowed countenance. "Your eyes shine like the rarest of fine gems. Your lips look as if they were carved from pink coral. Your teeth are like pearls—"

"No, no, I'd rather hear you praise my music. I was born with this face, but I've spent a lifetime training my voice."

As the bird completed a series of trills, Dare said, "Your singing reaches into my soul. And that wondrous rich voice

196

resides here, in a throat so delicate that my fingers can almost encircle it." His fingers curled around her slender neck. "The first song you sang tonight—I heard it in Liverpool, didn't I?"

" '*Frena le belle lagrime.*' Restrain not your lovely tears. Herr Abel composed it—Queen Charlotte's court musician."

"I had no idea what you were singing about, I knew only that it was the most poignant tune I'd ever heard."

"The lyric comes from a poem by Pietro Metastasio. His verses are beautiful, and many composers have set them to music. *Non destarmi almeno nuovi tumulti in seno,*" she quoted softly, "*bastano i dolci palpiti che vi cagiona amor.* Rouse not new turmoil in my breast, great is the sweet throbbing that love causes there."

His hand crept inside her cloak and sought her bosom, feeling its erratic rise and fall. "Yes, there is a turmoil here."

"Don't," she pleaded, "or I shall feel even more wretched."

"Clearly I need to improve my technique."

His wry comment produced a feeble burst of laughter. "No—as it is, you are difficult to resist. I shouldn't have come here."

"One kiss."

"You won't stop at that—you never have done. You'll want more."

"Much more," he drawled. "You promised I should have my answer tonight."

His reminder increased her agitation. "You might be content to dally with me for a little while, to pass the time in town, until you meet some suitable heiress with twice the riches you already possess. Eventually you must return to your home, with or without a bride."

He bestowed another chastening look. "You form your

judgments of me, and your expectations, by the way other men treated you—particularly that cad Thomas. Remember your anger and hurt when I treated you as one more in an endless parade of fortune hunters? It's unfair—and very foolish—to let our past misfortunes rob us of pleasure. Trust me, Oriana."

"I'm trying." Staring down at their joined hands, she confessed, "And I'm afraid."

"You needn't be. I seek only as much as you're willing to give. But if you say I must surrender all hope of having you, I must go away—soon. I want you too much," he said quietly.

This craving was leagues beyond merely wanting—his whole being pulsed with the need to possess, a force as powerful as it was elemental. Her heart, her soul, her mind . . . her naked body, wrapped in his arms.

He was desperate enough to suggest that she marry him. But should he?

No. Even if she wanted another husband—and she'd never hinted that she did—pride wouldn't permit him to wed a woman who wasn't in love with him. That was one mistake he would never repeat. But the fact that her heart wasn't fully his wouldn't prevent him from sleeping with her.

"Twice you deserted me, yet my desire for you grows stronger rather than weaker. Believe me, Oriana, your present wretchedness cannot possibly surpass mine. So many years I've evaded the snares of designing females, only to become enamored of a lady who cares nothing for me."

"I care," she broke in.

"Prove it," he challenged her.

She moved in closer, until her hips were framed by his and her long velvet cloak and silken skirt crumpled against his legs. Her hand reached for the back of his head, gently forcing him down to meet her parted mouth. The dart of her tongue between his lips sent a shudder through his frame. He clutched at her, and wondered how long he could survive this exquisite agony.

After the kiss, he told her, "You've proved very little, only your ability to torment me."

"And myself," she admitted, her eyes dark pools of uncertainty. "You seek a mistress—your own Nell Gwynn or Sally Vernon. And that is what I never wish to be."

"I am less familiar with such arrangements than you," he conceded, "but I do know they entail an exchange of money or property for sexual favors. I'm making no such offer. No allowance nor house, not a shilling of my money will you get. I won't barter for a bedmate. My greatest dream, my most fervent hope, is that from this night onward, we will belong exclusively to one another."

"While I dwell in London, and you on the Isle of Man? You're overlooking a crucial detail—geography."

"A minor problem with a simple solution. I'll divide my time between both places." He tried not to think of his lovely villa, empty and neglected, and the elegant furnishings he'd been choosing so carefully. And he closed off all thoughts of the Corlett Mining Company. His most vital concern stood before him—reluctant, undecided, breathtakingly beautiful.

"Constant travel grows wearisome," she said. "I might not be worth the trouble."

"If you weren't, I wouldn't be standing here," he pointed out. "That determination was made many weeks ago. Just when I was settling into complacency, my future clearly charted, you walked into my house and showed me what was missing. I didn't realize it then, but you do have impeccable timing."

"So say the critics," Oriana murmured. "Perfect pitch, also."

"Our greatest difficulty," he said heavily, "is that we've both grown too cautious. Maybe I should stop talking about what I intend to do, and do it. Now. You'd enjoy it—yes, you would, though you might not admit it. And I'd feel a hell of a lot better while it lasted. But afterward you'd be angry, and I'd be ashamed. And I can't let it happen that way. Why are you smiling at me like that, you witch?"

"Because you're the only man I've known who felt compelled to apologize for his decency."

"I don't. I curse it." Capturing her hand, he held it tightly. "My affection and devotion are yours. Not to mention fidelity, respect, and honesty—or as you might say, bluntness."

She said reflectively, "This is exactly how we began, all those weeks ago. You wanted to sleep with me before you even knew my name."

"It wasn't sleeping I had in mind, then or now." His hand smoothed her shoulder, brushing the nap of her garment. "That night I discovered my greatest weakness—a lovely lady in a blue-velvet cloak. Refuse me tonight, and I shall ask you again tomorrow. And the day after, and the day after . . ."

"I don't want to refuse."

At those wistful words, relief stilled his heart.

"I think about you all the time," she told him. "From morning to evening. When I lie in my bed, when I'm practicing at the pianoforte. I remember what happened at Skyhill, and wonder why I can't let it happen again. It isn't a lack of desire that holds me back, Dare, or a wish to make you miserable."

"Then why?"

"When I said I was afraid, I didn't mean that I feared you. It's scandal I dread—as you should."

"I've no intention of doing anything scandalous. I didn't set out to conquer Ana St. Albans to raise my own profile. I'm no sportsman, like your London rakes; I derive no great pleasure from the chase. I'm a miner, a seeker of treasure. Whenever I obtain a valuable gem, I hold on to it. I tell no one, and I hide it away in a private place. You may depend upon my discretion."

"I need more than that. I'm asking you to keep our— our liaison secret from everyone. No one can ever know about it."

"I promise. Will you be mine?"

"I think perhaps I already am."

"Look at me, Oriana." When she obeyed, he framed her face with his hands. "Say that again, leaving off the 'perhaps,' and I'll be the happiest of men."

"I'm yours—I am."

He rewarded her with a scalding kiss, striving to melt any icy remnants of resistance. And he did, setting free the wanton, willing creature she'd been in his library at Skyhill.

A loud titter broke through the nightingale's aria. When Dare turned his head, the silk flowers in Oriana's hair tickled his chin. He could just make out a couple sprawled across a nearby bench—the flighty Hetty and her swain Ralph. He spied their young friends farther on, the girl backed up against a tree trunk, her escort nuzzling her neck and bared breasts.

Oriana tugged on his coat button to get his attention. "Have you tired of me so soon?"

"No, but I think we should find a better place to consummate our pledge." He pulled up her hood and fastened her cloak to cover her.

"Where? And when?"

After much misery, he'd won what he wanted—or soon would. Now he could afford to toy with her. His mischievous intent showed in his grin when he replied, "At a time and place of *your* choosing."

The oars lay idle in their locks, for the steady current and an outgoing tide was drawing the rowboat downriver, toward Westminster Bridge. It was a heavier craft than the long, flat wherries that skimmed the water, carrying other revelers back to the city. It floated along in the pool of reflected light cast by the lanterns hanging from its bow and stern, and the candelabrum thoughtfully and generously supplied by the Vauxhall management.

Oriana, perched on the bench in the bow, was still dazed by her acceptance of Dare's proposition. Her choice was made, her fate was settled. Was this a surrender or a victory? A compromise, she decided. After a difficult siege, she'd succumbed to her own desire and his enticements, but in so doing had conquered her ingrained fear of sharing herself.

With uncharacteristic eloquence, he had revealed an emotional commitment that was gratifying as it was alarming. Neither of them, she suspected, could accurately define their feelings, but he'd been brave enough to try. After all, he was a scientist, accustomed to labeling specimens, and drawing conclusions about them. He'd courted her without mentioning love, offering in its stead his affection, devotion, honesty, faithfulness, and discretion. Few wives, she reflected, had received such firm assurances. But to make their bond more secure, she must become what she had vowed never to be.

What use was virtue, she reasoned, if by guarding it

she lost Dare? Whether she did or didn't share her body with the Manxman who had pilfered her heart, she'd continue to be damned by the gossips and the caricaturists and the printers of Fleet Street.

No longer content to let the silence drag on, she said, "My desire for concealment must seem strange to you."

"Not at all," he answered. "You've been performing since you were a little child. Fine ladies copy your clothes and hats. Girls in the street sing your ballads. Men follow after you when you walk in the Park. It's natural you should want to close off something of yourself from scrutiny. Even as a public figure, you have every right to lead a private life. I mean to help you in that effort, Oriana, not hinder you."

Propelled by his forceful stroke, the little craft surged ahead, cutting through the black waters. The lanterns wobbled, the candleholder tipped, and drops of wax spilled from the tapers. Oriana, mindful of the danger to her flounced hem, pulled up her skirt.

"Madame St. Albans, you're a wicked tease."

"I mustn't spoil my new gown," she defended herself. She refrained from pointing out that his coatless condition and open-necked shirt strained her own composure. She held out the goblet. "Here's the last of the champagne."

He released one oar to take it from her. After finishing it off, he said, "If only we had pen and paper, we could stick a note in the bottle and set it adrift."

Feeling about in her cloak's inner pocket, she reported, "I've got a pencil stub. And a crumpled playbill."

His grin flashed in the evening gloom. "If *you* write the message, it will be unreadable."

Bent on retaliation, she dipped her hand into the river and flicked cold water at him. It splashed upon his face and neck and dampened his white shirt. Where the material stuck to his dark skin it was nearly transparent, revealing dark skin and a delicate etching of black hairs.

"Do it again," he urged.

His eager response roused a yearning to pleasure him in other ways, and her whole body seemed to tingle with anticipation.

When he returned the wineglass, she let him have the pencil and paper. Resting her elbows on her knees, she watched him scribble, pause, then continue. When he presented his composition to her, she held it near the candlelight to read.

United by their pledge of mutual faith and hopefulness, Oriana & Dare, Saturday, 6 July, 1799.

Rolling the paper into a scroll, she tucked it inside the champagne bottle.

"Let's each contribute an item of personal significance." He dropped his cravat pin inside, and it fell with a clink.

Oriana couldn't settle on a sacrificial object. The St. Albans brooch was a memento of her father; her emerald eardrops had belonged to her mother. She wore no rings. Dare suggested that she give up one of the spangled silk flowers from her hair, so she stuffed it into the neck of the bottle.

To make a strong seal, she dipped the cork in a pool of rapidly congealing wax before inserting it into the mouth. "Shall I release it?"

He reached out to grip the neck, his fingers closing over hers. "Together."

Gently they laid the vessel in the water.

Oriana sat back to watch it bob on the surface. "I hope it doesn't wash ashore anywhere near London. Discovering my identity would be no great feat—my stage name is printed on that bill."

"And my surname is engraved on the pin." He brandished an oar. "I can pull it back."

"No," she answered. "Let it go."

Like the bottle, they had embarked upon a voyage to an unfamiliar region. Her destiny was entwined with his—for how long, she could not be sure.

Chapter 19

Drawn by a fresh set of horses, the post chaise sped along the familiar highway. Four times a year Oriana followed this route from London to Newmarket, and she knew every village, farmstead, and great house. Dare, on whose shoulder her head rested, viewed this terrain for the first time.

They had already passed by the posting inn at Epping where she often broke her journey to Suffolk. This time, to ensure their privacy, she would halt at Saffron Walden, a larger and busier town farther along the turnpike. There was less chance of encountering any of the sportsmen who knew her, for by now the majority would be in Newmarket.

At the start of their drive, intimidated by the presence of their London postilions, she and Dare had been content to hold hands beneath the billowing folds of her carriage habit. After the first change of horses and riders, they had kissed and cuddled. During the third stage, Oriana had dropped into a comfortable slumber, and for many miles had dozed in his arms. She needed her sleep—last night, tumultuous thoughts and emotions had kept her awake for hours, and she knew the evening ahead would not be restful.

Tonight she and Dare would share a room—and a bed.

To distract herself from this thrilling but unnerving

prospect, she told him, "Cousin Burford's horse runs tomorrow. Her name is Combustible, and she's got a very promising future ahead of her. Or so we hope." After a pause, she said, "Most of the lodgings in the town will be taken."

"Wherever you're staying suits me best."

"Gwynn Cottage is too small to accommodate you. But Mrs. Biggen, my landlady, will know of a farmhouse in the environs."

He smiled down at her. "I hope I've brought money enough to cover lodging and meals. Am I likely to incur other expenses during this excursion?"

"That depends on how many wagers you make, and how lucky you are."

"I hadn't planned on wagering. I wouldn't know how."

"Perfectly simple. You walk up to the betting post, where you'll find a slate printed with all the horses' names and the odds."

"It won't help me much."

"I'll advise you—I'm familiar with all the owners and their jockeys, and most of the horses. Burford knows even more than I do."

"Will the Duke of St. Albans be there?"

She shook her head. "At present, his chief occupation is rebuilding Hanworth."

"What about Lord Rushton?"

"He won't desert the House of Lords so near the end of the session, and he doesn't care for horseracing at all. He hunts foxes sometimes, and he shoots wildfowl on his estate. In autumn, he always sends me game birds. They come to Soho Square in a great hamper, all the way from Cheshire, every week. Annie complains mightily about having to pluck them, and Louis makes the most divine dishes." Sitting upright, she told him, "Not much farther to go."

"Let's hope the Sun can provide a vacant bedchamber."

A sudden attack of shyness deprived her of speech. To hide her flush, she averted her face.

For so very long, she'd avoided intimacy with a man. Running away, as Dare could attest, was a bad habit she'd developed during her celibate years. Nevertheless, she'd secretly cultivated a tiny seed of hope that she would find someone who would excite her senses and treat her with respect.

"In our effort to preserve secrecy," he said, "I suggest we keep to our room as much as possible."

His talent for brightening her moments of dim uncertainty with a jest was one of his most endearing qualities. He seemed to be aware of the vulnerability she tried to bury beneath her stubborn bravado and assertive independence.

They agreed that in the morning they would board separate conveyances and proceed to their different Newmarket lodgings, for a week of pretending to be casual acquaintances. After Race Week she would proceed to Bury St. Edmunds, to give a recital at the Assembly Rooms, and Dare would join her at the Angel Hotel. With luck, they could manage a few shared nights before returning to town.

A short time later, their chaise drew up before a whitewashed building of medieval origins. Its sharply pitched gables extended over the street, sheltering a gothic portal. The adjacent structure, similar in style, bore plasterwork decorations in a splendid display of the pargeter's artistry.

Oriana, head bowed, withdrew to a dim corner of the vestibule while Dare conversed with the landlord about their baggage. Within minutes, they were ascending a narrow stair to the upper level. Her heartbeat quickened, her fingers curled themselves tightly around the handle of her wooden mandoline case. She was eager—she was terrified.

Her thoughts carried her back to her wedding night. She and Henry had stayed at an inn far grander than this, because he'd wanted to impress her. She suspected Burford had actually paid the bill.

Thomas Teversal's arrangements had been more casual. She had been too ignorant to know that the site of their furtive encounters, a cramped lodging above a milliner's shop, wasn't the sort of place an honorable man took his future wife. But it served him well for meetings with his doxy.

She was three-and-twenty now. It was illogical—and so foolish—to feel this young and fluttery.

Their bedchamber was compact but clean. A servant deposited their trunks on the floor and withdrew, visibly awed by the largesse Dare bestowed upon him.

Oriana, still victim to her nerves, carefully set down her instrument case. Desperate for air, she crossed to the mullioned window and flung it open.

"Make yourself comfortable," Dare said. "I'll return shortly."

By the time she turned around he was gone, his footsteps fading as he went down the stair.

A maid came to wait upon her. She ordered a pot of tea to calm her apprehensions, and half a lemon. Her disappointment over Dare's unexpected desertion intensified, so she busied herself with unpacking—an experienced traveler, she felt the need to settle into her lodging as quickly as she could. She held up her nightshift, a delicate confection of sheer white lawn and spidery Brussels lace, its gathered yoke set with tiny satin bows. She wondered whether she'd need it.

Another quarter of an hour passed, and no sign of Dare.

Oriana took off her tight jacket and flounced skirt, intending to change for dinner. She loosened the front ties of her red-linen corset to relieve the constricting pressure of its rigid whalebone strips. Feeling much more comfortable, she also kicked off her low-heeled shoes and untied her garters and peeled off her stockings. Weary from five hours in the carriage and still feeling the effects of her sleepless night, she stretched out on the bed for just a few minutes. The checked-linen counterpane, softened by frequent laundering, was smooth and cool against one cheek, and a breeze from the open window drifted over the other. She hadn't realized the extent of her fatigue. Her breathing slowed; her eyelids fell.

She was wakened by a gentle, tickling pressure on her lips.

"You're back," she murmured.

Dare thrust a handful of flowers at her. "For you."

Pale blue larkspur, vibrantly pink everlasting peas, richly scented white stock, and trailing strands of deep green ivy. "Lovely. And so fragrant."

He removed his coat and began unwinding his cravat. "This town, I can tell you, is a very quiet place late on a Sunday afternoon."

"So is London." In a drowsy voice she reminded him, "Your island is no different."

"True. If anything, it's quieter, and I had only my books and my writing and my rock collection for enter-tainment. Here, I've got you—a beautiful, enticing female in a delectable state of undress—and what appears to be an exceedingly comfortable bed." He removed his boots and began unfastening the waistband of his breeches.

There was no mistaking his intentions. His eyes smol-dered, dark coals of desire.

Standing on a stage, she was fearless, confident of her

ability to please. In Dare's library, her passion for him had made her bold and reckless. But now, in a rented bed in this small, silent chamber, she was all too conscious of her limitations.

Stroking an azure petal, she confessed, "I'm nervous. At Skyhill you knew much less about me than you do now. And I haven't had much experience."

"I don't care about experience, Oriana. I want *you*."

It seemed like a year, thought Dare as he stripped off his shirt and flung it away, since the day he'd shown her his empty house. He was ready to feast upon her with the wild abandon of a ravenous beast. And yet he needed to hold himself in check and behave like a considerate and civilized gentleman. That's what he told himself as he quickly removed his breeches and smallclothes.

He joined her on the downy mattress, which dipped lower from their combined weight. "I'll be gentle," he promised her.

"I don't want gentle. I want *you*," she said, echoing his words to her. She reached out to him.

Placing his hand on her waist, he turned her around. Deftly he unhooked the corset and dropped it over the edge of the bed.

Her pleated petticoat was ruffled at the hem—even her underclothes had that St. Albans flounce. This one was threaded through with a cherry-satin ribbon, and decorated with bright rosettes and bows. "I've never received a present so elegantly wrapped," he commented as he removed it.

Her shift, transparent as gauze, revealed carmine-tipped breasts, firm and round. With tender deliberation, he paused to press his lips to each glorious discovery he unveiled—soft thighs, pale belly, smooth shoulders. Between her legs he found a tuft of crisp auburn curls to match her flowing locks.

He had bared the whole lovely length of her body. Like the earth itself, she was a collection of hills and valleys and caverns, and he roamed over her with an explorer's zeal. After crossing a sea and traveling countless miles, his quest had ended. He had found his promised land, and he was eager to claim it.

Her hands roamed across his forearms and chest and torso. With his every kiss, her yearning cries reverberated in the cavern of his mouth. Here was no ladylike acquiescence—this was lust, feral and primitive. His touch made her writhe and moan. Hers made him stiffen and swell.

He suckled her, the flicker of his tongue transforming each tender nipple into a firm pebble. His lips moved along the gentle underslope of one breast, down the flat plain of her midriff, and roamed across the slight rise of her belly.

He lifted his head. Through the dark fringe of hair hanging down over his forehead he saw that her eyes were half-lidded, and her mouth curved in a smile.

Finding the fragile spray of larkspur beneath his bent knees, he rescued it. "I'll get you another later," he promised. Discarding it, he dived at her for another bout of kissing, and she welcomed him with grasping arms, pliant lips.

Never, he thought, would he get his fill of her. There would be many more lazy afternoons, different rooms with grander bedsteads.

When he pried open her rose-pink folds, he felt the dewy proof of her readiness. He held her hand to his rampant flesh so she could guide him to his resting place. After a gradual, careful penetration, he was lodged inside her, pressing into her heated core.

She shifted her hips, drawing him even deeper into the well of delight.

Together they moved in eager lust, their hands and lips

and fervent sighs expressing the emotion they could not articulate. Each time he plunged, she gasped, and when he pulled back her embrace tightened, as though she couldn't bear to lose him.

He stroked her where she was most sensitive to his touch, his fingers urging her to the very summit of pleasure. From her desperate murmurs and the rake of her nails upon his back, he knew she was nearing the peak.

"I can take no more!" It was a cry of blissful agony, and a moment later her body quaked against him.

He continued his own quest, supporting himself with palms flattened against the mattress as he glided in and out. The exquisite friction rapidly brought him to the point of completion. With a groan of surrender, he sheathed himself one time more in a powerful, explosive thrust.

Collapsing, he laid his cheek upon her breast, savoring this moment of utter satisfaction.

Oriana lay beneath him, enfeebled by passion. Her nerves still rippled, her body was still shaken by the tremors he had caused.

"This," he declared gustily, "was worth waiting for. Your escapes and provoking teases are all forgiven. And so are the next dozen faults and mistakes and outrages you commit." He detached himself and crawled to the foot of the bed. When he had retrieved her frothy petticoat, he began to pull the red ribbon free of the flounce.

"What are you doing?" she asked, unable to watch the destruction of her exquisitely finished garment. "You'll spoil it."

"I'd better be the only person who'll see what's underneath your gowns." He returned with the strip of brightly colored silk. After tying one end around his wrist, he bound her to him. "You won't run away this time."

"I don't want to," she said, trying to free herself.

"Leave it. Just for tonight."

"Eating my dinner will be rather difficult," she protested.

"It's quite a long leash; it won't hamper you."

"When I'm ready for my bath it will. What if I need to—be alone?" Her gaze darted to the wooden cabinet housing items of necessity.

"Just tell me, and I'll step outside. But for the whole of the night, we'll be no farther away than this." He stretched out the ribbon to its full length. "Another experiment."

"I don't mind," she decided. "So long as you don't publish a treatise about it."

He swept her into his arms, holding her so close that she could feel the evidence of his arousal. Wantonly she pressed against him, her nipples budding as her bare bosom brushed against his broad chest. His hands were in her hair, tipping back her head. His mouth came nearer—she closed her eyes to receive his kiss.

When it didn't come, she opened them.

He was staring at her intently, yet he smiled. "I shall want you forever, Oriana."

She wasn't yet brave enough to echo his words, despite what they had just done, and what they were obviously about to do. And she certainly couldn't believe in them. Keeping her voice light, "Do you feel compelled to say that to every woman who shares your bed?"

"Only to you. After tonight, there can be no other."

As he laid her down, she tried to surrender her fear that eventually forever would end, and he'd regret his rash declarations.

Chapter 20

At midday, Dare made his initial foray onto Newmarket's hallowed heath. The first race had already begun, but he had several days of sport before him and saw no reason to join the eager crowd awaiting the outcome at the finishing post. He preferred to get his bearings, but it wasn't as simple as he'd expected. The haphazard and bewildering maze of courses included white-railed enclosures and various utility structures—troughs, betting posts, the weighing house, a movable judge's stand on wheels. White-canvas marquees and drinking booths added to the fairground atmosphere. Spectators had come on foot or horse, in common gigs and open carriages, creating an immense and active swarm of humanity. Newmarket racing bore no resemblance whatever to those casual contests that occasionally took place on the Isle of Man.

The sportsmen wore riding coats and breeches, fresh from the tailor's hands or shabby from frequent wear. The jockeys, lean, leathery-faced chaps stumping about on short, bowed legs, wore racing caps and colored silk waistcoats. Men were in the majority and females were easy to spot. Even so, he despaired of finding Oriana.

He'd last seen her that morning, boarding a post chaise for the final leg of the journey. He couldn't repress a satisfied grin, recalling the tumbled state of their bed when they left it. He'd never doubted that their physical union would be mutually rewarding, but to his delight it had also proved deliciously combustible. During the long night of many delights, they hadn't slept much. Wherever she might be, she surely experienced this same lassitude, and the sense of having woken from a pleasant dream and being summarily thrust into a noisy and active mob.

A remarkably flat stretch of earth spread out before him, and what hills it possessed were low and gently rounded. In the distance beyond the nearest racecourse, he could see clustered farm buildings and a patchwork of cultivated fields.

Striding across the springy turf, he noticed a raven-haired lady of fashion seated alone in a landau. After a faint prick of recognition, he couldn't shake the certainty that they'd met.

She returned his searching look, smiled, and beckoned to him. "Sir Darius Corlett! You haven't changed at all, though it must be six or seven years since we last met. You partnered me at the George Hotel assemblies in Douglas, and at Castletown, too. Or have you forgotten?"

Her silvery voice and clear gray eyes reinforced his recollection. "Lady Lavinia Cashin!" Gallantly, and in perfect truth, he declared, "Time has treated you most generously."

"It has indeed," she agreed. "For I'm married now, and a mother."

"Also a duchess."

"Yes, Garrick inherited the title last year. Sit with me, please—I'm desperate for interesting company. My husband is with his trainer; his horse is running the Beacon Course later today." With a laugh, she said, "During Race Week, the Duke of Halford is madly busy. He attends meetings of the Jockey Club, he shows people round his stud at Moulton Heath. He and his uncle give dinners at Monkwood Hall. In short, his children and I suffer the most pitiable neglect."

"You've got a pair of them, right?" he asked, taking the seat opposite hers.

"A girl and a boy." Her fine eyes shone with joy, and her cheeks turned rosy when she said, "And a new son or daughter coming next winter. I shall rely on you to prop me up, if I should swoon. I want all the island news! Now that Kerr and Ellin are parents, I rarely receive letters from Castle Cashin."

"I've been away for a full month and am behind on local affairs. What news from the castle? I hadn't even heard about Lord and Lady Garvain's happy event."

"My sister-in-law was delivered of a fine son. She and I are in competition to see who can produce the next set of twins in the family—they turn up in nearly every generation."

Dare's thoughts returned to Oriana. Their passion for one another, over time, might create a new life. Suddenly he wanted to know her feelings about that possibility. Illegitimacy was prevalent in her ancestry, recent and past, going all the way back to that pretty, witty blossom of an actress, Nell Gwynn. Oriana's status as a duke's by-blow had affected her profoundly, and he doubted that she would rejoice over bringing another bastard into the world.

Realizing that the duchess had questioned him, he had to ask her to repeat her words.

"Where are you staying?"

"In a hovel."

She raised her brows. "You must be exceedingly fond of the sport to endure privation."

"This is my first visit to Newmarket, and I've not yet seen a horse run."

"Did you travel here from your estate in—oh, dear, I can't recall its location."

"Derbyshire. No, I came from London." When she wrinkled up her nose in distaste, he laughed. "You don't care for the city?"

"Not much. Last year, when Garrick came into the title, we opened up Halford House and occupied it during the season. We spent time there this past Easter, but the children share my preference for country living, which is why we settled in Suffolk for much of the summer. After an initial burst of enthusiasm, Garrick grew bored with the House of Lords. He rarely attends, unless to cast his vote on matters of grave importance."

She waved at a striking, fair-haired gentleman making his way toward the landau. His features—prominent cheekbones and lean jaw, long aristocratic nose and cleft chin—seemed appropriate to a duke of the realm.

"So this is how you pay me out for abandoning you," he accused his duchess. "Are you setting up a flirt to make me jealous?"

"And the very best sort," she retorted. "A Manxman. Meet Sir Dare Corlett, by far the finest dancer from my island."

The duke's brown eyes fastened suspiciously on Dare, who told him, "I knew her grace when she was a slip of a girl, fresh from the schoolroom, and the undisputed belle of the assemblies there."

"That's right," she confirmed. "I was in my teens. You were very kind to partner a shy, uncertain girl as often as you did. I preferred you to all those raw soldiers from the garrison. Do stop glaring, Garrick. I never flirted with him—till I met you, I didn't now how. He wasn't my suitor."

"In that case," said the duke, "I'm very happy to meet

you, sir." Clasping his wife's gloved hand, he asked solic-
itously, "You are well, *carissima*?"

"Never better," she assured him. "We really must do
something for Sir Dare—his lodging sounds thoroughly
dismal. Wouldn't there be room for him at Moulton?"

"Certainly." Turning to Dare, the duke said, "I have a
racing box nearby, an old windmill converted to a residence. You're welcome to use it, and I urge you to stay
there instead, so long as you don't mind living among my
jockeys and grooms and horses. You'll find it adequately
furnished and staffed, and convenient to Newmarket."

"And after the racing," Lavinia interjected, "you must
join us at Monkwood Hall."

"You are most kind, and I wish I were free to accept.
But I've got an appointment in Bury St. Edmunds early
next week, and afterward I return to London."

"Splendid!" she cried. "We live only a few miles from
Bury! We'll take you to the subscription concert. I must
convince you to stay on a bit longer, so we can dance
together again at the upcoming assembly ball—I promise
I'll introduce you to all the loveliest girls in Suffolk."

The Duke of Halford tossed back his bright head,
laughing merrily. "My dear sir, I shall leave you to deal
with my duchess as best you can—but I warn you, when
she becomes enamored of a plan, it's impossible to dissuade her. Don't even try."

Considering the matter, Dare decided that attending
Oriana's concert as the Halford's guest would cover his
real reason for being there—and it wouldn't necessarily
interfere with their intended assignation at the Angel
Hotel.

"It's settled then," said Lavinia brightly. "And whenever you need to be in Bury, or anywhere else, our horses
and carriages will be yours to command."

"Uncle Bardy will wonder where I've got to," Garrick said. "Must return to the horses. Behave yourself, *carissima*, till next we meet."

"At the winning post," she told him confidently, leaning over the side of the carriage.

"I sincerely hope so." He kissed her fingers, and marched away.

"His uncle, Sir Bardolph Hyde, is devoted to the Turf," Lavinia confided.

As Oriana had done yesterday when describing her cousin's entries, the duchess informed Dare about the horses on which the Armitage Stud pinned its hopes of victory, reciting equine pedigrees with an acuity that the betting men would envy. Like Oriana, she possessed a well-worn copy of the *Racing Calendar.* Her years in Italy and England had endowed her with a veneer of sophistication, but beneath it was the unassuming and high-spirited girl he remembered. She treated him with a combination of deference and teasing, as if he were her older brother.

When the hour of her husband's race drew near, she climbed down from the carriage. On their way to the course, she pointed out notables to Dare—Sir Charles Bunbury, Mr. Concannon, Lord Darlington, Lord Clermont, Mr. Heathcote.

"At present there are several dukes actively involved in racing," she explained. "Halford and Grafton and Queensbury—chatting up a lady as usual, the old roué. She's Madame St. Albans, the singer. She dresses in excellent style, and is very popular among the gentlemen. I'm sure you can see why."

"She's the most beautiful woman I've ever seen. Present company excepted," he said with belated gallantry.

That morning he had fastened every one of those bright gilt buttons running down Oriana's dark green habit jacket. He'd handed her the smart hat, which had a gold chain encircling the crown and a jaunty plume pinned to the side. Around her neck was a longer chain with a dangling lorgnette. The desiccated old duke was leaning down to examine it—and from the way he leered, he also enjoyed his near view of her incomparable bosom.

Oriana returned Dare's gaze across a sea of strangers, her face expressionless. While he was perfectly willing to conceal their relationship, he would have liked some small acknowledgment of his existence. A polite nod or friendly smile would have been harmless enough. Her self-control nettled him.

"I give you leave to describe her as the most beautiful *Englishwoman*," Lavinia declared, smiling as she watched him watch Oriana. "That doesn't offend my vanity."

Tearing his eyes from his ladylove, he stated diplomatically, "Manxwomen are in a category all their own. It's unfortunate that the most charming ones desert the island."

"The same charge can be laid against eligible Manxmen," she responded. "You, sir, were seldom sighted in the years following our assembly-room encounters."

"Mining affairs in Derbyshire kept me away. But I've built a villa in Glen Auldyn, where I shall live in future." To forestall questions about his reasons for being in England, he asked her whether she had returned to the island since her marriage.

"Not yet. We go there in September, with the children, to meet the son and heir and visit my parents. And to see the heather blooming. Will we find you there?"

He admitted that he couldn't predict his movements so far in advance. Letting his gaze drift back to Oriana, he saw a younger man guiding her away from the elderly duke.

Lavinia said helpfully, "Her cousin Lord Burford, heir to the Duke of St. Albans. She'll be singing at that concert I mentioned. I don't know her, but if you like I can arrange an introduction."

Deciding that candor would be the safest policy, he replied, "That won't be necessary. I've met her."

And yearned for her, and kissed her, and bedded her—which, of course, he could not reveal.

The sight of her lover escorting a female to the finishing post was merely the latest of Oriana's frustrations.

She wasn't concerned that the lovely brunette sought to ensnare him, for the Halfords were a famously devoted couple. The duke belonged to the highest echelons of racing society. He was Sir Bardolph Hyde's nephew, descended from the Restoration courtiers who had followed her royal grandfather to Newmarket more than two centuries ago. But it was painful to see Dare advance into territory that was and would ever be closed to her. She didn't begrudge the Duchess of Halford's attention to him, but she was more keenly aware of her own lack of acceptability. The bastard daughter of the Duke of St. Albans and Sally Vernon performed for all these Newmarket grandees, she was related to several of them, and she'd received improper proposals from others. But the wives and daughters looked askance at her, no matter that they adorned their gowns with the St. Albans flounce, or wore their St. Albans spencers. She was used to it, and shouldn't mind. Yet she couldn't suppress a fear that Dare might, through association with them, absorb their prejudices against her.

Burford took her to a refreshment tent. She remained outside, while he pushed his way through the massed bodies to obtain drink. Because of the noise and commotion all around her, Dare was able to creep up on her unawares.

He said in a quiet confidential tone, "I couldn't keep away."

"The Duchess of Halford has befriended you, I see."

"We're former dancing partners, and have been reminiscing about past encounters in the island assembly rooms—which you were so careful to avoid. I know her family; they live in Maughold parish, near Ramsey. I needed to tell you that I'm transferring from my present quarters, grim beyond description, to the duke's racing box at Moulton Heath. Furthermore, his duchess commands that I make a visit to their estate near Bury after the races. They offered to take me to your concert. Should I accept?"

"Oh, yes. Halford is very important in racing, and is a Jockey Club member."

"I care less about his prestige than I do being separated from you. Where's that cottage of yours? I'll meet you later."

"On Mill Hill. But I can't let you come there, so please don't ask." She put a hand to her aching head.

"What's the matter?"

"Burford scratched Combustible from her race. She was entered against Sparrowhawk, another three-year-old, on the Rowley Mile this afternoon. But yesterday he learned about a stiffness in her lower leg, possibly a sprain, and couldn't risk running her. He had to pay ten guineas—ten percent of the prize—to Mr. Concannon. He's cross as two sticks, and threatens to sell the filly. It's madness."

"You told me she had the advantage."

Oriana nodded. "So I believed. With a win, she could've kept her place in Burford's stables, either as a racer or as broodmare. If I had a few hundred guineas laid by, I'd make him an offer myself—before he sends her to the Tattersall's auction. In his present mood, he's not likely to balk at a low price."

Her cousin returned with a tumbler of wine for her and a tankard of ale for himself.

Before she could begin an introduction, Dare spoke up.

"My lord Burford, I beg you to excuse my presumption, but I'm interested in acquiring a horse of good pedigree and wonder if you know any that might be available—for private sale. I've heard about your black horse, Deceit. And Weymouth, by Pharamond out of the stallion America, does he not belong to you?"

Oriana had supplied these facts during their journey. Reciting them back to her cousin, Dare sounded far more knowledgeable about racing than he actually was. It was an impressive performance.

Burford replied testily, "Neither horse is on the market, Mr.—"

"*Sir* Darius Corlett. From the Isle of Man."

The earl's reddish brows shot up, and he looked at Oriana. "Madame St. Albans has recently returned from there."

"Sir Darius is a friend of Halford's," she interjected.

"I've considered selling my black filly," Burford acknowledged. "If you and your trainer wish to examine Combustible, I invite you to do so. She was sired by Balloon, and finished third in a race at Brocket Hall."

What Dare intended to do with the animal if he actually bought it, she could not imagine. When he tucked Burford's card into an inside coat pocket, she spied a flash of red—the ribbon that had bound them together throughout the long night. She flushed from her crown to her toes, and very nearly choked on her wine.

"So dusty," she gasped, bringing her handkerchief to her lips.

"I've got myself into serious trouble," Dare confided to Lavinia when he rejoined her.

"How so?" She didn't look away from the string of horses plunging along the Flat.

"I am woefully ignorant about the care and feeding and other needs of a pedigreed courser, yet I've decided to purchase one." He lifted his tankard and drank deeply.

Her amusement burst forth in a ripple of laughter. "I'll never let you out of my sight again!"

"What, in your opinion, would be a reasonable offer for a three-year-old filly with a stiffness in her hock, who managed a third-place finish in her only race?"

Lavinia creased her snowy brow thoughtfully. "It depends how bad the injury is. Nick Cattermole, our trainer, could judge that for you. If she were perfectly sound, and her lineage is good enough, you wouldn't get her for less than five hundred pounds."

"I've been informed that she shows promise as a breeder."

"Not unless she can prove her merits with a win," Lavinia responded with a sagacity that he envied. Clutching his sleeve, she said eagerly, "The horses are coming! Mr. Wyndham's jockey wears the yellow silk and blue cap, he's riding a chestnut gelding. Lord Darlington's rider is in the pink-and-black stripes, on the dark horse."

"Why would anyone geld a racehorse?"

He never got his answer.

As the chestnut thundered past the post, the black pitched his rider out of the saddle. The band of followers riding in the wake of the two contestants tugged hard on their reins to divert their mounts before their hooves trampled the fallen jockey. Swerving, they endangered the spectators standing at the rail, whose excited, encouraging shouts were replaced by loud cries of fear and alarm.

Dare, mindful of Lavinia's safety—and her delicate condition—pulled her away from the scene of panic and chaos. He prayed that someone was doing the same to Oriana, wherever she might be—the riderless horse was running loose. Turning back, he saw two men lift the jockey from the ground and bear him away.

Lavinia's face was pressed against his arm, and her hands shielded her belly.

"It's all right," he said in relief. "They've caught the horse. Gelding him apparently engendered a terrible resentment against mankind."

She responded with a weak laugh.

"Can I take you back to your carriage?"

"I want to find my husband."

Dare saw the duke pushing through the crowd, evidently searching for his wife, and raised an arm to catch his attention.

Garrick hurried over. To Lavinia, he said gravely, "You shouldn't have left the landau."

"What happened to the jockey?" she asked.

"He's bruised and shaken, but otherwise unscathed. He's already standing on his own two feet. Which is more than you seem able to do, *carissima*," he said, tightening his hold on Lavinia. "Sir Dare, I'm deeply indebted to you. These accidents are uncommon, but when they do occur, all too often the consequences prove fatal—to rider or horse, or both."

As they walked toward the Halford carriage, Lavinia told her husband, "Sir Dare means to buy Burford's black filly."

Garrick looked at Dare. "He's selling Combustible? Who told you?"

"The earl himself."

"Reducing his stable again. I'm not surprised; he must have spent a considerable sum to acquire Weymouth. What are your plans for the filly?"

He wanted to give her to Oriana, who had once expressed a desire to own a racehorse. But that, he knew, was impractical. "I want to see her race," he said. "And win."

"So did Burford," the duke commented wryly.

"I've agreed to stop by his lordship's paddock later, so I can inspect the creature."

"Do you mean Burford's horse," Lavinia murmured, "or his beautiful cousin?"

Dare couldn't bring himself to glower at so charming a duchess, but he was sorely tempted. Not only did he understand Oriana's mania for privacy, he was beginning to share it.

Chapter 21

Oriana's fingers fluffed Combustible's mane, a short black fringe running the length of her glossy neck.

"Elegant, isn't she?" she heard Burford ask Dare.

"They both are," he responded. "The filly and the lady."

The earl laughed. "Only one is for sale, sir. And I doubt my cousin will let you examine her teeth."

"I wouldn't presume to ask." Dare marched in a circle around the horse, studying her from every angle. "I'm prepared to offer two hundred guineas."

"My dear Sir Darius, I've paid out that much in expenses. I can't accept less than six. And it's possible I'll get it—there's another interested buyer. The Duke of Halford and his trainer came by a little while ago to look her over."

"They did so at my request. If you and I reach an agreement, I'll be sending her to his grace's Moulton Heath stables."

That disclosure took the wind from Burford's sails, Oriana observed. Without a win, Combustible was worth only half of what he demanded.

For a long time she'd anticipated her favorite filly's debut season, cherishing hope of victory. This abrupt decision to sell was premature and unwise, and it made her cross. Burford's groom should have been more careful with Combustible. Muscle strain could occur when a coddled horse was moved from one location to another, because it was forced to cover rougher terrain than it had trained on. Her only comfort was that the injury seemed slight, and was certain to mend long before the filly's next scheduled Newmarket race.

Dare's willingness to purchase her *protegée* was as startling as Burford's plan to be rid of her. He had a good eye for horseflesh, demonstrated by his choice of Envoy for his island hack. He was also a skilled rider. But owning a pedigreed courser was a costly and demanding enterprise. The risks were many; the rewards were few and far between. Dare needed luck as well as patience and wealth, and plenty of it. But he never flinched at a challenge, and she believed that the dedication and persistence that had conquered her heart would stand him in good stead—if he could close the deal.

"Three hundred," Dare offered.

"I must point out that she's entered against Sir Charles Bunbury's Pamela at the October Meeting," Burford countered. "That engagement stands; it's included in the sale."

Oriana handed the halter rope to the stableboy. "Lead her over to the railing," she commanded.

The filly walked slowly, her gait affected by her injury.

"That sinew sprain in her left forefoot need not trouble you," Burford said. "We've taken the shoe off and applied a poultice of white-wine vinegar and egg whites. Any farrier will tell you that the problem can be cured in a couple of months. Perhaps sooner."

"And if it's not, she can't prepare for her next race. I stand by my price. Three hundred and not a guinea more."

In a tone of resignation, Burford replied, "Done. Though

it may not appear so at present, you've bought yourself a sound racehorse with a good disposition and an enviable pedigree. Meet me at the White Hart after the last race, and we'll seal our bargain with a glass of brandy."

"With pleasure." Dare smiled at Oriana, and invited her to join them.

"My reputation is dodgy enough, Sir Darius, and would suffer greatly if I invaded that solid bastion of masculinity."

Consulting his timepiece, Burford said to her, "We'd better hurry away if we mean to watch the two-year-olds race for the twenty guineas sweepstakes. I've bet on Vandal, Grafton's chestnut colt."

"Along with everybody else," she retorted. "I prefer the filly, Royala."

"Care to make a personal wager? We've got Corlett as witness. Ten guineas?"

"Twenty," she said daringly. She hoped her run of luck hadn't ended with Dare's purchase of her beloved filly.

"Agreed. Corlett, will you accompany us?"

Oriana handed Combustible's young caretaker a cartwheel penny and gave the velvety muzzle a parting caress. With her racing-mad relative on one side and her secret lover on the other, she left the paddock.

All the people of rank and fashion in the environs of Bury St. Edmunds had descended on the assembly rooms, and Angel Hill's flat, cobbled surface was thick with carriages. Dare and the Halfords arrived together, after dropping off his baggage at the inn where he would spend the night.

The master of ceremonies conducted the duke and duchess to a place of honor in the foremost row of chairs.

Sweeping his long coattails aside, Dare sat down beside Lavinia.

"I wish you'd stayed longer with us," she said while they waited for the concert to begin. "Kat and Jonathon will miss you—though their antics must have cured you of any desire to sire children of your own."

"Quite the contrary."

He'd developed an avuncular fondness for her daughter and son. If not for his desire to be with Oriana and return with her to London, he would gladly linger in the pleasant wilds of Suffolk, enjoying the domesticity of Monkwood Hall. He owned property here, after all—a black filly comfortably stabled at the duke's Moulton Heath stud. He would cover the cost of her feed and lodging, and the farrier's fee. As soon as she was judged ready, Nick Cattermole, his grace's trusted trainer, would prepare her for the October race meeting at Newmarket. Depending on her performance, she would either continue racing, or be covered by Don't Tell the Wife, a retired stallion of superior parentage who had won an impressive string of victories.

Madame St. Albans took her seat at the harpsichord. Conscious of Lavinia's watchful silvery eyes, Dare maintained an impassive face. Beneath his best waistcoat, his chest expanded with pride of possession.

A strand of pearls was wound through Oriana's coiffure, and she wore her St. Albans brooch. Her gown was a waterfall of cream satin, billowing down to the floor, with a foamy lace flounce at the bottom. He remembered the dress very well; she'd worn it at her dinner party.

She opened with a pensive ode to lost love, her soprano soaring to exquisite heights. Her artistry was sublime. Yet every time Dare confronted the famous Ana, the performer whose repertoire of music seemed infinite, his dream of sharing her life and fitting her more securely into his seemed threatened. In this rarefied setting, he couldn't envision her ever living with him at Skyhill—or wanting to. He'd sworn that he would take only what she was willing to give, but keeping his word was more difficult with each passing day.

In earlier years, his life had been more evenly divided between England and Man. Missing Tynwald Day hadn't concerned him, but he regretted his long absence from his lead mine and both his houses. Mr. Melton sent regular reports on the miners' progress on the new vein of lead, but predicted that it would falter with the onset of fishing season. Cousin Tom Gilchrist had written to assure him that Donny Corkhill and his father had cut and stacked the hay at Skyhill as ordered, and that Mrs. Stowell was still comfortably ensconced at Glencroft. If not for his chance encounter with the Halfords on Newmarket Heath, he wouldn't have known that Baron Garvain's lady had produced an heir for Castle Cashin. The Earl of Ballacraine, the infant's grandsire, planned a grand gala feast in September. The duke and duchess would attend, and so would all the island's gentry-folk—except Dare.

At the conclusion of the first piece, a multitude of gloved hands clapped approvingly, his included. But Lavinia's proximity required him to temper his enthusiasm.

The next offering was "No, my love, no!" Composed by her friend Michael Kelly; it was currently the most popular song in London. She then embarked on a selection of Manx airs. When she sang the opening line of *"Arrane y Lhondhoo,"* Lavinia turned her startled face in his direction. Her surprise was succeeded by a frown of confusion.

"I never thought to hear 'The Blackbird's Song' performed in England," she murmured to Dare during an interval. "I doubt Madame St. Albans has visited the Isle of Man, or knows anything about it."

"Perhaps she bought the song off a ballad singer in London," Garrick suggested. "Many performers do that."

"I suppose it's possible," Lavinia said doubtfully.

Dare could have offered an explanation. But, he told himself, he hadn't actually met the singer Ana St. Albans on the Isle of Man. Oriana Julian, a widow, had rented Glencroft.

In order to change the subject, he asked if Lavinia missed her girlhood home.

"I love Castle Cashin," she responded, "but I never expected to remain there. My family depended upon me to make a good marriage, and I always knew my fate would be settled in London."

"It was," said her husband, "the instant I first set eyes on you."

"He was a complete stranger, and he walked up and *kissed* me as I was walking along Cork Street," Lavinia said.

"And it changed your life."

Dare remembered the night in his Ramsey house, when he'd behaved with similar boldness.

Ignoring her spouse, Lavinia said, "I've lived very happily with that amorous stranger for five years, in Venice and in England. And now that he has his dukedom and the Langtree estate and so many responsibilities, we're tied to this country. But we're immensely fortunate; I have no reason to complain. I can't often return to the island, but I carry it with me always, in my heart and my memories."

Her cheerful declaration comforted Dare. Skyhill House belonged to him, whether or not he lived there—

exactly as Damerham did. The Glen Auldyn mine, like the Derbyshire ones, continued to provide employment and produce ore.

"I do want my children to see the place where I grew up," she continued. "I'll show them the castle's east tower, where my smuggling forefathers watched for the return of their ships. We'll climb North Barrule together—perhaps we'll make it to the summit of Snaefell!"

He didn't doubt that this intrepid and energetic young mother would achieve her ambition.

Before the recital resumed, the master of ceremonies shifted Oriana's chair to face the audience and placed a music stand beside it. When she reappeared with her *mandoline*, a hush fell over the room. Supporting her instrument's rounded body between thigh and knee, she plucked the strings with her quill end; her fingers danced upon the frets. Her songs were in Italian or French, some lively and others very soothing, and she performed a long piece without vocal accompaniment. Relinquishing her *mandoline,* she returned to the harpsichord to play a sonata. For an encore, she sang another Manx song, *"Te traa gall thie, as goll dy lhie."*

"Time to go home, to go and rest." After many busy weeks in England, the sentiment found favor with Dare. If only they could steal away to his peaceful glen, far from curious stares and probing questions.

After she made her final curtsy, the master of ceremonies led her over to the Duke of Grafton, who kissed her on both cheeks in the French fashion. The concertgoers mingled, chatting to one another, or headed for the adjoining refreshment room.

"I wish to speak with her," said Lavinia in a determined voice. "Garrick, I'm sure you need to discuss racing with Grafton—*don't* you?"

The duke obediently escorted his duchess across the room, and Dare, as their guest, went with them.

When they had all praised the singer's artistry, Grafton stated, "I take full credit for luring her here—this could rightly be termed a command performance. A most talented creature, my kinswoman." To Dare he said, "Like me, she's a direct descendant of Charles II—by a different mistress." With a smile, he explained to Oriana, "Sir Darius here is a fresh convert to our favorite pastime."

"I was at my cousin's paddock when he bought the filly," she responded.

Addressing his fellow duke, Grafton said, "We must convince Sir Darius to join us in the hunt, Halford."

"I'm not a hunting man," Dare admitted. "The country 'round Damerham is ill suited to the sport, and on the Isle of Man we've got no foxes."

"You should take it up," Lavinia urged him. "When we lived in Venice, hunting was what I missed most about England."

"An enchanting city," said Oriana, "despite the absence of horses. It's unlike any other. And the opera house is magnificent."

Clearly this comment captured Garrick's interest. "You performed at Venice?"

"Shortly after it opened," she replied.

"I suspected you'd been to Venice when you sang the gondolier's song. Didn't you recognize it, *carissima?*"

"Yes," Lavinia answered. "Madame St. Albans, I was more amazed to hear you sing in my native tongue. From whom did you learn 'Song of the Blackbird' and all the others?"

"A Manxman, your grace. A musician."

"You're quite clever, for it's not an easy language."

Smiling, Oriana replied, "My poor instructor had the harder task by far."

"My duchess might have preferred your Manx tunes, but I favor the Italian ones," Garrick told her. "One doesn't often encounter a *mandoline* in this country."

"I acquired mine in Naples, and gathered my music from many sources. I'm sure you are familiar with the operatic piece '*Deh, vieni alla finestra,*' from Mozart's *Don Giovanni.* The serenades, comic and serious, are popular tunes that I adapted myself, with the aid of my singing master, Signor Corri. The sonata by Gaudioso is one of the few pieces composed for a mandolinist."

"I sincerely hope that you'll perform in Bury often," said Lavinia. "Our London visits are infrequent, and we seldom attend the theater. When must you return to town?"

"Tomorrow."

The members of the group soon went their separate ways. Dare thanked the Halfords for their hospitality and wished them a safe and uneventful voyage to the island.

Leaving the assembly rooms, he made a swift progress across the cobblestones that paved Angel Hill and hurried up the steps of the hotel.

Even though Oriana expected it, the soft tap on her door made her jump. The old hinges rasped as Dare came into the room. Peering through the parted bedcurtains, she saw him come toward her, a chamber stick in his hand. He placed it on the nightstand beside hers, and removed his dressing gown. Her heart fluttered in anticipation.

"What are you reading?" Taking away her book, he turned its leaves one at a time, with maddening slowness. "Ah, yes. Your poet expresses my feelings most eloquently." Holding his finger on the chosen verse, he read it to her.

"This morning, timely rapt with holy fire,
I thought to form unto my zealous muse,
What kind of creature I could most desire,
To honour, serve, and love; as poets use.
I meant to make her fair, and free, and wise
Of greatest blood, and yet more good than great."

Flattered by the description, she knew she didn't deserve it. "The blood of kings runs in my veins, much diluted, but I've none of their greatness."

"For a famous woman, you have a very low opinion of yourself."

She laughed softly. "Truth is, I've pride enough for two. As for the rest of it—whenever you're with me, I'd rather *not* be good."

He joined her on the bed, and smilingly brushed aside the strands of hair trailing across her breast.

"Are you going to perform another experiment in animal behavior?" she asked hopefully.

"Not behavior." His fingertip drew a circle around her nipple, and the rosy tip drew itself into a bud. "Reflexes. Involuntary reactions. Allow me to test the limits of your self-control."

His palms drifted down her rib cage, along her sides, and spanned her hips. They swept behind to trace the curves of her bottom, then caressed the backs of her thighs. Oh, yes, the sensations he produced defied restraint.

She placed her hand low on his abdomen. His skin felt warm beneath her palm, and his muscles flexed into tautness. As she caressed him, she heard the hissing rush of air through his teeth and saw the upward thrust of his flesh, swollen with promise.

"You have reflexes, too." This observation earned her a

searing kiss. Afterward she said, "You've been drinking brandy."

"You've recently eaten marmalade," he said, the motion of his lips tickling hers. "You taste sugary, but slightly tart."

That was exactly how she was inside—all sticky and sweet, with a contrasting tangy sharpness. This pleasure was too seductive, deliciously intense, and she didn't want it to end. Trapped by his greater weight, maddened by desire, she couldn't remember why she'd fought so hard and long to preserve her celibacy—or her liberty. The joys of surrender were keener by far.

His restless fingers searched for the place where her passion pulsed. As his thumb stroked her sensitive inner flesh, little ripples of delight spread outward through her limbs, building into billowing, surging waves. She tensed, bracing herself for the largest breaker of all, which struck with a force so strong and uplifting that she was swept away entirely.

"A reflex," he whispered. The concentrated flare of the two candles shone upon his face, and their light was reflected in his dark eyes. "There's a whole collection of words and phrases to identify what you just experienced—some lofty and learned, some extremely crude." He nuzzled her cheek. "Tonight, Oriana, I mean to explore the process very thoroughly. Clear definitions are essential to the scientist's understanding, and the term I mean to concentrate on tonight is 'ravishment.'"

Stretched out upon this bed, her body exposed to his view, she should have felt vulnerable. His arousal, visible proof of her desirability, made her invincible. She grapsed his rigid flesh and ran the pad of her thumb over its rounded, velvety tip, brushing away a bead of dew. His eyelids fluttered and he clenched his jaw.

Another reflex.

"Who's ravishing whom?" he groaned, leaning forward and letting her guide him.

When he buried himself in her, she released a shuddering sigh. His body stilled, allowing them a moment to savor their closeness. She felt entirely filled, but wasn't yet satisfied.

He began to move, and so did she. Their friction kindled a rapturous heat that spread rapidly from her core. Her blood heated to the boiling point, it thickened like the marmalade she'd eaten and flowed sluggishly through her veins. He slid in and out of her, stoking the fire. She didn't feel ravished—she was burning up, and soon there would be nothing left of her, nothing at all but the scent of smoke in the air.

She cried out; he surged forward, and poured himself onto her embers.

Oriana's head fell back upon the pillow, dampened wisps of hair clinging to her forehead and temples.

"This isn't science," she panted. "It's magic."

For a long, lovely while they lay together, limbs entwined.

During the gradual recovery from their passionate coupling, Dare told her about his brief stay at Monkwood Hall and his thriving friendship with the Halfords.

"The children are delightful. Lady Kat sat upon my knee and let me teach her some Manx words. And I was permitted to cuddle her cat. Jonathon, the Marquis of Rotherfield, is a dignified young chap of two."

Beneath her hand, his chest heaved and sank in a sigh.

After a thoughtful silence, he asked, "What are your thoughts on motherhood?"

His simple question was an unwelcome reminder of the probable impermanence of their liaison. "If we produced a child, it would be awkward for you, and for me the worst scandal yet. I do what I can to prevent it."

"May I ask how?"

She stared up at the tester over their heads. "I use a lemon—cut in half."

He rolled over on his side. "What do you do, *eat* it?"

"Oh, don't ask," she pleaded. "You don't need to know."

"You've made me curious. Who told you about the preventive power of the lemon?"

"My mother. When I was first wed, she taught me how to—where to position the lemon. She visited the garrison for a long talk with Henry, and convinced him that an infant would interrupt my career. He could barely support me, never mind a child. We were young, he said; we could start our family when he returned from India."

He held up her fingers and kissed each one. "You do smell lemony."

"The scent is lasting."

"Your knowledge served you well, I gather, during your involvement that blackguard who treated you so ill."

She didn't want to remember Thomas while she was lying in Dare's embrace. "I didn't bother with it, because we were soon to marry. Or so I believed."

Dare's expression was inscrutable. Perhaps she shouldn't have spoken so candidly about her past. He might assume that Thomas Teversal was the only man whose child she'd been willing to bear. She could refute it, but the topic of pregnancy was not one she was eager to pursue. He seemed more amused than offended by her effort to avoid conception. Perhaps he was relieved. Most men would be—but then, Dare was in no way ordinary

He continued to hold her hand against his face, drawing her fingertips across his cheek. Reaching for the other, he did the same. "Feels different."

"Over time, the ends grow firm from pressing down on

the mandoline strings. I've been practicing so much lately."

"You deserved all the applause and approval you earned tonight."

"The audience was genteel and more attentive. These subscription concerts can also be more profitable for me. When I sing at a theater I must share the money with the proprietor, and not all of them deal fairly with performers or pay promptly. The crowds are larger and much noisier, and not very discriminating. They want popular or sentimental pieces—the ones I like the least."

"And yet you seek employment at the King's Theatre."

"I was trained for opera," she said simply. "And I enjoy it, despite the demands. Not only must I use my voice well, I'm required to interact with other characters." She laid her head on his shoulder. "You'll never guess my favorite place to sing."

"In bed?"

"In a church. For me, sacred music is the most marvelous of all. The oratorios by Bach—his *St. Matthew Passion* and *St. John Passion,* the *Christmas Oratorio.* Handel's *Messiah* and Arne's *Judith. Il Ritorno di Tobia,* by Herr Haydn. He's produced a new one, *The Creation,* which I long to perform. Nothing can compare to the hush and the holiness of a cathedral. I'm happy whether I'm a soloist, with a great organ playing in the background, or part of a large chorus. And the listeners—they are the true music lovers. They come to be uplifted, not merely entertained."

"What a surprising creature you are," he murmured. "When can I hear you sing one of these great religious works?"

"The Academy of Ancient Music sponsors concerts at

the Crown and Anchor Tavern, beginning in January. From February till May, Concerts of Ancient Music are held at the opera house on Wednesday evenings. I prefer employment with the latter, because the pay is better. But I long to sing in a cathedral again."

"I'll order one up for you, and hire musicians and choristers."

She kissed his cheek. "A lovely notion, but I wouldn't want to ruffle the sensibilities of the churchmen. I'll wait to be invited. Besides, you've incurred too many expenses already. Chasing me across England. Lodging charges at Nerot's and Morland's. The purchase of a racehorse."

"I got her at a bargain price," he reminded her. "It's only money. I've got plenty."

"And I'm only a woman."

"What does that mean?"

"There are so many others. Women who could please you better in bed. Women who are unencumbered by a profession as demanding as mine can be." *Women whom you might marry,* she thought despairingly.

His hand closed upon her shoulder. "But you are special, Oriana. No female in the entire world can surpass you. You're *mine.* Floating in the Thames somewhere, or out in the English Channel, or perhaps the ocean, is a champagne bottle containing our written pledge." He reached around to cup her breast, with tender possessiveness. "If your lemon should fail you, remember that I can afford to support a child. And I shall."

"You won't have to," she assured him.

"I want your promise that you'll deal with me honestly, whatever happens. No half-truths, and no subterfuge. No more running away. If by some accident I get you with child, let it be born on the island—it must grow up there. Bastardy is no stigma among the Manx."

And what would he do with her, send her back to London to resume her interrupted career? Keep her at Glencroft, conveniently down the hill from his villa?

She stared down at his broad, tanned hand as it toyed with her. "You should go back to your room."

"Not yet. For too many days, I haven't been able to touch you. Like this. Or kiss you here." He swept aside her long hair and his lips brushed her nape.

"I can't let you stay the night—not at this hotel, where I'm known. On our way back to town, we'll find some quiet, remote inn."

"And when we're back in London, what then?"

"I've not thought that far ahead."

She recalled her clandestine encounters with Thomas Teversal—rushed and stealthy, and so shaming. Her pride demanded a different arrangement, although she knew it wouldn't be easy to devise one.

Dare drew her into his embrace, and their mouths locked in a heady kiss. Casting off her concerns, Oriana decided to let the future resolve itself.

PART III

Why should we defer our joys?
Fame, and rumour, are but toys.
Cannot we delude the eyes
Of a few poor household spies?
Or his easier ears beguile,
So removèd by our wile?
'Tis no sin, love's fruit to steal,
But the sweet theft to reveal:
To be taken, to be seen,
These have crimes accounted been.

—BEN JONSON

Chapter 22

"**M**rs. Julian sings in theaters? *Vel shiu g'insh dou yn irriney*, Mainshtyr?"

"Of course I speak the truth."

Ned Crowe was in a perpetual state of wide-eyed incredulity, expressing his amazement at London's size and architectural magnificence, its traffic, the crowds. But his master's announcement that the former tenant of Croit ny Glionney was a famous vocalist startled him more than anything else.

"She performs at the public pleasure gardens."

The young Manxman rubbed his forehead. "Sweet is her voice, *dy-jarroo*. When I told her folk would pay to hear such sounds, how she laughed."

"She's paid very well," Dare responded. "Later this week she gives one of her Vauxhall concerts. I'll take you. You've never seen anything in your life like the illuminations, Ned—they will astound you."

"Everything does in London," the youth admitted with a grin.

The *Dorrity* had completed a smooth and swift sailing from Ramsey, and was now moored in Deptford. Her crew was enjoying a few days' leave, but they'd be busy again soon, for she was about to have her hull scraped and repainted, and get a new mast and rigging.

Ned, his arm fully mended, had delivered requested reports from the Glen Auldyn mine and copies of requisition orders to Morland's Hotel.

"What about that small pouch I asked for?" Dare wanted to know as he searched through the trunk. "It's supposed to be here. What've you done with it?"

Ned peered over his shoulder. "At the very bottom, Mainshtyr."

That was exactly where he found it, tucked into a corner. Emptying it onto a tabletop, Dare inspected the collection of prismlike crystals. He would restore them to Oriana, but not in their present state. The jeweler on Ludgate Hill must first transform them into an appropriate token of his affection.

He advised Ned to change his clothes. "Ask Wingate to give you all my old shirts. My brown coat should fit well enough without alteration, and he can shorten the black breeches for you. And have him trim your hair before you go out."

"*Vel oo cheet marym?*"

"No, I won't be going with you. I want you to deliver a message to Madame St. Albans, who lives close by, in Soho Square. Wingate can direct you to her house. Tell her that I must make a quick trip to Deptford to confer with the captain and give him orders for the refurbishing of the ship. I shall spend tonight on board and return tomorrow afternoon."

"*Ta,* Mainshtyr."

Wingate, coming into the parlor, said, "I can inform Madame of your plans myself, sir."

Since returning from Newmarket, Dare had noticed that his valet was never reluctant to visit the singer's house. Wingate claimed to have developed a comradeship with old Mr. Lumley, but Dare suspected the greater attraction was Oriana's waiting woman. Whether his servant's interest in Suke Barry was casual or reciprocal, he didn't know.

"Both of you may go." To Wingate, he added wryly, "Don't let me detain you. Lately I've had practice packing my valise; I can manage without you."

"I shall take care of it, sir. This came for you." Wingate presented a salver with a single letter and a silver knife to open it.

Oriana wasn't the sender—his name and direction were legibly written. Impatient to be away, Dare snatched it from the tray and unceremoniously stuck it in his pocket.

During his journey to Deptford, he read it.

Number 32, Soho Square
Sunday, 14th July, 1799

Sir,

My purpose in writing is twofold.
   Firstly, I commend your excellent treatise "Geology and Mineralogy of the Isle of Man." I found your investigations and their connection to Dr. Hutton's theories most intriguing.
   Secondly, if you are at leisure on Saturday evening, I would be honored by your presence at dinner. My wife Lady Banks and my sister send greetings, and look forward to seeing you in Soho Square.

Believe me, my dear Sir,
Very faithfully yours,
Jos. Banks, President, Royal Society

His treatise?

How the devil had Banks got hold of it? Dare had distributed copies to his circle of friends in Edinburgh—Hutton, Playfair, John Clerk of Eldin. The remainder languished in a dark cupboard at his Glen Auldyn mine office.

And there, he recalled, he'd presented one to Oriana . . . .

Not only had she read it, she'd shown it to her illustrious neighbor. She was responsible for this highly flattering invitation. He wasn't sure why she'd done it—but did it really matter? He was grateful, and he would definitely accept.

Ned Crowe's bow cut across the fiddle strings, producing a spirited *coda* to the lively ballad. Lowering his instrument, he suggested to Oriana, "Let's try '*Coontey-Ghiare Jeh Ellan Vannin.*' "

She searched among the sheaf of papers he'd brought with him. "It's got so very many verses. You're sure your arm is strong enough?" she asked, solicitous of his injury.

"I've been playing for more'n a fortnight," he informed her blithely. "During the voyage, I was sawing at this fiddle night and day, entertaining myself by day and the sailors at night."

When he had adjusted the tuning keys, he accompanied Oriana while she sang a lengthy ballad describing the isle's geography and its many beauties.

As soon as she finished, she collapsed on the nearest chair, saying, "The tune is simple, but the language is not!"

"You could sing the English words."

"That would detract from the novelty. I shall persevere."

She had been practicing yesterday when Ned arrived, and on being admitted to her sanctuary he had begged her to perform for him. Seating herself at the pianoforte, she'd played a Haydn composition, then took up her *mandoline* to entertain him with an Italian song. He'd rushed back to Morland's to fetch his fiddle, and they had spent the afternoon making music together. When she'd invited him to appear with her at Vauxhall, he agreed enthusiastially and helped her choose which pieces to insert into her repertoire. The famous Ana St. Albans, student of the finest music masters in the world, and a Manx miner with a remarkable talent—this collaboration might prove profitable for them both, financially as well as artistically.

"When we feel ready," she said, "I'll inform Mr. Barrett and Mr. Simpson that you'll be performing with me on Saturday night. If I say they should pay you three guineas a concert, they won't blink."

Ned's mouth dropped open. "Three gold pieces?"

"I doubt I can get you more. Not yet."

"I've never earned more than a *skillin* at a time, playing at weddings and wakes. I shall make my fortune here!" His gleeful outburst was followed by a sober question. "Which of us will be telling Mainshtyr Dare what we intend to do?"

"This was my idea. I'll do it," she said courageously. If he disliked her plan, she didn't want his blunt censure to fall upon Ned.

Rising, she returned to the music stand. "We should try the 'Courting Song' again."

"*Ta.*" Ned raised his violin, played a few notes, and sang out in his fine tenor.

"Lesh sooree ayns y geurey,
   An vennick beign ny lhie,
   Agh shooyll ayns y dorraghey,
   Scoan fakin yn raad thie.

With courting in the winter,
   I'd seldom be in bed,
   But walking in the darkness,
   Scarce seeing the road home."

The pounding of the knocker drew Lumley to the hall. Oriana heard Dare's deep tones, and smiled upon her accompanist, who had lowered his instrument. "Sing on," she instructed.

Dare entered the room just as the young man resumed his performance, and smiled at her. She held her finger to her lips, bidding him to keep silent.

"Veign goll gys ny unniagyn
   As crankal shirrey entreil
   Yn fillaghey yealley orrym
   As my lleckanyn gaase gial.

I would go to the windows,
   And rap seeking entrance,
   The rain pouring upon me,
   And my cheeks growing pale."

Remembering her criticisms of his untidiness—at his Ramsey home and the mining office—she regretted the disorder all around her. Music sheets were spread across the pianoforte, and instrument cases cluttered the floor. She mustn't draw attention to the chaos by trying to remedy it. Perhaps Dare hadn't noticed.

"My employees have transferred their allegiance to you, Madame," he complained. "Here is Ned, fiddling the day away. I suspect Wingate is belowstairs. He's certainly not where he should be—at Morland's, awaiting his master's return."

"He's with Lumley," Oriana replied. "They updated my cellar-book, and now they're bottling off claret from the pipe Berry Brothers delivered this morning."

"Finish your song," said Dare, a smile breaking through. "I know there's more."

Oriana glanced at Ned, who waited for her with poised bow. He played the introductory notes, and she picked up where he'd left off, singing the Manx girl's reply to her suitor.

"Fow royd voish yn unniag
Fow royd ta mee dy graa,
Son cha jean-ym lhiggey stlagh oo,
Ta fys aym's er ny shaare!

Get away from the window,
Get away I tell thee,
For I will not let you in,
I know better than that!

Dy bragh, ny dy bragh, guilley,
Cha bee ayms ayd son ben,
Son cha vell mee goll dy phoosey,
My taitnys hene vys aym.

No never, no never, young man,
Will I be thy woman,
For I'm not going to marry,
My own pleasure I will have."

Ned, resuming the man's part, described how his love crept out of the house, shawl over her head. They ended in a duet, singing of the joys they found in each other's arms.

Afterward, Oriana explained, "Ned and I are determined to perform together at Vauxhall. He'll be well compensated."

"But only if you permit it, Mainshtyr," the young man said quickly.

Dare's grave face revealed his reservations. "You want to do this?" he asked Ned.

"*Ta.* But not just for the money. I'd play for Mrs. Julian—St. Albans—even if I wasn't paid at all."

Evidently swayed by this assurance, Dare said, "Go to the tailor in Dean Street and have him measure you for a new suit of clothes—you should visit a hatter, too, and a wigmaker. Have all the bills sent to my bankers. The Vauxhall musicians dress very fine, and so must you."

Expressing profuse thanks, the youth tenderly laid his violin in its battered wooden case. He hurried away to procure the appropriate garments for his debut.

After he departed, a grim Dare confronted Oriana. "You are indeed a siren, and I hope Ned won't crash upon your rocks. He plays his fiddle for enjoyment, and to earn a few shillings now and again. He's never been off the island till now, and it's only his second day in London. He's entirely ignorant of the theater and its ways—he wasn't raised upon the stage, as you were."

"I know. But I never imagined there was harm in my suggestion."

"I'll not stand in his way—clearly he wants to perform with you. But I shall intervene, if I feel the need."

Oriana nodded her understanding. Ned's accident in the mine had proved how seriously Dare took his responsibility to the young Manxman. "Tell me about your visit to Deptford."

"I kept busy. The *Dorrity* will get new sails and rigging, a larger anchor, fresh caulk and paint—to the delight of her captain and the dismay of her owner. I'm dazed by the expense of this undertaking. The work can be done more cheaply here than in Ramsey, but even so, the estimates are higher than I expected." He put his arms around her waist. "If my funds run out, and I must give up my rooms at Morland's, would you take me in?"

Saucily she replied, "Certainly not, sir. I'll send you to the nearest poorhouse—all those sums I donate might as well benefit somebody I know."

"Have you no heart?"

She did, and when he looked at her that way, it jumped. "If not, I wouldn't be so lavish with my charitable contributions."

He shoved a letter at her. "Read this."

She unfolded it, laughing. "I never expected a *billet-doux* from a man whose pen produces scientific writings."

"I didn't write it, your neighbor Sir Joseph did. You showed him my geological treatise, you meddling hussy."

His tone was affectionate—he wasn't angry. "You got on so well with him, and he seemed interested in your work. An invitation to dine at his house—a high honor indeed! But Saturday is likely to be Ned's first Vauxhall appearance. Perhaps we can put it off for a fortnight."

"For Ned's sake, you'd better make the arrangements as speedily as possible. He's so excited about being your accompanist, he'll never notice I'm not there for his debut. There will be other performances, I'm sure."

Nodding, she replied, "I'll send a message to the master of ceremonies straightaway."

He went with her to the parlor, hovering over the chair of her writing desk. She felt as fluttery as those trees in the square gardens, branches swaying in the warm summer breeze. His hand on her shoulder affected her concentration, and she struggled to complete the simple task of penning and sealing her note to Mr. Simpson. With fumbling fingers, she replaced her pen and silver inkpot in their compartments.

When he leaned near, she saw the heat of desire glowing in his dark, black-lashed eyes. His curving mouth drifted ever closer, and gently collided with hers. His hand moved to her cheek, where the blood pulsed feverishly. Their kiss, which began as a soft brush of lips, turned into an incendiary exploration. She welcomed the invasion of his darting tongue, the slide of it across her teeth. Her body was heavy with longing. She could gladly shed her garments there and then, and let him take her—if not for their complete lack of privacy.

Belatedly recalling that that they were in full view of the window, she murmured a protest. He ignored it. Dragging her out of her chair, he pulled her into an intoxicatingly intimate embrace. His hands pressed against her arched back and his long legs, hidden by her voluminous skirts, imprisoned her. His mouth swept down, claiming and smothering her.

"No more," she pleaded, gasping for air.

"With you, Oriana, I always need more."

She glanced toward the hall to reassure herself that no servant had witnessed Dare's intimate assault upon her person. Reassured, she turned to the parlor window—and her erratic pulse stilled.

A pedestrian had paused to spy on them. Tapping on the pane, he glowered at her.

Matthew Powell.

Dare spun around. Oriana, horrified by this disaster in the making, rushed to the front door to admit the visitor herself.

"You're supposed to be in Cheshire," she said severely,

taking him to the parlor. "Rushton told me so."

"He was mistaken," Matthew Powell replied curtly, laying his hat and gloves on a chair. He gave Dare a long, assessing look. "I must inform you, sir, that Ana never permitted *me* to do what I just saw you doing." Turning back to Oriana, he intoned, "As for you, Madame—" His shoulders sagged, and he buried his face in his hands. "I cannot reproach you. You did not love me, or pretend that you could. Oh, the agonies I've suffered! Just when I believe I'm recovering from my rejection comes the torture of finding you in the arms of another. After all I've endured, the blow is too much to bear!" He drew a ragged sigh. "But bear it I must, else you will despise me."

Oriana returned to her desk. "I've not yet put away my writing paper—most fortunate. I'll inform Mr. Sheridan of your return, for he may well require fresh talent at Drury Lane in the coming season. The choice is yours, Matthew—matrimony or a stage career. You cannot have both. Rushton is too stuffy to have a son-in-law treading the boards."

The young man marched across the room and snatched the quill from her hand. "You're spoiling all my fun!"

"As you told me at our last meeting, my cruelty knows no bounds."

Said Dare, "Sir, I find myself in sympathy with you. I'm well acquainted with those agonies and tortures you mentioned."

The visitor grinned at Dare. "I'm Matthew Powell. May I know your name?"

"Sir Darius Corlett. Call me Dare."

Oriana, blushing to the roots of her hair, watched the two men shake hands.

"I'm curious to know how you managed to overcome her prudery."

"Persistence," said Dare, flashing a smile.

"Not that I ever tried to kiss her," he said. "She wouldn't have let me, and I wasn't brave enough to attempt it—with so many other chaps ogling her, I lived in fear of being challenged to a duel. I've got a healthy dislike of bullets and bloodshed, and my taste for melodrama does not extend to getting myself killed over Ana St. Albans."

Dare turned to Oriana. "Is he ever serious?"

"Rarely. When he asked me to marry him, he was laughing. And he continued to laugh when I refused him."

"Because I was so damned tipsy. Too much brandy that night. I was addled, yes, and my memory is hazy at best. But you can't deny that you were laughing, too. I thought you very unfeeling, for it's no easy task, wooing the most renowned singer in London. Have a care how you treat Sir Dare, Ana. Be kinder to him than you were to me."

"Ingrate," she accused him, "I did you a great kindness. My prudence saved your betrothal. When is the wedding to be?"

"Soon, I hope. Only, there's a snag, so tiresome—which is why I'm here. I've got a damned pesky problem, and to solve it I require the feminine perspective."

"I've caused more problems than I've ever cured," she said frankly. "And I can't imagine why you'd travel all the way from Cheshire to consult me, unless—" Narrowing her eyes, she asked suspiciously, "Have you quarreled with Lady Liza again?"

"No. I'm being good as gold."

"With Rushton?"

He shook his fair head. "The only time we had uncivil words, you were the cause."

She summoned Lumley with a tug on the bellpull, and requested a bottle of the good French brandy for her guests, and a glass of sherry for herself. "I want Sam to deliver this note to Mr. Simpson of Vauxhall," she instructed her butler.

While Oriana and Matthew chatted about the problem, Dare retreated to the desk to compose his acceptance of Sir Joseph's invitation.

"No more histrionics," he heard Oriana say impatiently.

"Trust me, my alarm is warranted. If you were in debt, you'd understand."

In explaining her fondness for Matthew Powell, Oriana had likened him to her late husband. Henry Julian, Dare deduced, must have been a merry fellow with bright hair and laughing eyes. She'd loved one enough to wed him, but not the other. That was a consolation and also a cause for concern. *Never, never, young man,* she'd sung a little while ago to Ned, *will I be your woman—for I won't marry, my own pleasure I will have.* She must have said something very similar when turning down Powell's offer of matrimony, doubtless substituting "pleasure" with "profession." Her unwavering dedication to her art formed her decisions and ruled her actions.

Dare wasn't entirely sure why this young fellow's drunken proposal had sent her flying off to Liverpool— and eventually to the Isle of Man—but he was glad of it.

Regretting that he lacked the power to transfer this cozy domestic scene to Skyhill House—without the young Englishman and his financial problems—he returned to his letter.

His dinner at Sir Joseph's house would, he hoped, resemble the ones he'd enjoyed so much in Edinburgh. During these two years since Dr. Hutton's death, he'd missed the opportunity to make scientific speculations and discuss intriguing observations with gentlemen who could appreciate them. His restricted social life on the island had grown wearisome, and though he greatly enjoyed the company of his cousin Tom and George

Quayle and Buck Whaley, he couldn't engage them in discussions of geology.

A familiar carriage had halted before the door, and the butler soon announced the Earl of Rushton. As the nobleman entered Oriana's parlor, Mr. Powell's face sobered, and he bounded to his feet.

Rushton cast wrathful eyes upon the young man. "You, sir, are not permitted to visit this house. Have you forgotten?"

Matthew clenched his jaw, then said, "I answer only to Liza. She knew I meant to come."

In a sorrowful voice, Oriana said, "I'm accustomed to other people making the worst assumptions about my character, Rushton, but not you. Do you really think I'd carry on an intrigue with a gentleman in my front parlor, in broad daylight?"

Matthew tugged at a trailing lock of her hair, and murmured, "Not your best defense, Ana. I was standing at your window long enough to know."

With less harshness, the earl said to Oriana, "Again and again I've warned you about the danger of this friendship with Matthew." He directed a stony glance at Dare before adding, "You should be wary of forming any attachments that might do you harm."

"It's far too late to remedy my lack of respectability. I hardly had any to lose. No effort of mine—or yours—can confer it upon me."

"I sincerely hope that time will prove you wrong," the earl replied.

Oriana cast desperate eyes upon Dare, wordlessly beseeching him to come to her aid.

Calmly he declared, "Mr. Powell has been telling Madame St. Albans of his wish to wed your daughter as soon as possible."

"That's right," Matthew confirmed. "In fact, I assured him that Ana never once tried to undermine my morals. I'm not his rival."

Rushton didn't appear to take comfort from this revelation. He turned to Oriana. "I trust you haven't yet done something you will later regret. Need I remind you of your shame and distress after—"

"I remember," she interrupted him. "But I prefer to forget. Can we not discuss Parliament, or the progress of the war, or anything else?"

Rushton softened his tone even more, and his expression. "I know how little you care for politics or war. I've come to speak on a topic of abiding interest to you: the theater."

Dare didn't like the way Oriana smiled back at the earl. "Really? They do say there's a first time for everything."

"Has Matthew informed you of our plan to stage a play at Rushton Hall?"

"He was just beginning to when you came in."

"The popularity of amateur theatricals continues unabated, and the young people of Cheshire are not immune. Soon I shall hold my annual shooting party, and Matthew and Liza are determined to entertain the guests with dramatics."

"We'll use the orangery for our theater," Matthew told Oriana. "And we want you to help us choose a suitable piece, and manage the actors."

"I'm not able to leave London until after the Vauxhall grand gala."

"We can promise you excellent dinners," said Rushton. "Grouse shooting begins on twelfth August, and we'll be out every day with our guns. Matthew speaks highly of your ability to manage a group of *dilettanti*."

"That's how we met," the young man informed Dare.

"I used to perform with a group of amateur players, and she assisted us. I say, Ana, wouldn't it be fun to attempt *Pizarro?* I picked up a copy at the bookseller's."

"You could've had mine, and saved yourself two shillings and sixpence."

"We've small hope of success without you," Matthew persisted.

"My friend Harriot Mellon will soon be at liberty," Oriana informed him. "And she's in Liverpool, just half a day's journey from Rushton Hall. As a member of the Drury Lane company, she's familiar with Sheridan's works and their staging."

The earl responded, "We could welcome her assistance. But only you can provide the music. We are content to delay our gathering until such time as you are able to join us."

After the nobleman and Mr. Powell departed, Oriana moved about the room in agitation. Pausing at the looking glass, she repositioned her St. Albans lion brooch.

Dare went to help her. When pinning the gold disk to her bodice, his fingers curled under the edge of the fabric to brush her warm, bare skin.

"In all the years I've known Rushton," she said, "he's never once suggested that I visit his estate. I can't imagine why he's so adamant about it now."

He didn't want her thinking about the earl when his hand was inside her dress. Masking his displeasure, and his dread that she might desert him yet again, Dare asked, "Will you go?"

"Not without you," she promised before kissing him.

Chapter 23

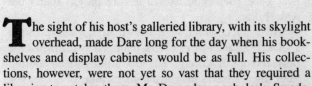

The sight of his host's galleried library, with its skylight overhead, made Dare long for the day when his book-shelves and display cabinets would be as full. His collections, however, were not yet so vast that they required a librarian to catalog them. Mr. Dryander, a scholarly Swede, diligently sorted through a stack of scientific volumes. He resumed his duties as soon as his employer led Dare out of the narrow room.

Sir Joseph Banks took him to a private study, decorated with portraits and busts of brilliant men and crowded with cabinets and bookcases. A broad window overlooked a courtyard. Picking up Dare's treatise from a baize-covered desk, he settled in an armchair.

"I'm curious about this document of yours," he said, his finger tapping the cover page. "What prompted its creation?"

"A lifelong fascination with my native island's landscape—and my curiosity about its origins. Since boyhood I've rambled over the mountains and through the glens, or sailed the coastline, trying to avoid the cliffs and rocks. Years later I recognized that their substance and layering and compaction matched what I'd seen when touring Scotland with Dr. Hutton and his associates."

Dare prowled the room while speaking about the mentor who had inspired and encouraged him.

"His illness prevented him from visiting Man—he suggested that I conduct the geological investigation myself. After collecting facts and refining my speculations, I paid a printer in Douglas to make up a few copies for my friends. My project is by no means complete—someday I shall make additions to the text, and include illustrations that clarify my observations."

"I hope your enthusiasm for your project didn't die with Hutton."

"No. I did, however, set it aside to design and construct a villa. That, and other matters, temporarily distracted me from geological writing." His love affair with an alluring Englishwoman was his current distraction.

"Your contribution to scientific literature will provoke controversy," Sir Joseph warned.

"I welcome it. I based my conclusions on direct observation—the evidence is there for anyone to see. My island may be compact—thirty-two miles from top to bottom, thirteen miles wide—but it's a splendid proving ground for Hutton's theories. He found his answers along Scotland's coast. Mine were waiting at Maughold Head and Langness and the Stack of Scarlett, where wind and sea have worn away the surface of the rocks and cliffs, exposing their inner structure."

His listener's keen eyes followed his movements attentively. "You subscribe to the prevailing theory that all rocks derive from the floor of a primeval ocean?"

"I do."

Returning Dare's treatise, Sir Joseph commented, "You are at odds with the vast majority of geological scientists, who declare that granite is the original and thus the oldest type of stone."

"I concur with Hutton. Granite is igneous." Dare

searched the pages for the section he wanted, then read, *"The Manx granites have undergone immense and various changes over time, judging from the number and types of crystals contained therein. There is clear evidence of igneous intrusion where the flow of molten granite penetrates the edges of the neighboring rock and remains there in clearly identifiable veins, differently colored. This granite, therefore, is of a later age than the rocks it has disrupted."*

His technical description of the phenomenon was also, he realized, an accurate description of his relationship with Oriana. She was the vulnerable slate, jostled and broken from cataclysmic events. He was molten granite, spreading into her cracks, and filling them to the greatest possible extent. But as he knew, even the most outwardly solid and substantial rocks were in a state of change. Stasis was impossible in the natural world—equally true for human relations.

Looking up, he said, "Any granite samples in your collection will affirm the validity of my conclusion."

The baronet left his chair and went to a cabinet. From one of its many drawers he took a fist-sized brown rock. "Will this serve?"

Dare inspected it carefully. On the underside, he found a narrow and jagged seam of white quartz. Tracing its path with his finger, he declared, "The granite existed when these cystals formed inside the crevice. This small specimen refutes the theory that crystalline rocks are older than all the rest."

Banks returned the rock to its case.

"As Hutton pointed out," Dare went on, "from the mountains to the seashore, everything is in a constant, though gradual, state of flux." Unable to keep still, he gestured with his hands, pounding and pushing the air with his fist to accent his steady flow of words. "We do not notice the action as it occurs, only the results. Rocks break down and dissolve to become soil, the rains and rivers carry that soil to the sea, and the agitation of the waves wears away the coastline. As it has been, so it is now, and ever shall be." After a pause for breath, he added, "Hutton explains it much better in *Theory of the Earth, with Proofs and Illustrations*."

"With so energetic a disciple," Banks commented, "his legacy is assured. But still I wonder whether these interesting assumptions can ever gain prominence."

The doubt in the older gentleman's tone compelled Dare to say, "Physical proofs of radical geological theories exist, sir—I've seen them myself. Before I met Hutton, I couldn't clearly understand *what* exactly I was seeing."

"My personal engraver, Mr. Mackenzie, can assist you by making plates of any pictures you wish to include in your report. He maintains a studio here, in the basement. I agree that you should illustrate your findings—that would be helpful."

"I could do it now, if I had paper and a pen."

Sir Joseph instantly provided both.

Remaining on his feet, Dare leaned over the table to produce the familiar, craggy outline of a Manx rock formation, sketching it with vertical and horizontal lines. After he'd added some shading and texture, he said, "This represents a rock I've examined on St. Patrick's Isle at Peel." He used the quill to point out the curving layers. "See how this slate has been compacted, then pushed upright? Originally these were layers of sediment on the ocean's floor. Over time, through many continuing cycles of heating and cooling, they were dramatically tilted and crumpled and folded."

"Yes, I do see." Said the baronet thoughtfully, "I've participated in many scientific expeditions, and I've sent explorers around the globe to discover as much as possible about our vast planetary home. Like your Scotsman friend, you've assisted science without straying terribly far from your birthplace. Some of my geologist acquaintances might care to hear your defense of Huttonian theory. In November, my Thursday morning scientific meetings will resume, as will my regular Sunday evening dinner parties. If you're still in London, I'll see that you receive an invitation."

"If I'm in London," Dare replied, uncertain whether he would be, "and invited, I shall attend."

"I daresay our discussions resemble those you had with Hutton and his associates."

"But in Edinburgh, nobody may participate without first declaring his preference for one of the rival theories, Neptunian or Huttonian."

"Informed debate is a necessary component of scientific advancement," Banks asserted. "Our Thursday breakfast gatherings are open to men only—the conversation is scientific and ideological. The dinners, while not as elegant or sophisticated as those given by my charming neighbor on the other side of the square, include ladies, and the topics are more general." Rising, he rubbed his hands together. "Now, sir, you must allow me to weigh you. When you've removed your boots and coat, you shall sit upon my scale."

Dare submitted to this curious command, following his host to an alcove where the apparatus was located. Obediently he lowered his body onto its seat, as though he were a Newmarket jockey after a race.

"Now I must add you to the record," said the baronet, taking from his shelves a stout book with a leather cover. "Corlett, Sir Darius. Thirteen stone, seven and a half pounds. You are very lean, for a man so large."

At his host's insistence, Dare glanced through the

alphabetized sections, and saw how the weights of all the members of the Banks household had increased over the years—with the exception of Mab the dog. "Ten pounds," he commented. "She must be a very small animal."

Farther on, he found the names and weights of aristocrats, authors, and geniuses of science. The addition of his obscure name to this impressive record made him feel as though he'd been admitted to a very select group. He rejoiced at his acceptance by this odd, brusque, and fascinating supporter of many remarkable discoveries and innovations.

He'd come to this house prepared to stand up for his beliefs. He left it determined to revise and submit his composition for publication by the Royal Society. Election to the membership would place him at the pinnacle of achievement, but he knew better than to set his hopes so high.

Impatient to tell Oriana about his meeting with Sir Joseph, he gazed at the house on the other side of Soho Square. But she was across the river at Vauxhall, singing with Ned. He must swallow his frustration and refrain from complaint when his need of her clashed with her professional obligations. His happiness was built upon an uncertain foundation, and he couldn't be sure how much strife it would withstand.

Oriana's desire to escape the crowded theater was tempered by a reluctance to curtail Ned Crowe's pleasure, and by the civility due her friends Mick Kelly and Mrs. Crouch, who had kindly shared their box at the Haymarket.

Although she didn't dislike *The Daughter,* a new comedy unfolding on the stage below, its deficiencies were apparent to one who had endured so many similar productions. The perennially popular device involving false identities was the chief reason she wasn't enjoying this performance as much as Ned, who chortled at every joke. On stage, when truth was revealed, forgiveness was instantly bestowed.

Real life is different, she thought, clapping at the conclusion of Mrs. Bland's song. Thomas Teversal's evasions and lies had broken her heart. Time had mended the crack but couldn't eradicate the scar.

By calling herself Mrs. Julian and disavowing her profession, she'd set herself up for trouble. Dare's discovery that she was also Ana St. Albans had shattered his faith in her honesty and had roused his anger. From the distance of several months, her early mistakes loomed larger than they had when she'd committed them, and now her conscience was heavier than it had been in Liverpool.

But if she hadn't presented herself to him as a respectable widow, he wouldn't have allowed her to live at Glen Auldyn for a memorable month of well-intentioned masquerade.

Their affair was taking its toll on her nerves. Although Dare seldom visited her house, they met in secret. Because they hadn't yet settled on a place where they could indulge their desire for each other, she was in a persistent state of yearning. In the hours following their brief, surreptitious encounters, she lay wakeful upon her lonely bed, her emotions in a tempest and her chaotic mind eagerly plotting out their next meeting.

After the curtain fell on the final tableau, she and her companions chatted about the performance. She was grateful to Mick Kelly for treating Ned so kindly, and told him so when the young man left the box to approach a fruit seller.

"It would be wrong," he declared, eyes twinkling, "for

a wine merchant's son to put on airs of superiority. Young Crowe is my equal in talent, is he not?"

"In truth, my dear," Mrs. Crouch said, smiling, "the Manxman's skill on the violin far exceeds yours."

"His popularity with the Vauxhall audiences is great," Oriana informed them. "He wasn't prepared for so much attention, after all his years living on the island, yet he thrives on it. He says he never worked so hard, not even in Sir Darius Corlett's lead mine."

"Ours is a demanding art," Mick concurred. "Signor Corri tells me that you are diligently preparing yourself for the rigors of opera. I am hopeful of soon restoring you to the exalted position to which your vocal gifts entitle you."

Bathed in his warm and luxuriant praise, she was in a cheerful mood when the Earl of Rushton entered the box.

"Still in town, my lord?" she asked in surprise. "His Majesty prorogued Parliament a fortnight ago." Her surprise increased when Matthew Powell followed the earl. "Shouldn't you both be at Rushton Hall?"

"Business in Downing Street kept me here," his lordship replied.

"I couldn't tear myself away from town without drinking to your health," the younger man said gaily. "Come into the box lobby and take a glass of wine with us."

Oriana suspected Matthew's stay had everything to do with his effort to settle his debts. She left her chair and accompanied them to the adjoining saloon, where refreshments were sold and served to the theater patrons.

"My daughter met with Miss Mellon in Chester and engaged her to direct the Rushton Hall players," the earl announced. "The chosen piece is *The Critic,* the satiric comedy by Sheridan, far more suitable for young ladies and gentlemen than *Pizarro.*"

Oriana was pleased to hear that her friend had secured

the Kingsleys' patronage. "Harri will manage it splendidly."

"But we still require your musical expertise," Matthew interjected. "Would you join our revels if they included your *cavaliere servante*?"

This smiling query greatly impaired her serenity. "I can't imagine whom you mean."

"Ana, Ana," he chided, "you know perfectly well I'm talking about Corlett, the Manxman you acquired during your travels."

She regarded the earl uncertainly. "Do you endorse the invitation, Rushton, or is this one of Matthew's teases?"

"I will agree to any plan that ensures your presence at Rushton Hall," he stated.

"I'm not sure Sir Darius would accept."

"I'll wager he does," Matthew predicted.

When the evening's entertainment came to an end, Oriana and Ned bade their theater companions farewell. She endured some good-natured teasing from Mrs. Crouch on her eccentric choice of summer cloak, a full-length, hooded garment of black silk.

"The high price of fame," Mick Kelly jested. "Even in the depths of night she must travel the town as an *incognita*, to avoid being mobbed."

A hackney delivered Oriana and a visibly weary Ned to Soho. After dropping him at Morland's Hotel, she returned to her square. At her orders, the jarvey halted at the entrance to the gardens, and she pulled up her hood and fastened her cloak before leaving the vehicle.

Oriana's midnight assignations with Dare occurred as often as the weather permitted, on evenings when she had social engagements. They relied on a simple signal—if she intended to meet him, in the morning she placed her cherished pelargonium plant outside the front door, ostensibly to partake of the fresh air and summer sunshine. During the day, when making his rounds of the furniture-makers or consulting with Sir Joseph's engraver, he passed near her house.

She reached into her reticule for the iron key that unlocked the garden gate. A tall, dark figure emerged from the surrounding darkness, and silently followed her into the enclosure. The night sky was thick with low-hanging clouds, which seemed to scrape the rooftops of the houses forming the boundaries of the square.

As soon as they reached the sheltered rendezvous place, he took her into his arms for a heady kiss.

"I'm late tonight," she apologized, as St. Anne's great bell clanged once. "Ned *would* stay for the farce, and I didn't like to spoil his fun by leaving before it ended. And then it seemed we'd never escape from Mick Kelly, he talks on and on—" Interrupted by Dare's demanding mouth, she abandoned her explanation.

"I saw a great deal more of you before our fateful journey to Newmarket," he complained.

"You saw me more *frequently.* Before our night in Saffron Walden, you hadn't seen so very much of me," she teased.

"I wish I could see all of you now—every glorious inch." Holding her, he said urgently, "Come with me to Deptford. It's not the most romantic destination, but at least we'd share a bed again."

She nodded. "I'll go. And will you accompany me to Cheshire? Rushton and Matthew were at the Haymarket tonight, and renewed the invitation—which includes you. Just think, Dare, it takes three days to travel to Rushton Hall, and three more back to London.' "

"Six nights," he said huskily, "of sleeping together. When do we leave?"

Softly laughing, she replied, "Not for another month."

He groaned, then expressed his impatience with hot, desperate kisses. "This sneaking about is maddening."

"I know." She sighed. "But it's necessary."

"Is it? Your friend Matthew caught us kissing. The earl is exceedingly sharp—he's surely guessed the truth."

"I hope not. But neither of them would gossip about me."

"Suppose some other friend—or enemy—asked you about the true nature of our relationship. Would you lie?"

With a few direct words, he revived the concern that had gnawed at her while watching the play: His doubts about her integrity persisted. "I would evade the question. But in my experience, people don't ask—they always assume the worst." She laid her head upon his chest. "You must think it ridiculous for a female of ill repute to be so careful."

"On occasion, you have struck me as misguided, frustrating, and damnably secretive. But never would I describe you as ridiculous."

"I'm sorry I must force you to be furtive and guarded—it's not in your character."

"You're worth it, Oriana. And there are rewards." Inserting his hand through a gap in her cloak, he stroked her bare skin. "We learn from each other. I teach you the virtue of candor, and you show me the value of privacy."

His fingers had plunged deep into her bodice, lighting fires that could not be quenched there and then. And how she wished they could express their passion in a place more secluded than Soho Square, more personal than the bedchamber of an inn.

Chapter 24

While their audience viewed the Grand Cascade's many marvels, Oriana soothed her throat with tea and lemon in the Vauxhall performers' green room. Ned waved his mug of porter as he gave his opinion of their performance in the first portion of the musical program.

Glancing down at his tailcoat, with gleaming brass buttons down the front and gold braid at the sleeves and pockets, he declared, "I'm as fine as any gentleman on the Isle of Man. What would Tom Lace and my other mates say, could they see me now?"

"They'd envy your good fortune," she responded. "Your labors at Vauxhall are less arduous than they were in the Corlett mine. And the pay is better."

"*Ta*. But I know not what I'll do with so fine a suit when we're home again."

Cold fingers of dread clutched Oriana's throat, briefly trapping her voice. "Has Sir Dare mentioned returning to the island?"

"The *Dorrity* will be ready to sail in a matter of weeks, he says. A full cargo she'll carry—Mainshtyr Dare's rooms are so full of furniture, there's no moving about. Every day more pieces are delivered to the hotel."

If Dare's departure was imminent, he wouldn't have

agreed to accompany her to Cheshire. In the weeks she'd known him, he'd held nothing back. Whatever his intentions, he was certain to reveal them. Dare Corlett didn't drop hints or leave room for speculation; he formed decisions and acted on them. At no time during their brief stay in Deptford, where his vessel was being refitted, had he implied that he planned to leave England.

If he did, he would return. Eventually.

While she was away at Rushton Hall, Ned would remain in London. His popularity here at Vauxhall, combined with Oriana's warm recommendation, had brought forth an invitation from the proprietor of a London theater. Mr. Hughes had engaged the Manx fiddler to perform his native music at Sadler's Wells for the next fortnight.

When he drained his mug, he said sympathetically, "You must be sorry to miss the fireworks."

She could look forward to a different sort of fireworks. Already sizzling with anticipation, she replied, "A gala night is no novelty for me, for I've been singing here since I was ten years old." She couldn't regret her early departure, knowing that Dare and a post chaise waited for her at the entrance to the gardens. The instant she completed her encore—a closing-night audience was certain to demand one—she and her lover would hasten to the Red Lion at Barnet, some ten miles out from London.

In the afternoon, a carriage bearing Suke Barry and Jonathon Wingate, with a collection of necessary baggage, had left town. Wingate's professional friendship with Lumley appeared to be genuine, yet Oriana felt certain it was Suke who drew him to Soho Square and was happiest to see him. Aware that her maidservant and the personable gentleman's gentleman had been carrying on a flirtation, she had refrained from comment. Complications could arise from a serious romance between Suke and Wingate, but from her own experience she knew how uncomfortable prying questions and interference could be.

The servants, no doubt, would enjoy the journey to Cheshire as much as she and Dare intended to, and she trusted them to behave just as discreetly.

Dare could hardly contain his impatience to leave Vauxhall. He endured successive disappointments each time an individual or a party exited through the gates. Oriana's concerts usually finished at eleven o'clock. When she failed to meet the post chaise at the appointed location—an alley off Vauxhall Road—he supposed that she'd been detained.

He trusted that the accommodations of the Red Lion in Barnet would please him better than the Anchor at Deptford. The dirtiest town in England could boast one of the filthiest inns. Oriana had proved her mettle on that occasion, making no complaint, but their hole-in-corner trysting place had been an appalling insult to her gentility. They could have spent a more comfortable night on board the *Dorrity,* if his cabin hadn't smelled of new paint and his crew hadn't been aboard.

Leaving the vehicle to search for his missing lady, he made his way to the brick facade that screened the gardens. Rockets burst, and after the successive explosions he saw the shimmer of sparks high above the treetops. The odor of singed gunpowder reminded him of the many times he'd stood at a safe distance, waiting for an earth-shuddering blast to open up a new mine shaft.

A multitude of carriages clogged the road, from cheap hackneys to costly private coaches. When he reached the passage through which the Vauxhall merrymakers passed in and out of the gardens, he witnessed the ejection of a rumpled gentleman who protested loudly at this treatment.

"Don't make no more trouble, sir," the doorkeeper advised, "or I'll call a constable and charge you with breaking the peace. Mr. Simpson said I could return your money—that's fair enough, ain't it? And if you stand here on t'other side of the carriageway, you might see some of the rockets going up."

"Bugger Mr. Simpson," said the culprit in an ugly tone, embracing a column for support. "And bugger the money, and bugger your blasted fireworks. I don't care a damn for any of it." He staggered forward a few steps before collapsing, and groaned in pain when his knees struck the cobbles.

The doorkeeper, having fulfilled his duty, retreated. Most of the passersby ignored the drunken gentleman, although a few glanced at him disdainfully.

Dare went over to help him rise. When he grasped the man's elbow he was shaken off.

"Go away." Struggling to his feet, the drunkard began a slow progress toward the main road. As he wove in and out among the waiting carriages, outraged coachmen shouted curses or mocked him.

An accident waiting to happen, thought Dare. Unwilling to stand by as a witness to disaster, he followed.

"Leave me be," the man said over his shoulder.

"Do you want a hackney to run you down?"

"That'd be a mercy."

"Not for the chap who cleans up the mess," Dare pointed out. He flung out a hand to keep the man from toppling over. "Steady now. Did you come here alone?"

"Lost my friend in the crowd—must've found himself a willing whore in one of the Dark Walks. I wasn't so lucky. Caught myself a plump little slut, but she played the coquette to get more money out of me. When I put her hand on my tackle, she started screeching. Then she struck me." The man rubbed his cheekbone. "A case of assault, pure and simple. And *I'm* the one who got tossed out on my arse." Head bowed, he muttered, "Shouldn't have come here. I wanted to see her again. There was a notice in the newspaper, I knew she'd be here." His jaw dropped lower still, and his muffled speech became incoherent. Glancing up, he asked sharply, "Who the devil are *you*?"

"A newcomer to London. Where I live, we help people in trouble."

The stranger's truculent face revealed all the ravages of excess. Drink had fleshed out his cheeks, blurring his once-fine features. "Then tell me, is there a public house nearby?"

That was the last place he needed to be, but Dare wasn't about to provoke an argument by saying so. "There's one at Vauxhall Stairs, where the watermen congregate."

The man lunged forward.

"Do you know where you're going?"

"Straight to hell, damn you."

Dare's altruistic impulse survived the insult. Unable to relinquish the duties of self-appointed guardian, he pursued the unsteady figure.

"Don't you have anything better to do than chase me around Southwark?"

"Yes." He cast a fleeting glance at his traveling chaise, its lamps glowing in the darkness. "But in your present condition, you shouldn't be wandering about alone. However great your difficulties seem now, they'll be far less daunting tomorrow."

"Much you know about it," the man retorted. "D'you think I'm about to throw myself into the river? She's not worth it. Never was."

Dare doubted he was referring to his screeching slut from the Dark Walk. "I gather you had a Vauxhall assignation, and something went amiss."

"Oh, I saw her—from a distance. Didn't want her to see me." With a shrug, he added, "Not that she'd recognize me. Three years of country living, not to mention the endless frustrations of married life, has taken a toll. I'm not the man I was before my lady wife disrupted a delightful bachelorhood." His cynical eyes focused on Dare, and he angled his disheveled head. "What d'you think of her? A prime article, isn't she?"

"Your wife?"

"The St. Albans. Sweet Ana, the Siren of Soho."

Unwilling to share his opinion of Oriana with an inebriated reveler, Dare responded, "She's exceptionally talented."

The stranger's smile was sly. "More talented than you can possibly know. Took me an age to get her under me, but I succeeded. Every man in London was after her, but I'm the one she lusted for."

He knew better than to believe a boast so patently false. The stream of salacious reminiscences that followed was the product of a drunken admirer's overexcited imagination. He was glad he'd removed the man before Oriana had exited the gardens.

"I was mad with desire for her. I grew reckless—I cared not at all that I had pledged to marry an eligible lady and was expected to breed strong grandsons for a wispy duke."

"You're not alone in losing your head over Madame St. Albans."

"No. But I'm the only one she fancied."

A baseless claim, Dare assured himself. If he gathered together all the men who had pursued Ana St. Albans, the line would stretch the length of Britain, from Land's End to John o' Groats. She treated them all exactly the same, whether prince or peer or commoner. He'd witnessed her behavior in Hyde Park, at Vauxhall, in her drawing room. In all situations, she exhibited charm and civility. This gentleman, entranced and desperate to possess her, had translated her politeness as encouragement.

"She'd had a man before—knew exactly what I was after. And wanted it as much as I did, even if she pretended not to. My marriage offer quieted her protests quick enough. I had the honor of swiving her once a week." Whirling around, the drunkard clutched Dare's coat lapels. "When I sheathed my sword inside her that first time, she liked it well enough. If she complained about our delayed nuptials, I gave her costly baubles— those diamonds cost me a fortune. Didn't object to the bedsport, oh, no, she just didn't want to be found out. It wasn't till she learned of my betrothal that she refused to see me again. Her scheme to catch a husband in her mantrap came to naught."

In essentials, the bitter, maudlin tirade corresponded uncannily with Oriana's account of her unhappy love affair.

"Nowadays, she prances 'round the town just as she always did, and parades herself on the stage. I'm told she plays the whore for any man who asks."

"You shouldn't believe everything you hear," Dare said roughly. Calling someone a liar—especially when he was drunk—inevitably resulted in violence. No good could come of an altercation, although he was sorely tempted to knock the sneer off the man's face.

"Trust me, I know far more about Ana St. Albans than you do—or ever will. I can tell you things . . ."

"Don't," he warned. "You'll regret it." Seeking verification of the suspicion that had swelled into certainty, he asked, "What's your name?"

"Teversal. Husband of Lady Penelope, son-in-law to the Duke of Wilminster."

"Thomas Teversal?"

"M'friends call me Tom. You can, too."

Dare was no friend to the villain who had lied to Oriana, seduced her, abandoned her, and capped his cruelties by publicizing their liaison.

Teversal put a hand to his brow. "Can't go to Soho Square—servants would turn me away. This was her last Vauxhall night, and my best chance of meeting her again. Shouldn't have swilled so much champagne, but I was nervous."

"I suggest you sober yourself up before presenting yourself to Madame St. Albans," said Dare. "I happen to know an excellent remedy for drunkenness."

"If you share it, I'll be forever in your debt."

"Gladly." With a grim smile, Dare guided Teversal toward the river. "Take a deep breath."

With one mighty push, he sent Oriana's betrayer into the Thames.

He waited until the soaked, sputtering head bobbed up to the surface, then called out, "Cold water—you'll want to remember it next time."

"Bastard!"

He turned to the coterie of oarsmen loitering nearby. Grinning at one of them, he said, "Toss him a rope."

"Right, guv'nor."

"I could've drowned! You'll pay for this," Teversal sputtered. "Don't walk away, you bugger—I'll know your name and direction. My friends will call upon you tomorrow, by God. So have your pistols ready!"

Dare ignored the implied challenge and left Teversal to the care of the watermen, who had thrown out a towline.

His rash act had given him some satisfaction. The perfidious Thomas was a greater ass than he'd imagined, and a temporary blot upon his peace of mind. On his way back to the alley where his carriage stood, he congratulated himself on saving Oriana from an unwanted and distressing encounter.

A gloved hand emerged from the post chaise, beckoning, and he quickened his pace. He flung the door open and climbed inside.

"Where were you?" Oriana asked.

"Strolling by the river. I guessed you'd been delayed."

She sighed. "Three encores tonight. And Mr. Simpson made one of his speeches, telling me how pleased he was with my performances this season. Most gratifying, but I was desperate to get away. Ned stayed for the fireworks—I wish you'd seen his face when the first rocket went up."

She was always like this after leaving her stage—talkative, bubbling with energy and spirits. He wouldn't douse them by bringing up Thomas Teversal.

Her detailed description of the concert concluded with a self-deprecating laugh. "I've been chattering too much. Tell me your news."

"What little I have to share came from Suffolk. I received a report on Combustible's training regimen and her progress from Nick Cattermole, the Duke of Halford's trainer. The lameness in her foot troubles her no more, and she joins in the morning gallops."

"What distance is he running her?"

"Five miles."

"That's promising."

"And he sweats her once a week. Whatever that means."

"It builds stamina," Oriana explained. "Her groom piles blankets on her back and her jockey takes her out for a long, hard run. Afterward, she's led to a shady place to be be scraped and dried off before they walk her back to her stable—very slowly."

"I hope she doesn't mind. I would."

"She's familiar with the routine."

"Cattermole should direct his letters to you," he commented wryly. "I'm too ignorant to appreciate or comprehend them. What's more, that filly should belong to you. I know you refuse to accept gifts, but couldn't you bend the rule?"

"If Mick Kelly makes good his promise to employ me at the opera house, my income would double. I could afford to buy Combustible, but I wouldn't be able to race her because I'm a female, and she'd never get her chance to prove herself." Laying her hand upon his knee, Oriana said contritely, "I've saddled you with too much responsibility—and expense."

"I don't complain. Much."

"When I found out Burford was selling Combustible, I couldn't let her go to just anyone. Too many owners are ruled by their desire to win at any cost, and their grooms and trainers behave accordingly. If she can attach a victory to her name in her next race, the Duke of Halford might take her. Any horse would be happy at Moulton Heath."

"Or I could take her to Skyhill. Would you object to that?"

For a fleeting moment, he saw alarm on her lovely face. "Only if you put her to work at your mine."

"Certainly not. She's been coddled all her life, and is bred for a different sort of labor."

For a long time she said nothing.

Curling an arm around her shoulders, he placed his lips against her ear, and murmured a suggestion.

"At the inn," she replied.

Her reluctance troubled him. He accepted that her mysterious ritual with the lemon was a necessary prelude to lovemaking, and tried to respect her pragmatism. Her unwillingness to bear his child might be a rejection of a permanent bond with him, or it could be that she feared the harm to her career. But she'd admitted to taking no such precautions with Teversal, and that nettled him.

"You aren't cross?" she asked him.

He shook his head. "A moving carriage is so much less comfortable than a mattress." To demonstrate his good-will, he ran his fingers lightly across her cheek. He wished he could know what she was thinking as she sat there still and silent.

Glancing out the window, she observed, "We've reached Islington—and later than I expected. Suke will give me up for lost."

"Is she likely to wait up for you?"

"I didn't ask her to. She'll be sleeping in a separate chamber. I'll be alone."

"No you won't be," he contradicted, squeezing her waist.

Her smile promised many delights, and he felt better.

When they had traveled a little farther, he said, "I've noticed Wingate's interest in the girl. Is she offering encouragement?"

"I'm sure she likes him. But she's no girl, she's a year younger than I am. I never interfere in my servants' private lives, but if your man means to seduce my Suke, I will. I'd do anything to keep her from suffering as I did, after Thomas—" She jerked her head as if shaking off the bad memory.

Completing her unfinished statement, he said, "After Thomas Teversal betrayed you."

She regarded him through narrowed eyes. Then she asked coolly, "How did you find out his surname?"

"Entirely by chance. I actually met him, less than an hour ago. He knew you were performing at Vauxhall tonight, and would've waylaid you—if the doorkeeper hadn't cast him out for unruliness."

"He wanted to see me?" She sank against the cushions, her expression one of horror. "If you think less of me for loving someone like that, my only excuse is that he concealed his true nature very well."

"A pity you never saw him when he was drunk," said Dare lightly. "Three years ago, he might have seemed dashing and seductive, but tonight he proved himself to be a boisterous sot with a foul tongue. I hope his ducking in the Thames sobered him."

"Dare, you *didn't*!"

"It was that or challenge him to a duel, which would bring about the sort of publicity you abhor. Don't fret, I didn't explain why he had infuriated me. As far as he's aware, I'm as much a stranger to you as I was to him." When she pressed her palms together, her face a study in dismay, he said, "Perhaps I shouldn't have told you."

"I'm glad you felt you could."

"You don't look glad."

"He's supposed to be in Wiltshire, not London—his father-in-law gated him. Matthew Powell shares all the best gossip with me, whether or not I figure in it."

"Do you ask him what people are saying about you?"

"Of course," she said blithely. "And he always tells. Whenever I ask Rushton for the latest Ana St. Albans stories, he prims up his mouth and changes the subject. During your weeks in London, you must have heard some choice gossip about me."

He didn't deny it. "But I know the truth, Oriana. The only time I was worried was my first day in town, when that imp Merton Pringle said you were immoral and depraved. And sang that detestable ballad."

"There's a songbird who makes the most glorious sound," Oriana caroled, *"her name is Ana St. Albans."*

His hand covered her mouth. "Don't." The verses inspired by her liaison with Teversal rankled more than ever, now that he'd met the man. Grasping her chin, he turned her head toward him, and declared, "It wouldn't have mattered if that brat's slander had been accurate. I wanted you so desperately, an entire legion of lovers wouldn't have daunted me."

"One lover is the most I can manage at a time. I'm too busy to entertain any more." Laying her hand upon his knee, she said earnestly, "I bear no happy memories of Thomas. He tricked me into relinquishing my heart and my virtue. He killed my love for him and trampled on my pride. For a long time afterward just hearing his name made me queasy." Her other hand crept to his chest as she said, "Whatever the future holds for us, Dare, I shall never regret knowing you."

He drew no comfort from her words, because the desperation in her kiss disturbed him. Her searching lips communicated uncertainty, perhaps anxiety, and he had no idea why.

Chapter 25

Rushton Hall, thought Harriot Mellon, must be the most civilized place in all England. Lady Liza Kingsley, born into privilege, was as gracious a hostess as a guest could wish, and her father's hauteur was less in evidence here at his country seat. Daily life in their beautifully appointed mansion was perfectly regulated. The household servants carried out their duties with cheerful efficiency, the women in neat gowns and starched aprons, the men in their livery. Her every request was attended to as though she were a lady born rather than a common stage player. And amazingly, her querulous parent had mellowed during their stay—an entire day had passed without a sharp comment or criticism.

Harriot's cup of contentment overflowed when Oriana arrived. She received the happy tidings while rehearsing her actors, and instantly dismissed them for the day. Together they all trooped out of the orangery and across the garden to the house to greet the travelers.

Eager to see Oriana and her handsome Manxman together for the first time, she was disappointed that the singer and Suke Barry had traveled in one chaise, the baronet and his manservant in another. Lord Rushton, who hadn't taken his gun out today because Oriana was expected, smiled upon her approvingly and nodded his silver-flecked head as if pleased.

Lady Liza, with her customary aplomb, presented Oriana to the other guests and various friends from the neighborhood. "And here is dear Miss Mellon, who has the thankless job of transforming us into Suetts and Kembles and Jordans."

"How does your play progress?" Oriana asked Harriot.

To avoid answering directly—and candidly—she replied, "I've offered the ladies and gentlemen advice on timing and inflection, and tell them when to move and where to stand. They're far easier to manage than professional players, and not so temperamental."

Said Mr. Powell to Oriana, "Would you be willing to favor our audience with a few of your Manx songs?"

The earl objected to this plan, saying firmly, "Madame St. Albans will not sing."

"But music is essential to the play," Lady Liza countered, turning earnest brown eyes upon her father. "The stage directions call for soft music at Tilburina's entrances. At the end of the last scene, the entire company sings 'Rule, Brittania.' Afterward there's a grand procession, and for that we must have Handel's *Water Music,* and a march."

Her betrothed complained, "We've got one of London's finest harpsichordists here—why can't she supply the necessary music?"

Oriana poured oil on troubled waters, saying serenely, "I shall. That's to be my sole contribution, for his lordship doesn't want me to take an acting role or perform any songs."

"The distinction strikes me as most odd," Mr. Powell declared.

Ignoring this comment, the earl turned to Oriana. "My daughter will show you to your chamber and see that you're comfortably settled. We hope you'll enjoy your first visit to the Hall."

Lady Liza led Oriana and Suke up the staircase, the earl retreated to his bookroom, and the young people scattered in many directions.

Rather than joining the other gentlemen in a game of billiards, Mr. Powell remained in the great hall with Harriot. "Ana ought to sing—I'm sure she'd like to. What d'you think of Rushton's edict?"

"He thinks it unsuitable for professionals to perform with gentlefolk."

"That's absurd."

"It's the way of the world," Harriot said simply. "*Your* world, sir. Oriana works at a trade, and so do I—a disreputable one at that."

"Don't you mind that sort of prejudice? Does she?"

"I know my place," she answered, without admitting her desire to improve it. "But my father wasn't a duke, and neither is my cousin. Unlike Oriana, I've known but one side of the footlights."

Although she gave the impression that she was resigned to her lot, a full week at Rushton Hall had shown her a richer, more luxurious existence that she couldn't help but envy. During her years laboring in the provincial theater circuits, local merchants and country squires had bestowed their patronage, taking her on carriage rides or inviting her to tea. Their houses, however fine, had lacked the splendor of this one.

Giving her a smile, Matthew Powell said, "I'll wager Corlett's presence won't improve his lordship's mood. An interesting week we've got ahead of us, Miss Mellon."

"You, sir, should worry more about mastering your speeches in Act I, Scene 2."

"Mangled them, didn't I?" he responded, unperturbed.

"I hope you're not cross with me—but of course not, you're too good-natured."

"I'll drill you," she offered helpfully, holding out her hand for the sheaf of pages he held. He failed to notice—Lady Liza was descending the stair, and his eyes were on her. "Better yet, why don't you ask her ladyship to do it?"

"Yes, an admirable suggestion," he murmured before leaving her side.

Her assumption that the engaged couple were genuinely in love had barely survived her first day as theater manageress. Lady Liza, who performed the role of the mock-heroine Tilburina, seemed more at ease in her playacting than she did in the company of her betrothed. And Mr. Powell, always so mirthful and jesting when he visited Soho Square, was strangely subdued at Rushton Hall.

"Trouble in paradise?" asked Oriana, when Harriot shared her observations. "I can't imagine it's serious. Matthew lost his heart to Lady Liza over a year ago. And she wouldn't have tried so hard to overcome her father's objections to the match if she didn't love him."

"What were the earl's objections?"

"Matthew's lack of money, and his mania for the theater. He'd make a wonderful actor, if he hadn't been born a gentleman,.." To her maid, Oriana said, "Take my blue silk to the laundry to be pressed for this evening. Tomorrow I'll need the white muslin."

"New, aren't they?" Harriot commented as Suke tossed the requested garments over her arm and left the bedchamber.

"I've been very extravagant this summer, and must practice many economies in the coming months."

"Sir Darius doesn't give you an allowance?"

"Heavens, no. I wouldn't have accepted if he'd offered one."

"Oh." But there was no doubt that their relationship was an intimate one. Oriana had never looked more beautiful, as if she'd been feasting on love. After an embarrassed pause, Harriot said, "I saw him in Liverpool, after you left in such a hurry. If a man like that came after me—I don't know if I could refuse him."

Amused, Oriana gently pinched her friend's scarlet cheek. "Don't let your mother hear you say that."

"If he asked you to wed him, wouldn't you accept?"

She felt her smile slipping away. "He won't ask."

"You sound so certain."

"I am." Though Oriana wouldn't admit it, she'd be surprised if Dare remained in England after the October Meeting at Newmarket. She hadn't forgotten his suggestion that he take Combustible to Skyhill if she failed to win her race.

In a disappointed voice, the actress said, "I hoped Sir Darius would turn out to be different than all those other men."

"Oh, but he is," she declared fervently. "He's unlike anyone I've ever known. If Mick Kelly offers me employment at the opera house, I'll have everything I could possibly wish for."

"Except a husband."

"I'm not so sure I want one." From her small trunk, Oriana removed several music books. After her break with Thomas, singing had been her solace. If she lost Dare, she relied on Providence to return her to the King's Theatre. When handing over the volumes, she told Harriot, "I brought all the pieces that seemed appropriately lively for background accompaniment. I must say, I'm eager to see how Matthew conducts himself as Mr. Puff."

"Mr. Sheridan would applaud his performance. He's more comfortable in his role, and more serious, than his fellow players. To them, acting is a game. Lady Liza, as

Tilburina, is by far the best of the young ladies. Some of the gentlemen have taken double roles. If Sir Darius wishes to join our company, we've room for him."

"Like me, he prefers to make himself useful in a less visible capacity."

"I'm afraid we'll want a good prompter," said Harriot candidly. "The young men spend more time out with their guns than they do perfecting their speeches, and the ladies constantly chatter—mostly about the gentlemen. If they worked at Drury Lane, their salaries would hardly cover the sums they'd forfeit for tardiness and dereliction of duty."

Mrs. Entwistle swept in majestically, greeted Oriana in a perfunctory fashion, and made the pithy observation that this room was superior to her daughter's.

"These hangings are damask, not chintz—and the bed is as prettily curtained as Lady Liza's. I shouldn't wonder if this had been Lady Rushton's chamber, when she lived."

"My room is perfectly nice, Mother," Harriot stated.

"Pinch your cheeks, child, and retie your hair ribbons. A fine gentleman has just arrived with his servant, and you'll want to look your best."

Exchanging glances with Oriana, the actress replied, "It will serve no purpose. I cannot compare favorably to the lady he most admires."

"Well, she's not here, and you must seize your chance to captivate him. Come along with me."

Said Oriana, "Before you go, Harri, direct me to the orangery. I must see your theater."

Harriot bobbed up from her seat and led Oriana to the window. "There," she said, pointing to a white building in the distance. In a complicit whisper, she added, "When I see Sir Darius, I'll tell him where to find you."

On her way through the house, Oriana found much to

admire. Handsome paintings of people and places lined the walls, and elegant carpets covered its floors with bursts of colors. The furnishings were exactly what she expected to see in the Kingsleys' ancestral home. Here was grandeur without ostentation.

She followed a stony path across a tidy expanse of lawn to the glass-walled building Harriot had shown her. As she approached, she could see a male figure striding back and forth, flinging one hand about with abandon and carrying a book in the other. She stood outside the open double doors, shamelessly eavesdropping.

"Ever while you live, have two plots to your tragedy," Matthew Powell declaimed, facing his invisible audience. "The grand point in managing them is only to let your under plot have as little connection with your main plot as possible. I flatter myself nothing can be more distinct than mine. For as in my chief plot the characters are all great people, I have laid my under plot in low life. And as the former is to end in deep distress, I make the other end as happy as a farce."

Oriana clapped softly. "Very well expressed, sir."

"Ana!"

"I was just telling Harri it's a crime you were born a gentleman."

"But an even greater one that you were not born a ladyship."

He wasn't jesting, which was most unusual. "I'd rather be a *prima donna* at an opera house, thank you."

"I may yet be forced to seek my fortune on the boards," he said glumly. "This betrothal of mine doesn't prosper. The financial difficulties I told you about weeks ago threaten my future with Liza."

"How so?"

"You said I oughtn't to keep my debts secret, that I should be honest with her, and your eloquent arguments swayed me. I followed your advice, and it's put me in the devil of a mess." He flung his playbook aside, and it struck the stone floor. "It's not your fault. After explaining that I was desperately short of funds, I suggested we have a hasty wedding, else the bailiffs would seize me and put me behind bars. As a joke, mind you."

"Oh, Matthew." She shook her head at him. What was the matter with men. Why couldn't they *think* before speaking?

"I was serious about the quick wedding, but it's nothing to do with money. As you know, it took me forever and a day to convince her that my proposal was inspired by true affection. And then, with a few ill-chosen words in an attempt to be clever, I gave the impression of being a fortune hunter. She no longer seeks my company— wouldn't even help me study my part when I asked. I'm not absolutely sure that I *am* still engaged."

Oriana ached for him, he looked so distraught. "Should I have a word with her?"

"Words are no use. I need money. I can raise a thousand, half what I owe. I've already sold my phaeton and the bays. I mean to give up both my hunters next."

"You're so fond of them." For her, the sale of a favorite horse would be a calamity.

With a semblance of his cocksure smile, he said, "I'm fonder of Liza by far."

"Rushton will pay off the rest of your creditors after the wedding."

"No. I won't be beholden to my father-in-law. When I marry, I want to stand beside my bride without a cloud of dependency hanging over me. Rushton doesn't know the extent of my indebtedness—unless Liza told him. I hope she didn't."

Oriana picked up his discarded book and brushed off the paper cover. "I've got an idea."

"Better than your last one?"

"*I* never suggested that you make foolish jokes about debtors' prison," she retorted.

"That's true. Right, then. What do I do now?"

"Settle up with your creditors as quickly as possible. I can help. I'll get my jewels from my attorney, and—"

"No, Ana. You're not selling your trinkets to cover my debts."

"Of course not. My man-at-law will dispose of them."

"What would Corlett say?"

"He doesn't know these gems exist. Don't look so grave. They aren't heirlooms, and have no sentimental value."

"They must have considerable value, if you think they'll fetch a thousand quid."

"I have no doubt of it. They're Brazilian diamonds."

He regarded her with amazement. "The ones Teversal gave you? I never guessed you'd kept them."

"It's a female's prerogative to keep all gifts she receives from an admirer. When Thomas presented me with the diamond set, he said it came to him from his great-aunt and was intended for his bride. I believed him—just as I believed in his promise of marriage—and gave them to my attorney for safekeeping. He asked a jeweler to give a valuation. Mr. Rundell recognized the stones, because he'd sold them to Thomas the previous month, and one of his goldsmiths made the settings. My attorney advised me to keep them, as it was easier than mounting a breach of promise suit. I was angry enough to toss them down a well, or into the sea. For three years they've been shut away in a vault. I've long wished to be rid of them, but until today I couldn't decide how."

"I can't possibly accept your offer."

"You must, Matthew. Believe me, the diamonds mean nothing to me. I won't ever wear them, or exchange them for money. They are relics of a shameful and distressing episode, and you'd be doing me a favor by taking them off my hands. I would be comforted by the knowledge that anything connected to the man who caused me so much unhappiness could ensure the happiness of others."

He came over to her, his eyes bright. "For both our sakes, I'll take them. But what if their worth exceeds a thousand pounds?"

"You'll be able to keep at least one of your hunters."

"And what do I tell Liza?"

"Nothing. Rushton, either—he'd be livid if he found out."

Gently he taunted, "Your pretty policy of honesty just flew right out the door."

That didn't trouble her much. "If you feel you should inform them, wait till *after* the knot is tied."

"I could kiss you, Ana, but I don't dare in front of all these windows. Someone might see, and there'd be no end of a fuss. But one day I'll repay you."

She shook her head. "Don't even try. In effect, I'd be taking money from Thomas. I can't. For some reason, I need to preserve the illusion that he presented those diamonds to his future wife, not his whore."

Dare had attended few country-house parties, and this one reminded him how tedious they could be. Their function was as much dynastic as social, an attempt to pair off the sons and daughters of the gentry and aristocracy, although he doubted any matches would arise from this gathering. Rehearsals for *The Critic* were punctuated by petty squabbles. The participants were too well acquainted for romance to sprout, and the play was too satirical to put its performers in a tender mood.

An outsider, and the most mature of the bachelors present, he was regarded by the young ladies with flirtatious interest, to which he was immune. Their conversations centered on dances they had attended or would attend, and novels they had read. Nice girls, all of them, extremely decorative in their light-colored summer gowns, but they could not compete with Oriana's elegance and sparkle and sophisticated conversation.

"I've visited Matlock," the handsome Miss Haygarth informed him during dinner one evening. "You have a property near that town, I understand."

"I do," he confirmed.

"I *long* to see the Peak," said the lady seated on his other side. "To me, mountains are delightful beyond anything. You must command some magnificent views from your estate, Sir Darius."

"Damerham lies some forty miles from the Peak, Miss Mainwaring." He refrained from stating his preference for the Manx mountains, dreading a fresh set of questions about his island home.

Lady Liza Kingsley's physical resemblance to her enigmatic father was striking, and she exhibited a similar reticence. Her influence would calm the erratic Matthew, Dare suspected, just as his liveliness complemented her quietude. He had detected an estrangement between them, but Oriana predicted it would be brief. She seemed quite certain.

His encounters with her inevitably occurred in full view of the Kingsleys and their guests, at meals or rehearsals. The rest of the time, he was tramping across an endless expanse of moorland with Lord Rushton and Matthew Powell and the other gentlemen, in search of red-legged grouse. His gun, procured in London, was a lighter model than he'd previously used, but it was perfectly balanced. His satisfaction was assured by his companions' envious glances. Unfortunately, he had to rely on the diminishing skills of his host's most decrepit setter bitch, who hadn't yet lost her enthusiasm for her job but was growing too old for it. He bagged as many birds as others in the shooting party but fewer than Lord Rushton, and tried not to let it bother him.

The men stayed out in the field from eight in the morning till two in the afternoon. On their return to the house, they refreshed themselves with brandy and claret in the earl's library, then changed into evening attire. After dinner, those participating in the play gathered in the orangery to rehearse.

As the day of the performance grew closer, the amateurs' tempers wore thinner and the quarrels over costumes and properties were more frequent. Harriot Mellon acquitted herself nobly, and with great patience. Oriana, busy at the harpsichord, remained aloof from the proceedings, but from his makeshift prompter's box Dare saw how often she pressed her lips together in mute frustration.

"Will they be ready, do you think?" he asked after a particularly harrowing session.

"It hardly matters. Their audience will consist of relations and neighbors, who will dismiss any errors—the ones they notice."

They were the last to leave the orangery. A thick evening fog had descended upon the gardens, and the house's lighted windows seemed farther away than they really were.

"Are you wishing I hadn't dragged you into the wilds of Cheshire?" Oriana asked.

"I was perfectly happy to be lured here, and my sole regret is our lack of privacy. I'm begging off from tomorrow's shoot. That poor spaniel has worn herself out on my behalf and needs to rest, and I've been neglecting my correspondence. I mean to write Melton and a Derbyshire acquaintance. And I'm determined to meet you somewhere alone, if we can manage it without drawing attention to our absence. What about that place where we had the picnic, that stand of trees far beyond the park?"

"I'm supposed to help the ladies with finishing touches to their costumes. But I could easily steal away for a little while," she said.

"Make it a long while. I've got a week's worth of pent-up kisses to bestow."

"That sounds heavenly."

"Stop smiling at me like that," he commanded softly. "Or I'll give you one right now."

She paused on the pathway and extended her hand. "Hand me your prompt copy."

"Why?"

"You'll see." When he held it out, she took it. "Oh, *dear*," she said, before deliberately dropping the book. "Where did it fall? Can you help me find it?"

They both knelt down at the same moment. He placed his hands on her shoulders, she clutched his lapels, and their mouths merged. The furtive contact was brief, and left him wanting much more.

"Here it is," she said, retrieving his book and returning it to him. "Pray forgive me, sir."

Following her example, he let the volume fall once more. "Clumsiness has its rewards," he said, and stole another kiss.

The next day, after writing his letters, Dare visited the earl's stable to inspect the horses and lingered there until he saw Oriana leave the house. After a circuitous ramble through the park, he found her waiting for him in a coppice offering the seclusion they craved.

Her face was luminous, her hazel eyes reflected all the colors of the surrounding wood—green and brown and gold. "I've never made love *al fresco*," she told him, with a shyness that was unique in a mistress, and utterly bewitching. The excited tremor in her voice assured him that she welcomed her new adventure.

His lips ravished hers, expressing his savage need. Her eyelids fell, her neck arched. The delicious contact could not satisfy him long. He was eager to take her, his refined, royal-blooded singer, in this uncivilized setting. They sank to the bare ground, cool and hard, unlike the beds they'd shared. Their bodies crushed the grass, releasing its fresh scent, and he could imagine himself in Glen Auldyn again.

Opening her bodice, he discovered that she'd dispensed with her corset—and her petticoat, too. Beneath the simple gown, easily removed, she wore only her chemise. He let her keep it but pulled it down her shoulders to gain access to her creamy breasts, warm and smooth.

Her hands were in his hair, he felt her nails against his scalp. Her ardent pleas delighted him, and he gloried in this proof of her desire. His fists clutched her skirt, bunching the fabric and pushing it out of his way. Between her legs he found heat and slick moisture. He slid his rampant flesh into the gap and was welcomed, as always, with a moan of joy. Her desire fanned his into a flame, and he drove into her.

Every time was like the first time—the heady sense of exploration, the rewards of discovery. He could endure days of privation, their careful pretense of a platonic relationship, knowing this magnificent creature was his to enjoy and to pleasure.

"I'll never stop wanting this," he declared in the aftermath of climax.

Oriana should have made a similar admission, and her quietness disturbed him. As she nestled against him, he longed to know the state of her heart. In her lovemaking she lost her inhibitions; when it ended she locked her emotions away. The one plausible reason for such reticence, he mused, was her protective instinct—she hadn't relinquished her lingering fears of pain and loss.

This, he reminded himself, was what he'd wanted ever since she'd come to his Ramsey town house. He should be thoroughly satisfied with their undemanding arrangement. She willingly bestowed all that he'd sought. Why, then, did he feel a greater hunger gnawing at him?

Because she'd imposed silence and secrecy upon him, and he yearned to acknowledge their bond—to claim her as his love and to declare himself her lover. This being impossible, he was determined to provide her with a token of his affection. No one, not even Oriana, could refuse a birthday present.

Turning his head to gaze upon her, the creature who had altered his life in the most marvelous way, he hoped there would not be too lengthy a drought until the next flood of passion.

Chapter 26

Anticipation and excitement reigned at Rushton Hall on the day of the theatrical performance. Servants bustled about the house readying its reception rooms, while the kitchen staff prepared a grand dinner for the invited guests. The young gentlemen abandoned their sport in order to rehearse once more. Only Dare, who had excused himself the previous day, accompanied the earl to the moors. From her window, Oriana had watched the two men set off on foot, with dogs and guns and attendants.

In her effort to be useful, she was helping Suke with the final embellishments to the ladies' costumes. As they plied their needles, she detected an anxiety in the deft-fingered young woman.

"Did you find trouble at home, Suke?" she inquired. "You've been very quiet since you came back from Chester."

The maidservant set a few more stitches before raising her pretty face. "Not for any bad reason. A wonderful thing has happened—*might* happen. I wanted to mention it, only I wasn't sure how to begin. Mr. Wingate went with me to my parents' house. He wished to meet them."

Oriana's hands settled in her lap, crushing the satin gown she was trimming. "He's courting you."

"He is, ma'am."

The disclosure brought relief and sadness both. "Then you'll soon be giving your notice."

"I should like to continue in service, if Jonathon—Mr. Wingate—and I could work in the same household. But because you've already got Mr. Lumley, you don't need a butler."

The Lumleys had served her mother and herself devotedly and would always have a place in her home. But their advancing age made it unlikely that they could continue their duties for more than a few years. Wingate would be a valuable addition, if she could avoid ruffling the sensibilities of her valued retainers.

Before she could speak her mind, Suke continued, "Jonathon—Mr. Wingate—would be sorry to leave his master. He's been with Sir Dare twice as long as I've been with you." After a very long pause, she said softly, "The Isle of Man, as he describes it, seems a pleasant place to live."

"It is."

Her maid was explaining, as delicately as possible, that her marriage would sever this relationship. Dare, she realized, had not only suspected this could happen, he'd even tried to prepare her. Fondness for her efficient, discreet handmaiden required her to conceal her distress.

In a neutral tone, she said, "Sir Dare has a lovely new home and will require a larger staff. Be assured that I shall provide you with a highly favorable recommendation—although he knows your merits well enough by this time."

"Mr. Wingate posed a question to me, concerning you and his master, but I didn't know how to answer. It's not my place to ask, ma'am, but we've both wondered if perhaps you and Sir Dare might become engaged yourselves."

"There are a host of reasons why I shall not marry Sir

Dare Corlett." Fearing that she might have given the erroneous impression that he might want her to, she added, "Nor do I expect an offer from him."

She returned her attention to the garment, stabbing the shiny fabric with her needle.

"Mr. Wingate hasn't yet stated his intentions," Suke confided. "But he spent half an hour with my father."

"Very proper of him to request permission to pay his addresses," said Oriana. "And though it may be a trifle premature, I wish you both every happiness in your marriage."

"Thank you, ma'am. I've been saving up my money, as my mother told me to, for a dowry. But I never imagined meeting anyone who'd want me for his wife." Ducking her head, the young woman sliced a thread with her scissors.

"Whyever not, Suke?"

As soon as she asked the question, the logical answer presented itself. A maidservant's reputation matched that of her mistress. Suke Barry, therefore, shared her notoriety and had been similarly damaged by it.

"I've always been too busy for a sweetheart. Just like you, ma'am."

A diplomatic response, intended to spare Oriana's feelings—which did absolutely nothing to quell her remorse.

The earl's explosive shot broke the silence of the moor, and his shotgun's double barrels smoked.

The grouse's inert body dropped to the ground.

At her master's command, the setter darted forward.

The other birds, lying low in the covert, suddenly soared above the brushy wasteland.

Dare fired, bringing down one bird, and his lordship, armed with a second gun, took another. The scent of black powder hung heavy in the damp air.

"Well done," Rushton congratulated him. "A worthwhile outing—our numbers must be equal now."

"Four birds each, m'lord," reported one of the servants, slinging a game bag over his shoulder.

Dare wasn't enough of a sportsman to care about his numbers, but he would have disliked being bested by this man.

They handed over their weapons to the attendants and began their walk back to the Hall. The weary dogs padded along after them, tongues lolling.

Here in his native shire, Rushton was less chilling a personality than he'd been in London. Nineteen years a widower, after his young wife's death in childbed, he was an attentive parent who had raised his daughter alone and enjoyed a warm relationship with her. His strong sense of responsibility made him seem older than his years—he wasn't yet forty—but at Rushton Hall he demonstrated a fondness for the company of his friends and neighbors, and his devotion to sport. His hospitality to his guests could not be faulted.

The camaraderie engendered by their morning on the moors had lulled Dare's jealousy to some extent, and he was consoled by the knowledge that tomorrow he would remove Oriana from Rushton Hall. But all his dislike came rushing back when the earl asked how much longer he intended to stay in England.

"There are vessels that make regular sailings to your island from Liverpool—which is no great distance from here."

Dare knew he could be home within a day and a half, but wasn't tempted to go. "I've no need to return," he replied, "for I've not yet completed my business in London."

"Haven't you?" asked Rushton. "It seems to me that

you've done exactly what you intended to. You seduced Oriana."

Loyalty to Oriana demanded that Dare keep silent, and he couldn't defend himself against the accusation. Flashing an angry glance at the nobleman, he said, "You have a very poor opinion of me. And of her."

"I hold her in the highest regard, but I know how her impulses lead her into trouble. Has she ever spoken to you about a man called Thomas?"

He nodded.

"His failure to treat her honorably caused her great unhappiness. You can't possibly understand what she suffered—or why, afterward, she held herself aloof from all men. She found solace in her music, and her professional pursuits. When she sought my counsel, I suggested that she limit herself to the most exclusive engagements and cultivate her blood connection to the Beauclerks. Her efforts to overcome past scandal would have succeeded, had Matthew not scuttled them."

"Did you arrange Powell's marriage to your daughter as a means of separating him from Oriana?"

"Certainly not. Their attachment existed long before Matthew met Oriana. He has his faults—volatility, extravagance—but I'm convinced of his devotion to Liza and hers to him. As my sole heiress, she can marry without regard to fortune, and I shall settle the London house upon her when she marries. She spent the season in town, establishing herself in society and ordering her bride clothes. When a ridiculous household dispute arose over a set of Wedgwood china, Matthew reacted badly. He got drunk, and for consolation turned to Oriana."

"At the theater. Yes, I know. She removed herself from London."

"From England, in fact. To my eternal regret, she let a whim carry her off to the Isle of Man."

One man's loss was another's gain. "So I *didn't* imagine your dog-in-the-manger attitude."

"I guard what is mine, Corlett."

"In what sense does Oriana belong to *you*?"

"Moderate your tone, sir," Rushton advised him, "unless you want my servants to overhear."

He glanced over his shoulder and saw the men ambling behind them, passing a brandy flask back and forth. In a low voice, he asked, "What the devil do you mean, she's yours? If so, she failed to mention it."

"Circumstances have prevented me from declaring myself," he said coolly. "Oriana required sufficient time to recover from the Teversal episode. And I couldn't create a scandal with an opera singer while planning my daughter's wedding festivities."

They were passing the coppice where Dare and Oriana had disported themselves, and his memories bolstered his certainty that she belonged more to him than to Rushton. A shared passion, he assured himself, trumped years of platonic friendship. She'd exchanged a pledge with him.

"As soon as Liza and Matthew are married, I shall be at liberty to court Oriana."

"You want her for your mistress?" asked Dare grimly. "Or your countess?"

"For the past week, she has occupied my late wife's bedchamber." The earl's smile was triumphant. "I would not have insisted upon that, unless I intended to become her husband. Which I do."

Dare would have felt the same alarm if Rushton suddenly seized one of the shotguns and pointed it at him. "She won't have you. Given the choice between marriage and music, she'd choose the latter."

"Her music would cease to be a public spectacle, and become a private pleasure. Yes, she would relinquish her career, but the rewards would be substantial—a title, a fortune, a country house. Through me, she can gain the respectability she desires above anything. I will ensure that she leaves her house in Soho Square, a monument to her unseemly heritage. With you, she must endure the shame of a secret dalliance that is unlikely to last. Her choice, Corlett, is simple."

If he denied his affair with Oriana, he'd be lying. But silence would confirm the earl's suspicion. "Your assumptions belittle Oriana, and do you no credit. She's not a helpless, abandoned creature in need of guidance, my lord, but a uniquely talented woman who cherishes her independence. I predict she'll refuse your proposal—and with a delicacy that preserves a valued friendship."

With what sounded like grudging respect, Rushton said, "You would not deliberately wound her—but it's inevitable that you will. If you break with her sooner than later, you'd be doing her a favor."

Dare doubted that Oriana would regard his desertion in that light. Squaring his shoulders, he stared into his rival's flinty eyes. "I regard your remarks, and your advice, as an intrusion."

"A necessary one. As Oriana's future husband, I must state my objections to your—your intimacy with her."

"Until she agrees to become Lady Rushton," he retorted, "she's free to live as she pleases, not as you ordain."

He would cede nothing to this toplofty lord, who implied that Dare's connection to the singer was both ephemeral and degrading. Their tense dialogue had shaken his confidence only slightly. He was a scientist, trained to observe and draw fact-based conclusions, and he'd seen nothing, heard nothing to prove that Oriana would turn away from her profession—and her para-mour—to marry the Earl of Rushton.

* * *

A grand success, thought Harriot Mellon, was hardly an apt description of the Rushton Hall players' version of *The Critic*. Her assessment of the performance was quite different from that of the gentry-folk, so effusive in their compliments to the young actors and actresses. In her judgment, they had acquitted themselves reasonably well, but the only one who truly deserved the accolades was Mr. Powell.

Her duty done, she could enjoy herself at the grandest party she had ever attended. Although her pink gown was made of sheer muslin, not silk, Oriana said it favored her coloring. Her pearls weren't real, and her lacy shawl had been loaned by her more fashionable friend, but her occasional glances at the nearest gilt-framed mirror showed an impressively elegant image.

"A pity there are so few aristocrats here," her mother commented. "Squires and baronets are well enough, *if* they've got riches—and no wife." Her sharp eyes moved to the one gentleman matching that description. "Sir Darius Corlett must be pleased with you, Harriot, for he chose you as his dinner partner."

Sir Dare's invitation to sit beside him had thrown her mother into a state of ecstasy. During the meal, the Manxman had quizzed her about Mr. Sheridan's eccentricities and expressed a flattering desire to see her perform. Grateful though she was for his interest in her career, and his kind attention, she understood perfectly well that his friendliness was a product of his devotion to her dear friend.

The theatrical season would soon begin, and the Drury Lane proprietors had summoned her back for rehearsals. Tomorrow she would travel to London on the mail coach—no stops along the way, except for meals—and all the way her mother would grumble enviously about Oriana, who would make the journey in an unhurried and more comfortable fashion.

Her parent, still carping about the absence of titled persons from this gathering, was yet again holding up another actress as a model. "When Miss Farren managed the players at the Duke of Richmond's house, she was able to push herself into high society—and marry the Earl of Derby." Mrs. Entwistle took one of Harriot's trailing black ringlets, and draped it more picturesquely. "You must thank Lord Rushton for asking us to stay."

"It was Lady Liza who invited me," Harriot reminded her.

"Yes, but his lordship is your host. If we leave him with a good impression, he will remember you—and perhaps will seek you out when he's in London. What has become of him, I wonder?"

"He stepped out into the gardens a little while ago." He'd taken Oriana with him, but saying so would provoke a tirade.

"Then I suggest you improve your acquaintance with Sir Darius—until the earl returns." When Harriot stood her ground, her mother pinched her waist, hard enough to make her flinch. "Go along, now—and do remember to hold your head high, it makes your neck look longer."

Angry and ashamed, Harriot crossed to the drawing-room window to join Sir Dare, as commanded. His warm smile failed to comfort her. She wondered how he'd react if she surrendered to her emotions, pressed her flushed face against his chest, and wept all over his coat lapel. He'd seen her tears before, when he'd come to her Liverpool lodging in search of Oriana.

"Your mother sent you," he said, his voice softened by compassion.

Ignoring her parent's recommendation about holding

up her head, she bowed it. "She's always telling me that unless I put myself forward, no one will notice me."

"By no one, she must mean eligible gentlemen."

Harriot nodded. "She expects me to marry a rich nobleman, as Miss Farren did."

The baronet's dark head turned toward the window. "Every female player's dream," he said wryly.

"It is. And Mother resents Oriana because she's likely to make a brilliant match before I do."

His jet-black brows angled downward, and his eyes fastened on hers. "With whom?"

"Someone—anyone—who has a title and a great deal of money."

"If such a person made her an offer, would she accept it?"

Rolling her sham pearls between her fingers, Harriot decided that he needed encouragement. "If she cared for the gentleman, and he for her, I'm certain she would."

"Even if the marriage curtailed her career?"

"When she eloped with Captain Julian, she didn't mind about that."

"She was much younger then, and madly in love."

"She also felt trapped by her mother's expectations. Sally Vernon put Oriana on the stage, but she also reared her as a duke's daughter, a royal descendant. She longs to be honorably married, and she's a slave to her music. No wonder she feels so torn," Harriot said sympathetically. "She expects to be asked back to the King's Theatre—as *prima donna*. But if she became a ladyship instead, her Beauclerk relations—the duke and the earl—would be so pleased. And people couldn't say rude things about her any longer."

"True," he said heavily. "That consideration hadn't even occurred to me."

Gazing up at his weary face, Harriot perceived that he,

too, was exhausted from a long and busy day, and all the evening's activities. Summoning a smile, she said, "This week you've learned how demanding a profession ours is. It's equally unpredictable. Oriana and I don't wish to end up like our mothers—embittered by misfortune, fearful of what the future might bring."

Smiling, he said, "I can't imagine your spirits being dampened for very long, not even by the most dismal occurrence. You deserve a husband with a fortune larger than the King's, and whose title will place you at the pinnacle of the aristocracy—you'd make a magnificent duchess. And may your consort be as handsome and charming as you are lovely and talented."

Harriot laughed. "You are generous, sir. But if I had a suitor so rich, or was courted by a duke, I wouldn't care if he looked like a toad!"

From the earl's darkened gardens, Oriana could clearly see the figures standing near the tall and well-lit drawing room windows. Dare and Harri had been speaking to one another for several minutes, and now were laughing. She was pleased that they got on so well.

Rushton placed a hand beneath her elbow, guiding her away from the house and deeper into the shadows. "Are you in love with him?" he asked.

"He doesn't want my love," she confided.

The earl had comforted her in bereavement, after her mother's death, and supported her through scandals great and small. But by requiring Dare to conceal their relationship, she'd forced herself to conceal the truth from all the kind, uncritical people who cared about her—Rushton and Harri and Matthew.

"I recall a time, not so long ago, when you vowed never to give your heart to a man who can't wed you—or won't. You must know that Corlett has but one use for an Ana St. Albans. He made that perfectly clear."

"Did he?" she couldn't help asking. "When?"

"I overheard him talking with the young men during our shoot the other day. I cannot reveal exactly what terms he used when referring to you. But from his tone and the ribald laughter his comments produced, I know they were disrespectful."

Stricken, Oriana stared up at the earl. "I can't believe that of him." But the pity in his ascetic face confirmed his revelation.

Men talked among themselves, that she knew, trying to impress one another. They told tales of their conquests—real and imaginary. As a female who valued her privacy, she couldn't understand the masculine urge to establish prowess through coarse boasting. She was vastly disappointed that Dare had broken his promise. But his betrayal had most probably been accidental, not deliberate—he was so tactless. To collapse in despair because he turned out to be a fallible human, not a saint, would be absurd. She was stronger and more sensible than that.

If she confronted Dare with his transgression, she might imperil their relationship. By feigning ignorance, she could hold on to him a little while longer.

"When Dare does seek a bride," Oriana told her concerned friend, "he won't choose a professional singer. Or a duke's bastard. *Or* a reputed courtesan. I'm all three." To remove any impression that she dreamed of becoming Lady Corlett, she lightened her tone, saying, "I've left no room for a husband in my plans for the future."

"You refer to your anticipated return to the King's Theatre."

She nodded.

"It must have occurred to you that employment at the

opera house will revive past controversies. You've become accustomed to the sedate and attentive audiences at your oratorios, and the middle-class pleasure-seekers of Vauxhall. People of fashion attend the opera, and they don't necessarily go to hear the music. It's London's temple of gossip and intrigue. The ladies shred the characters of the performers, with or without cause. The gentlemen in the boxes and in Fop's Alley ogle the prettiest singers and dancers, and vie for their favors. Your visibility will cause you much misery, I fear."

His prediction disturbed her, for she knew the truth of it better than he.

"If ever you feel the need to retire from public life, Oriana, you must let me know. When you were in Liverpool, and sought a quiet retreat, you could have come to Rushton Hall." Lowering his voice, he added, "How I wish you had done."

He was clearly worried that her sojourn on the Isle of Man would lead to her greatest sorrow yet. Deep down, she feared he might be right.

Chapter 27

The short supply of bedchambers at the George Inn prevented Dare from trysting with Oriana during their night in Stafford. Privacy was denied them, for Suke Barry shared her chamber and slept on a truckle bed.

Before they resumed their journey, he joined her in a cramped dining parlor for a breakfast of toast, boiled eggs, and coffee, served by a chatty waiter. Assisting him was a young female, whose downcast face and red-rimmed, teary eyes stirred Oriana's sympathy. When the girl stepped out of the room she asked the cause.

"Her brother was a miner, and lost his life in an accident," the man replied.

Dare glanced up from the newspaper. "What happened to him?"

"He drowned, sir. The lead mine he worked in flooded during the rains. Her other brother brought back his body yesterday, and the funeral's this afternoon."

"Which mine was it?"

"I can't say, sir. You'd have to ask Liddy. I'll take you to the kitchen." The servant hoisted his tray and moved to the door.

Oriana knew Dare's fears without being told, and waited for his return with increasing trepidation.

When he came back, she asked, "Did the accident happen at Damerham?"

"No. But conditions there will be just as bad—and as dangerous. The August rains caused much flooding, and left the ground saturated and unstable. When water collects in a mine shaft, it must be pumped out."

His intentions became apparent when he picked up her copy of *Paterson's Roads,* lying on the table, and unfolded its map of turnpike roads.

"You're going to Derbyshire."

"I must. Although I leased the mineral rights of the various Corlett properties to another, the land is still mine, and I feel responsible for the men who work it. I've already instructed Wingate to load all my baggage in one chaise, and yours in the other."

"You may take my book, if you need it," she offered. "I know my way back to London."

She refrained from asking when she would see him again—it depended on too many uncertainties. To tell him how much she'd miss him would be equally unwise.

He came over to her. "You may come with me, if you wish. I don't like parting from you so near your birthday."

Believing that his invitation rose from his sense of obligation, she shook her head. "My presence would be impossible to explain in a place where you're so well known. And I'm not at all sure I want you watching me grow older before your eyes."

"You needn't whine to me about turning twenty-four. We met the day I attained my thirtieth year, remember."

"It's different for men," she declared. "I don't mind traveling back to town by myself. It's time I resumed my voice lessons with Signor Corri, and I also need to confer with my solicitor about the sale of some property."

"What property?" he asked sharply.

She gave the only answer that presented itself. "This isn't the best time to discuss it."

His lips thinned, and he gave her the stony stare she recalled from long ago. He could glower as long as he liked, but she wasn't telling him about Thomas Teversal's diamonds.

When he spoke again, he said, "I'll be out of favor with my butler for parting him from his sweetheart at a crucial stage in their romance. They'll soon be betrothed, if they aren't already."

"My maid has already given notice," Oriana admitted. "Not in so many words, but her meaning was unmistakable. I can't imagine Wingate would leave you, even if I could offer him a place in my household. I'm confident that Suke will be extremely happy on the Isle of Man, and she'll have easier access to her relatives in Cheshire than she does living with me in London."

"You took her on at Lord Rushton's behest. Doubtless *he'll* find a suitable candidate to fill the vacancy." When Dare mentioned the earl, the crease between his black brows deepened. "How much longer will he remain in Cheshire, reducing the grouse population?"

"The grouse will be safe again in a fortnight, when Parliament reconvenes."

"I'll be in London before him. If not, I'll meet you in Newmarket at the end of the month—to watch Combustible run her race."

The possibility that their separation might stretch as long as two weeks dismayed Oriana. This was the man who couldn't let two days go by without seeing her, who had insisted on all those midnight meetings in the Soho Square gardens.

Had his passion for her faded?

Her husband's love had lasted until death. She'd severed her relationship with a lover whose marriage promise had been false but whose desire had been constant.

Rejection by Dare, so ardent and possessive, would be a shattering and unprecedented experience. From the moment she'd reached womanhood, men had pursued her. No previous admirer had abandoned her—but none had been given the chance. As Dare frequently pointed out, she had a habit of running away.

She could do it again, right now. With a few firm words, she could declare the end of this affair and board a swift coach to London. That might be easier to bear than the agony of a slow demise.

But she loved him too much to give him up. And therefore she must set aside all her aching uncertainties about their future and pretend they didn't exist.

From the Manxman's very first kiss, she'd been enthralled. His initial dislike had wounded her, but during her residence at Glen Auldyn a form of friendship had sprouted. Her control over her emotions had failed her at Skyhill, in an episode that hadn't cured their passion for each other but had whetted it. All those seemingly divisive truths she'd revealed in Liverpool and London hadn't deterred him. He'd wrung from her a pledge that she could never have made, she now realized, unless she'd been in love. To spare her pride, she'd concealed her feelings, realizing that someday he must return to the Isle of Man—without her.

Dare had been her tormenter, her closest companion, her adoring lover—but he could never be her husband. And his solitary journey from Stafford to Damerham, she feared, was his first step on the road back to the life he'd known before their memorable meeting.

She walked up to him, taking his stern face between

her hands, and rising on her toes to kiss him. His hands settled on her waist, and his mouth gentled. Elation and sorrow tumbled about inside her. Love was a test of endurance, and a great adventure. She would be faithful to the end.

When Wingate strode briskly into the parlor to announce that Dare's chaise was ready, Oriana buried her regret beneath a facade of serenity and accompanied him to the inn yard.

The butler boldly kissed Suke Barry, in full view of his master and her mistress. They exchanged a few confidential words before he climbed into the carriage.

Oriana smiled valiantly and waved as Dare lifted his hat to her.

Suke, holding a handkerchief to her eyes, walked back to the inn.

Oriana put a consoling arm around her shoulders. "You'll soon see him again," she said reassuringly.

"I know." The young woman drew a long, labored breath. "It's not for sadness that I'm weeping, but for joy. He just asked me to wed him, and I said I would."

A blade of envy sliced through Oriana's soul.

In that moment of vivid understanding Oriana knew that she would surrender anything, everything—her talent, her fame, her lovely dresses, Nell Gwynn's diamonds—if only she could become Dare Corlett's bride.

"I'm happy for you both," she declared in a tremulous voice, determined to share in her servant's happiness rather than dwell on her looming sorrow.

Dare's lantern augmented the feeble glow of coals in the grate and a pair of malodorous tallow candles, but could not overpower the pervasive darkness of Dan Bonsall's cramped, low-ceilinged cottage. He nodded as his hostess held the spout of her teapot over his cup and added more of the weak brew. Wingate, seated beside him on the wooden bench, declined her offer.

Her husband, Dare noted, had not received a second serving of tea, a privilege accorded only to guests.

From the next room came whispers and childish giggles.

Mrs. Bonsall looked in upon her many offspring, piled onto one of the two beds. "Quiet, every one of you." Turning back to Dare, she explained apologetically, "The excitement of having you here, sir. Late as it is, they'll soon settle into sleep."

Dan Bonsall sat at the opposite end of the kitchen table, shoulders bowed from exhaustion, chin propped by his dirty hands. "As I told you," he said, "we all fared better with Mr. Melton as manager. He treated his miners fairly, and they respected him. He knew our wives' names, and paid us enough to keep our cottages in good repair. The man who followed him wasn't at all popular with us—until he went away."

"And what about his successor, the current manager?"

"Eh, I don't like to complain to you, Sir Dare, when there's nowt you can do. But he's the worst in Derbyshire, I'd wager—if I had any coppers to lose. Conditions at Dale End Mine have worsened since he came. First he reduced the pay, during the coldest winter in memory. There was much illness, but none of the men can afford to leave their work. Then we had the wettest of summers, with floods and damp, and our pumps were in such ill repair that for days on end the mines were closed. The price of wheat has already gone up four pence—it's certain to rise much higher, for harvest will come late and food will be sparse."

Mrs. Bonsall's white cap moved up and down in an emphatic nod. "Bread's goin' to be even more costly this autumn—and worse in winter. We've decided to send our Laura, young as she is, to the cotton factory."

The impoverished inhabitants of this cottage represented countless families living in these dales and moors, struggling for survival. Their disclosures made him wish that he'd come here much sooner.

"Tomorrow I'll make an unannounced visit to all the mines—especially Dale End," he said. "I don't know whether that will help matters, but it can't do any harm."

"It will encourage the men," Bonsall said, "to know they're not forgotten."

Dare reached into his coat pocket for his writing case. "I want the names of any men you know who may be injured or ill, or have sickness in their households. And those with the fewest resources—be it money, food, or fuel. I mean to assist as many as possible, but first I must know which are the very worst cases."

The miner required no time to think. As the names spilled from his cracked lips, Dare listed them—the column grew longer, and with each addition his spirits sank ever lower. He recognized most of the surnames, and could associate faces with the majority of them.

Tomorrow, after touring the mines, he'd visit his bankers in Wirksworth to withdraw enough money to alleviate the ills caused by poverty and poor working conditions. Never before had he felt so blessed by his wealth—and a vast portion of it had come from the labor of men like Dan Bonsall, their sons and fathers and grandsires.

When the miner concluded the grim recital, Dare pocketed his writing materials. He took out his pouch, plucked out a gold coin, and laid it on the table.

"Eh, sir," Mrs. Bonsall breathed. "What's that?"

"Half a guinea. It's worth ten shillings and sixpence."

Bursting into tears, she hid her streaming face with her apron. Dan jumped up from the bench and went to comfort her.

"I'm going now," Dare told them. "But I'll return as soon as I can."

He held his lantern high as he led Wingate away from the cottage and toward the tollhouse where they had left their innkeeper's gig.

"Not a very pleasant homecoming," he commented. "Affairs here are in a deplorable state."

"Will you go to Damerham, sir? We'll pass it by on our way to Wirksworth."

"I don't know," Dare answered frankly. "Under the terms of the lease, I have a right to make an annual visit—which I've not yet exercised. It's no longer my home, and won't revert to my possession for four years. You thought me mad to give it up, I know. What a long time ago it seems," he reflected. "I wonder whether anyone here remembers I was engaged to Miss Bradfield."

"Sir, though I had no right to object or approve your decision to leave Derbyshire, I understood it."

"My choice had unfortunate consequences for the miners, which I must remedy as best I can. However long it takes." As he marched into uneven terrain, he said, "If you dislike being away from Suke Barry, I shall pack you off to London."

"That won't be necessary, sir," said Wingate's disembodied voice. "I shall stay with you because it's my duty, and also my most earnest wish. You've got used to having a companion. And though I'm a poor substitute for Madame St. Albans, I shall endeavor to keep your spirits up."

Dare laughed softly. "Thank you, Wingate. I'm more grateful than I can express." Feeling the soil beneath him shift, he flung up an arm and warned, "Come no closer!" He held the light out in front of him as far as his arm would stretch, but before he could ascertain what lay ahead, the earth opened up.

Down he tumbled, scraping against a hard, rough surface, deafened by the rumble of loose rocks. His descent was broken by a solid barrier, but the impact pounded the air from his lungs.

Numb and immobile, he waited tensely for burial by the inevitable avalanche from above.

It didn't come.

He tried to open his eyes—and saw nothing.

I'm blinded, he thought, frantically blinking to clear away the grit. Blackness surrounded him. He flexed his fists and gingerly shifted his legs. Groaning, he sat up. His entire body ached, but it wasn't broken.

"Sir?"

"I'm down here!" His shout echoed in the well-like chamber. "I lost my lantern." Was that the reason he couldn't see? "I've landed on a wooden platform—a portion of the scaffolding, I think. And not at all sturdy."

"I'll go back to the miner's cottage—we'll bring some men to help you out."

"Be careful," Dare cautioned.

There was no answer.

After combing his fingers through his hair to remove the sharp pebbles and grit, he pressed them to the stinging scratch on his cheek. He suspected it was bleeding but couldn't tell, because his entire face was moist.

Striving for a more comfortable position, he bent his knees. The right one hurt like hell.

Nothing to do but sit and wait. He chafed at his helplessness, but had too much knowledge of mines to attempt an escape. This one, he surmised, hadn't been worked for years. Frequent rains and waterlogged soil had weakened the support timbers, which likely had been rotten. The planks beneath him were damp and muddy, and he prayed they were in better condition.

He shoved aside the harsh suspicion that this accident was a form of divine retribution, his penance for neglecting the many people dependent on the various Corlett mines. For three years he'd stayed away from Derbyshire, determined not to interfere in an enterprise that he'd entrusted to someone else's management. Although he had no legal authority to make changes, he would consult with his attorney. They should ascertain whether or not his tenant cared to break the lease.

As he waited, his thoughts turned toward Oriana, by far the greatest mystery in his life.

In recent days he hadn't been able to banish his recurring suspicion that she'd used him to make Rushton jealous, to prompt the honorable proposal that would transform her from a hardworking social pariah into a pampered countess. Harriot Mellon's enlightening conversation had undermined his certainty that the singer would never abandon her career to marry the earl. And Rushton himself had pointed out that her rise in the world would please the noble Beauclerks, proud of their descent from an English monarch and his Drury Lane mistress.

Doubts and false assumptions, Dare reminded himself, had too often misled him, and he mustn't let them undermine his plans for her happiness. He could not lose Oriana to Rushton, or any other man, because no one else understood her as he did.

But he remembered their parting, and how she'd kissed him as though they might never kiss again. She had also mentioned selling property—presumably her house.

Rushton had been adamant about removing her from Soho Square.

The earl would impose his lofty notions of respectability upon Oriana—motivated, Dare believed, by genuine affection. But he doubted that his independent, free-spirited songstress, accustomed to turning heads and setting fashions, would be content to dwell in obscurity at Rushton Hall.

He'd often assured her that his passion was boundless, but he hadn't yet proved that he loved her with his entire being—body, heart, and soul. His infatuation with Willa Bradfield was feeble by comparison to what he felt for Oriana. These emotions were deeper and richer, they nourished and sustained him.

By making her his wife, he could proclaim to her and all the world that they were bonded for eternity. They could live in the same house—or houses. Share a marital bed. Make love at any hour of the day or night. Bring children into the world and rear them together. He'd give her horses and goats and dogs and cats. Chickens. Cows. Even geese, if Oriana wanted them.

Unable to contain his joy, he laughed aloud. He pounded the planks with his fist—and the platform shuddered.

At any moment he could plunge to his death, and Oriana would never know about his dream. Dare forced himself to lie perfectly still.

He drew slow, calming breaths as he traced the progress of their relationship. Early on, they had each flatly stated their disinterest—he to guard his privacy, she to refute his belief that she was a fortune hunter. But time had brought understanding, and they had altered their opinions of each other. Desperate to hold on to her, he'd chased her from the island to Liverpool. After learning her identity, he had continued his pursuit in London. And throughout, she'd steadfastly denied any desire to wed—an attempt, he suspected, to shield herself from loss and betrayal.

Easy to oppose marriage when nobody had offered it.

In the near future, she would have her pick of two suitors. One possessed an earldom, the other a baronetcy. Each could give her a respected name, and considerable wealth. Which would she choose?

The man who loved her best, Dare hoped, and who needed her the most.

Did she need him? He didn't expect her to readily admit it. She refused all gifts or any semblance of financial support. He was confident of his ability to arouse and satisfy her passions. He'd been discretion personified. Yet her love was elusive, and he must court it with care and sensitivity.

He had no means of knowing whether his servant had been gone for minutes or hours. His injured knee ached more as time passed. His damp clothes stuck uncomfortably to his skin. He had so much to accomplish—in Derbyshire, in London, at Newmarket—and was impatient to escape his dark, silent prison.

Wingate finally returned with Dan Bonsall and a rescue party. The miners, many of them roused from their beds, brought lanterns and torches; they had buckets and shovels, wooden ladders and coils of rope. Their first order of business was to lower a light into the pit, followed by a bottle of spirits and a blanket.

Dare's apology for causing trouble prompted many a hearty laugh.

"I remember when you and your grandfather stood vigil with the families all night, waiting to see if the miners would come out again. You've come to our aid time and again, sir."

The complicated process of extricating him was long and arduous. The men decided it was too dangerous to haul him up with ropes—their combined weight could cause another collapse. Dare, mindful of the risk, waited till they unblocked the original entrance to the shaft, enabling him to crawl out.

The first pale light of dawn welcomed him when he emerged from the earth's depths. *Oriana's birthday,* he thought, while the cheering men thumped his shoulder and gripped his hand.

Unlike his rescuers, who collected their implements and trudged off to the mine for a full day of work, Dare was free to return to his lodging for several hours of rest. At Wingate's urging, he sent for the local physician and grudgingly let him inspect the cut on his cheek and bandage his bruised and swollen knee. This also gave him an opportunity to find out whether the number of serious accidents had increased since the arrival of the current manager.

"It's possible," the doctor replied. "But I do know there's more sickness than I can remember. Any fever that strikes here runs rampant. The men are working themselves into a state of exhaustion, and too many of their wives and children are underfed."

With a renewed sense of purpose, Dare left his inn. At Wirksworth, he stopped at the banking establishment of Arkwright and Toplis but found neither man at his desk. Amenable to Wingate's suggestion that they press on to Matlock, the spa town, he left a message for his bankers.

"I doubt a dose of the waters can heal my injuries," he commented, as the gig crossed the bridge to the other side of the River Derwent.

"Perhaps not, sir," his servant replied, "but the new

hotel is superior to any in Wirksworth, with views of the dale and the mountains."

In the morning, Mr. Toplis arrived at their lodging with a document box. Dare's announcement that he wished to withdraw a substantial sum from his account prompted frowns, and what could only be described as a lecture.

"I've brought your account record, Sir Darius," said the banker. "In recent months, you have drastically drawn down your funds. Almost daily we receive payment requests from our London associates at Down, Thornton, Free, and Cornwall." He opened his box and removed a narrow ledger.

Confronted by his expenditures, Dare fell silent. The withdrawals represented payments made to innkeepers, furniture-makers, tailors, Lord Burford, the horse trainer at Moulton Heath, posting houses all over the country, and the Ludgate Hill jeweler. He was dismayed to learn that the amount on deposit wouldn't help the miners to the extent he'd hoped.

"I need to raise cash," he said. "Heaps of it."

When he had explained his purpose, the banker said ponderously, "A very worthwhile endeavor. However, your present balance does not enable you to take on so many projects. You must determine which of them you are most eager to pursue. Perhaps the fencing of disused mine shafts can be put off?"

"Not for long," Dare answered. "Can't I rely on my capital?"

"I strongly advise against it. The consols and annuities are rising, as are bank stocks and India stocks. If you will permit me to make a suggestion?"

He nodded.

"Your quarterly payment for mineral rights falls due

next week, at Michaelmas," Mr. Toplis pointed out. "If you remain here to collect it yourself, you can immediately disburse it to the miners. In the meantime, I shall assist you in setting up a charitable fund."

Dare endorsed this reasonable course of action reluctantly, knowing that it would delay his proposal to the dearly beloved mistress he intended to win as his wife.

"Our London winters are so detrimental to Signora Banti's health that the management of the King's Theatre cannot depend on her to perform in every opera. Therefore, I have persuaded Mr. Taylor that an Italian-trained Englishwoman is exactly what we require to fill out our company." Michael Kelly's cheeks plumped in a puckish grin. "We can offer you a salary of fifteen hundred guineas for the full season, plus proceeds from a benefit. As our *prima donna,* you may claim 'right of the book,' should you prefer to substitute an aria of your choosing over the one supplied by the composer."

Hearing these highly advantageous terms, Oriana realized she was being courted. The reason for this change, she guessed, was Signora Banti's tendency to sicken and the debt-plagued proprietor's inability to keep his best performers for successive seasons. Her acquaintances in the orchestra often complained that salaries were in arrears.

"Signor Federici will conduct our singers from the harpsichord, and Saloman leads the orchestra. I, of course, continue in my position as stage manager. I can't yet tell you when the King's Theatre will reopen," the Irishman admitted. "But sometime after the turn of the year, you will begin rehearsing a comic piece new to Londoners: von Winter's *I Fratelli Rivalli.*"

As an Englishwoman performing a work by a German

composer, she would be opposed by the cabal. These partisans of Italian-born singers and musicians congregated in the opera house gallery, hissing loudly and shouting insults. They would resent her prominence, and exert themselves to interrupt her solos.

"Will I be performing *opera seria*?" she asked hopefully.

"I can offer you Gluck's *Alceste*."

A French libretto, she thought in dismay, certain to stir the cabal's resentment.

"We may stage a revival of Paisiello's *Nina*—you remember how popular it was two seasons ago. Your delicacy and naturalness are exquisitely suited to the pathos and sentiment of the title role."

Now that this opportunity had come to her, Oriana was startled by her wish to discuss it with Dare. In the years since her mother's death she'd followed her own inclinations, without regard for any other person's opinion.

He'd been a long time in Derbyshire. She'd received one letter, brief and affectionate, which had done nothing to allay her fears of an impending break. It was so easy to feign affection in writing, from afar. She needed to see his face, his eyes, to believe in the sentiments he'd penned from Matlock. They had seldom been apart since becoming lovers, and she'd been unprepared for the effects of this separation. She found herself dwelling on past conversations, wishing she'd expressed her affection more fully. Often she cheered herself by remembering the delightful hours they'd spent in bed—making love, sharing secret dreams and ambitions, falling asleep still locked in an embrace.

"My dear Ana, your silence makes me nervous. If Sheridan has already made a rival offer to lure you to

Drury Lane, I hope you'll grant us the opportunity to improve upon it."

"I've received none."

"Then I may assure Mr. Taylor that you accept his terms?"

"Not yet." Her reply brought a frown to his face. Leaving the sofa, she went to him and said, "I'm grateful for your loyal campaign on my behalf. But I was too unsure of the outcome to let my hopes run away with me. I couldn't even consider Mr. Taylor's offer until it was formally presented."

"I understand. But we are impatient to settle the matter."

"Tomorrow I depart for Newmarket. While I'm there, you and the opera house will be in my thoughts."

After he left, Oriana fell prey to an attack of restlessness. She climbed the two flights of stairs to her bedchamber, where Suke was preparing for the journey to Suffolk. This room, her private retreat, was unchanged from her girlhood. The intricately carved bedstead with its rose damask tester and curtains, the inlaid chests and ladylike French chairs, had all been chosen by her mother as worthy of the duke's daughter. The Poussin oil painting, purchased from Cousin Aubrey, was one of Oriana's favorite possessions—it had belonged to father.

"I've come for my redingote and a bonnet," she explained on her way to her dressing room. "And my umbrella."

"A bad afternoon for walking out," said the maidservant, bending down to lay a stack of neatly folded petticoats in one of the trunks.

Oriana's errand was important; she would brave the heavy rains. For days she'd waited for another communication from Dare, but it hadn't come, and she was desperate to know his whereabouts. Each time her brass door knocker announced a visitor, her hopes of his return were dashed. Harriot was her most regular visitor, bubbling with excitement over her role as Celia in *As You Like It*. Matthew Powell had come once, straight from her solicitor's office, enriched by the sale of her diamonds. Freed from debt, he'd been almost incoherent with relief and gratitude. Today Mick Kelly had come to fulfill her cherished dream.

And in the midst of these events, she could concentrate only on Dare.

Bracing herself against the wind and angling her umbrella to keep the rain off her face, she crossed the square and strolled down Dean Street in the direction of Morland's Hotel. She handed her dripping umbrella to a servant, and informed the proprietor that she needed to see Ned Crowe.

Henry Morland grinned and jerked his thumb toward the stair. "You'll find him upstairs, with Sir Darius Corlett's furniture."

She discovered the Manxman in a parlor, winding holland cloth around the delicate leg of a an Adam-style console table. An array of similarly shrouded objects surrounded him, and many more waiting to be wrapped—tables, chairs, a set of library steps. Against the wall stood those glass-topped display cabinets made to hold Dare's minerals and rocks.

"You're hard at work," she observed, her buoyant voice at odds with her leaden spirits.

"*Ta*," he muttered, securing the protective cloth with a piece of twine. "Mainshtyr Dare sent instructions that I should make everything ready for transport to Deptford. The wagons come in two days to carry his purchases to the docks."

A sharp spray of raindrops against the glass drew Oriana's gaze to the window. Watching the water stream down the panes, she asked, "When does the *Dorrity* set sail?

Ned shrugged. "I'll be aboard her, that's all I know—my fiddle, too. I've been away from the island long enough."

"Your master will be in Newmarket. Have you any message I can convey?"

"Tell Mainshtyr Dare he bought too much furniture," Ned grumbled, moving on to the next piece. "What you see here is only a part of what he's got—there are three more rooms, crammed full."

She forced out a laugh. "I'll send Sam over to help; that will make your task go quicker."

This impromptu trip to Morland's Hotel had leached the few remaining drops of hope from her heart. Here was visible, umistakable evidence of Dare's intent—he would soon return to his island home. Why hadn't he mentioned it in his letter?

Because, she realized with dire certainty, he believed it would be kinder to break the news in person. In Newmarket.

Leaving Ned to continue his labors, she made her way downstairs. The attendant opened the door for her, and returned her umbrella. She unfurled it, and set out for home. Unshed tears misted her vision, and her breath came in short, sobbing gasps.

Fate had seldom treated her gently. With one hand it bestowed the coveted position of *prima donna*. With the other, it towed Dare away from her.

Much to her amazement—and dismay—she saw the Earl of Rushton's town carriage standing before her house. The coachman's head was bowed in discomfort as the rain pelted him, and the capes of his greatcoat flapped in the breeze. Unwilling to reveal her distress to Rushton, she forced her chin higher. The first test of her composure came when she walked past the square gardens, the setting for so many midnight assignations with her lost lover.

Chapter 28

⟡⟡⟡

This Newmarket journey was a stark contrast to Oriana's previous one. No cuddles and kisses, or halting for carnal delights at a roadside inn. This time, unlike the last, she would have preferred to travel alone.

Through lowered lashes, she glanced at the gentleman beside her. Why she'd accepted his offer to escort her to Suffolk, she wasn't sure—perhaps because she'd been too astonished by it to refuse. Rushton wasn't fond of racing, and she'd wondered why he wished to attend October Meeting.

When he informed her that his daughter was married, she understood: He felt lonely.

"Her ladyship's wedding came about so suddenly," she said. The bridegroom had not, it seemed, exposed her efforts to bring about the match.

"Matthew dashed off to London in a great hurry, and returned to Rushton Hall the following week with a special license. The next morning, in the drawing room, Liza became his wife. Later that same day, they set out for his aunt's house in Wales."

"How happy they must be." She was pleased that her detested diamonds had paved the couple's way to marital bliss.

"When I shall next set eyes on them, I can't say," the earl told her. "I return to Cheshire before they take up residence at Rushton House."

His daughter's changed circumstances had altered him. He was withdrawn and subdued, and his long silences were symptomatic of his discomfiture.

He knew her full history and, unlike Dare, wouldn't be entertained by tales of her childhood and youth. Nor did he want to hear theatrical reminiscences, or her experiences while living on the Continent. And she cared not at all for his dry description of recent parliamentary business. With Dare, the constant flow of dialogue ceased only when they were kissing or making love. Sometimes not even then, she remembered, faintly smiling.

"Rushton Hall will seem very empty," Rushton commented. "But I have hopes of finding companionship." The silver-streaked head turned toward her, and his hand settled over hers. His palm was unexpectedly damp. "For a very long time I've wanted to bare my heart to you. I waited till the furor over the Teversal affair died down. I couldn't involve myself in scandal while Liza was establishing herself in London society, but her future is settled. Now I am free as never before. Oriana, you deserve a better life—and I mean to give it to you."

"Better in what way?" she wondered.

"You'll find out when you marry me. Be my wife, and you will want for nothing."

Astonished, she replied swiftly, "I can't."

"You say that without considering how we will both benefit," he responded. "When you become a peeress, your days of currying favor with theater managers—and a fickle public—will end. I shall protect you from men like Corlett, who impose themselves on you to bolster their reputations as libertines."

Pulling her hand away, she said, "For you, marriage to

Ana St. Albans, the Siren of Soho, would be a liability, not a benefit. Imagine the gossip!"

"We'll never hear it," he said soothingly. "We shall conduct ourselves with discretion. I won't mean to flaunt our union, or present you at court, or even live in town. As Lady Rushton, you'll make your home in Cheshire. I've instructed my solicitor to seek a buyer for your Soho Square house, so you can sell it."

Stung that he should take her acquiescence for granted, Oriana shook her head. "I cannot—I will not accept your offer, my lord. You do me great honor, and I regret disappointing you with a refusal, but I love—" She hesitated. "Believe me, it's quite impossible."

His expression was guarded. "Your infatuation with that Manxman clouds your judgment."

"Not entirely. My answer would be the same if I'd never met him."

A loveless, passionless marriage, however respectable, was unthinkable. Exile from London, hiding herself in the country—it sounded like a punishment for her waywardness.

"He is unworthy of you, Oriana, and proved it with his scurrilous boasts. I heard him characterize you as a shameless wanton, lying down for him and raising up your skirts and—"

"Don't," she choked. "I won't let you disparage him."

"I'll never mention Corlett's name again, if you agree to marry me."

She owed him a credible reason for her decision, and easily found one. "My singing, as you well know, is important to me. I couldn't possibly give it up."

"You may sing as often as you please, at home. Is it the music you crave, or the acclaim it brings you?" he asked shrewdly.

"I want both," she admitted. "My art *and* my audience.

I do enjoy singing for myself, alone in my music room, or for my close friends. But I also need a stage or concert hall. If that makes me a selfish, shallow person, there's no help for it."

To become his countess, she must abandon the career she'd begun at six years old and the richly varied existence filled with music and racing and interesting, creative people. Even worse, she'd have to sever her relationship with Dare.

As a *prima donna* she would remain in London from winter until summer, when the opera season concluded. More than ever before, she'd be the target of unwanted attentions. The pro-Italian claque would create disturbances, controversy would overshadow her artistry, and all the worst gossip about her private life would be resurrected. But her liaison with Dare could continue, and that, she realized, was the greatest advantage.

As she examined the two opportunities fate had presented, she found both of them lacking. She was no longer entirely comfortable with the familiar existence of Ana St. Albans. But she'd be miserable if she married the earl for convenience, just so she could call herself Lady Rushton.

Their long and awkward journey through Essex and Suffolk ended that night at Gwynn Cottage on Mill Hill. Rushton led her up to the door and kissed her hand before driving back to the Wheatsheaf, the nearest public inn, to seek lodging. She didn't expect him to remain in the vicinity longer than a single evening. He hadn't joined her because he liked racing, but to propose matrimony.

"You shouldn't ought've come all the way from London in a day," Mrs. Biggen scolded her gently. "Poor dear, you're looking wan and weary."

"I'm not surprised," Oriana replied, accepting a cup of tea.

"Did you dine on the road?"

"Twice. First at Epping, and later at the Crown in Bishop's Stortford."

"Fancy a bit of fish?"

"This is all I need." She sipped the hot brew gratefully.

A countess, she marveled. *I could have been a countess—still could be, if I wanted.* Only she didn't. *A prima donna, that's what I shall be, just as my mother dreamed.* But the price of her success was terribly high—an inevitable separation from the man she loved. Their love affair afforded her many joys, but it also brought despair. Because it was no longer their secret, she must prepare herself for a raging storm of scandal in the days and weeks to come. And she knew he could not remain in London indefinitely.

"A gentleman stopped in to see you no more than an hour ago."

"My cousin Burford?"

"Nay, 'twasn't his lordship. A fine, black-haired fellow, looking like he'd got the worst of it in a brawl. He'd come over from Moulton Heath to hear the reading of the Steward's list."

Dare Corlett, in a fight? "Does he mean to return?"

Mrs. Biggen's jowls waggled when she shook her head. "Didn't say. Likely you'll see him at the course tomorrow."

Oriana did not doubt it. His filly was running.

The Beauclerk contingent had cause for celebration when Lord Burford's black horse Weymouth won the very first race, besting Lord Clermont's entry on the Flat. Dare, at the Armitage stables, heard the cheers but didn't learn the result until the Duke of Halford announced it.

Lavinia, her willowy figure significantly rounder than it had been in July, said, "Madame St. Albans will be pleased at her cousin's victory. I hope she laid money on Weymouth." When Dare failed to respond, she asked, "Have you placed your bet?"

"Twenty-five guineas, to win."

"A paltry sum—for an owner!" The duchess shook her sleek black head. "You mystify me, Sir Dare, really you do."

"I'm a shining example of Manx thrift," he pointed out virtuously. His unwillingness to risk a large sum on his filly stemmed from his need to hoard his money for the Derbyshire miners. He explained to Lavinia, "I'm more a guardian to Combustible than a master. I feel responsible for her, but ours is a distant relationship."

"Why did you buy her?"

He couldn't admit that he'd been persuaded by Oriana's conviction that the filly was a winner, or his own need to please her and strengthen their connection. "Because she's beautiful and gifted, and deserves a chance to prove her breeding and her talent."

Like Oriana, he remembered with a pang, whose career might well turn out to be an obstacle to marriage.

He and his companions looked toward the stable as the groom led out the black filly.

"I've watched her during her weeks at Moulton," said Garrick. "She ran a good trial yesterday. If she wins today, I'm prepared to make a generous offer."

Con Finbar, the jockey, carried his racing saddle over his arm. The stableboy was leading the filly back and forth. Head erect, she moved with sinuous grace. The black mane, sheared into a short fringe, exposed the sinews of her neck; her tail was docked into a stiff brush. Trainer Nick Cattermole trotted alongside her on spindly bowed legs, telling Con how to run his race.

Sir Charles Bunbury, his horse and rider in pink-and-white-striped livery, and a large crowd of hangers-on proceeded toward the Rowley Mile.

"She's overexcited," Lavinia commented.

"Who?"

"Pamela. See how she jerks at her reins?"

"The odds are greatly in her favor." Dare knew about the rival's victories, which Oriana had documented for him. "She won at Epsom and at Ipswich."

"But she hasn't been as lucky on the Newmarket course," Garrick reminded him, "for during July Meeting, she came in next to the last—in a large field. At Brighton and Lewes, she finished third, and had a very poor showing at Bedford."

"Combustible is untried." He wanted her to win, for Oriana's sake and because he needed the purchase money for his miners, and his nerves were stretched thin.

The colors of his racing silks honored his native island: grass green for the Manx hills, pale blue for the sky above. He held the filly's bridle while her groom tossed the saddle onto her back and cinched the girth around her belly.

"Look who's here to wish you luck," said the duchess in an undertone that conveyed sharp interest.

He saw Oriana coming toward them, flanked by two earls. Threaded through the flounce of her blue habit was a green ribbon. His heart lifted at this proof of her loyalties. "A partisan."

"Her cousin I recognize, but not the other man."

"Lord Rushton."

Garrick was welcoming the threesome to his enclosure.

Burford, flushed and beaming, heartily shook Dare's hand. "May your luck match mine. She looks well," he said of the filly. "No more trouble with that hock?"

"None, my lord."

Oriana tugged off her glove and stroked Combustible's velvety muzzle. "Run fast as you can," she murmured to her favorite.

After so many days apart, Dare couldn't stop staring at Oriana's lilylike face. If not for the crowd gathered around them, he could kiss those delectable, pouting lips.

In a concerned voice, audible only to Dare, she said, "You've hurt yourself."

Touching his cheek, he said ruefully, "I'll have a lasting scar, I fear." No time to explain, for Rushton was closing in on them, cutting off their surreptitious exchange.

The Duke of Halford insisted that his duchess view the race from her landau. When Rushton urged Oriana to do the same, rebellion flashed in her hazel eyes.

"Do join me," her grace entreated. "We shall have an excellent view of the course, I assure you."

Oriana longed to stand beside Dare during his race but was trapped into accepting the Duchess of Halford's invitation. Not so long ago she would have rejoiced at this gesture of acceptance from one of racing's elite, but like all the good fortune that had come to her lately, it was a mixed blessing. As they proceeded to the ducal carriage, she cast a backward glance at the gentlemen. Dare favored his right leg.

What had happened to him in Derbyshire?

Letting curiosity sweep away her caution, she asked, "How did Sir Dare injure his face?"

"He tumbled into a mine shaft while visiting his Derbyshire property. The ground opened up beneath him, he said."

All these many days, she'd assumed his lack of communication signified his waning affection, when in fact he'd been in grave danger—and in pain. She sank down onto the cushioned leather seat, avoiding the gentle scrutiny of the other woman's gray eyes.

As she focused on her grace's waistline, she felt the familiar nip of envy. Suke's betrothal had provoked the last attack, and now she was unsettled by a visibly pregnant duchess. Although she certainly didn't begrudge these women their joy, she keenly regretted her inability to experience it.

"Garrick and I recently returned from a long visit to my parents and brother on the Isle of Man."

Overcoming her distraction, Oriana replied, "That must have been pleasant—for all of you."

"I particularly enjoyed sharing my birthplace with my son and daughter. During our stay, Garrick drove me to Glen Auldyn to see Sir Dare's new villa."

Memories of a verdant hillside crowned by a graceful white house flooded her mind. Saying nothing, she relied upon her lowered lashes to shield her secrets.

"We ventured as far as the lead mine, and very busy it is." Leaning forward, the duchess continued, "On our way back down the glen, we met an old woman driving her goats up to the hills to graze. I spoke to her in Manx, and mentioned our acquaintance with the baronet. She pointed out a nearby cottage, and told me it had been occupied by an English fairy. Mine is a superstitious race, and I'm familiar with a variety of local legends. But this one was of very recent origin. The *ferish,* whose great beauty she described in detail, cast a spell on Mainshtyr Dare, and lured him away. *Dys Sostyn*—to England."

Oriana would not sully her precious love with lies and pretense. "Her spell has faded. He's free to return to his island and his people. Soon he will."

"Why do you say so?"

"I *know* him." The second of those three simple words revealed the wealth of emotion she'd been hoarding.

"If I've made you uncomfortable, I'm sorry. But when you looked so bereft just now, I wanted you to know you've got a friend." The duchess reached over and lightly touched Oriana's wrist. "I remember being at Newmarket, desperately in love and terribly confused. And feeling lonely, despite the throng. Or even because of it." Smiling, she continued, "At your concert in Bury St. Edmunds, you neglected to tell me *where* you learned all those Manx songs. Now I know."

"Have you informed Dare of your discovery?" asked Oriana.

"Not yet."

"Don't—please."

But the secret was already out, she reminded herself. Her companion's warm sincerity was melting her reserve, but still she was reluctant to share the full history of her latest ill-fated romance.

Looking toward the Flat, she said thankfully, "The race has begun."

Dare's mind exploded with curses. What the devil was Rushton doing here at Newmarket, hovering around Oriana?

He and the other gentleman were gathered at the rail. The official's box had been wheeled into place near the finishing post.

Two minutes, or thereabouts, and the race would be over.

It was the longest two minutes of his life.

His head rang from the shouting—it seemed that everyone standing along the Rowley Mile supported the popular Sir Charles Bunbury and his Pamela.

The two horses flew past him at exactly the same moment, and he could not distinguish which was the leader. The followers cantering in their wake blocked the judge's box, and it was the spectators' startled reaction that told him the outcome. The shouts of "Pamela! Bunbury!" suddenly ceased, and a murmuring broke out.

"Combustible—by a nose!" someone yelped.

Garrick was grinning ear to ear. "She did it! Let's find Con—they'll be weighing him."

Sir Charles Bunbury proved his sportsmanship by walking up to Dare and grasping his hand. "Well done, sir," he said graciously, "very well done, indeed. Courage and good management wins out over confidence and experience. You should be pleased with your filly and her rider."

"Extremely," said Dare.

A host of strangers clamored for his attention. He nodded and smiled at them indiscriminately, until they moved away to the betting circle to pay up or be paid. Garrick conversed with Con Finbar, whose cherubic face was flecked with mud.

"Corlett."

Dare spun around.

Rushton marched toward him. "We both have cause to rejoice, having won something here at Newmarket. For you, a handsome purse. For me, a bride."

After a lengthy silence, during which the nobleman's steely gaze faltered, Dare said, "That surprises me." In fact, it half killed him.

A siren, he reminded himself, sang out many a false promise that she never intended to keep.

"I tried to warn you." The earl exhibited a sealed letter. "I've written my solicitor, requesting that he undertake the sale of the Soho Square house. Oriana accepts the necessity of surrendering it—along with all her disreputable friendships."

A category that included Dare. "Is the wedding date decided?"

"Not yet," the earl answered, meeting his stare. "It would be a kindness if you departed for the Isle of Man without seeing Oriana again. That would spare her the awkwardness of a final parting. Her recent conduct causes her much shame. And regret."

To Dare's ears, Rushton's claim didn't ring true. His rival hadn't seen Oriana's face when she noticed his wounded cheek, or heard her words. She wouldn't, she *couldn't* marry a man she didn't love, not even if it repaired her reputation and gained her a title.

After receiving his prize money, he and his entourage led Combustible back to the Armitage stable, where he accepted Garrick's purchase offer.

Like Oriana and the other dedicated racegoers, he passed from course to course to witness each contest. Rushton and Burford were always at her side, and he couldn't wrest her away from them without creating a scene. She often smiled but seldom laughed. Her remarks were mostly directed to her cousin, and she tended to drift away from the earl. These observations confirmed his belief that Rushton had lied to make him think there was an engagement.

The earl's interference made him more desperate than ever to marry Oriana. They could travel to London that night—get a special license in the morning. By noon, they'd be man and wife.

He declined Garrick's invitation to join the Jockey Club members at the Coffee House, and set out for Moulton in a fast chaise to collect his baggage and his servant. Returning to Newmarket, he left the vehicle in the High Street and made his way up Mill Hill.

As he approached Gwynn Cottage, he heard her rich voice, accompanied by the *mandoline*. By the door was a wooden bench, and he sat down to revel in her music.

Whether she married a Manx baronet or an English

earl, she deserved to cultivate and share her talents. After days of searching in vain for a solution to his thorniest problem, he found it in her soaring notes. Her gift, he realized, could enrich other lives besides her own—and his.

When she finished, he rapped lightly on the window-pane to get her attention.

Oriana opened the door to him, but not all the way.

Her unexpected visitor wore his hat low on his brow, and the collar of his greatcoat was turned up, giving him a furtive appearance. She gazed up at the wounded face, and to prevent her landlady from overhearing, asked quietly, "Shouldn't you be celebrating your victory?"

"I did. Halford bought the filly, and means to race her one season more. I imposed a condition on the sale, that you are allowed to visit her at Moulton whenever you wish."

From the heart of the town came the sounds of roistering. Oriana peeked out and saw two parties of men on opposite sides of the street, waving at each other and shouting. To avoid attracting their attention, she asked Dare to come inside.

"Only if our privacy is assured."

"Mrs. Biggen is here."

"Then come walking with me. There's something important I must tell you. And ask you."

Leaving the clustered houses of Mill Hill, they strolled through one of the hedge-bound fields that stretched along the Exning road. Dare, his hand clasped around hers, described the plight of his Derbyshire miners.

"The people suffer many hardships—declining wages, disease, and hazardous working conditions. Though the mines are no longer in my direct control, I'm doing everything in my power to help and seek assistance from anyone able to offer it." He recounted a meeting with Sir

Joseph Banks at his Overton Hall estate near Matlock. "He made a sizable contribution to the charitable fund I've established. Now I must solicit your aid."

"I'll support your fund," she assured him. "How much money do you need?"

"It's not your money I want, but your voice." Facing her, he explained, "I've decided to sponsor charity concerts, with the profits going to the Benevolent Society for the Relief of Distressed Miners."

"And you want me to perform? Certainly I will. It's a splendid plan."

He raised her hand to his lips. "I haven't worked out any of the details, but I soon will."

"I can help you."

"My conversations with Sir Joseph were devoted to philanthropy rather than geology, but he did encourage me to deliver my revised treatise to the Royal Society."

"Dare, how wonderful—oh, you must be so pleased! I have some happy news of my own," she told him. "I've received a most exciting offer."

Pain flashed in his dark eyes. "So I heard."

His answer was unexpected. "You did?"

"The earl told me. He declared his intentions when we were at Rushton Hall. And don't expect me to express all the proper sentiments." He drew a long breath. "Human lives, like igneous rocks, are shaped and marked by past events. Your experiences, good and bad, make you the unique and remarkable creature that you are. If Rushton doesn't understand that, you can't marry him."

"I don't intend to."

Dare grinned—and with a groan quickly pressed his fingers over his lacerated cheek.

"Does it pain you?" she asked.

"Only when I smile. The earl said you accepted him.

He has already directed his solicitor to find a buyer for your house."

"Perhaps you misunderstood."

"The misunderstanding appears to be on his side—he showed me the letter. Your refusal must've been less than emphatic."

"I was extremely emphatic. If I marry Rushton, he'll banish me to Cheshire and make me do penance for my indiscretions. He'll keep me away from race meetings. And throw out all my low-cut dresses."

"How unenlightened of him."

"I've been telling you for months, I don't want a husband."

"At twenty-four, you're rather young to commit to a solitary life."

"I'm old enough to know my mind," she insisted.

A steady breeze gusted around them, billowing her skirts and his greatcoat. The coming rain scented the air.

The earl's manipulation of the facts reminded her of another instance when she'd doubted him. "During our visit to Rushton's estate, did you say anything—purposely or by accident—about our relationship?"

"Absolutely not."

His denial rang true, but it was at odds with what she'd been told. "According to Rushton, you made jests about me to the other men, on the grouse moor. He overheard you boasting about my—my eagerness when you come to my bed."

"Never," he replied forcefully. "The only conversation concerned the number of birds we bagged. And sometimes they made sport of my bitch."

"Who?"

"That poor old setter. Half-lame, always eager to rest. Once I made them laugh by saying she never needed a command to sit, or lie down. Perhaps Rushton mistook my meaning. I've always been careful around him," Dare assured her. "Whatever he thinks he knows about us, he learned none of it from me."

Vastly relieved, Oriana tucked her arm through his. "I've had a musical offer, as well as a matrimonial one. Mick Kelly asked me to sing at the King's Theatre next season, as *prima donna*."

In a tender, caressing tone, he said, "The honor is long overdue. You deserve the highest place in the company, and a salary to match."

Unlike the earl, he was proud of her, and she loved him for it. "We've both got what we most wanted, haven't we? The Royal Society will publish your writings, and I'll be singing at the opera once more." Glancing up at him, she caught him wearing a bleak, almost tragic expression.

He slowed his long stride to match hers as they crossed the darkening field. "How much longer do you stay here?"

"Burford's horse runs on Thursday. It's one of the last races."

"I'm afraid I must miss it."

"You're returning to Derbyshire?"

"London. I've got a post chaise waiting for me even now."

The words fell ominously on Oriana's ears. Having made many an escape of her own, she was troubled by his sudden bolt. His eventual destination, she felt sure, would be Deptford docks, where his ship waited.

Many weeks ago, at Vauxhall, he'd said he would divide his time between London and the island—for her sake. She could not keep him away from his lead mine and his new house. As she'd already explained to Rushton, she couldn't surrender her own dear home, or her audience. Therefore, she must endure the many weeks—or months—that Dare chose to be elsewhere.

When they arrived at her door, he unlinked his arm from hers and reached into his coat. "I want you to have this." He presented a small velvet pouch.

"If it's money—"

Laughing—and wincing—he said, "I haven't any to spare."

Still she wouldn't take it from him. "I can't, Dare."

"You shall. It's a birthday present." The wind whipped strands of hair across her face, and gently he brushed them aside. "I wasn't with you then. But I was thinking of you, wishing I could do this." His mouth fastened on hers.

The passion in his kiss scalded her. And it ended with such tenderness that incredibly, a bud of hope unfurled in her breast.

"A love that's solid like rock, as clear as crystal," he said. "That's what you deserve, Oriana. Not blame, not penance."

He opened the pouch and poured the contents into her palms.

Rock and crystal was exactly what he'd given her. Here were those twenty-three quartz pieces she'd left behind at Glencroft, cut and faceted and set in shining gold. Five of the smallest stones had gone into a half-hoop ring, two more had been fashioned into a pair of dangling eardrops, and the remainder made up a necklace.

"Wear them when you sing," he told her. "At the opera house."

Would he be there to see her, hear her? She wouldn't spoil this moment by asking.

Nor could she respond to his loving declaration with one of her own. She was afraid to expose the depth of her need and her wretchedness at this separation. There would be many more, for as long as their affair lasted. She didn't want his memories of her to include a teary face and mournful farewells.

If I want to hold him, she thought, *I must learn to let him go.*

A brave decision, and a wise one. But the weight of her unspoken love felt heavier than her most shameful scandal.

Nothing bound her to him but a pledge made on a summer night, and the nights of passion they had enjoyed in a succession of roadside inns. She'd believed that was enough to satisfy her. Watching his tall figure walk down the hill, Oriana discovered that she needed much more— but had no expectation of getting it.

Chapter 29

Oriana's enthusiasm for racing was stifled by heartache, and her temper was stretched to its limit by Lord Rushton's behavior. His unrelenting attentions were tiresome, and worse, he'd confided his hopes to Burford, who was utterly mystified by her reluctance to become a countess.

"You should rejoice at so respectable an offer," her cousin pointed out one afternoon. "Rushton's a good man, devoted to you. You'll want for nothing."

She raised her brows. "Did he ask you to plead his case?"

"Yes," he admitted. "What's more, he sought assurance that your Beauclerk relations approve the match. My brother Fred was with me. He told Rushton that our opinion wouldn't alter your decision, because you're damnably stubborn."

Oriana smiled at Lord Frederick Beauclerk's pungent phrasing—for a clergyman, he was refreshingly impious.

"But I can't approve the earl's wish to sell your house," Burford added. "The freehold of a London residential property is too valuable to discard."

"That's not for him to choose," she said pithily. "And never will be. I belong at the King's Theatre in the Haymarket, not at Rushton Hall."

Her anger simmered, and not even a second Newmarket victory by Burford's horse Weymouth improved her mood. When Rushton came to the paddock to congratulate the Beauclerks, she did not smile upon him.

He held his glass of celebratory champagne aloft, and said in a low voice, "To our future happiness. Mine will be assured if we declare our betrothal here, in your cousins' presence."

She stared into his unfathomable eyes. "I refused you, Rushton. Burford and Cousin Fred know that. So does Dare. You misled him into thinking we were engaged."

His smile was perfunctory. "I warned him away."

"You did more than that. And you were misleading *me,* when you said he was gossiping on your grouse moor. Did you hear Dare, or any of the other sportsmen, utter my name?"

"I did not."

A sigh escaped her.

"I believed—still believe—you will be better off as my baroness than as Corlett's mistress. We have been friends so long, you simply need more time to feel comfortable about a different connection between us."

He was forcing her to speak directly, without regard for his pride or his position. "My lord, your manipulations have broken my faith in that friendship. You seek to change me—to wrest away my very past."

"A past that you secretly deplore," he responded. "As my wife, you will occupy the position that you might have held, had you been lawfully born."

"My mother and father never made me feel ashamed—not about them, nor myself. My Beauclerk cousins accept me as a part of their family. *You* are the one who regards my origins as disgraceful, and my career as a blemish. You assure me that our marriage would improve my social standing, and yet you want to shut me away at Rushton Hall. I need more than that."

His lips thinned in a humorless smile. "Your many conquests have spoiled you. Must I make some grand, dramatic gesture to convince you of my affection? I thought an honorable proposal of marriage was the greatest possible compliment."

"So did I," she responded, "until you tarnished it with falsehood." Anger made her voice so strident that she hardly recognized it as her own. "I'm leaving for London straightaway to rescind those instructions to your solicitor. I will never give up my house. I shall continue to live as I choose—to do whatever I please. Whether I'm in a public place, or in my private bedchamber."

"You're going to him, aren't you?"

"I'm going *home*."

"Wait." The earl reached for her hands, his face a cauldron of emotion. "If you care so much for the Manxman, tell him. Don't hold back, as I did, until too late." His silvered head bowed. Without looking at her, he said, "That is the most difficult, the most agonizing speech I have made in all my life."

"I thank you for it," she said gently.

She would follow the advice he'd given so unselfishly.

She could no longer let pride or fear restrain her. With the same recklessness and candor she expected from Dare, she must proclaim her love for him. Whether or not he intended to leave England, she owed him the truth.

As her post chaise turned off Oxford Street into Charles Street, Oriana pressed her face to the window. Her square was a peaceful oasis in the midst of London's noise and bustle, and never had she been so relieved to return to it. She stepped out of the carriage and paid her post-boys, earning compliments for her liberal payments. One removed her trunks from the vehicle and set them down by the area railing.

Entering the house, she found a collection of large packing cases standing in the hall, with *J. Broadwood* stencilled on the side. Somebody had taken delivery of a pianoforte, or a harpsichord. Both, it seemed.

She also found a stranger seated on the hall bench, his hat resting on his knees. He wore a clergyman's bands at his neck, and a black coat and breeches. *A prospective buyer,* she thought, her optimism fading.

"Sir, if you're here to look over my house—"

"Madame St. Albans!" He bounded up from the bench.

Her mind blank, she focused on the long thin nose and dark, close-set eyes, which reminded her of a whippet. "Have we met?"

"We sang together—last winter. Before I came to St. Anne's, Soho, I was a Vicar Choral at St. Paul's Cathedral. It was Mr. Attwood, the organist, who introduced us. But I don't expect you to remember."

"The night of the Bach oratorio," she said, though her recollection of the choristers was hazy at best. "Do these cases belong to you? There's been a mistake, so if you wish to purchase my house—"

"No, ma'am, I'm waiting to be paid my fee. I've just performed a wedding."

"Here?" The answer came in a loud burst of merriment from the servants' hall. "I'm too late," she murmured in regret.

She started down the stairway, only to find the passage blocked by a large body surging up from below.

"Dare!"

A relieved grin brightened his damaged face. "Welcome home. As ever, your timing is impeccable."

"It couldn't be worse," she contradicted. "My maid has married your valet, and I wasn't here."

"They refused to wait any longer. A sentiment I understood perfectly." Taking her arm, he spun her around.

"What are you doing? I want to see Suke."

"Later. Right now, I need you more than she does."

"Do those boxes in the hall belong to you?" she asked, while he marched her back up the steps.

"They're yours." He towed her through the hall to where the clergyman stood. "Wait here, sir—I may require your services once again." Still clutching Oriana's hand, Dare led her to the parlor and shut the door.

"Are you responsible for this appalling mess? Oh, Dare, what have you been doing?"

"Sir Joseph suggested that I revise and illustrate my treatise on Manx rocks, and I've begun preliminary notes and sketches."

While he sorted through the rough drawings scattered across the chairs, Oriana slipped her reticule off her wrist and placed it on the mantel shelf next to a lopsided stack of books. "Where did these come from?"

"Sir Joseph's library. His assistant let me borrow them."

"I'm glad you're here," she said. "I was worried I might miss you, that you'd be in Deptford, preparing to set sail."

"The *Dorrity* is on her way to the island, and so is Ned, with all my furniture." Going to her writing desk, he shoved aside a sheaf of pages. "Now what the devil have I done with—ah, here it is."

He handed her a printed certificate with their names clearly inscribed upon it: *Oriana Vera St. Albans Julian, widow,* and *Darius Gilchrist Corlett, bachelor.* A marriage license.

"How did you get it?"

"Couldn't have been simpler. Wingate and I went to Doctors' Commons and answered some questions. We each paid five pounds, and left with one of these." Carefully, he pried the license from her grasp. "I decided it might be convenient to have one in readiness, just in case Miss Mellon is correct about your secret longing to be a wife."

A sudden blush put fire in her cheeks. "Harri and I often jest about husband hunting."

"To me, however, you've rigorously denied any interest in wedlock. You refused Rushton, you said, because you don't care to spend the rest of your days buried in the country, cut off from the theaters and racing. Wasting your talent, and giving up your low-cut gowns."

"I never meant to sound so frivolous," she defended herself. "The real reason is that I don't love Rushton enough to make those sacrifices."

"If he loved you, he wouldn't require them," Dare countered. "A marriage should be founded on tolerance and trust. Compromise. Humor. And a passion like the one I feel for you, and you seem to feel for me."

She couldn't speak, and she couldn't wrest her gaze from his. "Perhaps," she said in a very odd voice, "you should record your philosophies in a treatise."

"Not till *after* our wedding. I must test my theories before I publish them. Oriana, do you love me? I don't want a wife who doesn't."

"Yes," she answered. "That's why I came back to London—to say all the things I should have said a long time ago, but didn't know how. I'm used to singing them in front of an audience, not speaking them."

"Please try," he urged.

"I've kept my feelings to myself because—because I couldn't imagine you would remain faithful to Ana St.

Albans, the disreputable singer. You want to marry someone like the virtuous widow, Mrs. Julian."

"I didn't propose in spite of who you are, but *because*
of who you are."

"What about that highbred heiress you've always
wanted, with the large fortune?"

"I despair of finding one who can play the instruments
I purchased at Broadwood's," he responded. "And who
has watched Mount Vesuvius erupt. And who happens to
be a neighbor of Sir Joseph Banks, President of the Royal
Society. He means to propose me as a member. Living in
Soho Square might improve my chances of election, it's
so very convenient for all the scientific meetings and dinners at his house. And the sad truth is, I can no longer
afford to stay at Morland's," he said with dubious sincerity.

"You needn't marry me to get a London house," she
said. "I suspect you could purchase the entire square if
you wanted."

"My banker won't let me. In future I must practice
stringent economies, and curtail my expenses as best I
can. This is your chance to prove that you're no fortune
hunter, because mine is hopelessly tied up, and I can't get
my hands on it just now."

"Then I'd better have Rushton instead," Oriana said
playfully. "He offered a very generous settlement."

Humor warmed his eyes, belying his sober tone when
he told her, "I'll provide you with enough pin money to
supply essentials—the annual edition of the *Racing Calendar,* a few yards of lace to make a petticoat flounce. I
fully understand that you'll want to set fashions in Douglas and Castletown during the winter. Don't you think
you can do it with the gowns you possess already?"

Not really caring whether or not he was serious, she
said thoughtfully, "I daresay London modes would create

a sensation at island assemblies, even if they were a season behind."

He took her into the music room. "I won't take this away from you, either. If you want to delay the marriage until you've had your season at the opera house—"

"I don't care about that."

"No? How can you be so sure?"

"Being asked to return is my triumph," she responded. "After I considered Mick Kelly's offer, I discovered my reluctance to stir up old scandals. Rushton was right when he predicted that I would be miserable if I returned to the King's Theatre."

"Make no mistake, I still want you to give those benefit concerts."

Oriana stared at him. "As Lady Corlett?"

"You'll draw larger crowds if you appear on the bill as Ana St. Albans."

Pressing her fingers down on the ivory keys of the pianoforte, she said, "My mother told me that if I wanted to be wife and singer both, I must wed another professional. Marriage, I believed, would curtail my career, not preserve it."

"It might be an unconventional thing for a ladyship to do, but I can't imagine anyone objecting if you sing and play on behalf of a worthy cause like the Benevolent Society for the Relief of Distressed Miners."

"Mr. Sheridan permitted his first wife, Elizabeth Linley, to sing in public after they married," she recalled. "But that was many years ago."

"I'm not merely permitting," said Dare, "I'm encouraging you. However, if you dislike the notion, we'll find some other way to raise funds."

We. That tiny, magnificent word reassured her that their marriage would be the true partnership she desired, based upon passion and love, and this profound, soul-stirring need.

An entire lifetime of lovemaking, she thought when Dare began kissing her. At night she would slumber in his arms, and in the morning she'd wake up at his side. They would share a home openly—no more stealth, and no shame. She would belong to a man as unshakable as a Manx mountain, whether confronted by her evasions and uncertainties, her motley collection of friends and cousins, or an obnoxious man from her past. Before meeting him, she had endured a lonely, self-absorbed existence, and because of him her future would be unimaginably fulfilling.

He surfaced from their heated embrace to say, "Marry me, here and now. There's a parson with his prayer book in the hall, and a host of witnesses downstairs." He kissed her again. "I've already supplied you with the ring."

She returned to the adjoining room for her reticule, and emptied its contents onto a chair cushion. Among the pile of sparkling ornaments he'd bestowed in Newmarket, she found the gem-encrusted band and handed it to him. "Call in the priest and tell the servants to meet us in the drawing room. I'll not conduct my wedding in the midst of so much untidiness."

When he hurried away, she confronted the looking glass hanging over the mantel. Beneath her hat, her chignon was in fairly good order, but she rearranged some of the tendrils that had escaped it. A carriage costume for a wedding dress—for the second time. She wouldn't bother to change her gown, for she was as eager as Dare to seal their love with all possible haste. She clasped her crystal necklace around her throat, and replaced her earrings with the ones he'd given her.

His summons brought all of her servants trooping into

the drawing room. Suke, her pretty face glowing with joy, entered on her husband's arm. The clergyman read through the service with feeling, and after Dare slipped the ring on Oriana's finger, he joined their hands and declared them man and wife. The framed oil portraits of King Charles and Nell Gwynn smiled upon the proceedings.

After the ceremony, Oriana accepted her servants' felicitations. Suke, still dazed by her own nuptials, wished her all happiness, and Oriana returned the sentiment. Both of the Lumleys were misty-eyed.

Said the housekeeper, "Your mother never dreamed you'd become a ladyship."

"No more did we," her butler added.

Louis vowed to serve up a splendid wedding supper made up of all her favorite dishes. The crowd dispersed; the clergyman, handsomely compensated, took his leave.

Her husband took her left hand, holding it up to admire the gem-encrusted band she wore. "Manx stone and London gold. A suitable symbol for this marriage." He held her fingers to her lips. "You've made me very happy, Oriana."

Marriage was a holy estate, but Dare's first kiss as her husband made her made her feel spectacularly wicked. "Come with me," she invited him.

They walked around the packing cases in the hall, and ascended the staircase together.

"I've lived in this house as a girl, and as a widow," she said when they entered her chamber. "Not a soul in London would believe it, but you're the first man I've invited to share this bed."

Dare inspected her Poussin painting of the bacchante crossing a river, and after commenting on her pulchritude, he faced her. He removed every article of Oriana's clothing, until she was in the same disrobed state as the girl in the picture.

"You're much lovelier," he said, when they lay together on the bed. He filled his hands with her hair, spreading it across the pillow. "And infinitely more respectable."

It was a term that she didn't readily associate with herself—perhaps in time she would grow accustomed to it.

She traced the contours of his chest, then felt the strength of the muscled arms that enfolded her. Desire flowed hot and thick in her veins, pulsing though her eager limbs, but she sought more than carnal pleasure; she wanted to give—her soul, her body, all of her senses.

This new respectability was being undermined by what Dare was doing to her with his hands and his lips. Oriana didn't care. Other gifts, tangible and intangible—music and minerals, love and passion—were far more precious.

Epilogue

Glen Auldyn, Isle of Man
April 1800

Oriana rejoiced in the mild warmth of spring, for it
enabled her to bring her _mandoline_ into the old
orchard. She sat among the blossom-laden trees, plucking
the strings, while her pony Glistree cropped the grass
nearby. As she played, she cast her eyes toward the villa in
which she and her husband had spent many happy months,
devoting themselves to private pleasures.

Very little time remained to revel in the peace and beauty
of the glen—in two days she and Dare would sail for England.

"_For Love's sake, kiss me once again,_" she sang, "_I long
and should not beg in vain._" At Dare's suggestion, she was
setting his favorite Jonson verses to music.

When her final note faded, a mistle thrush broke into
song. Oriana sat perfectly still, listening to her fellow performer.

A short time later she spied her husband coming up the
path from his mine, where he'd been giving final instructions to the manager.

"What fair creature is this?" he inquired, feigning surprise. "Lady Corlett, you should be devising your seating plan for tonight's dinner."

"Wingate and Suke will do it for me. I'm taking advantage of the leisurely hours left to me, for we shall be very busy in England."

They would travel first to Derbyshire to inspect the improvements made to the miners' dwellings, funded by the proceeds from her initial subscription concerts. After the Spring Meeting at Newmarket, she'd give a recital at the Bury St. Edmunds Guildhall on behalf of their charity. Its success was already assured: The Duchess of Halford had vigorously peddled tickets.

"How many guests are we expecting tonight?"

"Your cousins the Gilchrists, Lord and Lady Garvain, the Curpheys, and the newest newlyweds, Mr. and Mrs. Buck Whaley." She leaned her instrument against the trunk of the nearest tree. "Ned will play for us afterward—and it was no small feat snaring him; his services are in high demand."

Grinning, Dare quoted, " 'Mr. Crowe, the celebrated performer of London's Vauxhall and Sadler's Wells Theater.' With that impressive title, small wonder he's the most-sought-after musician on our island." He leaned down and dropped a handful of pebbles into her lap. "Care to classify these for me?"

Oriana held up each glittering specimen, proudly giving its name. "Pyrite. Calcite. Quartz. Galena."

"What a clever assistant," said her husband approvingly. "I'm taking these to London. I can donate them to the British Museum, or use them during my presentation to the Royal Society."

Within a month of their marriage, Sir Joseph Banks had presented Dare as a candidate for membership in that illustrious body. Confirmation of his election had come in a letter early in the year, and he'd been invited to speak at a meeting and submit his writings for publication. Oriana would never forget his pride the first time he added the initials *R.S.* after his signature. Throughout the winter he had revised and expanded his treatise, and finished the illustrations. She'd accompanied him on his rambles across the island to sketch the geological phenomena he referred to in his text.

Previously, she'd had no need of thick-soled walking boots. The ones poking out from under her blue flounce were now scuffed from regular wear. She rubbed one of the toes, and said, "I must remember to order a new pair from my London shoemaker."

He pulled out his memorandum book and pencil. "I'll add it to the list. Anything else?" When Oriana shook her head, he asked, "No gowns, no hats? A town coach?"

"Not if we're trying to avoid extravagance."

"That was last year. As far as my bankers are concerned, a new year began at Lady Day. My finances are greatly improved. I can afford to indulge your fashionable impulses, and settle all your dressmakers' and milliners' bills. My own needs are few—although I do intend to acquire one very desirable object that Skyhill lacks."

Oriana couldn't think of a single necessity that was missing from their exquisitely appointed house. "What might that be?"

"A portrait of my beautiful and talented wife. But I haven't yet decided whether to have her painted with the *mandoline,* or seated at a harpsichord."

"It should be a double portrait," she insisted. "The illustrious geologist writing his next treatise, or perusing Dr. Hutton's *Theory of the Earth.* And on his desk— these." She gave him the shiny stones.

"*Art and Science,*" he said, warming to her idea.

Her smile faded as she said, "I wish I could attend your lecture."

"After you've heard me practice over and over, you won't. Unlike you, I'm not accustomed to making addresses, or appearing in front of an audience."

"You can witness my performances whenever you like, but I'm excluded from yours. Most unfair."

"Your concerts are open to anyone with the means to buy a ticket. This will be a private meeting—members only. Don't forget, Banks invited me to make a presentation at the Royal Institution. I've decided my subject should be my campaign to ensure greater safety for miners, and you must definitely be there." Dare rose and reached high to pull clusters of frilly blossoms from the tree. When he rejoined Oriana on the grass, he tucked one into her hair and used the St. Albans brooch to fasten the other to her chemisette. "I mean to credit you for raising all that money. The first series of subscription concerts succeeded beyond my wildest dreams."

"I'm eager to resume them. You've very nearly depleted the coffers of the Benevolent Society for the Relief of Distressed Miners." She drew a quick breath as his hands settled on her waist.

"Come let us here enjoy the shade, as your poet says. *For love in shadow best is made.* . . . You, Lady Corlett, have the nicest, most ruffly petticoats of any female on this island."

"How do you know?" she asked suspiciously. "Whose skirts have you been peeking under, besides mine?"

"Only a theory," he replied, his lips grazing her knee. "Be assured, I have absolutely no intention of proving it. My investigation ends here." His hand settled on her thigh.

The security of marriage permitted her to share herself

fearlessly, and the privacy they enjoyed at Skyhill emboldened her. Her hands eagerly caressed his broad shoulders, and her mouth meshed with his.

Her lips still tingled from the kiss when she said wistfully, "We needn't stay in England any longer than absolutely necessary. I want you to be at home to watch our apples ripen."

"Home," he murmured against her neck, "has nothing to do with which house I occupy, Oriana. My residence of choice is your heart, and I rejoice that you invited me to live there."

The missel thrush resumed her song, sweetly serenading the lovers while they took full advantage of their seclusion.

Author's Note

The primary characters of *Improper Advances* are my fictional creations. Nearly all the secondary characters are real people.

Actress Harriot Mellon eventually left the stage to marry Thomas Coutts, the millionaire banker, when she was thirty-seven and he was eighty. At his death, she became the richest widow in Great Britain. In her fiftieth year she wed her second husband, the twenty-six-year-old Duke of St. Albans—a nephew of the Lord Burford who appears in this story. She was never fully accepted by high society, although her enormous fortune and grand title ensured her entrée at Court.

It is true that in 1799, Michael Kelly needed a *prima donna* for the opera house; eventually, he hired an Italian one. He and Anna Maria Crouch remained a devoted couple until her death in 1803. He pursued his theatrical endeavors as singer, composer, musical director, and seller of music until he was debilitated by gout and debts.

Sir Joseph Banks, his wife, and his eccentric sister continued to live at Number 32, Soho Square, all three living to a great age. The Royal Society and the Royal Institution of Great Britain are two of his many legacies. Less well known is the leather-bound volume in which he recorded the weights of his family members and visitors.

In January 1800, Thomas "Buck" Whaley, Irish adventurer, politician, and dog-lover, wed the Honorable Mary Lawless, sister of Lord Cloncurry. She raised his illegitimate children as her own, edited his memoirs, and arranged their publication.

At the close of the eighteenth century, Dr. James Hutton's theories were discounted by all except his closest associates. His observations of igneous coastal rocks, basalt and granite, supported his belief that our earth's true age should be counted in millions of years. As scientific methods and dating procedures grew more sophisticated and precise, they proved the accuracy of Hutton's radical—for his time—pronouncements. Not only was he a founder of modern geology, he also promoted the concept of natural selection a generation before Charles Darwin. As far as I'm aware, no one besides Sir Darius Corlett has aligned the geology of the Isle of Man with Huttonian theory.

The paintings in Oriana's possession correspond to items listed on inventories, sold or otherwise disposed of, by the third and fourth Dukes of St. Albans.

I welcome reader letters (SASE appreciated for a response), either at P.O. Box 437, Epsom, NH 03234-0437, or in email to *MargEvaPor@aol.com.* Visit my website *http://members.aol.com/MargEvaPor* for information about my life, my travels, my dogs, previous books, and a virtual tour of the Isle of Man.

Margaret Evans Porter

Coming in January from Avon Romance
Two historical love stories that are guaranteed
to leave you utterly breathless . . .
and longing for more . . .

The Wicked One
by **Danelle Harmon**

"Provocative and passionate!"
Lisa Kleypas

Meet Lucien, the Duke of Blackheath—head of the
noble de Montforte family—and one of the most infuri-
ating, manipulative, irresistible men in England. He
never expects that his plans will be foiled by beautiful
Eva de la Mouriére . . .

A Belated Bride
by **Karen Hawkins**

"[She] knows how to keep a reader entranced
from first page to last!"
Joan Johnston

From the author of *The Abduction of Julia* comes a
provocative, passionate love story. Arabella Hadley has
vowed she would never wed the dissolute Duke of
Wexford—except she still finds the power of his kisses too
strong to ignore . . .

Coming in February 2001

One of the most breathlessly awaited
love stories of the year
from one of romance's most adored writers

All About Love
A Cynster Novel
By Stephanie Laurens

Six notorious cousins, known to the *ton* as the Bar
Cynster, have cut a swath through the ballrooms of
London. One by one, each has fallen in love and
married the woman of his heart . . . until only one is
left unclaimed. He's the most rakish of Stephanie
Laurens's captivating clan . . . and he's not about to
go easily.

Alasdair Cynster, known to his intimates as Lucifer,
is about to meet his match in Phyllida Tallent. She's
willful, beautiful and independent.

She's just right to become a Cynster bride.

America Loves Lindsey!
The Timeless Romances
of #1 Bestselling Author